Dangerous Depths

The Sea Monster Memoirs, #2

Karen Amanda Hooper

Starry Sky Publishing

"I am once again blown away by just how beautiful Hooper's writing is. *Dangerous Depths* is every bit as amazing as *Tangled Tides* with more heart pulling moments added in for good measure. I was hooked, flipping the pages to see how my favorite characters were going to pull off the impossible... again. This is one of the best mermaid series out there."

~ Tiffany Mahaffy, *ESCAPING ONE BOOK AT A TIME*

"*Dangerous Depths* is filled with life altering moments that will leave your eyes filled with tears and danger that will have you on the edge of your seat. A wonderful YA read that will change the way you think about life under the water forever."

~ Windie Butera, *NOVEL HOARDERS*

"I am in love with every aspect of the world that Hooper has created, and I cannot wait to read more. A tale filled with adventure, magic, and the power of love, *Dangerous Depths* will leave you enchanted."

~ Chiara Sullivan, *BOOKS FOR A DELICATE ETERNITY*

Starry Sky Publishing

ISBN ebook: 978-0-9855899-0-5
ISBN paperback: 978-0-9855899-3-6

Cover art by Melissa Williams
http://mwcoverdesign.blogspot.com

Interior art by Steve Graham
http://avurt.com

Visit author Karen Amanda Hooper on the Web at
http://www.karenamandahooper.com

Dedication

For my Father

Whenever the waves crashed into me,
you held my hand and helped me stay on my feet.
Thank you for teaching me that the world is *truly wondrous*.

Dangerous Depths

The Sea Monster Memoirs, #2

Karen Amanda Hooper

No matter how much I adored—or disliked—my new sea monster traits, I still relished returning to human form and feeling sand between my toes.

Three days had passed since my almost-death, my negotiations with Medusa and Poseidon, and my transformation into a mixture of mer, selkie, siren, gorgon, and human. Technically, the realm of Rathe was my new home, but Earth—particularly Eden's Hammock—would fill a part of my heart that could never be replaced. Nothing and no one would ever change my love for the tiny island. Same with my love for sand between my toes. Some things just feel right.

Up ahead, my uncle's lighthouse stood tall and proud against a clear azure sky. Palm trees shimmered in the sunlight with each waft of tropical breeze. A chorus of birds sang from the beach and sky. Our tiny island hadn't changed at all.

My brown hair draped over my shoulders was a welcomed contrast to my white mermaid hair. Temporarily, I was regular old me again. No fins, no wings, no pressure of life-or-death responsibilities, no new magical realm to learn about and navigate. I let out a sigh of relief and lifted my face skyward to bask in the moment of familiarity and temporary freedom.

"You are the most beautiful thing I've ever seen," Treygan said.

I couldn't contain the grin that spread across my face. His thumb caressed my cheek as his cobalt eyes gazed down at me. I reached up and ran my fingers through his wet black hair. He looked just as gorgeous in human form. "Ditto."

My grin faded when I realized he had said those same words to me at Koraline's healing ceremony. The thought of her ripped away my moment of bliss.

Koraline had woken from her coma, but I hadn't found the courage to visit her yet. I planned to soon, but how could I properly thank her for saving me from bloodthirsty sharks? Or adequately apologize for putting her in harm's way?

"What's the matter?" Treygan asked. "You look sad."

"I'm fine." Since we were in human form, my emotions weren't given away by the changing color of my skin. When my emotions literally showed all over me, it was much harder to lie to him. For days I had been worried about how he'd react when he discovered I could lie. Merfolk didn't possess the ability to lie, but I had negotiated a reprieve from that inconvenient restriction during my meeting with Medusa. Some lies were necessary to protect loved ones. If Medusa wanted me to help rule her realm of sea creatures, I needed the option of hiding some truths from people.

I didn't want to dampen the mood by explaining how worried I was about seeing Koraline again, or stressing over a million other issues. Instead, I changed the subject.

"This dress isn't too wrinkled?" I twirled around, kicking up sand as my billowing skirt kissed the top of my knees.

"We're attending a party filled with merfolk and selkies, all of whom are probably wearing clothes that were hidden around the island. Most likely everyone's outfit will be wrinkled."

I eyed his khaki shorts and unbuttoned dress shirt. His shirt was more wrinkled than my sundress, but he looked incredible. His bangs dripped as he finished rolling up his sleeves. A bead of water ran down his forearm, momentarily revealing a silver and indigo hallmark in its path. Then it faded away, like a living tattoo flickering in and out of existence.

Treygan pulled me close to him and lifted my chin. "Stop looking at me like that or we will never make it to the party. We're already late as it is."

I rose up on my tippy toes and wrapped my arms around his neck. "Let's just skip it."

"Lloyd has been waiting days to see you. It would break his heart if you didn't attend."

The mention of Uncle Lloyd rooted my feet back into the sand. Treygan had visited him while I was stuck in Rathe, but I needed to see my uncle and make sure he was okay. Plus, I really missed him. "You're right. Let's go."

Treygan took my hand and we walked along the path to Uncle Lloyd's house. "Are you excited to see everyone?"

"Kind of. It's still hard to believe the selkies will be happy to see me. Last time I saw any of them they wanted me dead."

"Only because they thought it was their way to return home. To survive. You showed them a different way. You saved their lives, and they are grateful for that."

Treygan and Nixie were the only friendly faces I had seen since the Triple Eighteen. Most of my time had been spent sequestered in the grotto, taking care of crucial business with the gorgon sisters. Stheno and Euryale tolerated me, but I could tell they didn't like me. I assumed that's how most of my new fellow sea creatures would feel about me—with the exception of merfolk.

The merfolk had become my treasured family over the last few weeks. I would do anything for them. Oddly, since the Triple Eighteen that same devotion filled me when I thought of the selkies. And the sirens. Even the menacing gorgons.

A breeze blew my hair across my face. "Do you think they'll recognize me now that I'm a brunette again in human form?"

"They'll recognize you. Light or dark, you're still the same radiant soul."

I shot him my best attempt at a seductive glance. "Are you saying you like my dark side?"

"Your dark side balances out my excessively joyful, overly optimistic, and cheerfully blinding bright side."

His sarcasm made me break out laughing. "Joyful? You were the most brooding person ever before I came along."

"My brooding was endearing, and you know it."

"It was not." I playfully shoved his shoulder. "I didn't even think you were attractive until the first time you laughed."

"Really?" He stopped walking and faced me. "What did I laugh at?"

"Me."

"That makes sense." He winked. "So, my laughter is what hooked you?"

My cheeks warmed, recalling some of the many qualities that made me fall for him: strength, loyalty, selflessness. Even his brooding had been attractive at times, but I would never admit it to him. "Among other things."

"See, light and dark. We balance each other." He twisted a lock of my hair around his finger. "I love you no matter what form you're in, but wait until everyone sees you in the water with your white hair and tail. You look like an agape pearl."

I pressed my hand against my armband, confirming the agape pearl Treygan gave me was still safe in its secret pouch, and I rested my head on his shoulder. "I'll miss looking like everyone else."

His hard bicep bounced against my cheek as he silently chuckled. "Yamabuki, you have never looked like everyone else. It's one of the many reasons I'm so in love with you."

I sighed, deliriously happy but still a little in disbelief. Treygan was in love with me. *Me*. A small-island girl who was a hodgepodge of human and sea creature, and whom, I shamefully admit, wasn't all that nice to him in the beginning of our relationship. At least, the parts of our relationship I could remember.

Most of the memories Delmar removed from my mind during my mermaid transformation were still gone, but I had a few moments from my past I could still recall. Like Treygan saving my life when I was five, and every minute of every day since I was turned mer. Happily, many of those minutes had been spent with Treygan.

As we rounded the bend, it hit me that we were together for good. No impending doom, no more impossible decisions about sparing my life or his, no one forbidding us to see each other, no bloodthirsty gang of selkies wanting me sacrificed. Treygan and I had fought our way out of the darkness, together.

"Hmm, that's odd," Treygan said, snapping me out of my thoughts.

Uncle Lloyd's house was in sight, but it didn't look any different. "What's odd?"

Treygan picked up his pace, so I walked faster to keep up with him. "Merfolk should be surrounding the house in celebration. And selkies, for that matter."

"They're probably inside."

"The selkies, maybe." Treygan shook his head. "But merfolk would be outside in the sun. Besides, I don't sense any merfolk. The party must have ended early." His hand tightened around mine and his voice turned stony. "Something is wrong."

I pulled out of his grasp and ran ahead of him.

"Uncle Lloyd!" I yelled, barreling up the porch steps and through the front door. He didn't answer me. He was standing in the living room with his hand resting against a carved wood panel hung on the wall. "Where'd everybody go?"

Nixie strutted into the room. She leaned against the doorframe and crossed her arms over her red corset. "Not the best time for a celebration, given the circumstances."

"What circumstances? What's wrong?" I inched toward Uncle Lloyd, terrified of what he might tell me. Terrified of why the house felt ominous and why he looked so distraught. "Is it your kidneys?"

He lifted his head, but didn't look at me. Instead, he pulled a cloth out of his shirt pocket and polished the wood panel on the wall in front of him. "He was right, you know. I didn't even have him represented in my own home."

"Who? What are you talking about?" I reached his side. The new portrait was an intricate carving of a male selkie. Dark hair, big dark eyes, broad shoulders, six-pack abs that led to his strong seal-like tail, and deadly claws opened proudly at his waist. Even his goatee had been etched into the wood. His name escaped my lips in a whisper, "Rownan." I cleared my throat and pulled my focus away. "I'm surprised you had enough strength to carve it."

"Strength." Uncle Lloyd huffed. "What does an old fool like me know about strength?"

Nixie's high-heeled boots clicked across the tile floors as she headed for the front door. "I'll wait outside. You three have a lot to discuss."

My mer senses never detected Treygan walking up behind me—probably another glitch in my new sea monster wiring—so the sound of his voice was a surprise, and so were his words. "Is my brother all right?"

Treygan had never spoken about Rownan with such concern. Yes, Treygan and Rownan were half-brothers, but they had been at war for eighteen years and despised each other. They had almost killed each other on the Triple Eighteen. The gate opening had ended the battle between the selkies and merfolk, but had it instantly repaired the damage between Treygan and Rownan?

Uncle Lloyd stepped backward. His knees shook as if struggling to support his weight. He lowered himself into his chair, letting out a sigh. I couldn't tell if it was relief, sadness, or exhaustion. "I'm afraid he won't be all right."

"Why?" Treygan and I both asked at the same time.

I walked over to my uncle and kneeled by his side. "Tell us what's going on."

He finally looked at me, and I gasped. Based on his appearance, I would've guessed ten years had passed since I last saw him, but it had only been a few days. His face looked thinner, his skin was pale as a jellyfish, and milky clouds hovered over his slate gray eyes. "Uncle Lloyd," I whispered, "can you see?"

"My sweet, strong Yara." He aimlessly moved his peeling, calloused hand between us until I took it and pressed it against my cheek.

"I'm right here." I fought back tears. His vision was failing. My worst fear was coming true. The man who had always been the sunshine of my life was fading into permanent darkness.

He sank back into his chair and tried taking a deep breath, but it stuck in his chest. "Treygan."

Treygan rushed to his side. Deep worry lines creased his forehead. "I'm here."

Uncle Lloyd wheezed. "Rownan needs the two of you now more than ever."

"What do you mean?" Treygan asked.

"Vienna." Uncle Lloyd went into a coughing fit, so I hurried to the kitchen to get him a glass of water.

Vienna. Rownan's wife and true love. I said a silent prayer that she was okay. The gate to the sea creature realm had been sealed for eighteen years. What if, gods forbid, Vienna had become sick or died? After Uncle Lloyd took a few sips of water, his coughing calmed down.

"What about Vienna?" Treygan pressed.

Uncle Lloyd held the cool glass to his forehead. "She didn't wait."

My heart deflated. Vienna didn't wait for Rownan. She was with someone else. How could she? As much as Rownan loved her, he would have done anything to be reunited with her. He would have swum through hell itself to be with her again, and she couldn't wait a measly eighteen years? "What a bitch."

"Bite your tongue, young lady," Uncle Lloyd said. Was her really scolding me for bad language? I was eighteen. I had faced Poseidon and Medusa and demanded a position in the gorgon sister trinity. I pretty much had say over everything that happened in regards to sea creatures. Did he actually think he could still order me around? "Go get me a cough drop from the top drawer in the kitchen."

"Yes, sir." I jumped up and hurried back to the kitchen. Okay, apparently he *could* still order me around.

Treygan was pacing when I came back. I unwrapped a cough drop and placed it in Uncle Lloyd's shaking hand. "So, where is Rownan?" I asked. "Drinking himself into a coma somewhere?"

Uncle Lloyd popped the lozenge into his mouth and after a few seconds managed to say, "He's going after her."

Treygan stopped pacing. "He can't. That's suicide."

"Yes, well." Uncle Lloyd swallowed hard. "He believes life isn't worth living without her, so he's willing to risk it."

"Wait," I said. "What are we talking about? Going after her … and finding her where? With some other guy?"

"No." Treygan pinched the bridge of his nose. "She didn't wait for the gate to open. She tried getting back to Rownan a different way—an insane and perilous way."

Apparently, I was the only one who didn't understand what was going on. "Elaborate, Treygan."

His eyes locked with mine. All of his inner light had been snuffed out. "She went to the damned realm. The realm of darkness and evil."

My head throbbed and my back burned. My sea monster traits tried to surface, but I kept them at bay. "There's another realm? Besides here and Rathe?"

"Yes," Treygan said. "Harte."

He pronounced it "Hartay." The name was foreign to me. "Why didn't anyone tell me?"

"We don't discuss that place." His tone made the hairs on my arms stand up.

"Why? What's so evil about it?"

"You don't want to know," Uncle Lloyd grumbled.

"Why would Vienna go there?"

Treygan sat on the couch and rubbed his hands over his face. "She probably thought she could find another way back to this realm to be with Rownan."

"But I thought the gate was the only way."

"It is," Uncle Lloyd confirmed.

"Then why would she go to some damned world thinking she could find another way?"

Treygan cracked his neck. "Because for decades there have been rumors that one soul in Harte figured out a way to travel into Earth's realm. But the Violets say it isn't possible."

Uncle Lloyd took another sip of water. "Legend says the gateway to Harte only works one way. Once you enter, there's no returning."

"Then Rownan can't go after her," I shrieked. "He'll never be able to come back!"

"He has already made up his mind," Treygan said. "When it comes to Vienna, there's no stopping him."

"Sharkshit," I argued. "I'll stop him. I'll ask Stheno and Euryale to close the gate to Harte."

"They won't." Uncle Lloyd sighed. "Medusa tried the same thing centuries ago. Stheno and Euryale wouldn't listen."

If Medusa couldn't make them do it, they definitely wouldn't do it for me. "Where is Rownan right now?"

"He left this morning." Uncle Lloyd turned toward Treygan. "He said to tell you thank you. And that he wished things could have been better between you two for these last eighteen years."

"How can he be gone already?" My voice rose. "How could you let him go? Why didn't you have Nixie send me a message?"

"Yara, I'm at my rope's end. My last bit of interfering caused me to lose my sight. I can hardly breathe. My kidneys are kaput." Uncle Lloyd rubbed his neck, like holding up his head was too much effort. Like his life had become too much to bear. I wished I could carry all of his guilt, sorrow, and pain for him. "If I interfered one more time, even one gesture, one conversation with any intent to meddle, I might have died before I saw you again. Before I could say goodbye to you and Treygan."

Tears welled in my eyes. "But …."

Treygan rested his hand on Uncle Lloyd's—his father's—shoulder. "You're the wisest and bravest man I have ever known. I'm honored and grateful to be your son."

A tear rolled down my cheek as I stared at them. I couldn't imagine my world, or any other world, without Uncle Lloyd in it. He would get better. He had to.

I wiped away my tears and stood. "You're going to be okay, and I'll find Rownan and Vienna and bring them back. You didn't interfere. This is my choice and mine alone." I threw my head back and shouted at the ceiling, loud enough to go through the roof, through this world, and into the Inbetween, or wherever our gods existed. "You hear me, Medusa and Poseidon? This is my free will! He didn't meddle! Don't you inflict one more inkling of pain on him!"

Treygan held my face in his hands, forcing me to stop shouting and look at him. "Enough. If we have any hope of stopping Rownan from going to Harte, we need to leave now."

I nodded.

Uncle Lloyd struggled to stand up then hobbled toward the den. "There is a gateway to Harte on the darkest border of Rathe. No one goes near it, but that's where Rownan is headed."

Treygan held my hand. "We'll find him. He has a head start, but it would take him all day to swim back to our realm then to Harte's gateway. I swim much faster than him. I can make up for the lead he has on us."

"No," I argued, full of hope. "I can fly to him. I fly faster than you can swim."

Treygan flinched, but I didn't have time to soothe his ego.

Uncle Lloyd turned to face me. Knowing he couldn't see me tore a hole through my soul. He reached forward and I placed my hands in his. "Yara, please listen to me. And listen carefully. I'm honored you consider me family." He coughed and wheezed, trying to pull air into his lungs. "Words can't express how proud I am of you, or how much I love you. My soul will rest in peace knowing you and Treygan have each other."

"Stop it." My eyes burned again. "Stop talking about dying. That's not happening."

He squeezed my fingers tighter. "Remember, once upon a time I was a gorgon. I grew up hearing our kinds' stories. One of them was about a merman who went into Harte, and he made it back alive." More wet and strained coughing. My lungs burned from sympathy pain. "But he only lived to tell one other soul about it."

"You mean there is a way?" Treygan asked.

"It's a longshot, but it's your only shot." Uncle Lloyd wiped a drop of blood from his mouth with a handkerchief.

"Don't say another word." I tried pulling away, but he kept a tight grip on me. "No more meddling. Nothing is worth losing you."

"Rownan is my son. I'd gladly give up my life for him, Treygan, or you. In this case, Rownan needs me to meddle, and you and Treygan need to hear what I have to say."

"No." I shook my head and closed my eyes, as if that could keep him from talking.

"It tears me apart to think of any of my children entering that evil place, but there's no stopping Rownan—that I'm sure of. You two are his only chance of surviving. He's not strong enough to find his own way out. I'm sure of that too."

"You're not putting yourself at risk," I told Treygan. "I'll go with Rownan."

Treygan smirked. "I promised you I'd always be your guardian, and you think I'm letting you go to Harte without me?"

Truth be told, I didn't want to go without him, but it seemed awful and selfish not to put up some kind of fight. Rownan wanted to swim through hell to find Vienna, and Treygan and I would either have to stop him or go with him.

Rowan

My muscles felt like limp tentacles, my back ached, and my broken wrist still throbbed.

Treygan came out the winner of our fight on the Triple Eighteen, and he deserved to win. Maybe I deserved all the bad things that happened—and were still happening—to me. I deceived Yara. I kissed someone other than my wife. I lied to my own kind. Sure, I did it all to survive and get back to Vienna, but karma doesn't care about reasoning. Wrong is wrong, and eventually consequences must be paid.

I was severely paying.

Vienna's brother said she sank into a deep depression as soon as the gate closed. No one could snap her out of it, not even her mother. Vienna was convinced that the gate between Earth and Rathe would never open again. Everyone in Rathe assumed we were as good as dead, sealed away permanently from our realm. No one believed we could last eighteen years without Rathe's suns, moons, and water.

Vienna only waited two years. Her mother said she grew more crazed and impatient until she couldn't take anymore. One night she disappeared, leaving a note saying she went to Harte to find the legendary secret gateway to Earth's realm. That's the last anyone heard from her.

A stabbing pain shot through my wrist. The broken bone bulged beneath my skin, threatening to break through. I should have let the Violets heal me like Dina suggested, but I had been without Vienna for almost two decades. I couldn't wait a minute longer, and I couldn't risk anyone trying to stop me.

Cradling my injured wrist against my chest, I dove deeper, weaving between giant buttress trees and ignoring the macaw fish swimming behind me. Why Medusa felt the need to create swimming parrots was beyond me. They served no purpose except to pollute the ocean with their cackling gibberish that no one wanted to hear.

I waited for them to stop following me. The elders told me I would know I was getting close to Rathe's border by the lack of plant life—or any other life. They said to look for black rock formations rising out of the water. One would look like a mountainous trident. A lightless pass between the trident's spears would allow me access to Harte. I hoped it was cold on the outskirts of Rathe. The colder the water, the faster I'd be able to swim.

A burst of red exploded to the side of me. When the bubbles cleared, Nixie's ruby eyes glowed in front of me. Her red hair rose around her head like flames.

What are you doing here? I mentally asked her.

She smiled and dipped down, then snaked her body against mine. *I'm here to entice you to stay.*

I'm going to Harte. No one can stop me.

She raked her talons over my chest then ran her hands through my hair. *I promise, once you get a taste of me, you won't worry about Vienna anymore.*

I pushed her away from me. *As always, thanks for the offer, but no. I'm going to find my wife.*

She looped behind me, and then I was launched upward. We broke through the surface and Nixie hovered above the water, holding me under my arms. I hated that sirens were so strong.

"Let go of me!" I demanded. "You have no right to interfere."

"Maybe I don't, but Yara does. She ordered me to find you and stop you from swimming any farther."

"Screw Yara! I don't care how much power she has. She can't control me."

"Apparently she can, because here we are. You don't seem to be going anywhere."

I whipped my tail back and forth, trying to hit her or wiggle free, but it was pointless. Nixie had a firm grip on me. "What are we going to do, hang here until Yara arrives?"

"I offered to make the wait more enjoyable." She purred in my ear. "The offer still stands if you'd like to learn why redheads are more fun."

She knew I'd never take her up on it. "This is bullshit."

Nixie let out one of her shrill bird calls and it echoed across the ocean. A similar cry answered back. "She's on her way."

"You wouldn't fly me to Harte's gate like I asked, but you'll fly here to stop me just because Yara says so?"

"I'm Yara's siren. I do what she tells me."

"You're just going to accept that and let her control you for the rest of your life?"

"It's my duty."

"You're deranged, Nix."

"No, I'm content. I have a purpose. I'm assigned to the most powerful and unique member of the gorgon sister trinity. I lucked out."

I had heard about Yara's transformation, but I didn't believe it until I saw it with my own eyes. She was flying toward us. *Flying.* She had giant, sparkling white wings that matched her hair. As she got closer, I saw a silver serpent hissing above her left shoulder.

She halted in front of me and Nixie. Her wings flapped hard, blowing us backward.

"Easy, Yara!" Nixie barked.

Yara's wings slowed, but stayed high and wide in the air. The wind around us calmed. "Sorry about that," Yara said. "Still getting used to all of my accessories."

I looked her up and down. "I don't see any selkie features."

Pearl-colored claws shot out from her fingertips with impressive speed. She pressed the razor-sharp tips under my chin. "Do these clear up any doubts about my selkie side?"

"Crystal clear. Now come with me and save one of your kind."

Yara's chest turned red. I had learned that color meant sadness for her. "Rownan, I know you want to go to Harte and search for Vienna, but it's a suicide mission."

"Living without her is worse than suicide."

Her voice softened. "Don't say that."

"Why not? It's the truth. You've been in love with Treygan for a few weeks. Vienna and I have loved each other since we were kids. Imagine how heartbroken you'd be if you lost Treygan—if he was trapped in some damned world alone. Take the pain that you can only imagine and amplify it by infinity. After that, if you still have the nerve to stop me from going after her, then you don't have a fraction of the heart and soul people think you do."

Her jaw went slack and sadness filled her eyes. The snake rose beside her head and hissed at me.

"And what the hell is that?" I asked. "Does that thing bite?"

"Only if I want her to."

I tilted my head, trying to get a better look at the white-eyed serpent. "Wait, is he—"

"She," Yara corrected. "Her name is Sage."

"Whatever. Is she physically attached to you?"

Yara petted the snake, who was still hissing at me.

"Of course she is," Nixie answered. "Yara is part gorgon now."

I laughed. "That's priceless. So, you and Treygan always have an audience when you're together. Creepy."

"First of all," Yara started, "she's not creepy. She enhances my intelligence and helps me make decisions. Second, it's not like she watches me and Treygan all the time. If we want privacy, she goes to sleep. And she disappears when I'm in human form."

Nixie curved her wings so they brushed up the front of my tail. "And all the good stuff happens when they're in human form."

"Nixie," Yara snapped. "Don't be disrespectful."

"What?" Nixie shrugged, momentarily lifting me higher. "Treygan is devourable."

"You think all men are devourable."

"True," Nixie said, "but I bet Treygan is exceptionally delicious."

"Shut up." I groaned. As if I wanted to hear them talk about my brother that way. "We all know Treygan can't get it on with Yara. He'd turn her to stone again."

Yara called me an idiot just as Nixie dropped me into the water. Totally unexpected, but at least I didn't feel like a worm hanging from a hook anymore. I swam back to the surface where Nixie and Yara were waiting for me.

"Let's get back to the bigger and more important issue," Yara said. "Rownan, are you one hundred percent sure you want to go to Harte? You do know your odds of coming out alive are, like, non-existent, right?"

My anger dispersed into the ocean around me. I swam closer, letting down my guard, hoping Yara would try to look past our rough history together. "You'll probably never forgive me for lying to you and mysting you into believing we were a couple. I don't blame you for that. I'm disgusted with myself for doing it, but I thought I had no choice. All of that horribleness, all of my lies and schemes, I did them for love. Not because I'm a bad person, not because I wanted to hurt you, not even so the gate would open and all the selkies could go home. I did it for Vienna. Every move I made was so I could return to Vienna."

Yara took a deep breath. Her weird snake relaxed against her shoulder, and I met her unblinking eyes again. "When I finally made it back here, Vienna was gone. She risked her life and soul, went to some damned, dreadful place, *alone*, on the slim chance she'd find a way to get back to me and be trapped with me in Earth's realm. That's the kind of stuff we do for each other. That's how unstoppable our love is. No torture could be worse than living without Vienna." My heart ached at the thought. I had to keep moving. Too much time to think would destroy me. "But I don't expect you to understand that."

Yara leaned down and lifted my chin. "I do understand. So does Treygan. That's why we're coming with you."

I shrieked so loud my vocal cords ached. "You're what?"

Yara looked up at me. "We can't let Rownan go to Harte alone."

Why should she care what happened to Rownan? "Don't fall for that pathetic speech of his. He deceived you," I reminded her. "He planned to kill you."

"But he didn't go through with it. In the end, he helped me. He even endured being tortured by Jack so Treygan and I could be together."

I flew backward, putting distance between us, then crossed my arms over my chest. "I am *not* going into that realm."

Yara flew up to meet me. "No one asked you to."

Yara was my assigned gorgon. My job was to serve her. How could she consider traveling to somewhere like Harte without me? I spoke quietly so Rownan wouldn't hear. "You told me I'd be your first in command. You said you had big plans for Rathe and needed my help."

"All of that is still true." Yara's focus drifted to Rownan. "This is just a detour."

"Detour? You won't come back if you go to Harte." I hovered in front of her face, forcing her to look at me again. "No one comes back."

"Come on, Nixie. Have some faith in me."

"It's not about faith. You don't even know how to use all of your abilities yet. You hardly know anything about our realm, but you're going to blindly enter Harte and expect to come back?"

"I know what I'm capable of." Yara's snake slithered over her shoulder and our noses almost touched.

"You're delusional," I snapped. Sage hissed at me, and I hissed back.

Yara flew down to Rownan. He was watching us with a mixed look of shock and confusion.

"Treygan and I are going with you," she repeated, "but we need to be smart about this. We have to give ourselves the best chance at finding Vienna and making it back to Rathe."

I landed on the water, pacing beside them, my eyes burning holes into Rownan's thick, stupid skull. Rownan had to tell Yara no. Even if he didn't care what happened to Treygan, he had to care about Yara and the future of Rathe.

Rownan—the useless twit—didn't argue with her. "I can't believe what you're saying. Actually, I sort of believe you'd do something like this, but Treygan? He agreed?"

"I didn't even ask him." Yara shrugged. "He insisted. He's on his way here."

Rownan almost smiled. "I'll be damned."

"Exactly!" I kicked the water, sending the spray directly into Rownan's face. "You *will* be damned! All of you will be damned." Gusts of wind blew so hard that Rownan drifted away from us in the churning waves.

Yara grabbed my arm. "Calm down, Nixie!"

But it was too late. I had lost my temper. I would conjure up a storm that would put Yara's birthday hurricane to shame. Anything to stop her from entering Harte. "My job is to protect you. If I have to blow this realm to oblivion to stop you from going, I will."

"You're forgetting I can create storms of my own."

"I have much more experience."

Yara squared her shoulders and lifted her chin. "Don't test me."

Of all the nerve. I threw my hands above my head and dark clouds boiled into being. I gritted my teeth and thunder rumbled.

Yara's wings rose high and wide. Lightning split the sky with three distinct bolts. She raised her arms and the lightning rotated so it was parallel with the horizon.

I gasped.

She circled her hands above her head and the bolts stretched and linked together, creating a belt of flashing light around us. I had never seen a siren manipulate lightning that way. We could create it, even direct it where to strike, but this was different. My skin buzzed with electric current and my hair stood on end. Yara didn't look the least bit affected. Maybe she had learned more about her abilities than I thought.

"Now, that's impressive," Rownan shouted, swimming toward us.

I took a few deep breaths. My wind and waves calmed. The clouds I had created dispersed and the sky returned to its normal shade of violet. With a flick of Yara's fingers the band of lightning around us fizzled into smoke that drifted away.

I gripped Yara's shoulders. "You'll lose your soul if you go to that world. We'll never see you again. Think about everyone here who needs you. You just filled the empty place in the gorgon trinity, and now you're going to give it up?"

"I promise I'll come back." Yara stroked my hair. "With my soul intact."

"You can't promise that!" I shoved her hand away. "You're already breaking promises. I liked you better when you couldn't lie."

"Wait." Rownan bobbed in the waves below us. He was like a pesky eel that wouldn't go away. "Yara can lie again? What other changes should I know about?"

Yara shushed us. "I'd never lie about important things, but sometimes white lies are necessary." She practically whispered,

"The no lying rule is outdated and makes for some awkward situations."

Rownan smirked at Yara. "I knew you had a devious side."

Yara's transformation into a mixed breed left her equally balanced with dark and light, warm and cold. I wondered, if the time ever came, which species she would defend first. Given the current situation, I guessed it wouldn't be me and my siren sisters.

"So, this preparation stuff you're talking about," Rownan said. "What's the plan? Gather supplies, heal my arm, and come back tomorrow?"

Yara tilted her head. "Yes, yes, and no. We'll need a couple of weeks to—"

"Weeks?" Rownan repeated. "No way. That's too long. In a couple of weeks Vienna could be dead."

"You crazy fools!" I shouted. "She went in there sixteen years ago. She's already dead."

"Shut up, you loveless harpy!" Rownan's claws shot out and he swatted at me, but I swooped out of his reach.

"If not dead, she's an empty shell of herself." I snapped my teeth at Rownan. "You're risking Yara's life for someone who is either gone or soulless."

"Don't talk about her like that!" His nostrils flared as he thrashed his arms. "I hope your wings fall off!"

"Both of you, stop it!" Yara ordered.

Rownan kept his eyes on me and spit in the water. Knowing he really wanted to spit at me, I stuck out my tongue at him.

He rolled his eyes. "Yara will be fine. Even if she does die, Medusa will just send her back again."

That thought hadn't occurred to me, and it momentarily gave me hope, but then I looked at Yara.

"Not true," she said. "Medusa and Poseidon set some terms in our bargain too. Medusa made it very clear that I will not get a third chance at life. When I die again, it will be permanent."

We were all silent for a few moments. Medusa had reigned over Rathe for hundreds of years. Her sisters had reigned for centuries. How long would Yara live if she didn't do anything stupid and get herself killed? What would happen to me and my position if Yara was gone?

"You're not dying anytime soon," I told her. I shot Rownan a fiery glare. "Especially not in Harte."

"Whatever," Rownan said. "I'm going to Harte. Today."

"No, you're not!" Yara yelled.

Rownan dipped under the water and Yara dove in after him. They wrestled beneath the surface. I had no intentions of interfering, but then he used his claws on her. I cried out in pain as he sliced open her chest. I felt her injury as if it was my own. Part of me relished the pain because it meant my connection with Yara was strengthening. The other part of me rushed to her defense and dove down, tearing him off her.

I grabbed him by his hair, burst out of the water, and flew straight for a colony of jagged rocks. I pinned him down with my talons, screeching and snapping at his face.

"Nixie, stop!" Yara shouted.

She wrapped her arms around my waist and pulled me off him, but not before I kicked him in the jaw. "Don't ever hurt her again, you useless seal!"

Yara grabbed my chin and forced me to look at her. She was angry and flustered. "You didn't need to attack him!"

"I'm your siren. My duty is to protect you."

"I don't need you to protect me. I just need you to follow my orders."

My wings drooped, but I couldn't look away from her. How could she say something like that? How could she deprive me of reacting to my natural instincts? "But I—"

"No arguing." She let go of me and flew to Rownan's side. "Are you okay?"

Rownan's face and arms were bleeding. He rubbed and stretched his back, but he looked as arrogant as ever. "Just keep your attack bird away from me."

I imagined ripping every hair out of his head, making a nest out of it, then setting it on fire with my anger.

Treygan leaped out of the water and pulled Rownan under so fast that Yara and I were momentarily stunned. Then Yara dove beneath the water, and I followed.

Treygan had Rownan in a chokehold with one of Rownan's arms pinned behind his back. He must have seen Rownan attack me and Yara.

I pumped my fist. *Break his other arm!*

Yara was beside them in an instant, pulling Treygan's hand from Rownan's throat.

Apologize to both of them, Treygan commanded Rownan while extending his sight so we could hear his thoughts.

I'm sorry, Rownan said. *You don't understand how desperate I am to find Vienna.*

Treygan pulled Rownan so close their noses almost touched. I didn't hear everything Treygan said to him, but I caught his last words: … *ever again, I'll destroy you.*

Please, Yara begged. *No more fighting. Rownan, we want to help you, but the violence needs to stop and you need to heal.*

After all that, she still wanted to help Rownan. She didn't even glance in my direction. She had no consideration for me whatsoever. Our bond meant nothing to her.

How quickly the tide had turned.

While I appreciated Treygan defending me and Nixie, I sympathized with Rownan.

Let him go, I said to Treygan.

Rownan drifted backward, holding his injured wrist and looking mostly defeated. A few days ago I would've strangled him myself for all his lies and deceit. I'd had to hide from the selkies because they wanted to kill me. Now I was part selkie, and I felt a fierce and protective loyalty to him.

That same instinct burned inside of me for every sea creature: merfolk, selkies, sirens, gorgons, even Sage.

When I first discovered a snake attached to my head I was horrified, but it didn't take long for me to grow fond of her. Sometimes I heard whispers in my mind and wondered if Sage communicated like the rest of us did underwater, or if I was just imagining she had a voice. I never could have predicted I would become so attached to a serpent—literally and emotionally. Feeling my affection for her, Sage rubbed against my neck.

My love for Rathe and its creatures, even those I hadn't met yet, was almost overwhelming at times. Medusa told me I would inherit her instincts, but had I also inherited her love for this realm and everything in it?

I didn't want to fight with Rownan or Nixie. I was terrified to enter Harte, but I couldn't sit back and wave goodbye and good luck as Rownan went on an eternal vacation to hell.

You can't go like this, I told Rownan, swimming closer to him. *Let me take you to the Violets so they can heal you.*

I'm fine. I'm going now. If the three of you want to try to stop me, then so be it, but you'll have to kill me because I won't give up.

Damn it, Rownan, Treygan said. *You're injured. Don't you want to give yourself the best chance of surviving? You need to be as healthy and strong as possible.*

Heartbreak makes me invincible. No amount of physical pain can stop me from getting to Vienna as soon as possible.

I flashed a worried glance at Treygan, knowing we would never win this argument. Treygan wouldn't hurt Rownan badly enough to stop him from going into Harte. Neither would I.

Fine, Treygan said. *Be stubborn. We'll go now.*

I took a deep breath. We were really doing this. My eyes locked with Rownan's. I nodded in agreement with Treygan. *But when you can't keep up and we have to carry you, expect a resentful I-told-you-so.*

Don't worry your pearly little head. I'll keep up.

You are mad! Insane! Nixie mentally shouted at me. *You are throwing away your new position and your entire life.*

You know my philosophy, Nixie. Love until it kills you, because there's nothing better worth dying for.

Stheno and Euryale were right, she hissed. *You're not nearly intelligent enough to take Medusa's place.*

I flinched. I would expect Stheno and Euryale to say something like that, but it hurt to hear Nixie agree with them. *We'll see about that.*

I turned and swam away. Rownan and Treygan followed. I heard Nixie break through the surface. I didn't know if she would travel to the gate with us or desert me, but it didn't matter.

Treygan, Rownan, and I didn't say anything else to each other as we swam closer to the dark border of Rathe. I had so many things I wanted to discuss with Rownan. I wanted to thank him for helping me on the Triple Eighteen, for enduring torture from Jack so that Treygan and I could be together, and for protecting me from being sacrificed by the selkies. I wanted to tell him his father truly did love him and was proud of him. But everything I had rehearsed in my head didn't feel adequate. We all stared ahead and swam in silence.

Rownan was first to spot Poseidon's marker. The rocks were taller than I pictured, but there was no mistaking the black mountain made to look like a trident. That alone should have been a severe enough warning to stay away from it.

"Never cross Poseidon's trident," Treygan recited.

A legendary proverb we were foolishly choosing to disobey. I realized everything had gone still and quiet. There had been no plant life for miles. No creatures in the sea or air except for us. Even the waves crashing against the rocks made no sound.

My hands were shaking. I looked at Treygan. His jaw was tense, and he was breathing hard. I glanced at Rownan. I had never seen him so pale. I spotted a vibrant red shimmering in the far distance. Nixie was perched on the ledge of a cliff several peaks to the right of Trident Rock. She hadn't deserted me after all.

My tail felt ice-cold beneath the water, probably because all my blood was being used to fuel the supersonic beating of my heart. I stared up at the towering pillars of rock. I tried swallowing, but my mouth was bone-dry. "You're sure we're doing this?"

Treygan squeezed my hand. Rownan gave one firm nod. I took a deep breath, and we swam into a foreboding mist, entering the shadow between two of the spears.

A burning jolt shot through me. We were thrown backward by a curtain of electricity. The shock was so powerful that we were launched up out of the water. I landed in a hard belly flop that stung the whole front of my body. All of my hair was standing on end. My skin felt like a crackling fire.

"What the hell was that?" Rownan gasped.

Treygan shook his head as if trying to shake off the pain. "It felt like lightning hit us."

I searched the sky to see if Nixie had created an electrical storm to stop us, but saw nothing except spires of black rock silently mocking us.

Rownan swam forward again, only to be thrown back even harder. His body flew in an arc as if he had been punched with a powerful uppercut from an invisible giant. He skidded across the water. He was much more shaken up by the second jolt.

Nixie flew toward us.

"Stay right here," I told Treygan. "And don't let him try again until I get back. We don't need him shocking himself to death."

I flew up into the sky to meet Nixie.

"I thought this would be one of the most depressing moments of my life," Nixie said, grinning. She was biting her lip so hard I couldn't tell if it was bleeding or just her natural shade of crimson. "But Rownan getting trounced a second time was pure bliss."

"We couldn't cross. Do you have any idea why?"

Nixie shrugged. "No clue."

Sage curved forward, her diamond-like eyes blinking at me as her scales warmed against my skin. *Sea monster worlds. Part human.*

My wings drooped as I looked over my shoulder at Treygan and Rownan waiting below. I muttered to myself as the truth hit me. "It's a gate between two sea monster worlds. The three of us are all part human."

"What?" Nixie asked.

Of course. I swooped down to Treygan and Rownan. "We can't pass through the gateway because we all have human blood in us. Only pure-blooded sea monsters can pass through it."

"Ohhhh," Nixie cooed behind me.

"No! No way!" Rownan punched the water while yelling like a maniac. Treygan and I let him throw his fit. He deserved to lose control. I would have too if someone had told me there was no way to save Treygan from a damned world.

I looked at Treygan and tried to imagine it. What if he was in Harte and I couldn't get to him? Technically, we had only been together for weeks, but our bond was already so strong. Rownan and Vienna had years together before they were separated. How does someone ever accept that they have to give up on reuniting with their soul mate?

Rownan finally stopped punching and yelling. He clutched his face in his hands. "This can't be happening."

Treygan and I kept silent. Nothing we could say would help. My heart broke for Rownan, but I felt heinous because a big part of me was relieved that we couldn't enter Harte. If we couldn't enter, we couldn't not come back.

"I'll kill him." Rownan dove beneath the water. His tail shot away from us faster than I had ever seen him swim.

"Where is he going?" I asked Treygan. "Who is he going to kill?"

Treygan shut his eyes and pinched the bridge of his nose. "Our father."

The long swim hadn't calmed me down at all. Treygan caught up to me and stayed by my side the whole way. He only attempted to stop me once.

I scrambled up the ladder to the pier. Yara was already standing there, waiting with clothes for us. I pushed past her.

"At least put some shorts on," she yelled, trying to keep up with me. "It's tourist season!"

I turned around, snatched a pair of shorts from her, pulled them on, and stormed off. Yara and Treygan followed close behind.

I stomped up the porch steps of Lloyd's house and kicked the door open. He was sitting in his recliner with a drink in his hand, like he didn't have a care in the world.

"I couldn't pass through the gate! Do you want to know why?" I leaned down, bracing my arms on either side of his chair. I was so close to his face I could smell the orange juice he was drinking. "Because I'm part human. Because you tainted me with your human blood, and now I can't save Vienna!"

Yara and Treygan stayed on the other side of the room.

"Did you know about this?" I asked through clenched teeth.

My meddling father said nothing. Just downed his juice and rattled the ice cubes around his empty glass. His silence said it all.

I grabbed a vase and smashed it on the tile floor. It didn't put a dent in my anger. I grabbed the side table by Lloyd's chair.

"Rownan!" Yara yelled, but I didn't stop.

I lifted the table over my head and threw it at the floor-to-ceiling aquarium. The glass cracked, but didn't break. My chest heaved up and down. My eyes met Treygan's.

"Feel better?" he asked.

I shook my head.

He bent down, knocked books off the coffee table, and picked it up. He handed me the table, and I hurled it at the aquarium. The glass shattered. Water and fish poured out onto the floor.

"Rownan, stop!" Yara sprang forward, but Treygan stopped her.

"Let him be," Lloyd said. "At least that's a mess we can clean up."

"How could you do this to me?" I yelled at Lloyd. "Why did you allow me to have hope? Haven't I suffered enough already?"

Lloyd shifted in his seat, his joints cracking and popping. "I suspected you might not be able to pass through the gate, but I wasn't certain."

"You should have told me!"

Yara and Treygan were working together to clean up the aquarium mess, but Yara stepped away to shout in my face. "He can't meddle, Rownan. At all."

"He meddles to protect you and Treygan," I snarled.

Yara opened her mouth to argue, but my worthless father cut her off.

"I should have told you," he said. "I'm very sorry. There are many things I should have done differently."

"You've got that right."

"Ease up," Yara snapped at me. "He's in no condition to be yelled at. He feels bad enough as it is, and you're making things worse."

"Worse? How can things be worse? Vienna is trapped in hell, and I can't even attempt to save her! I'm never going to see her again."

Yara's eyes lowered and she sat on the arm of Lloyd's chair.

I glanced at Treygan, but he was busy ushering waves of water and fish into a new stone tank he had just created.

My knees grew weaker as the truth of my words settled deeper into my soul. I was never going to see Vienna again. She was alone, trapped in the damned realm for eternity.

I shook my head hard. "No. I refuse to let her be trapped in there." I started pacing. "I couldn't pass through the gate because I have human blood, but a pure mer or selkie could get through. I'll ask the selkies. Someone will do it." Even as I spoke the words I knew I was lying to myself. I had asked for volunteers when I first found out where Vienna had gone. No one would go with me, not even her own brother. "Or maybe Delmar or Pango. They're brave and strong."

Treygan and Yara shot each other skeptical glances.

"What should I do?" I asked desperately.

No one said anything. The room became hotter. I couldn't stand around doing nothing, losing more hope with every second. "Please, someone come up with an idea to save the day, because I'm going out of my mind!"

More deafening silence. Treygan leaned against the wall and stared at the floor. Yara stared at the new stone fish tank.

Lloyd cleared his throat then reached up and held Yara's hand. "How's Koraline doing?"

My jaw went slack. Then I punched a wall. My fist went through the plaster. "Koraline? I'm standing here begging for help at the most desperate and agonizing point in my entire life, and you're changing the subject?" I punched three more holes in the wall.

"Rownan, stop!" Yara stood, but my selfish father kept a grip on her hand so she couldn't leave his side.

"I need a drink. Or twenty." I stomped out the front door, and then slammed it behind me as hard as I could.

Jack Frost's was the nearest place with vodka. As much as I didn't want to see Jack again, I needed a serious fix. Not that any amount of drinking would ever fix my obliterated heart.

Physically, I swam alone to the Keys, but memories of Vienna and images of where she was and what might happen to her suffocated me every second. I was almost to the pier near Jack Frost's when I spotted a blur of green and yellow swimming in my direction.

I tried to dart away before they saw me, but Pango called out to me.

Fancy meeting you here, Pango said as we reached each other.

Merrick's eyes narrowed. *Aren't you supposed to be in Harte?*

We couldn't pass through the gate because of our human blood.

Pango's eyes widened. *Oh, goodness, that throws a wrench in things, doesn't it?*

To say the least. I need to find someone of pure sea monster blood who is brave enough to go in and find her.

Merrick's brow lifted.

Pango pursed his lips. *Hmm, yes, splendid plan.* He tilted his head side to side. *Impossible, but splendid nonetheless. Who are you thinking of asking?*

I looked pointedly at him. *You were the first one that came to mind.*

His eyes widened. *Me? Whaaaat?* he shrieked. *Dear, sweet seal boy, did someone club you over the head? I have a life here, and family, and Merrick. I'm not giving all that up for an eternal romp in hell.*

Merrick shook his head. *Agreed. Sorry, Rownan, but absolutely not.*

I grasped Pango's huge shoulders. *Please help me. I'll do anything.*

Pango laid his hands over mine. *Rownan, I can't imagine how difficult this is. I can honestly say I don't think you'll ever get over it, but you have to accept it. Vienna entered Harte sixteen years ago. She's gone. Even if a superhero of the sea could find her, she wouldn't be the Vienna you knew and loved.*

I pushed him away. *That's not true. She's strong enough to remain herself. She'd never stop looking for me. I know that with everything inside me. She knows I'll find her.*

Merrick swam closer. *But you can't. You can't go to Harte, and I'm sorry, but no one is going to go for you.*

I shook my head, not wanting to accept what they were saying. *Delmar. He might go.*

Merrick's shaking head mirrored mine, but for the opposite reason.

Pango touched my cheek. *It's over, Rownan. I'm deeply sorry to say it, but it's time to let go and start the grieving process.*

I turned away and swam as hard and fast as I could. I prayed Jack's bar had a bottle of vodka deeper than the ocean, because I planned on drowning myself in it.

Echo Bayou was peaceful and quiet.

The water was so still it acted as a mirror, reflecting a blur of red as I flew above it. I dipped beneath the canopy of weeping willows, gliding above the river to my old village.

I landed on a tree branch and gazed longingly at all the floating water lilies below. I missed my water lily. I missed my brothers and sisters. Many times I wished I had never accepted the promotion to a siren.

When Cleo died, my siren sisters panicked. Otabia and Mariza needed a replacement for Cleo or they wouldn't be as powerful. They came to my village and tempted us with stories of the amazing and adventurous life one of us would be gifted with. The chosen one would control weather, fly faster and farther than any sprite had ever dreamed, and be directly connected to the spirit of our almighty Medusa.

I yearned to be bigger, faster, more powerful—*special*. I trained and competed like my life depended on it. I wanted that sacred spot as a siren so badly. Years later, after seducing countless men and stealing even more memories, after being bossed around by Otabia and Mariza and never once feeling a true connection to Medusa, I realized the grass wasn't greener on the other side. If I could go back and do it all over, I would choose to remain a sprite. Homesickness is a wretched disease, and I would never be cured of it.

Reminiscing about the merrier days of my life, I started humming an old sprite hymn. The water lilies lit up one by one as my family stirred awake. Keeley was the first to poke her tiny head out from the petals of her electric blue flower.

"Nixie!" Her high-pitched voice buzzed through the air, followed by the happy cries of dozens more water sprites. Their voices sounded like pennies dropping into a copper wishing well.

Keeley zoomed at my head then stopped short and stood on the tip of my nose. "We've missed you so!" She threw her arms open and hugged the bridge of my nose, then flitted around kissing my eyelids and forehead.

"I've missed you too." I sighed. "More than you can imagine."

More of my brothers and sisters swarmed me, landing on my shoulders, arms, legs, and anywhere else they could find room. My skin was speckled with all the colors of the rainbow as they tickled me with kisses and loving pinches.

"Tell us news!" Jenna circled my head. Her radiant grin was almost as bright as her sunflower-colored skin. "What great adventures will you be having with Yara?"

"No adventures," I confessed. "Not even any work to be done."

Echoes of "what" and "why" and "what do you mean" reverberated off me and the trees. I wanted to tell them everything, how Yara had chosen Rownan over me and everyone else in Rathe, how Yara spent most of her time with Treygan, and how she had bonded more with Sage than with me. Now that I thought about it, I had felt a stronger connection to Yara before she was transformed. She was so powerful now that she didn't need me. I hated being the orphaned siren who would never live up to the reputation of her sisters.

My lips parted as I started to explain, but then, there beneath the weeping willows, with dozens of sprites watching me, a tear rolled down my cheek. It was unexpected, and something I could never let happen in front of Otabia or Mariza.

"Why so sad?" Keeley asked as she pushed away my tear. "That's not a happy tear, and sad tears shouldn't fall from such a pretty face. If I could, I'd weave a spell to make you our size again so I could give you a big hug, but as it is I can only hug one of your fingers at a time and somehow I think that wouldn't be enough unless maybe we all hugged you at the same time and—"

"Keeley, shush." Jenna said. "Sometimes I don't understand how your mouth can keep up with your mind. Let Nixie tell us what's upsetting her."

They all looked at me, wide-eyed and full of concern. My huge family of tiny, beautiful souls surrounded me and supported me, even though I deserted them to become a siren. I couldn't tell them that I had made a horrible mistake. I couldn't admit the tear I shed was due to my own sadness. A siren would never behave that way.

"It's just Yara's emotions," I lied. "Our bond is so strong that I feel her sadness as if it's my own."

"Ooooh," Jenna cooed. "It must be amazing to feel so connected to Rathe's new ruler."

All the sprites sparkled and fluttered, intrigued and excited by my lie.

I nodded. "Words can't express how I feel."

Only a few minutes had passed until something inside me ached to fly again. Since my transformation I never felt content. If I was flying, I ached to be in the water. If I was swimming, my wings yearned to break free. When I was hot, I craved the chill of the moon. When I was cold, I craved the sun. The internal battle was daunting. Had I made a mistake by thinking I could handle being a combination of human, mer, selkie, siren, and gorgon? Would I ever feel at peace?

Sage slithered up against my cheek, silently assuring me I would find a way.

I rounded a stretch of glowing coral then shot upward and broke through the surface. Pink and green rays of Medusa's sun stretched through the sky.

Rathe's suns were different from the sun that shined on Earth. Three huge, oval-shaped suns floated high in our sky. *In* our sky, not millions of miles away. Rathe's suns had rays that stretched, curved, and coiled in all directions. The beams changed from very short to so long that the ends wrapped around the horizon. They weaved through the sky, linking together, crisscrossing, and creating a blanket of colorful strings over Rathe.

The best part was our suns weren't blinding. I could stare at them for hours, watching them pulse, grow, shrink, stretch, change colors, get brighter or dimmer, but never did I have to squint or shield my eyes.

The three suns represented Medusa, Stheno, and Euryale. Medusa's sun changed almost constantly. Stheno's and Euryale's stayed pretty much the same, never glowing as bright as they should, their beams never stretching and weaving like Medusa's. I tried imagining what the sky must have looked like when the three sisters were still together. Were Stheno and Euryale happier then? Did their suns become duller the longer they were shut away in their dark and lonely cave? As beautiful as Rathe was, some aspects of it seemed so unfair.

On the cold selkie side of Rathe, three moons never slept. Again, Stheno and Euryale's moons were pale and dull compared to Medusa's. I had heard about the colors that streaked the dark sky; not in radiant sunbeams like the mer side, but as showers of what appeared to be shooting stars. I hadn't witnessed them for myself yet because I had been so busy taking care of my obligations with my new gorgon sisters. I hadn't explored much of my new world, or met many of its inhabitants, but Treygan assured me I would soon.

The area of Rathe where Treygan lived reminded me so much of Solis. Houses made of all-natural materials were connected by waterways. Unlike Solis, homes here were sometimes miles apart. They were surrounded by lush landscapes with many waterfalls, trees, plants, and flowers I had never seen before.

Nature in Rathe was different in many ways from Earth. Colorful trees and buildings made of sparkling rock existed above and below the water. Coral and plants changed color all the time. Beaches had unexpected colors of sand like lavender or mint green. Even the clouds, stars, and Rathe's three moons were tinted different shades of the rainbow. Medusa had created a masterpiece when she designed this world.

Treygan paced the beach in front of his half-in-the-water, half-on-land house. His attention snapped to the sky when he sensed me, then his eyes lowered and he spotted me flying inches above the water.

The sight of him momentarily stole my breath. His hallmarks glimmered in the sunlight, and his skin's silvery hue enhanced the dark blue color of his hair. In Rathe, we didn't have to worry about humans seeing us in sea creature form. We didn't have to hide who we were. It was one of the many things I loved about my new realm.

"Nixie wasn't at the nest," I told Treygan as I landed in front of him. "Neither were Mariza and Otabia." I leaned into him as he hugged me.

"You can catch up with her later. You must be exhausted."

"Getting there."

"Let's go inside."

We swam through the stream that led into Treygan's home. As it got shallower, we both transformed our tails into legs and waded through his main entrance.

"I still can't believe rivers run through the houses here."

"Rivulets," Treygan corrected me. "No one's home is big enough for a river."

"You know what I mean. All the waterways and pools throughout everyone's houses are so cool."

"What about you?" he asked. "Where do you want your home to be?" He had an expectant look in his eyes.

"Technically, I live in the gorgon grotto."

He squinted. "Do you even have any of your belongings in there?"

"No, but ..." Stheno and Euryale each had their own den, and there was a third den that used to be Medusa's, but I was forbidden to go in it. That was fine with me because, in my opinion, Medusa's room was sacred. I took her place in the trinity to do a job, but I would never try taking over her previous private space. "The grotto doesn't exactly have a homey ambiance. I'd rather keep my stuff at my house on Eden's Hammock."

"I see."

"Why are you upset?"

His chest was speckled with blue and green. He was definitely upset, or disappointed. He ran his fingers through his wet hair, tugging harder than normal. "I hoped you'd want to live here, with me, but maybe it's too soon for that."

He wanted me to move into his house? Impose on his personal space?

"Forget I asked," he said. "It's obviously too soon for you."

"No, it's just … I guess I hadn't thought about it. So much has been on my mind, and then the Harte thing. Everything happened so fast."

He nodded, but still seemed let down. "We can discuss it whenever you're ready. Just know the invitation stands."

We walked up a few steps of carved rock and into Treygan's kitchen. I sat at the table and grabbed an odd-looking fruit, running my fingers over its green, scaly skin. It looked like a mutated cornhusk. "What is this?"

"Monstera fruit."

"Monstera fruit for monsters, of course."

Treygan grinned. "It grows in Earth too. It's just not as common as apples or oranges."

"I've never heard of it."

"It was one of the few things Medusa contributed to that realm that still exists. Poseidon wanted to make sure some parts of her would always live on in the mortal world."

"What else is there?"

"Jellyfish."

"Jellyfish?" I repeated.

"Medusozoa. Commonly referred to as, and I know this will be tough to remember," he winked at me, "Medusa."

I playfully smacked him with the monstera fruit. "I've never heard jellyfish called that."

"I suppose it's not common knowledge for most humans."

"Uncle Lloyd should have told me that sort of stuff."

"My father tried to shelter you. I'm sure he assumed the less you knew about our world, the better."

"I didn't imagine Rathe would be similar to Earth in so many ways. I mean, the houses, and all the modern conveniences. I figured everything would be underwater and more … *20,000 Leagues Under the Sea*, or something."

Treygan laughed. "Merfolk and selkies were created as land and sea dwellers. We like our legs and land just as much as we like our tails and water."

I eyed Treygan from head to toe. I was still getting used to us being somewhat naked around each other. Between our satiny, color-changing skin and the hallmarks covering our bodies I never felt truly naked or exposed, but I still had moments when I missed clothes.

I sniffed the fruit in my hands. It reminded me of pineapple. "Can I eat this?"

"Not yet. You have to wait for the scales to lift away." He silently stared out the window for a minute, then his shoulders slumped. "I'm worried about Rownan."

"Me too. I can't imagine what he's going through."

Treygan shook his head. "I still can't believe we almost went to Harte. Unprepared, no less."

"We couldn't let him go alone."

"He was going with a broken arm. He was exhausted and beat up. He never would have survived. With or without us."

"He's in love. People do crazy things for love." I pointedly raised a brow at him. "You know, like fight their own family, or volunteer to die."

Years ago, Treygan agreed to give up his life and future so I could have one, and so the sea creatures could return home to Rathe. After I found out about Treygan voluntarily sacrificing himself, I would have done anything to spare him from turning his life and soul over to the gorgon sisters. We were just as reckless as Rownan, but in different ways.

"Thank the gods we weren't able to enter Harte," Treygan said, as if suddenly realizing how dangerous it really was. "All three of us are deeply disturbed. You do realize that, right?"

"You know the saying. 'Heaven doesn't want us and Hell is afraid we'd take over.'"

"I've never heard that before."

"Must be a human thing," I snickered. "What is Harte, anyway? I mean, I know it's an evil place, but how and why is it connected to Rathe?"

"Have you ever heard the story of Pandora's box?"

"Sure. Uncle Lloyd told me Pandora was the wife of some important guy, and they were given a box as a gift but told never to open it. Pandora got curious and opened it anyway, and unleashed all kinds of bad stuff."

"Correct. That box Pandora opened was a gift from Zeus. Not long after Poseidon created Rathe for Medusa, his wife, Amphitrite, found out about their continuing love affair and sought revenge. She asked Zeus for help, and Zeus obliged. With his assistance, Amphitrite created a mirror similar to Pandora's box. Zeus sent Pegasus to take the mirror into Rathe and deliver it to Medusa."

"Wait. Pegasus? The flying horse?"

"Yes."

"Wow." I sat back in my chair. "It's hard to comprehend that some of these supposedly mythical creatures were real."

"Some were not only real, but they still exist. As you've witnessed firsthand."

"Who else is still hanging around? Is Pegasus? Because I would love to go flying with him."

Treygan smiled. "Do you want to hear the story or not?"

"Okay, okay, but eventually you will have to answer my questions about which creatures still exist."

Ignoring me, Treygan continued. "As I was saying, Pegasus delivered the mirror to Medusa. A note was attached that said the mirror was a gift so she could always see what she looked like before she was turned into a monster, but the price for her vanity would be costly. Each time she gazed into the mirror, evil would be unleashed into the world."

I sat forward, resting my elbows on the table. "Don't tell me she looked in the mirror."

"Not only did she look, she stared into the mirror more times than anyone could have guessed."

"What? I've met her. She's not that stupid."

"Wisdom comes with experience. She was sequestered in her grotto. She had no idea what was going on in the world outside. She thought evil would be unleashed on Earth, not Rathe. And, well, she didn't care much for Earth, seeing as how she was banished from it."

"So, what happened?"

"When Poseidon visited her next, he found a dark nightmare world. He questioned Medusa and she showed him the mirror and explained what happened. Poseidon removed the curse from the mirror by putting his own spell on it. From that point forward, when Medusa looked into the mirror, all she could see was Rathe. She was horrified by all the ugliness it contained, and she begged for forgiveness. Poseidon could never deny her, so he created a second realm, Harte. He spent a long time rounding up all the evil and wickedness and locking it away."

"How?"

"How what?"

"How did he round up the evil? I mean, was there some big magical net and he just scooped it all up and flung it into this other world? Seems a bit, you know, out there."

Treygan leaned back and covered his face with his hands, groaning.

"What?" I pulled his hands away. "You're telling me you never questioned this? I mean, what kind of evil was it? Evil creatures? Because that I can believe. But, like, greed, hate, all the stuff that supposedly came out of Pandora's box, how do you gather that up and get rid of it?"

"I don't question how our gods did most of what they did."

"Maybe you should."

"You question enough for both of us, Yamabuki."

I crinkled my nose at him, and then turned as a faint, high-pitched squeal caught my attention. Outside the kitchen window, dolphin fins bobbed through the water. "I've seen a lot of dolphins in Rathe. Do sharks live here too?"

"A few small breeds are permitted to come and go, but they rarely visit here."

I glanced at him, and again, he seemed to read my mind. "No tiger or bull sharks. You'll always be safe swimming in Rathe."

The awful image of Koraline fighting off sharks flashed through my mind. "I need to see Koraline and thank her for saving my life."

"I already told Pango we would visit her today. But if you're too tired we can go later."

Treygan knowing me so well was a comfort at times. "No, I'm okay. I feel bad that I haven't visited her yet." I paused, then took a deep breath. "Does she hate me?"

"No. I don't think Koraline is capable of hatred."

I stood and we made our way outside.

"Do you want to swim or fly?" Treygan asked.

"You said you didn't like me flying you around."

"I don't. I can swim while you fly." His chin lowered slightly. "I want you to fly if that's how you want to travel."

A flashing neon elephant had been dancing between us ever since I transformed into more than just a mermaid, but neither one of us wanted to acknowledge it. I had powers that Treygan didn't. I could conjure up storms. I had fierce selkie claws. I could fly faster than he swam. I didn't know much about dating or relationships, but I was pretty sure he was feeling emasculated.

"Does it bother you that I ..." I couldn't think of the proper words to describe what I wanted to say without making the situation worse. "That I can fly?"

If we left it as just flying, maybe he wouldn't feel so uncomfortable.

"I'm envious that you can fly. And I'm sure one day I will be okay with you flying me around. Right now it reminds me too much of the siren sisters. They're manipulative and live a lifestyle I have never agreed with. I know you'd never do the despicable things they do, but Otabia and Mariza have rubbed me the wrong way too many times. And flown me around too much lately."

"Oh!" What a relief. "So, it has nothing to do with me being faster than you."

His head snapped up.

Crap. Did I really just say that out loud?

Half a grin pulled at one corner of his mouth and he crossed his arms over his chest. "Ah, you thought my manhood was being threatened because you can fly faster than I swim?" The sand under my feet was the only place I could look. "Yara, I'm much more secure than that."

"I figured you were. It's just all these new abilities are overwhelming me, so I figured they might be overwhelming you too."

"They are a lot to take in, but I can handle it, I assure you." He reached forward and cupped my chin. "Besides, I'm still more experienced in many areas. I'd beat you in a swimming race any day. And I'm not sure if you'll ever be able to do this." He turned to the left. A nearby sea grape tree crackled and turned to stone.

Sage hissed to life beside my head.

"Treygan!" I exclaimed.

He blinked his eyes a few times before looking at me again.

I playfully shoved his chest. "You said you avoid using your gorgon side whenever possible."

"That was before the love of my life turned part gorgon and acquired a charming snake as her sidekick. I suddenly feel proud to be gorgon."

I smiled so big it made my cheeks ache.

Sage reached forward, and Treygan rubbed her head. "Gorgons unite, isn't that right, Sage?"

She purred and wrapped herself around his hand in what looked like her version of a hug, then returned to her place on my shoulder.

"I like seeing you like this," I told Treygan.

"Like what?"

"Proud of who and what you are."

He stood taller, his shoulders spread wider. "You helped me realize my gorgon side is nothing to be ashamed of."

"Good." I threw my arms around his neck. "Now teach me how to turn things to stone."

He lifted me off my feet. "Later. First, we have a date with Koraline and Pango."

"I've decided I want to swim there." I bit my lip, fighting back a smile. "So we can race."

Treygan kissed me while carrying me into the water. Confidently—bordering on cocky—he said, "I apologize in advance for leaving you in a cloud of bubbles."

He did win. I could barely keep him in sight underwater, so I had to fly to catch up.

Koraline's private oasis was almost as pretty and green as she was. Treygan held my hand as we walked onto her beach, which had the softest lime green sand my feet had ever felt. My stomach, however, was queasy.

I retracted my wings and told Sage to get some rest. She faded away, leaving only a dull tingling at the base of my skull. Treygan's brow rose.

"Koraline lost half of her tail," I explained. "It would be rude to walk in there flaunting all the new additions to my body when she just lost a crucial part of hers."

He nodded and squeezed my hand.

"I don't know what to say to her," I admitted.

"Speak from your heart. The words will come."

Pango's green, curly hair popped through a window of the sandstone house. "Hello, love birds! We've been expecting you."

I waved to Pango then shot Treygan one last worried look, but he was already shouting back to Pango. "Good to see you!"

Koraline's home had a rope bridge porch just like her house on Solis. We went up the steps and Treygan walked right in. Pango met us just inside the door and barreled us over with one of his not-so-gentle hugs. "It warms my heart to see you sugar babies alive and well. We're home!" He spun around with his arms above his head. "Can you believe it?"

"Feels good to be back," Treygan said.

"What do you think of our lovely world?" Pango asked me. "Isn't it like Disney World on steroids?"

I grinned. "It's more gorgeous than I imagined."

"And now, little miss queen of our magical kingdom, you are the grand master of it. How's that feel?"

"It's a lot of pressure."

Pango laughed. "I bet it is. I would not want to trade places with you. No offense."

"None taken."

"Hello?" Koraline called from another room. "Rotting away like unwanted sushi in here! I thought this visit was for me."

Treygan led me into what would be considered the living room in a human house. Koraline was sitting in a pool with stone seating carved into the walls. My focus immediately shot to her tail. The tip where her fins should have been was wrapped in material that looked like palm fronds. I was glad the foliage and water prevented me from seeing further details. I wasn't sure I could handle seeing what the sharks did to her.

"How are you feeling?" I asked her.

"Much better." She was smiling as if she didn't mind getting eaten half to death by sharks. "How are you doing?"

"A lot has changed since we were last together."

"It sure has. You're a White, which no one has ever seen before. You're breathtaking."

My cheeks roared with warmth that spread down my chest where orange splotches appeared.

Koraline was still smiling. "I'm sorry. I didn't mean to embarrass you."

I wrung my hands, trying to mellow out so my chest would go back to its normal color. "It's okay."

Koraline looked at Treygan. "Good gods, look at you, Treygan. I've never seen you so happy. Love looks amazing on you."

Treygan flashed me a smitten grin. "Thank you, Koraline. We were a very unlikely couple, but somehow, here we are."

"A perfect and adorable couple." Pango clapped his hands. "Let's celebrate all these good tidings with baked goods. I've been whipping up all kinds of deliciousness."

Treygan stepped into the pool and sat beside Koraline. "The Violets tell us you're healing better than they expected."

"I'm feeling so much better." Koraline rubbed the scales around her hips. "Anything is an improvement from a coma, right?"

She shouldered Treygan, and they both smiled. I wasn't ready to joke about the disabling injuries I had caused her, so I offered to help Pango in the kitchen.

"Need any help?" He was shoveling cookies from a pan onto a plate.

"Thank you, but I have everything under control."

I lowered my voice so Koraline wouldn't overhear me. "Is Koraline upset with me for what happened to her?"

"Why would she be? You didn't tell those heathen sharks to eat her tail."

I cringed at the memory of their gnashing teeth and all that blood in the water. "But she was attacked because of me."

"Sweet potato, stop it. All of us are alive and back home because of you. She came out of her coma because she returned to the strong energy of our world. Did you consider that?" He wiped his hands on his apron and hugged me. "We can split hairs all you'd like, but we're all victorious because we are home, alive, and well."

"Do you honestly think Koraline will ever be able to swim again?"

With his huge hands that smelled like cookies, Pango lifted my chin. "Yara, that's like asking if the sun will ever shine again."

Half a smile broke through my tense lips.

"Yes! That's what I want to see. Smiles all around. Now, come on, we have cookies to consume!"

Koraline and Treygan were talking quietly, but they stopped as soon as Pango and I entered the room. An awkward indication they had been talking about me.

Koraline motioned to the empty seat beside her. "Yara, sit with me. We have lots to catch up on."

I sat down in the pool, almost letting my legs transform into my tail, but then I realized how inconsiderate that would be. "How deep is this thing?"

"Deep. It has a couple of rooms down there."

I figured. Treygan's house had the same kind of set-up. I just didn't know what else to talk about.

Koraline shifted so she was facing me. "When you died, what happened?"

"Koraline!" Pango almost choked on his cookie. "Have manners somehow escaped you?"

"It's okay," I said. "I don't mind discussing it."

Koraline splashed water at Pango, but didn't take her eyes off me. "Treygan said you met Medusa and Poseidon."

"I did. It was the most incredible thing I've ever experienced."

Her sea-green eyes were wide and sparkling. "And you talked to them?"

"Yup."

"Holy mackerel. What was that like?"

"Very intimidating."

"I can imagine!" She threw her head back. "You were shooting the breeze with our makers! A god and goddess. Do you realize how epic that is? You're my hero, you know that? Seriously, I want to hear every detail from start to finish. I might even take notes."

"Later." Pango held out the plate of cookies. "Right now it's time for treats, and you need to reassure our worry wart here that you're going to recover and that all is well in the land of Koraline."

Koraline grabbed two cookies, practically inhaling the first one. "I'm *fine*." She waved her hand, sending crumbs dropping into the pool. Pango tsked her and tried scooping them out of the water while Koraline kept talking. "At least tell me what you said to convince them to send you back. I mean, you were dead!"

"I told Medusa I was her only shot at filling her place in the gorgon trinity. That I couldn't die. I demanded she send me back."

"And she just agreed?"

"At first she said no, but my uncle and—" I didn't want to get into a long explanation about how Liora was a ghost that still communicated with Uncle Lloyd. "Let's just say I had wise advisors who told me not to take no for an answer."

Koraline nibbled on a cookie with a giddy smile. "It reminds me of one of my favorite quotes by Harriet Stowe. Never give up, for that is the place and time that the tide will turn."

Koraline truly didn't seem upset with me at all. It felt just like it did when she was my teacher, educating me about my new life as a mermaid. The ease of our conversation didn't make me feel any less guilty, but at least communication wasn't awkward between us. I took one of Pango's cookies and handed another one to Koraline. "I've missed hearing your quotes."

"Tell me more," Koraline said. "I'm living vicariously through your adventures."

I finished telling her the story of everything that had happened after the Triple Eighteen. I told her about Rownan and Vienna, and how we couldn't pass through the gate to Harte, how Rownan trashed Uncle Lloyd's house, and how, in the middle of all the drama and tension, Uncle Lloyd asked me how she was doing.

"Me?" Koraline's green eyes widened. "He asked about me?"

"Out of nowhere. I think he was trying to tell me you might be able to help, but without actually meddling. Maybe you know something or someone that can help Rownan?"

"Me? I don't know any—" She paused, then sucked air through her teeth.

She did know something. A glimmer of hope sparked inside me. "What is it?"

She pressed her palms over her eyelids. Pango and Treygan stared at her with intrigued expressions.

"Koraline?" Treygan scooted closer to her. "Please, if you can think of anything that might help Rownan, you have to tell us. You're the smartest person I've ever met. If anyone can figure this out, it's you."

She dropped her hands and half-smiled. "Actually, it's not me. If there is any way around this dilemma, I don't have the solution." She glanced apprehensively at us. "But I know someone who might."

"Who?" I asked.

She rubbed her forehead. "It's been sixteen years. Do you realize how minute the chances are that Vienna is still alive? Or worse yet, what if Harte has transformed her into something evil?"

"I know," Treygan said. "But you didn't see Rownan. You can't imagine how this is destroying him."

I touched her arm. "If there's any chance of going to Harte, even if it's to prove that Vienna is gone, then Rownan deserves that chance. He deserves closure."

"And what about you and Treygan? What if your souls are tainted just by going there? What if you don't come back?"

"It's a risk we're willing to take."

Pango whimpered and started chewing his nails. "I don't like where this conversation is heading."

Koraline crossed her arms, gripping her own shoulders. "More people would be involved this way. More people could get hurt, or in trouble."

"Trouble?" Treygan asked. "What do you mean?"

Koraline had transformed over the last few minutes. When I arrived, she was the same radiant and confident Koraline I had first met as my teacher, but now she looked like a guilty child caught doing something wrong.

"You're a White," she said to me. "What exactly does that mean? Do you have authority over the Violets?"

"Huh?" I had never thought about my status in the mer ranks. I was too busy figuring out how to be accepted by Stheno and Euryale, or master my new abilities, or understand and learn my way around Rathe.

"For example," Koraline said, "If I had broken a rule, and the Violets wanted me punished, would you be able to overrule them?"

I glanced at Treygan. He looked as confused as me. I looked at Pango, but his focus was on the water in front of him.

"I have no idea," I admitted. "Why would you be punished?"

"Pango?" Koraline said weakly.

He lifted his gaze to meet hers. After a few moments of silence, he nodded.

She sighed deeply. "I have this friend, a human friend, and he's a genius when it comes to ocean life and history. He also knows a lot about our kind, and our legends. He could probably help."

"A human?" I asked. "But I thought we kept our existence a secret."

"We do," Treygan said.

"We go to great lengths to keep everything about us top secret," Pango added. "Sometimes information slips through the cracks. And once humans find out about us, they become obsessed with learning as much as possible. Just like Koraline's friend did."

"Is this guy dangerous?" I asked.

"Not at all." Koraline grabbed my hand. "He's one of the kindest souls I've ever met." There was a gleam in her eye. Was she more than just friends with this human? Now wasn't the time to open that can of worms. "But I could get in trouble for associating with him if the Violets found out."

"I won't tell anyone," I assured her. "You have my word. I won't ever tell another soul. Your secret is safe with me."

Koraline nodded, but didn't look convinced. Behind her, Treygan squinted at me.

"I swear on my life," I said. "Please, Koraline, if this guy can help, we have to talk to him."

Her mouth opened, but it took a while for her words to surface. "He works in a bookstore on the mainland. His name is Joel."

"Will you go with us?" I asked her.

"Me? Hello? In case you haven't noticed, I'm missing half of my tail."

"I'll fly and carry you."

"What? No. I don't want Joel seeing me with half a tail. I look like something from a horror movie."

"You can go in human form." The words came out without thinking, but the pain that filled Koraline's eyes slapped me with a heavy realization.

Sadness radiated from everyone, filling the pool. I hadn't thought about what would happen if she tried transforming and using her legs. Her tail had been eaten by sharks, not her legs.

"In human form I'd require a wheelchair," she said softly. "Which is why I now prefer to be in the water at all times."

I couldn't breathe for a minute. My stomach turned imagining what her legs must look like, and how much she must be suffering behind her strong and optimistic exterior. "Koraline, I'm so sorry. I didn't realize."

"It's okay. I wasn't sure either, until I tried changing. It's not a pretty sight. And it hurts worse than anything I've ever felt."

I put my hand over my mouth, half in shock and half at a loss for words. Pango slid off his seat and drifted over to her, resting his hand on her tail and silently comforting his sister.

"I'll take you to him," Pango said to me. "I know where to find him."

"You should go now," Treygan said. "It's getting late."

"You're not coming?" I asked.

He shook his head. "You'll get there much faster if you fly and carry Pango."

I wanted Treygan to come too, but I couldn't carry both of them, and if I didn't fly the store would probably be closed by the time we got there. I wanted to get past this roadblock as soon as possible. Before Rownan did something crazy or irreversible.

Treygan and Pango stepped out of the pool, so I hugged Koraline and prepared to leave.

"Thank you," I told her. "Rownan would say the same."

"Yara?" Koraline wouldn't look at me. "Tell Joel I'm very sorry."

"For what?"

She kept her head down, picking at her fingernails. "He'll know."

Jenna and Keeley braided flowers in my hair while I stacked twigs and leaves to make a new hut for them. Most likely, no one would ever use the building—they preferred being outside or in their water lilies—but constructing something for them made me feel useful.

Keeley finished singing another one of her made-up songs, then sat on my shoulder and petted my cheek. "Sometimes I wish you could change back and be one of us again."

"Me too." I sighed. "Me too."

"But isn't it fun to be so big?" Jenna asked. "You're so strong." She flew in front of me with her balled fists punching the air. "Nobody can mess with you."

I gently pressed one of my knuckles to her punching hand. "You two are just as strong as I am."

"That's not true," Keeley argued. "Remember that time you lifted that fallen tree? You saved twelve sprites that day."

Jenna nodded vigorously. "And that was before they made you a siren! I could never lift a tree by myself."

"You could if you really needed to," I assured her. "Something clicks inside when people you love are in danger. You summon strength you didn't know you were capable of."

Keeley flexed her biceps and evaluated her pea-sized muscles. "I could do it. If the time came, I bet I could lift a tree."

Jenna snickered, but I liked seeing Keeley so confident.

"I bet you could lift a tree with each hand," I told her.

Her eyes widened, and I could tell she was mentally picturing herself achieving such a feat. She flew in front of me and kissed the tip of my nose. "Don't be silly! No sprite is that strong."

"If physical strength is equal to emotional strength, you and Jenna could move mountains."

Jenna and Keeley both laughed so hard they flipped backward.

"Move mountains," Jenna repeated, still laughing. "How preposterous!" She flew over to a patch of wild flowers and changed each one to varying shades of yellow. "I'd rather decorate the mountains with billions of yellow flowers."

I picked one and inhaled its lemony scent. I missed having a connection with flowers. I missed being able to color things in beautiful shades of red. "They would be the prettiest mountains in all the worlds."

"Prettier than Medusa's," Keeley said.

Jenna's buttercup skin blushed to almost orange. "Shucks, nothing is prettier than Medusa's creations."

We all nodded in agreement.

"Well," I stretched my arms over my head. "I should probably get going."

"No, come to our dinner party," Jenna pleaded. "I'm making berry tarts!"

"I can't. Otabia and Mariza will already be upset that I've been gone so long. I have to get back to them."

When I was with the sprites, I felt more like myself. I could laugh, have fun, and not feel judged by my siren sisters. Otabia and Mariza always urged me to be more seductive, to entrap more men, to steal more memories, and devour more souls. With them it was always take, take, take, and never give. I worried that no matter how hard I tried to please them, I would never live up to the expectations they had for me.

"Come back soon, yes?" Keeley rubbed my eyebrow.

"Of course."

Jenna kissed my nose. "I'll save you a tart or two—or twelve."

"Twelve would make a decent appetizer." I spread my wings and glanced over my shoulder at my two favorite souls in the world. Jenna and Keeley waved goodbye and blew kisses at me.

I turned my back, wanting so badly to stay with them, but I did what was expected of me and flew to Sybarites Nest.

I still wasn't used to how large our nest was compared to the smaller imitation we had built in Earth.

Our real nest sat atop three sky-scraping trees with trunks made of water and huge, hollow branches that I could crawl into. Leaves were everywhere, inside and out, and they could be frosted and on fire all in the same day, but they never died or fell from our trees. The walls of our nest were made of clouds that shifted and adapted to the seasons and our moods. My sisters would hide in the thicker pockets, making them difficult to find, and when we sang or called out for each other the mist would swallow our voices.

I preferred our nest in Earth. It was cozier, and I didn't have to search multiple rooms to find Otabia or Mariza.

"You're getting weak," Mariza said, appearing like a brown shadow from her den.

Otabia flew in above her in a blur of black. "We can feel how drained you are. Prepare to travel to the human realm. You must feed."

"That's fine." I waved my hand dismissively. "But I don't think it's a physical drain as much as it is emotional."

"Feeding will help that too," Mariza said.

I rolled my eyes. "Don't you want to know why I'm upset?"

Otabia preened her wings. Tiny black feathers disappeared into the floor of clouds below her. "Because Yara doesn't *need* you. We already know that. It's not our problem. However, you're bringing us down with you, and we can't allow it."

Sometimes I hated being connected to two sisters who barely gave a squat about me. "What's the point of stealing human memories if I have no one to pass them on to? Yara is repulsed by the way we regurgitate."

Otabia's tongue flicked away a lingering feather from her ebony lips. "Some siren you turned out to be."

"It's so addicting." Mariza strutted around the room, her hands gliding up and down her body. "The attention, the rush, the ecstasy. Men's heads snapping up like dogs, zeroing in on you the instant they hear you sing. The way they can't blink or look away, even as you tell them in delicious detail how you're going to suck them dry and make them beg for mercy." She nibbled on her pinky talon, seductively smiling at me. "The way they give themselves over, doing anything we ask, because they think their lust is going to be satisfied."

I walked over to a window, disinterested in Mariza's play-by-play. "And then we take what we want and leave them a disheveled mess with a few less memories, a lot of insecurity, and doubting their own sanity. I know. I've done it plenty of times."

Mariza cooed as her wings rustled. The clouds around us buzzed with whispers of an electrical storm. She cackled loud and shrill. "Let's go! I'm excited just thinking about it."

Maybe feeding would make me feel better. I used to enjoy being a siren. I used to get off on the hunt almost as much as Mariza. I wasn't a water sprite anymore. Life wasn't all innocent fun. Darkness would always be needed to balance out the light, and I was now a member of the dark side.

"Fine," I conceded. "Let's go, but we're only hunting for morally ambiguous men." My mouth watered. "And I get first pick."

We made it to the bookstore just before closing. Joel's private office was like a shrine to the ocean. Maps, nautical charts, items salvaged from shipwrecks, even miniature skeletal models of sea mammals—including a mermaid. Pango and I sat side by side in two antique chairs pirated from the sunken ship, Cristobal Colon—or so Joel told us.

"For real, who is this guy?" I asked Pango as we waited for Joel to come back.

"He's a history buff."

"I can see that. Who is he in relation to Koraline?"

Pango shrugged. "Koraline is exceptionally intelligent. She enjoys the company of other intelligent people."

I suspected there was much more to it than that, but the office door opened and Joel walked in, so I dropped the subject.

"So sorry for making you wait," Joel said.

"It's no problem," I replied. "We're sorry to bother you at work. Especially when you were getting ready to go home for the night."

"I'm almost always at work, and it's no bother. Any friend of Koraline's is a friend of mine."

"How long have you and Koraline known each other?" I asked.

Pango cleared his throat. "Yara, let's not take up Joel's time with chitchat. I'm sure he wants to lock up and go home."

"Right. Sorry," I said.

"We'll tell you all we can, Joel," Pango started, "but, as you know, that doesn't leave room for much explaining, so I request that you only ask the most necessary questions."

Joel nodded like he was familiar with the rules of confidential sea creature conversation.

Pango continued. "A couple of merfolk tried to pass through a gateway between Rathe and Harte." I watched Joel, waiting for him to ask what Rathe and Harte were, but he didn't flinch. "They couldn't do it."

"Why not?" Joel asked.

Pango shifted in his seat. The chair creaked so loud I worried his six-foot-five heavy frame might break the treasured antique. "Because." Pango hesitated. "Because they have human blood in their genes, so they were unable to cross between two sea monster realms."

"Human blood." Joel straightened his glasses. "How is that possible?"

"We'd prefer not to elaborate on that detail," Pango said. Joel nodded again. "Rumor has it you might be able to help us figure out a way around this restriction."

Joel tapped his fingers on the desk while he glanced back and forth between me and Pango. "To clarify, these," he looked directly at me, "*individuals* can't cross because of their human blood. Only pure-blooded sea creatures can pass through the gate between Harte and Rathe?"

"Correct," Pango replied.

"What about between Earth and Rathe? Could a human-blooded being cross that gateway?"

Pango raised his head and squinted for a few moments before answering. "Not relevant."

Joel squinted too and leaned back in his chair. "You're sure the only issue here is the human blood factor?"

"What other factors could there be?" Pango asked.

Joel folded his hands on top of his stomach. "Are you sure there isn't fear or apprehension to enter Harte? I mean, it's a very evil place."

"Of course there was some fear," I interjected a little too defensively. "But they were going to do it anyway. They tried. They swam right up to the gate, but they were thrown back by a powerful force."

I didn't know why I couldn't be straightforward with him. Joel had obviously figured out I was one of the merfolk who couldn't cross over, but I had promised to let Pango decide what we could and couldn't reveal.

Joel's eyes darted between me and Pango. "I see." He spun around in his chair, searching the overflowing bookshelves behind him. "I have a vague memory of my grandfather telling me about … well, hang on. Let's not get ahead of ourselves."

"What?" I asked. "Your grandfather told you about what?"

Joel stood up and faced us again. "Give me a few minutes to search for an old book. I think it might be in the vault."

"Take all the time you need," Pango said.

Joel walked over to the corner of his office. He slid a couple of books from a shelf, reached through the opening, and grunted as he pushed on some kind of lever. A large framed map, which was actually a door, slid open and revealed a secret passageway.

I stood up. "What the—? Where does that go?"

Joel grinned at me over his shoulder. "We humans have secrets too."

Pango took my hand and pulled me back into my chair. "Sit, my curious crusader. It's none of our business."

Joel ducked through the doorway, and the painting slid shut behind him.

"Do you know where that goes?" I asked Pango.

"Koraline says there's a secret room full of his family's prized possessions."

"Wow. I've seen that stuff in movies, but I didn't know it really existed."

Pango chuckled. "You've discovered other realms full of creatures and magic, but a secret door to a hidden room is what boggles your mind?"

"You know what I mean. I just didn't expect there to be secret passageways and hidden rooms in what appears to be a regular old bookstore."

Pango flicked a strand of my brown human hair and winked at me. "Appearances can be deceiving."

Joel returned several minutes later. He seemed tense.

"Did you find anything that might help us?" Pango asked.

Joel sat on the edge of his desk, so close to us that his knees almost touched Pango's. He stared down at us over his glasses. "My father's journal confirmed something I remembered from a story my grandfather told me when I was a child. It could be of help, but I also worry it would … let's see, how shall I put this?" Joel looked directly at me and swallowed. "If you pursue this route, it will most likely be your final journey."

He definitely knew I was one of the souls trying to enter Harte.

"Continue," Pango urged.

"First," Joel said. "I need to know if Koraline is one of the merfolk you mentioned."

"No," Pango replied firmly.

Joel looked apprehensive and concerned. "You give me your word that she is not involved in this madness in any way, and that she won't go near any gates to hell?"

"Yes," Pango said. "And you know I can't lie."

Joel focused on me again and continued. "Harte is a damned realm filled with ravenous creatures and the most negative emotions. Just like this world, the gods had their hand in the creation of Harte, and many gods have enjoyed using humans as their playthings. If their playthings didn't play by the rules or stepped out of line, the gods had ways of punishing them. One of those ways being a one-way ticket to the eternal nightmare of Harte."

My pulse quickened. "There's another way in?"

Joel nodded slowly. "But I have never heard of any soul purposefully wanting to go there. Yes, there's an entrance from our human world, but no return ticket is offered."

He didn't know what I knew. That one sea creature had found an exit, and Uncle Lloyd had told me and Treygan where it was and how to get through it. One exit was enough for me to believe we would make it out alive. I leaned toward Joel. "I already know the risks involved."

"Do you really?" Joel crossed his arms over his chest. "How much have you studied about Harte? Do you have any idea what happens there? What horrible, unthinkable monsters or torture devices exist there? No, because no one has ever made it back. Many people claim to have glimpsed the afterlife or Heaven, but how many accounts have you ever heard of anyone returning from a visit to hell?"

To say I wasn't scared would have been a lie, and I could have tried to fool him, but my trembling voice would have betrayed me. "If there's a way in, you have to tell us."

"Please, Joel," Pango urged quietly.

Joel sighed and walked to the other side of his office. He stood with his back toward us, staring at an old, tattered map hung on the wall. "Come here and I'll show you."

Pango and I walked over and stood on either side of him.

Joel took off his glasses and rubbed his hand over his face. "I don't feel good about this. I'm basically showing you the way into the lion's den."

I pulled his hand away from his face. "We understand what we're getting ourselves into. You are in no way responsible for what happens. But you would be helping in a way more important than you can imagine."

He stared at me for several silent heartbeats. I still wasn't sure how Koraline knew Joel, but I could see why she trusted him. He had abyss eyes. Uncle Lloyd used to tell me that his wife had abyss eyes. The first time he met her, he knew her goodness had no end because he could see into her soul, and no matter how deep or long he looked, he never saw one hint of bad. Joel's eyes were the same way. He didn't want anyone to get hurt. He didn't even know me, but he was concerned about me.

"Some things are worth the risk," I told him.

"How about dying? Is this worth dying for?"

A close-lipped grin struggled to surface as Koraline's famous words echoed through my mind. The words I had died by, and now lived by.

"Love until it kills you," I recited with a smile. Joel's eyes widened with recognition. "Because there's nothing better worth dying for."

Joel slid his glasses back on and squared his shoulders. "The other gateway, the only one a human, or part human, could pass through is here."

He pointed to the map. His finger landed on an open area of blue to the right of Florida. I leaned forward to examine the thin lines making a triangle around the tip of his finger.

"Oh, dear gods," Pango gasped.

I read the tiny words handwritten above Joel's chewed fingernail. *The Devil's Triangle.*

The worst part about having the same dream over and over was that I always woke up and felt the loss all over again.

The dream felt so real while it was happening. My dreams were why I slept so much while we were trapped in Earth's realm. I always gave in and allowed myself to be pulled into memories of Vienna.

I would never forget our wedding. Dreaming about it was almost as good as the real thing had been.

Vienna was covered from head to toe in snowflakes. Her skin looked like it had been covered in a glistening, frosted fishing net. Behind her, the pulsing colors of the aurora borealis lit up the dark December sky. She took my hand and stepped into the water.

"You put those snowflakes to shame," I whispered to her. "They aren't half as beautiful as you."

She blushed and wrapped her tailfin around mine beneath the surface. "I wish we could skip right to the kiss."

It took all of my willpower not to pull her underwater and swim away with her right then and there.

All of our selkie guests were circled around us in the icy water. Merfolk lined the shore, like a midnight rainbow. The High Priestess hovered above me and Vienna, giving her spiel and making our union official. Our mothers swam forward to wrap sea kelp around our wrists—a symbolic gesture to solidify our eternal bond.

But that's where the memory ended and my dream turned into a nightmare.

All of our guests sank into the black water. The High Priestess screamed like a banshee. Hissing snakes grew out of her head. Long fangs tore through her bottom lip and her jaw stretched down to her feet.

Vienna screamed. I turned to see the sea kelp branching out and moving, creeping and crawling up our arms and around our torsos. I tried to break my hands free, but the plants were too strong.

A long vine wrapped itself around Vienna's neck, strangling her and gagging her screams. I flailed and fought with all my might, trying to rip free of my restraints, but they were like boa constrictors that wouldn't stop squeezing. Vienna's eyes bulged out of her head as the seaweed pulled her under and out of my sight. Then it pulled me under too. Beneath the surface, the water was pitch-black. I couldn't see anything, but it was so hot my skin burned. A fire ignited in front of me. The raging flames momentarily blinded me, but then, in the middle of the fire, I saw my beautiful bride. Her face was flawless and she kept calling my name, but the rest of her skin was charred to the bone.

I bolted upright.

Vienna was gone. The flames were gone.

I was sitting on a beach on the selkie side of Rathe. My tail was in the water, partially buried in the sand. A calm indigo sky stretched out above me. Stars twinkled and the moons shined.

"Just a nightmare," I told myself.

Vienna and I had sat on this beach, and so many others in Rathe, more times than I could count. I turned my head and the glittering sand turned into a mirage of a young Vienna. I wasn't delusional, I knew it was just me reminiscing, but there she was, skipping down the beach several yards away. She saw me, waved, and ran over to me.

She looked so real. My mind retained every detail, right down to the sand in her black, windblown hair. "Have you seen all the shells that washed ashore?"

Of all the conversations we ever had, this one was my favorite. One of the first times we discussed being more than friends. "Yeah." I smiled. "How many have you collected?"

She bent down and picked up a piece of sea glass, holding it up and admiring it in the moonlight. "Only one. The rest belong here, on the beach—or in the ocean, if the tide chooses to carry them away." She tossed the sea glass back into the sand and sat down beside me. "I don't keep them. I just like admiring them, holding them between my fingers and feeling how different each one is. Except for this one." She removed a shell from her armband. At first it looked all white, but then I noticed the hints of green and silver. "Feel it. It's hard and soft at the same time. The edges are ragged, but run your fingers along the silver veins—they're soft as silk."

I rubbed it, noting all the different textures. "You're right."

"It reminds me of you." Her ivory cheeks blushed and she looked down, studying the shell in my fingers. "Something so unique should be treasured. Forever."

"The shell?"

She leaned toward me—barely an inch—but it was enough to feel the energy building between us. "You, Rownan. I would treasure you forever."

It was the first time I kissed her. The first time I had kissed anyone. We were barely teenagers, but I remembered it like it happened yesterday.

I pulled away and smiled at her.

She groaned, frustrated. "I was afraid that would happen."

"What's wrong?" Panic flooded me. Had I turned some part of her to stone like Treygan had done when he kissed Kimber?

"I knew if you kissed me, I'd be forever ruined for anyone else. No other selkie, or any creature for that matter, will ever top that."

Sweet relief. "Good. Because I hope you never kiss anyone else." I handed her shell back to her. "I want to keep you—I mean, treasure you. Forever."

Her smile spread so wide it outshined the moons above us. "Forever? You promise?"

"I promise." I kissed her again. "Was there ever any doubt? You're my best friend."

"I guess I had some fears."

"What kind of fears?"

She held my hand in hers. "My grandmother says we have a rare kind of love. Love that's only gifted to the world when the tides and moons align just right, and it happens so rarely. She said it means we'll be faced with more challenges than most."

"You talked to your grandmother about us?"

Vienna giggled. "I talk to everyone about you."

My cheeks warmed.

"Gran says our love will be tested in ways we might not be strong enough to survive."

"And you believe that? The bad part, I mean."

"Gran knows these things."

I picked sand out of Vienna's hair. "I believe we create our own fate."

"Part of me believes that too, but you know how my family is. They've drilled all the fate and fortune stuff into my head."

"Don't worry, whatever the world wants to throw at us, we'll get through it."

She closed both of her hands around mine. "Together, right?"

"Together."

"That's my biggest fear," Vienna said. "Losing you."

"You won't lose me. Even if you do, I'll always find you again."

She smiled so radiantly it made my heart overflow. "Say it again."

"What?"

"That I won't lose you. And if I do, you'll always find me again."

I held her delicate face in my hands. "You won't lose me. Even if you do, I swear on the oceans and heavens, I will always find you again."

I leaned in to kiss her, but she was gone.

Sand sifted through my fingers as I tried clinging to her, but all I found was an empty beach.

"Do you know what I fear?" I said aloud, pretending Vienna was still beside me. "I fear you were in Harte so long that you stopped believing I would find you. I fear you'll never forgive me for breaking my promise to you. I'm terrified you'll never forgive me for whatever torture you've suffered all these years—because I know I'll never forgive myself. I'm so sorry, V."

Some part of me hoped she'd reply. Wishful thinking that her voice would carry across the sky, the ocean, the worlds, and somehow whisper forgiveness in my ear.

But there was no reply. No sound at all except the tide washing in and out. I threw my second empty vodka bottle into the waves then popped open the tequila from Jack Frost's. I chugged until I reached rock bottom.

I was by myself when I first knew something was wrong. Minding my own business, I had been flying to Echo Bayou, and that's when the fear hit me.

The most intense part was brief, but it was much stronger than I'd ever felt before. I had never known Otabia or Mariza to be terrified of anything, so that only left Yara.

First, I checked the grotto, thinking maybe Stheno and Euryale had scared her again. She wasn't there, so I flew to Treygan's house, which is where I found her. I sort of wish I hadn't, because it ruined my perfectly good mood.

Yara and Treygan were sitting at the kitchen table with books and papers spread out everywhere.

"What's going on?" I asked.

Neither one of them looked up. They were too engrossed in reading. I have never liked repeating myself, so I spread my wings wide and flapped them so hard that papers flew off the table and Yara's hair blew over her eyes.

"Nixie!" Treygan yelled. "What is your problem?"

"I don't like being ignored."

"We weren't ignoring you." Yara pulled her white hair into a ponytail. Such an odd human thing, the ponytail. I'd never be a fan of not allowing my hair to flow freely and blow in the wind. "We didn't even hear you come in."

Exactly. They were too self-absorbed to even notice me. "You were scared earlier," I said to Yara. "Unbelievably scared. Why?"

Yara glanced at Treygan. He watched her with a look of concern. Sage swayed over Yara's shoulder.

"There's another way in," Yara said.

"Another way in where?"

She swallowed. "Harte."

"What?" My wings rustled involuntarily. "How?"

Treygan carried a map over to me and held it up so I could see where he was pointing. *The Devil's Triangle.*

I knocked the map out of his hand, wanting to break his finger for pointing out such a dreaded place. "You can't do this!"

Yara stood up and snatched the map off the floor. "We can and we are. You can either help us or not. I don't want to leave on bad terms with you. I need your help if we stand any chance of surviving this."

"You need me? Since when?"

Yara's eyes softened. "Have you ever doubted that I needed your help?"

"Many times." *And if you ever attempted to tune in to my feelings, you'd know that.* I should have told her that, but I didn't want to look weak in front of Treygan.

"Do I need to remind you that you saved my life on more than one occasion?"

I did save her from being eaten by sharks, but the incident when she was a child was owed to Treygan. "Technically, Treygan saved you from drowning."

"He wouldn't have known I was drowning if it weren't for you." Yara nodded once, slowly, as if to signal the discussion was over. She walked to the table and shuffled through papers. "We need you to help us train and prepare."

"Train and prepare? That doesn't even sound like a real job. I thought you wanted me to come with you."

She didn't glance up from the paper in her hands. "I'd never put your soul in jeopardy by taking you into Harte."

I walked over and leaned on the table, trying to make her look at me. "Treygan is going with you. Why is he allowed to go and I'm not?"

Yara looked up, but only at Treygan. He sat silently at the table, watching us. "Rownan is his brother," Yara said. "He has the right to go, and he's insisting. I can't deny him the chance to help save his own brother's life."

"But you're part siren. That makes you my sister. I demand to go so I can save your life."

She finally looked at me. "It's not the same, Nixie."

"How is it not the same?"

"They are more help to each other by being in the same realm together. I need you here as my link to this world."

My interest was piqued. "Your *link*?"

"You feel my emotions, right? I've been thinking that you can monitor how I'm feeling while I'm in Harte. If you feel me get scared or anxious, Indrea can calm you, and it will make me calm too. We could have multiple Violets standing by to help with any negative emotions that may surface."

"That *would* be a brilliant plan, except what if our connection doesn't work in Harte?"

"It works between Rathe and Earth." She was so naïve. As if Rathe and Earth were anything like Harte.

"What if it doesn't work because you're dead or your soul has been banished to hell?"

Yara slammed her palms on the table. "Nixie!"

"What? It's the truth! Stop acting like this is going to be some leisure vacation. It's going to be hell. Literally, you are going to hell. Don't you understand that?"

"Of course I understand that."

"Then why aren't you recruiting an army to accompany you? Why are you being so foolish about your odds of making it back alive?" Sage rose high in the air, and Yara's anger vanished quickly and completely. "Holy Medusa!" I shouted. "Sage is controlling your emotions!"

"No, she just helps me stay focused."

A long, irritated growl poured out of me. "You're lying! You don't need me or the Violets to help with your emotions. You have your sidekick serpent to do our jobs!"

"Merfolk don't lie," Treygan interjected.

I snarled at him. Yara could lie. I had already witnessed it a couple of times since her transformation. He was so blinded by love that he couldn't see how different she was in her new form.

Yara replied before I could shatter Treygan's delusion. "It's not like that. Sage keeps me thinking clearly. She reminds me that I can't be scared or angry. If I give in to those negative emotions, I lose strength. My will gets weaker. I can't afford to be weak in Harte. Not even for a second. My soul depends on it." She lowered her head and mumbled, "So do Treygan's and Rownan's."

I stared at Sage, drifting back and forth beside Yara's head like a kite in the wind. "You better keep her safe, you self-righteous, glorified worm."

Sage hissed at me, but Yara pulled her back. Yara smoothed down my hair then squeezed my shoulder. "Everything is going to work out. You'll see."

I tapped my foot, trying to curb my anger. I didn't want to fight with Yara any more than I wanted her going to Harte. "If I can't feel you anymore—if we lose our connection—I'll go mad."

"We won't lose our connection. Our bond is too strong."

Pango's loud voice startled all of us. "Knock knock! I found our drunken sailor!"

Yara and Treygan hurried into the other room, and I followed. Pango waded through the water and up the steps into the living room. He was dragging Rownan beside him. Rownan's arm was draped around Pango's shoulder. He looked like he'd slide right back down the steps and into the water if Pango didn't keep hold of him.

"Drunk, huh?" Yara asked.

"Positively wasted," Pango said. "I've got a contact buzz from all the alcohol leaking out of his pores."

"Thanks, Pango." Treygan dipped under Rownan's other arm and took the heavy load off Pango. "I'll take him from here." Treygan assisted him into the kitchen as we all followed. He dumped Rownan into a chair and he slumped forward, his forehead landing with a thwack on the table.

"Good grief," Yara said. "He can't even hold up his own head."

Treygan grabbed him by the hair and pulled his head up. Rownan's eyes stayed closed as Treygan loudly said, "There's been a major turn of events." Rownan didn't utter a word, not even a groan. "Maybe now isn't the time to update him," Treygan said to Yara. "He's not even coherent."

Yara nodded. Treygan released his hold on Rownan's hair and let his head fall forward, slamming against the table again. I snickered.

"I'm going to lay him down in the den." Treygan scooped Rownan into his arms. "He needs to sleep it off."

Treygan's hallmarks stretched across his bulging muscles. Desire stirred inside me, but I didn't know if it was mine or Yara's. We were both staring at him like he was a juicy piece of prime meat.

"Thank you, Pango," Yara said. "I appreciate all of your help. I owe you more paybacks than I can count."

"You owe me nothing," Pango insisted. "It was my pleasure. But if you are no longer in need of my gallant services, I'd like to go home and spend some quality time with Merrick."

"Of course," Yara said. "Tell him I said hello."

Pango winked at me. "Goodbye, winged Ruby Goddess. Don't hurt anyone."

I nodded, and half waved goodbye, not realizing how much I felt like an intrusive observer until Pango acknowledged me.

"I'm sorry," Yara said to me. "We were interrupted. What were we talking about?"

That you need me. Or maybe you don't and you're just pretending you do to shut me up. "If you don't remember, it must not have been important."

Treygan came out of the den. "He's out cold." He glanced between me and Yara. "Did I interrupt something?"

"No, we're fine," Yara said, assuming she knew how I felt.

"Nix," Treygan said. "Would you do us and Rownan a huge favor?" I glowered, but didn't reply. "Yara, you may be repulsed by this, so don't listen."

"Oh no," Yara groaned, but continued listening anyway.

Treygan stepped closer to me. He glanced sideways at Yara and tried not to grin. "Could you please filter out some of the alcohol in Rownan's blood?"

Yara's head snapped back. "Gross!"

Treygan shrugged. "We need him in semi-good condition when he wakes up. If Nixie can help ease his hangover, then we'll be much better off."

"Sure," I said, wanting to prove to Yara that I was useful for something—regardless of whether she appreciated my talents or not. "I'll drink as much as I can without killing him."

Treygan looked down his nose at me. "Don't come anywhere close to that point. Just take enough so he can walk and talk without throwing up."

"Why do you always put a damper on my fun?"

"Thank you." Treygan gently squeezed my forearm. Since when had he become so affectionate?

Yara sat at the table again, thumbing through a book. "Nixie, don't you get drunk too. But don't regurgitate in the house. That sound makes me sick, and we're not cleaning up the mess."

I flinched. Not even a thank you from her. Just a reminder that me doing what comes naturally makes her sick.

"You're part siren too," I reminded her.

She didn't look up from her page. "Yes, but my other instincts cancel out any desire to drink blood."

"Whatever." I stomped off into the den where Rownan was passed out on the floor.

I kicked Rownan's arm. He was as limp as a dead eel.

"This won't be much fun," I said to him. "You're not even going to put up a fight."

I straddled him and sat down on his pelvis. My siren instincts stirred, and I leaned forward and breathed in his scent. "My, my, you are soaked in alcohol. I can hardly smell your blood at all."

I ran my talons along his cheek, down his chest, and then lifted his arm.

My mouth wrapped around his wrist and I licked up the inside of his forearm, savoring the build-up to the moment where I'd sink my teeth into his flesh and drink a good portion of his life force. "Don't worry," I purred. "It will only hurt for a long time."

If anything, he owed me a big thank you when he woke up. I was saving him from an arduous hangover. I nibbled at his forearm and he stirred.

"There, there," I petted his jaw, the coarse hair of his goatee prickling my fingertips. "Just pretend I'm Vienna. You'll enjoy it much more."

Of course, he didn't reply. I smiled at him hungrily. Then I got tired of foreplay and sank my teeth into his arm. The first sip burned my tongue and throat. "Gods, Rownan, how much did you drink? Bleh."

Treygan owed me big time for this. I'd be lucky if I could drink and regurgitate fast enough that I didn't get intoxicated too. I drank again, and Rownan groaned. I assumed he was dreaming about Vienna drinking from him. He was probably enjoying this feeding more than me.

It wasn't until he whispered, "Nixie," that I stopped sucking on his arm.

His eyes were open. They were glassy and bloodshot, but he seemed somewhat coherent. "Nix, is that you?"

"I'm saving you from a wicked hangover. Just lay there and be quiet. You can thank me later."

His eyes fluttered closed. I continued draining him of vodka and, much to my dismay, tequila. I gagged on the awful taste.

"I need your help."

I wasn't sure I had heard him right, so I paused and glanced down at him. "What?"

He opened his eyes again. "Help me."

"I am helping you."

"No, I need you to …."

He tried sitting up, but I pressed on his chest to keep him down. "Don't move. You'll end up vomiting on me. And if that happens, I will feed you to a killer whale."

"Steal my songs," he muttered.

My heart tripled its pace. "What?"

"Take all my memories of Vienna." He sighed, long but weak. "Please."

"You're drunk. You don't know what you're saying."

His bloodshot eyes focused on me. "I know what I'm saying. I can't live like this. If I have no memories of her, then it won't hurt anymore."

"But …" He didn't know about the other way into Harte yet. Treygan and Yara were waiting until he sobered up to tell him. "Trust me, that's not what you want."

"It is." He gripped my wrist tight. "I'll do whatever you ask, just please take all memory of her out of my soul."

I started to tell him that their mission was still a go, that I didn't need to do anything to his soul because Harte would obliterate it soon enough. But it occurred to me that if Rownan had no memories of Vienna—no more love or feelings for her, no more pain of being without her—then there would be no reason for him to go to Harte. And Yara and Treygan wouldn't need to go either.

"It's the perfect solution," I muttered to myself, but Rownan thought I was talking to him.

"I know. Do it. Fast." His eyes closed again. "Don't leave any memories of her. None."

Never had anyone offered themselves to me with such ease, and such an appetizing buffet of songs to steal. The thought of it made me light-headed. Or was the alcohol starting to kick in?

I stood up and walked over to the doorway. I peeked around the corner to see if Yara and Treygan were within hearing range, but I didn't see them anywhere. I hurried back over to Rownan. My siren song was aching to burst out of me.

"We'll have to be quiet," I told him. A slight twist of his arms was my invitation to begin feasting, but to take so many memories I would need to go for the mainline.

I sang as quietly as I could, not that I needed to seduce him, but it was part of the process. I brushed my lips against his and they parted. So many times I had tried to seduce Rownan, to make him share a song with me, just one tiny memory, but he always refused. So many selkies had tried to share their blood directly with him, but he refused that too. He was fiercely loyal to Vienna. And now, after countless rejections, Rownan was letting me steal volumes of his songs. A smile spread across my lips.

"This is going to hurt," I warned him.

His only reply was breathing into my mouth, and the coolness of his breath set me into motion. I bit his bottom lip and he groaned. The frenzy of ecstasy spread through my entire body. I closed my eyes and enjoyed the ride into Rownan's soul.

Right away, I found memory after memory of Vienna.

A beach in Rathe. Vienna was so much younger. She skipped toward him. She handed him a shell. They talked. They kissed. Love. Devotion. Desire. All of it so delectable because he cherished the memory so deeply. I inhaled it in and snatched it away from him, feeling its deliciousness on my tongue, and then it was inside me. Later, I would regurgitate it into the ocean and let the moment in time be washed away forever.

Another memory rushed through me. Vienna curled up in his arms. They stared at Rathe's moons. She held up the same shell again, running her fingers along its silver and green veins. Loyalty. Gratitude. More love. I devoured the memory—along with a dozen more of her with the same shell and all the same sappy feelings.

Then I hit the mother lode. Their wedding.

When Vienna first appeared in her white fur cape, I was obliterated. Rownan's love for her ripped through my heart in a way I didn't know was possible. Rownan's feelings were overwhelming. His love for her was so intense, so transcendental. Suns, moons, even the stars would have to move over to make room for such a boundless connection. I could never have fathomed loving someone so profoundly if I hadn't felt his emotions for myself.

I reared back. As impossible as it was, I pulled my mouth away from Rownan's.

"I can't do this." I stumbled backward, putting distance between us. The urge to take more was so powerful. I had met many humans who were addicted to drugs. I had stolen their songs and got high off their craving and desire. But that desperation and yearning was nothing compared to what Rownan felt for Vienna.

I wanted more. So much more. I hugged myself tightly, fighting the fervor rushing through me.

"Nixie?" Rownan rolled onto his side, scanning the room for me. I backed into the corner, trying to hide in the shadows. His blood and soul tingled on my lips. "Vienna is still part of me. I can't close my eyes without seeing her."

"I know." I wiped my mouth, feeling guilty but also frenzied with hunger at the sight of Rownan's blood on my palm.

I sank to my knees, spreading my wings and wrapping them around me, cowering in the dark protection of my own feathery walls. Part of me wanted to claw my way out and devour every last drop from him. But another part of me knew what a rare and beautiful bond I would be erasing.

I sank my talons into my thighs, using my own pain to center me and ease my turmoil. Humans. I could leave here and drain as many human men as I wanted. But not Rownan. I had already taken too much from him. So many precious memories. I didn't even want to regurgitate them. Doing so felt like a waste of such beauty.

My own rapid breaths made the shelter of my wings feel like a sweltering cocoon. I opened my wings and gasped for fresh air.

Rownan was pale, sweating, and trying to crawl toward me. He looked so weak and sick. The room was probably spinning for him; it was already wobbling for me. "Nixie, please. You have no idea what it's like."

I crawled toward him, conjuring up strength and willpower I didn't know I possessed. I lifted his face. His head was so heavy. The blood dripping down his chin made my mouth water, but I resisted. "I know, Rownan. But I can't take any more from you. You have to keep all that love you feel for her."

"No," he murmured. Tears streamed from his eyes and ran down my thumbs.

"Yes," I told him. "You're still going to Harte."

His head shook as his teary red eyes met mine. "I can't pass through the gate. I can't save her."

I smiled in spite of all the blood and tears. "They found another way in."

At first he didn't react. Then, as my words registered, his eyes widened and focused on mine. "What?"

"Sober up, Rownan. You're in for the fight of your life. And you better not fail."

"No more drinking alcohol," Treygan told me. "At all."

I sipped the god-awful concoction Yara had made to help me with my hangover. "I'm not stupid." I took another sip and gagged. "Seriously, what am I drinking?"

Yara smirked. "You don't want to know. But the Violets said it will help, so choke it down."

"I still don't understand why Nixie didn't take more alcohol out of your system." Treygan sat beside me. "You shouldn't be feeling this bad."

Only Nixie and I knew why she didn't keep drinking from me. After she told me about the Devil's Triangle, she couldn't get away from me fast enough. She was feeling the effects of the liquor in my blood. She was worried she wouldn't be able to control her desire to steal more of my songs. She had told me they were a rare commodity, and then she was gone.

Nixie had always been more level-headed then Otabia and Mariza, but the restraint she had shown in such a tempting situation left me forever in her debt.

"She did all she could." I took another sip. "I drank so much I should be dead right now."

"Very responsible of you," Treygan said. His sarcasm was the last thing my pounding head needed.

"You might have done the same if it was Yara trapped in hell and you thought you'd never see her again." I didn't look up, but I was sure Yara and Treygan were exchanging glances and agreeing. I had a valid point. "Love isn't responsible. Love can make you the strongest you've ever been, or it can shatter you into useless pieces."

"No argument there." Yara leaned forward, resting her elbows on the table. "Are you feeling well enough to discuss our game plan?"

I nodded, then gripped the edge of the table to stop the room from spinning.

"The gate only opens when certain factors align." Yara rambled on about the moon and tides, but it all sounded like screeching static until she said, "The next time it opens is three days from now."

Three more days without Vienna. "That's too long."

Treygan smirked. "Do you know how fortunate you are that it's opening so soon? The last time it opened was eighteen months ago. After this time, it probably won't happen again for another eighteen months. Imagine if you had to wait that long."

"I'd rip the bitch open and claw my way in."

"Ambitious thought." Yara leaned back and kicked her feet up, resting them on the table. "But I don't think you could pull the moon closer to Earth, rip open the ocean, and claw your way into a portal that only exists when the heavens perfectly align."

"I'd find a way."

"You can't even find the strength to chug that drink." Yara laughed. "Come on, Hercules, we don't have much time. You ready to start training?"

I rolled my eyes. "Don't call me Hercules."

Treygan grinned and opened his mouth to say something, but I cut him off. "If you make an Achilles heel joke I will throw this drink in your annoyingly happy face."

He put his hands up in surrender. "We all have weaknesses."

I reached out, resting my hand on top of Yara's. "Thank you. For not giving up on Vienna. For finding another way in."

She smiled. "Thank your father and Koraline."

Treygan and I worked on our tracking skills. Shadowing was the one gorgon trait that we shared. Yara flew one of us farther away each time we practiced. She started out planting us in people's homes so we'd have company while we waited to be found, but it progressed to hiding us in caves, inside the trunks of trees, or in the deepest canyons of Rathe's ocean.

During our last round of hide-and-seek it took Treygan hours to track me. Yara refused to tell him where I was. He finally found me in an underwater crevasse in the bedrock of Pontus Glacier.

He shook me awake. *Come on, I'm so cold I can't feel my fins. Took you long enough.*

Do you know how many glaciers I had to search? They all look the same. His skin was covered with goose bumps. *And my brain doesn't work so well with icicles forming around it.*

We swam out of the crevasse together and into open water.

What if Harte is one big world of ice? I asked. *We need to anticipate anything and everything.*

Yara is way ahead of you. The Violets are having temperature adjusting suits made for us.

Suits? I'm not wearing a suit. I have my coat. That's all I need.

So, if Harte is a fiery world of ever-burning flames, your coat will miraculously be fireproof?

I cringed at the thought of burning to death. *Maybe special suits are a good idea.*

What was Vienna suffering through? Fire? Deadly beasts? Physical pain? She'd been in Harte for years. I was pretty sure no one had made her a flame resistant suit. I couldn't think about all the dreadful possibilities. I had to stay focused. *What other surprises does Yara have in store for us?*

She's working diligently. While we're out here shadowing each other, she's making preparations for every worst case scenario.

You're sure she doesn't have any shadowing abilities? She's part gorgon, maybe it's there but she doesn't know how to access it.

She keeps trying. She even asked Lloyd to help her, but he said she's a mix of too many species. Not quite enough of a gorgon for us to hone in on her.

She has a snake coming out of her skull. How much more gorgon can she get? All of our shadowing practice had been to help us locate Vienna. And maybe each other if needed, but Yara was the anomaly we couldn't track. *That's a shame. It would come in handy if we become separated from her.*

Treygan stopped swimming. He did that eerie thing where somehow he kept completely still, even as water flowed all around him. I eyed his fins. Seriously, how was it possible that his fins didn't even sway?

No matter what happens, Treygan said, *we cannot separate.*

And what happens if we do?

Treygan glared at me.

Hey, I'm just playing devil's advocate.

We have to stay together at all times. Not just for Yara's sake, but for ours too.

I nodded. We swam the rest of the way to the gorgon grotto in silence.

The worry lines had deepened around Treygan's eyes when we surfaced outside the grotto. I still had time to talk Yara and Treygan out of going with me. As much as I'd appreciate help finding Vienna, and as scared as I was to go alone, I didn't want Yara and Treygan risking everything.

"What do you think about us going through the Devil's Triangle?" I asked him.

Treygan shrugged. "How we get to Harte makes no difference."

"You know the stories as well as I do. Lloyd warned us about the Hoodoo Sea."

Treygan raised himself onto a rock and sat. "He also warned us not to go to Harte. We've never been good at following our father's advice."

I chuckled.

Treygan lifted his face toward the side of Rathe where Medusa's sunbeams weaved through the sky. "Lloyd wants us to visit him so he can tell us everything he knows about Harte."

"Won't that be considered meddling?"

"Probably."

"He's on his last leg. If he tells us anything else, it might kill him."

Treygan looked down at his half-submerged tail. His jaw tensed. "I argued the same thing, but he says it's worth the risk."

"What could he possibly tell us? Hardly anything is known about Harte."

"Do you remember the story about the one soul who visited Harte and lived to tell about it?"

"The crazy merman? I've heard rumors, but I also heard the guy died a day or two after he returned."

"Killed himself, actually," Treygan said. "His soul was too affected. Waking nightmares and hallucinations made him snap. He chose death over living with his memories of hell."

"That can't be true."

"Lloyd says it's true, and I believe him."

"How would he know?"

"Haven't you also heard that the tortured soul only spoke to one gorgon about his time in Harte?"

"Yeah."

Treygan's brows rose.

"The gorgon he talked to was our father?"

"The one and only."

I shook my head. "That man has a knack for finding trouble."

"Looks like we inherited that from him."

"I guess we're visiting dear old dad again." I drifted backward. "Let's find Yara."

Treygan stiffened. "No."

"No?"

"As much as I don't agree with it, Lloyd says Yara can't know. She'll fight tooth and talons to stop him from meddling."

Yara loved that man. Maybe even more than Treygan and I did. "What if he does die because of this?"

"He said he'd rather die helping to save you and Vienna than live and watch you suffer."

I raked my fingers over my goatee. Lloyd couldn't die. Not like this. Not because of me and my stupid mistakes. I couldn't let that happen. "Sometimes I wish he'd just be the bastard father I accuse him of being."

"We both know that's impossible."

The suns were dimmer as Rathe shifted to what would be considered nighttime. The mer side of Rathe didn't get dark like the selkie side, just dimmer, similar to dusk. I stared at the sky through the opening in Treygan's roof as we floated in his resting pool.

"I can't rest anymore." I sat up, treading water. "Maybe Indrea and Caspian are awake and can answer some more questions I thought of."

Treygan turned his head and smiled at me. "You and I have plans elsewhere."

"We do? Where? What plans?"

He placed his hands on my hips and pulled me close to him. "Remember when I said you smell like apple blossoms, and you told me you had never smelled them?"

"Yes."

"It's time to change that."

"But we have to train, and—"

Treygan silenced me with a kiss that made my fins flutter. He pulled back and lightly brushed his nose against mine. "Rownan will be asleep for hours. We shouldn't train without him anyway."

"We could work on our combat skills."

Treygan looked away then sighed. He laced his fingers through mine and squeezed, bringing his eyes back to meet mine. "Please, let me have this one thing. There's so much more I want to show you in Rathe, but we don't have enough time. Give me this one thing before we go." Worry lines creased his forehead. They silently spoke a truth he hadn't wanted to say out loud. He was worried we would never return from Harte. "Take some time out to stop and smell the apple blossoms. For me."

The pleading way he looked at me dissolved all of my defenses. How could I say no to him? "Okay. I'll take a break. For you."

He smiled and kissed the top of my head. Hands still locked together, we swam out of his house and away from the looming burdens of our dangerous trip to Harte, and all the pressures of me finding my place in this new world. I had to admit, the break was a welcomed reprieve.

You ready? Treygan asked me.

Ahead of us was an underwater forest. I glanced back and forth between him and the dense array of trees in front of us. *We're swimming in there? It looks like a scary maze we'll never find our way out of.*

I know this place as well as the scales on my tail. It's far from scary, and we won't get lost. He winked mischievously. *Unless you want to.*

I flicked him with my fins, sending bubbles floating up around us. *Lead the way.*

He took off in front of me, darting around branches and swimming deeper into the labyrinth of trees. His muscular body propelled him through the water, strong and graceful. I kept reaching out, needing to touch him over and over—his tail, his side, his arm, wherever. He flashed me approving grins, but he kept swimming—until beams of sunlight illuminated a patch of trees in front of us.

Treygan flipped over and looked at me. His bright silver skin and huge smile revealed how happy he was, but his face flushed with orange which meant he was super excited. *Normally, I'd insist you go first, but I want to be up there when you break through the surface so I can see your reaction.*

Clearly, this place meant a lot to Treygan. I motioned upward. *After you.*

He shot toward the circle of glowing water above us. I waited a few seconds, contemplating what might be up there. I couldn't imagine anything being more beautiful than what I'd already seen in Rathe. No matter what awaited me, even if it wasn't all that spectacular, I'd fake being impressed because it meant so much to Treygan.

I took my time, swimming upward in figure eights until I saw Treygan's tail swaying above me. I closed my eyes, propelled myself up the last few feet, and enjoyed the transition from cool water against my face to warm air.

I opened my eyes, taking in the sparkling trees surrounding me. My mouth fell open, but I couldn't make a sound. I stuck my face in the water again, rubbed my eyes, and did a double take. It was even more mesmerizing at second glance.

"Forbidden Apple Lagoon," Treygan whispered respectfully, as if we had entered a sacred temple.

"It's …" I spun around, taking in the acres of apple trees blooming with white and pink flowers. Twinkling flowers. Gold, silver, and white apples dangled from the branches. "It's incredible."

Treygan smiled. "Poseidon's handiwork."

Treygan educating me about Rathe and sea folk had become one of my favorite hobbies, but stories about Medusa and Poseidon's love were my very favorite. "Tell me the story."

He positioned himself behind me and held on to my hips, slowly spinning us in a circle to give us a panoramic view as he spoke. "Medusa loved flowers. In the formative years of Rathe, she hinted to Poseidon about how much she missed them. Like most males, he didn't take the hint, so after a few years of no flowers, Medusa became furious and refused to see him. Stheno and Euryale told Poseidon why their sister was so upset, and he made it up to Medusa by creating this place."

"The flowers are gorgeous, but why the apples?"

"There's an ancient belief among gods and goddesses that the offering of an apple is the declaration of one's love. Poseidon told Medusa one apple could never be sufficient, so he gave her an eternal orchard. Of course, it's also fitting that the apple was the forbidden fruit, and Poseidon and Medusa's love was forbidden by many."

"What makes the flowers sparkle like that?"

Treygan pressed his chest against my back and rested his chin on my shoulder. "That's the best part. Poseidon took fragments of stars from all of Medusa's favorite constellations and placed them inside each flower."

I spun to face him, zeroing in on Treygan's freckles that formed the Canis Major constellation. I loved those freckles. They had helped me remember who I was and kept me tied to the living world when I was being tempted in the Inbetween.

"They never stop shining," Treygan continued. "I could never decide if this place was prettier at night or in the full light of the suns."

The star-flowers blossomed everywhere. I glided toward a thick, curved branch that dipped below the surface. "Can I touch them?"

"Sure. The stardust in the center is warm, but not enough to burn." He plucked one and held it between us.

I touched its silky petals while inhaling. "They smell so good."

"I pictured this place every time I smelled you." He tucked the flower behind my ear and it warmed the side of my head. "You always reminded me of here—of home, and star-flowers that smell like heaven."

He looked gorgeous, with his wet hair all slicked back and his intense eyes staring at me with a million beautiful twinkling flowers behind him. I wanted to tell him how deeply in love with him I had fallen, how I couldn't stand the thought of ever being without him, and how scared I was about what might happen to us in Harte. But those thoughts felt too heavy for such a magical place. Instead, I teased him. "You've become a total sap."

He laughed. "It's disturbing. I toss and turn every night, wondering how I let myself get this bad. I finally understand what it's like to lose sleep because you can't stop thinking about someone."

I mocked the words he had told me just weeks ago when I first became a mermaid. "Merfolk don't sleep."

"Touché." He pulled me against him. "But we do rest, and even when I'm resting, I never stop thinking about you."

The tingling in my fins spread through my entire body. If I didn't lighten the mood, I'd end up losing all rational thoughts. I climbed onto the cascading branch and sat in its curve. I could hardly see my tail because of all the twinkling flowers surrounding me. "There's one thing I don't understand. Medusa couldn't leave the grotto, so she would've never been able to come here and see this beautiful place."

"True, but she could use the all-seeing mirror." Treygan draped his arms over the branch, lifting himself halfway out of the water. His wet, rippling muscles were distracting and much too enticing. "The stories say this was one of her favorite places to gaze at for days on end."

"Mm, yes, I can see why."

Sage purred, forcing me to hone in on the topic of the mirror. Treygan had mentioned the gorgon's mirror before, and I remembered reading about it in the history books. "I don't think that mirror still exists. I haven't seen it anywhere in the grotto."

"Well, it was a very long time ago. Legend says it stopped working when Medusa was killed. Maybe Stheno and Euryale destroyed it out of anger or frustration."

Stheno and Euryale destroying anything wouldn't surprise me. I was pretty sure they wanted to destroy me.

"So, was the trip worth it?" Treygan maneuvered himself onto the branch so he was sitting beside me. "To see this place?"

"Absolutely. I've never seen anything in Earth this breathtaking."

"Considering you didn't travel much beyond your island and some parts of Florida, you don't have much to compare it to, but based on my extensive traveling, you're right. Nowhere else do stars shine all the time—or inside flowers."

"Am I the first girl you've ever brought here?"

He laughed. "You're the only girl I've ever taken anywhere in any sort of romantic sense."

I blushed.

"Also," he added, "only gorgons can enter this place."

"Really? Why?"

"I'm not sure. I tried bringing Delmar and Kimber here when we were kids, but they couldn't enter the forest. They said it was like an invisible brick wall stopped them from swimming forward. They tried a few more times throughout the years, but always with the same result. I could only let them see it through my memories."

"So, no one else has been here except for you?"

"I'm sure some of the gorgon kin have been here at some point. And Rownan came here with me when we were kids."

"Rownan came here?" I couldn't picture it. "Doesn't seem like his type of place."

Treygan grinned, scanning the area around us like he was watching memories play out in front of him. "We used to play Treasure Hunting."

"Treasure Hunting?"

"A children's game. Rownan always won."

I wanted to bask in the moment and enjoy our alone time. I wanted to hear more stories about Treygan as a child, but the mention of Rownan had me distracted and worried again. "Treygan, I want to know what Vienna is like."

A short huff escaped his lips. I had ruined the moment he had created for us. I felt awful that I couldn't give him my undivided attention, but he quickly recovered before I could apologize. "Vienna was a true—"

"Is." I corrected him.

"Is?"

"She *is* a true … whatever you were about to say. You said was. Like she doesn't exist anymore."

"Sorry. I didn't mean it that way. It's just been so long since I last saw her."

I shifted my weight. The tree branch wasn't the most comfortable seat. "We should speak about her as if she's alive and well. That will help us be more confident about our mission."

"You're right. Okay, Vienna *is* a true romantic. She and Rownan had the best relationship I've ever witnessed. They always put each other first and made selfless displays of affection and appreciation for each other."

"It's hard to picture Rownan that way."

Treygan looked vexed. "Really? He never faked being romantic those couple of weeks you dated?"

"Whoa. Let's clear this up so there's no more confusion. Rownan and I never *really* dated. You know that. He mysted me into thinking we were a couple. None of our so-called relationship was based on truth or real feelings."

"You never felt anything for him?"

"During those weeks we fake-dated, I don't know what I felt because none of it was real. But after the fact, there were many times I wanted to throw Rownan into a tank of killer jellyfish and let them sting the stupid out of him. I don't think anyone would describe that as lovey-dovey feelings."

Treygan smiled. "Point taken." He fidgeted with some flowers beside him. "I've been worried that maybe you would have had feelings for him if circumstances were different."

What circumstances? Did he mean if Rownan wasn't married? Or if I had been turned selkie instead of mer? My feelings for

Treygan would have been the same no matter what, I was sure of that. "It doesn't matter what the circumstances might have been. Like it or not, you are stuck with me and my hodgepodge sea monster craziness. *You* are my destiny, Treygan."

His eyes lit up. "Destiny? Now who's talking romantic?" His fingers traced the vines of hallmarks where my tail melded into skin.

My fins curled in response to his touch. I closed my eyes, relishing the way his fingertips stirred my insides. My reply came out breathless. "We're romantics. We need to accept our shame and carry on."

He kissed along my collarbone. "You make me proud to be a romantic."

His closeness to my ear made me realize Sage was gone. Her absence reminded me that Vienna was gone too. Guilt sucker-punched me back into the severity of our situation. Hard as it was, I pulled away from Treygan's kisses. "We strayed off track. Let's get back to Vienna."

"Vienna who?" he whispered.

I playfully splashed water on him. "Stop it! We need to focus."

"Fine," he sighed, wiping water from his face. "Let's see. More about Vienna. I have so many memories of her and Rownan."

"Perfect! Why didn't we think of that earlier?" One of the most amazing gifts merfolk had was the ability to share memories with other merfolk. Treygan and I had linked souls and lived each other's memories several times, and every time it strengthened our bond. "Share some memories of her with me."

"Let me think of one or two good ones." His eyes shifted to the sky. "I have one."

His cobalt eyes focused on mine. Water lapped gently between us. We both held our breath. The calm before the storm was my favorite part of the soul sharing process. So much could be said in the silence between two people. Treygan and I had some of our most meaningful conversations in complete silence. He knew how much I loved the build-up, so he took his time, but eventually clouds passed over his eyes. My soul connected with his as I was pulled out of the present and into Treygan's past.

I became him, Treygan in a time and place long ago.

For the first time ever, I saw Vienna. With Rownan. And if I had any traces of doubt about them before, they vanished the moment I witnessed them together.

I had a new understanding and appreciation for who, and what, we were saving.

Treygan and Yara were determined to return home. I would come back with Vienna. I had never been surer of anything in my life.

Schools of fish circled nearby. And a pod of dolphins. And a few sea turtles. Everywhere we went, Rathe's creatures were all trying to meet Yara, or at least watch what she was doing. The crowds were annoying, especially when we were trying to work.

Once we're in Harte, I explained to Yara and Treygan, *we'll shadow Vienna. I'm sure she'll be easy for me to find since our connection is so strong.*

Yara waved away two curious manatees. *I agree. Your relationship was like something from a fairy tale.*

I snickered. *You have no idea.*

Yes, I do. I've lived several of Treygan's memories of her and witnessed you two together. I sort of feel like I know her now.

My body tensed from my forehead to my fins. Treygan's eyes met mine and he squared his shoulders. I wanted to body slam him. My teeth were clenched so hard I thought they might crack. *You shared memories of Vienna with her?*

She needs to know what Vienna looks like. She's helping us find her.

I lurched forward. *You had no right!*

Why are you so upset? Yara asked. *Me knowing what she looks like can only help us.*

Look, Treygan said, swimming closer to me. *I'm sure it's infuriating that you can't relive memories of her, but I thought it—*

You didn't think anything! I shouted. *Even if you two did do something so violating behind my back,* I pointed at Yara, *you should have been smart enough not to tell me about it.*

She flinched. *I'm sorry, Rownan. I didn't mean to—*

I don't want to hear another word from either of you. I swam away, angry and hurt, but then turned back. I felt emotionally out of control. I grabbed Yara by her upper arms. *I changed my mind. What memories did he share with you? What was she doing?*

Treygan grabbed my forearm and pulled me off Yara. *Calm down. And don't ever grab her like that again.*

Don't tell me to calm down. I wriggled out of his grip. *Was I there? Was I in the memories?*

Treygan's eyes were still narrowed, but I saw sympathy seep in. *Of course you were.*

Was she ... happy? The water around me felt heavier, like it was trying to crush me from the outside. *Were we happy?*

Treygan's tone was much calmer. *You already know the answer to that.*

Of course we were happy. I sank to the bottom of the shallow ocean and sat in the sand. Yara and Treygan both swam down after me. I caught a snippet of Treygan's mental conversation with Yara as he asked her to give us a minute alone.

Treygan hovered in front of me. *I'm sorry. I should have realized how upsetting that would be for you. I'd give you my ability if I could. I swear it.*

A throbbing pain burned in my chest. I closed my eyes, not wanting Treygan invading my thoughts. I didn't need Treygan's ability. I relived my memories of Vienna all day, every day. Intimate moments that no one else could ever re-experience. What had me so upset was knowing I might have ruined everything. Our powerful love, and Vienna's soul and life, had been jeopardized because of my stupid decisions. Memories were all I had left. And they weren't nearly enough. I opened my eyes. *I miss her so much.*

I know, Treygan said.

Less than a week ago we were at each other's throats and doing physical harm to one another. Treygan was noble, but it was still hard for me to believe that he and Yara were risking their souls, and the rest of their happy lives together, to help me find Vienna. He had to have some kind of ulterior motive. *Why are you doing this?*

Doing what?

Helping me rescue Vienna. Risking your life and your future with Yara.

You're my brother.

Half-brother.

His eyes had a faraway look, much farther than the ocean stretched. He finally refocused on me and said, *Trivialities.*

What's that supposed to mean?

It means we share blood. You're my family. I'd do anything to protect my family.

Last week you wanted to kill me.

Last week you were an arrogant bastard who needed some sense beaten into him.

I couldn't argue with that.

And, truth be told, he continued, *you're probably going to be an arrogant bastard when we get to Harte. Your emotions will lead instead of your head. You'll make risky moves and life-threatening decisions, so if I need to beat sense into you while we're there, I will.*

I tried not to crack a smile, but I couldn't help it. Treygan had my back. Just like when we were kids. *Fine. But fair warning: don't come between me and Vienna. If you do, my claws will come out.*

He cracked a smile too. *You're forgetting that no one and nothing could ever come between you and Vienna.*

I glanced around, wanting to apologize to Yara for overreacting. Maybe even tell her she landed herself one hell of a guy, but she was gone. *Where'd Yara go?*

I don't know. But this is the perfect opportunity for us to try shadowing her again.

I thought you said that was impossible.

Isn't this whole mission supposedly impossible?

We couldn't find Yara through shadowing, but we did spot her after only a few minutes of regular searching. Her white hair and tail were bright beacons we could've spotted from miles away. She had found the two manatees from earlier. They had joined three more manatees, and Yara was petting and hugging all of them like they were old friends.

Should we join her? I asked Treygan.

No, she looks happy and relaxed. Let her have some alone time with them. She's under a lot of pressure.

I watched her grab one of the manatees by the sides of his face and kiss his snout. He nuzzled her and she giggled. *Yeah, she does look happy.*

As we swam away, Treygan asked, *How's your arm?*

Seems to be back to normal.

Ah, as weak as usual, then?

I punched him in the shoulder. *Shut up.*

I missed this. I missed getting along with my brother. We had been closer than ever before the gate closed—almost inseparable. I finally asked the question I had been wondering for years. *Did you know something awful was going to happen?*

What?

Ever since my wedding, you were different. So cautious about everything. You kept a much closer watch over Vienna and me. I kind of suspected you knew something and were afraid to tell me.

He looked away, staring at the ocean in front of us. I clutched his shoulder and forced him to stop swimming. *Tell me, Treygan. I won't be mad.*

I can't.

What do you mean you can't? We're about to enter hell together. There can't be any secrets between us.

He hesitated, but then, *At your wedding, when you and Vienna did your future reading with the High Priestess, she told you she didn't see anything ... but that wasn't true.*

I tensed, remembering how flustered the High Priestess had seemed during our reading. She had told Vienna she couldn't make a connection because of the energy from the Northern Lights, that we were too far from our realm, that nothing she saw was clear. *What did she tell you?*

She said a time would come when I'd have to decide how far I'd go to protect you.

What?

Treygan shrugged. *She emphasized the words 'far' and 'protect.' For years I wondered what she meant. Even when the gate closed, it didn't make sense because we were together, and there wasn't much to protect you from—except your own stupidity.*

Seriously, don't make me hurt you before our trip.

Treygan almost smiled, but then seriousness reclaimed him. *The day our father told us you were going to Harte to try to find Vienna, I knew this was it. This is what the High Priestess warned me about.*

That's why you're going? Because of one conversation with some old lady you hardly knew?

I had no idea what she meant that day. You can't imagine the horrible scenarios that ran through my head. But I always knew I'd do whatever it took. I didn't care how far I'd have to go.

I didn't want to get all sappy, but I was touched. Would I have done the same for him? I wasn't sure. Treygan had always been the noble one. *Did she say how it would turn out?*

No. I just know you're going to need me.

Don't be so cocky.

It's not me being cocky. This was written in the waters long ago. I have to go with you.

I didn't know if that High Priestess was still alive, but I either owed her a thank you for preparing my brother for this mission, or I needed to curse her for making him feel obligated to go with me.

Of course, Yara had to bring Sage to the sprites' party. Heaven forbid she should do anything without her favorite pet. I flew beside them, unsettled by Sage occasionally glancing at me with her glowing eyes. "I'm surprised you didn't insist on bringing Treygan and Rownan too."

"I already witnessed them almost kill each other," Yara said. "I didn't feel like hanging around to watch them break each other's bones again. We're supposed to start a suicide mission tomorrow, and they're already fighting."

My wings ruffled. "Don't call it a suicide mission."

"Sorry."

The three of them had been inseparable since they started their "training." As if any preparation could prepare them for Harte. I despised Rownan for dragging Yara into his mess. "I'd like to break a few of Rownan's bones."

"Please don't. The Violets just finished repairing your first demolition job."

"He had it coming."

As we entered Echo Bayou, I zigzagged and weaved around the weeping willows. Yara followed, matching my every move. I slowed as we approached the village of water lilies. Everyone was bustling around. The celebration had already begun.

We landed on top of the water. Yara's eyes widened at the scene in front of us. "There's so many of them! And so many different colors. The flower petals and leaves look like they're really attached to them."

I paused, realizing Yara wasn't used to seeing creatures naturally adorned with foliage. "They *are* attached to them."

"They aren't dressed up for the party?"

I snickered. "No, those accessories are part of them. They naturally develop that way."

"I don't remember the sprite I saw in Treygan's memory having any leaves or petals."

"Did the sprite's skin look fluid? His or her predominant trait might have been water."

She stared to the side of me as if replaying the memory. "You're right. She did have watery skin. That's so cool."

I touched my own forearm, missing the way my skin used to resemble the leaves of Calliandra plants. Hundreds of water sprites shouted my name, and then the chatter began about Yara. The buzz of excitement grew louder as more sprites flew over to greet us. They swarmed Yara, so I backed away and walked to the riverbank.

After meeting everyone and answering a hundred and one questions, Yara excused herself and joined me by the log of tiny desserts. "They're so adorable and friendly, and there are so many of them."

"Yes, Medusa cried a lot when she was first banished to this world."

Yara turned to face me. "What does crying have to do with the sprites?"

"Each sprite was formed from one of Medusa's tears."

She glanced at all my flitting brothers and sisters then gaped at me. "You're kidding."

"Why would I kid about my own former species?" I grabbed a berry tart then flew up to a branch.

Yara followed me, perching on a neighboring tree limb. "Tell me more."

I sighed. History was my least favorite subject, so I summarized. "Medusa was lonely and missed all the colors of Earth's realm. This was long before she started creating the world you see now. Poseidon vowed she'd never cry lonely tears again, so every tear she cried from that point on blossomed to life as a water sprite. Until she died. Now her tears are just shooting stars."

Yara's eyes were practically sparkling. "That's amazing."

I popped the barely bite-sized tart into my mouth. "You think everything Medusa and Poseidon created is amazing."

Jenna flew over and landed on Yara's shoulder, pointing at Sage. "Oh, my goodness, you have a snake attached to your head!"

Sage bent down and sniffed her. Sage's head was almost as big as Jenna's entire body, but Jenna showed no fear.

"Hello, silver snake!" She kissed Sage's nose, and Sage's tongue darted out and grazed her forehead. "Ahhh!" Jenna wiped her face, giggling. "Snake breath is stinky."

"You are too cute for words," Yara said to Jenna.

"Why, thank you." Jenna blushed. "We've been anxiously waiting to meet you."

Keeley flew over with a grin so big her lips took up half of her azure face. "Such a pleasure to meet you, Yara. Nixie has told us stories about you, and we've heard all about your wings, claws, snake, how you can control lightning, and … and look how pretty your hair and wings are! They truly are like diamonds because when the light hits you a certain way I see all the colors of the rainbow and—"

"Keeley, give someone else a chance to speak!" Jenna brushed her leafy bangs out of her eyes and shrugged at Yara. "Her favorite hobby is talking."

I held back a laugh. Yara seemed to do the same.

"I'm sorry," Keeley said, darting in front of Yara. "I'm just in awe of you and have so many questions."

"My goodness," Yara said. "So much energy and personality for such little creatures."

I winked at my sisters. "The best things come in small packages."

Jenna and Keeley both nodded happily.

Yara moved from her branch and sat beside me. "I've never seen you smile so much."

"Me?" I hadn't noticed the permanent grin on my face until Yara mentioned it. I tried to wipe it away and maintain a neutral expression.

"You're different around the sprites—softer or something."

I stared out at the bayou, watching water lilies float along and bump into each other while my brothers and sisters celebrated. They lived a playful and joyful existence—so different from a siren's. I couldn't imagine a sprite drinking blood or stealing human memories. They didn't have a mean bone in their bodies. "You never forget where you came from. At least, I don't. The sprites remind me of a different time in my life."

"Nixie, were you happier as a sprite?" Yara spoke quietly. "Do you regret becoming a siren?"

I turned to look her in the eyes. "We all have regrets. Anyone who says they have none is a liar, and anyone who thinks they'll live without acquiring some is a fool."

Yara's brows wrinkled together and her lips parted, but whatever she wanted to say was cut off by the giddy chatter of sprites. A few of the older sprites pulled Yara away. Keeley and Jenna hovered on either side of my head.

"I like her very much," Keeley said.

"Me too." Jenna landed on my shoulder. "She has vine markings on her. Nature must be fond of her."

"She needs some foliage sprouting out of her head to go with that snake." Keeley combed her fingers through her hair of blue leaves.

Unconsciously, I touched the top of my own head, but my sprite features were long gone. Emptiness tugged at me, but then Jenna appeared in front of my face and batted her long, golden eyelashes. "We made you a crown. I arranged the flowers myself. Come on!"

That put the smile back on my face. She grabbed hold of my pinky and together we flew up into the trees where my beautiful crown hung from a branch. It didn't matter that I had become a siren. My family of sprites made sure that the bayou would always be my home.

Later, we all danced under the weeping willows.

"Hold out your hand," I told Yara. She did, but it was limp. "No, keep your palm and fingers flat."

Jenna landed in the center of Yara's hand and twirled. "See, and now we dance."

Yara laughed. "It tickles."

"You'll get used to it," I assured her, opening my own hands in front of me. Sprites landed on each of my palms, already dancing. Their joy was contagious. I had never seen anyone resist their charm. Even Sage swayed and bounced.

The musically inclined sprites played upbeat songs for hours. Yara chatted with them about how they used water reeds, cattails, shells, and tree bark as instruments.

"How'd she do it?" Yara asked me.

"How did who do what?"

"Medusa. She created this world full of magic, beauty, and so many amazing and gifted creatures. Then she just handed over the reins to a nobody like me and expects me to know what to do. I have no clue how to manage a world. Especially a world like this."

I wanted to tell her she didn't need to worry about it. That she would go to Harte and never come back. But I was tired of being the one to preach the ugly truth. Tonight, I'd keep my mouth shut so she could enjoy her last night in Rathe. "Don't worry about it," I told her. "Everything will be fine."

The words felt like venom on my lips because I knew it was a lie.

"Do you think you're ready for Harte?" I asked her.

"Ready as we'll ever be." Yara sat on the muddy riverbank and dipped her feet in the water. "I wish I could empower all three of us with the same abilities."

I sat beside her. "What do you mean?"

"I wish Rownan and Treygan could fly like me. I wish I could shadow the guys. I wish Rownan had the ability to relive memories of Vienna the way merfolk can."

"Why don't you talk to Stheno and Euryale? Ask them if you can grant all those abilities."

Her wings spread a tad, bumping into mine. "Stheno and Euryale can't just give us new powers. Can they?"

I brushed some glowing pollen off her shoulder. "Medusa used to create new rules all the time. She gifted everyone with the abilities they now have. You're taking her place. Seems logical that you'd be able to do the same things she did."

Yara's eyes were wide with possibilities. She grabbed my head and kissed me on the cheek. "Nixie, you're a genius!"

Genius. I liked the sound of that.

Trips to the grotto to visit Stheno and Euryale were about as pleasurable as getting cavities filled. The sisters did not like me. I had no faith they'd want to help me, but my request could save the lives of two true sea creatures—both of whom were part gorgon. Surely, Stheno and Euryale would want to help Rownan and Treygan.

I flew to the grotto, shape-shifting into heron form. I flew around the massive cliffs then dove into the water and through the small entrance. I darted inside, navigating through the dark, murky tunnels, then exploded into the main chamber and transformed back into my regular self.

The grotto, as always, smelled like mildew and saltwater. The eternal torches burned at average strength, which meant Stheno and Euryale were awake. At least I wouldn't have to disturb their sleep.

I walked toward the sound of their tails slithering along the damp floor of the cave. Then the all-too-familiar sound of Mariza vomiting stopped me in my tracks.

I gagged a little too loudly, and Euryale slithered around the corner.

She looked disappointed to see me. As if it could have been anyone else visiting this awful place. "What do you want? It is not our scheduled meeting day."

"I wanted to talk with you and Stheno, if you have a few minutes."

"I'm feeding on the memories Mariza brought me."

"By all means, go ahead. I'll wait in the den."

Several minutes later, the torches in the grotto burned weaker. It meant my gorgon sisters were relaxed and well fed. Stheno and Euryale slithered into the room.

"What do *you* want?" Stheno hissed.

I hesitated, second-guessing my plan to ask them for help, but for Treygan and Rownan's sake, I had to try. "How did it work when Medusa wanted to … change something, or create something new?"

"Be specific, child." Stheno sounded exasperated. She usually napped after feeding, so if I drew out the conversation too long she would get even crankier.

"Say I wanted to gift Rownan with an ability that merfolk have. Do you two need to approve it?"

Euryale cackled sinisterly, her mustard-colored fangs still had blood on the tips.

Stheno smirked. "We would never approve such a thing. You cannot alter what Medusa created."

"It's not a big change, just, like, a present to one of her children."

"No," Stheno snapped.

"Why not?"

"This is her world!" Stheno's bottom fangs extended as she snarled. "Our world. Not yours."

Euryale slithered closer to me, the end of her tail ticking like a rattlesnake. "We do not like that she sent you here. We did not agree and we do not approve of her decision. If you think we are going to let you redesign what we spent centuries creating, then you are gravely mistaken."

Sage purred beside me and rose into the air. I stood taller. "I would never try to replace your sister, but Medusa assigned me this job, and you need to respect your sister's decision."

Stheno rose up several feet, her body stretching forward like a snake. Blue pinwheels of fire spun in her eyes. Her tone made Sage retreat into my hair. "Do not attempt to tell us what to do ever again."

I glanced at Euryale. Her eyes were spinning flames too. The torches on the walls roared so high they burned the tips of the stalactites hanging from the ceiling.

Great. I had pissed off both of them. "I'm sorry. I just wanted to give us the best chance of returning to Rathe. As it stands," my voice cracked, "I'm not sure we'll make it back."

They both laughed, but not out loud. They went through all the motions of a full-blown hysterical fit. Heads tossed back, mouths wide open, eyes dancing, but they didn't make any sound. My shaky breaths rattled inside my head. The drip-drip-drip of stalactites made each moment of Stheno and Euryale's mocking feel so much longer.

At the exact same moment, they stopped, slithered away from me, and stood side by side. I hated when they did their synchronized sister speeches. They were going to start talking like Siamese twins completing each other's sentences. It always made me hyper aware of the fact that it was two against one.

"As we said," Stheno began.

"Do not attempt to tell us what to do," Euryale said.

Stheno didn't miss a beat. "Ever again."

"But we accept your apology," Euryale continued.

"Because you cannot help how pitiful you are."

I wanted to raise my chin and keep my eyes locked with theirs, but my body betrayed me. My gaze drifted to my own feet. My toes—even with hallmarks scrolling over my skin—seemed so weak and ordinary. I could hardly stand up to Stheno and Euryale. How would I ever be strong enough to face what awaited us in Harte?

"We leave tomorrow," I mumbled. "Is there anything you could offer to help us?"

They smiled mischievously at each other, then looked at me. In unison, they both snarled, "No."

Medusa was wrong. They didn't want a third to restore their power. They had lived so long without her that they didn't want things to change. They would never accept me. They didn't care if I lived or died.

I stood at the tide pool, preparing to morph into my bird form and fly out of the grotto, but I stopped, remembering the story Treygan had told me. I turned around. "Stheno, Euryale?"

Their heads swiveled one-hundred-eighty degrees to look at me.

"The all-seeing mirror," I said. "What happened to it?"

Stheno smirked. "Even if we knew."

"We would not tell you," Euryale hissed.

I flipped them off then dove into the tunnel as fast as I could, hoping they didn't know what my extended middle fingers meant. I couldn't verbally tell them what I thought of them, but human sign language was surprisingly satisfying.

Rowan

My good luck party reminded me why I loved being a selkie.

This was the world I had missed so much: glacier homes and arctic pools, dancing under the moonlight, bonding with everyone. The beauty of the selkie side of Rathe was endless. In Earth's realm, ice and snow only existed in shades of white. In Rathe, the trees were frosted in shades of blue, green, and silver, and the leaves never died.

Call me biased, but our part of Rathe was so much prettier than the mer's. Our world constantly glistened. Our three moons always reflected their light off something: the water, ice, or even a snowflake falling from the sky. Ours was a world of colorful, sparkling, unbreakable glass. The constant frigid temperatures kept my soul warm.

Lavender snow-capped mountains stretched tall into the always-dark sky. Ice paths of all lengths and inclines had been carved into the nearest mountain like massive sliding boards. Selkies slid down them, laughing and enjoying the twists and turns before splashing into the water. And, of course, there was music.

For the first time in a long time, I let loose. I danced until my lungs and muscles hurt, and then I danced some more. No one forced me to drink because they knew the rush that blood or vodka would give me was nothing compared to my excitement about finding Vienna.

"You seem confident," Dina said, dancing with me for the fifth time. She hadn't tried flirting with me. Everyone knew where my head and heart were—with Vienna. The same place they had been since I was a kid.

"I know I'm coming back. And I'm bringing Vienna back with me."

"No doubts at all?"

I took a swig of my water. "None."

"Are you scared?"

"I was, but not anymore."

She raised her glass. "I admire your courage, Rownan. I wouldn't dare go into Harte."

"You might if your soul mate was trapped in there."

Dina bobbed her head, but I'd never known her to date anyone more than a few weeks. She had no concept of what it felt like to know another soul was "the one."

A slower song began. I stopped dancing and wiped sweat from my face. "I need to take a breather."

"Okay." Dina hugged me, squeezing me an extra time before she let go. "See you when you come home."

She always saw through my lies. I was leaving the party, and she knew it. I didn't want a bunch of emotional goodbyes. I didn't want to see so many selkies look at me with worry or sadness. Silently sneaking away was best for everyone.

I tousled her wet hair. "Tell everyone I said thanks for the party."

She nodded and smiled. "Sure thing."

I headed home so I could pass out much earlier than usual. The sooner I fell asleep, the sooner tomorrow would arrive.

I jolted awake, haunted by the same reoccurring nightmare of Vienna burning to death.

I was on the beach of our home, sleeping under the moonlight.

"I'll find you," I vowed, staring up at the moons. "I swear, I'll find a way, Vienna. Hold on just a little while longer."

One green star shot across the dark sky and faded into the horizon. Medusa could shed as many tears as she wanted. I was not going to fail Vienna again.

The waves gently ebbed and flowed, calming me. But I was too calm. It usually took me a good hour or more to recover from that nightmare. Something was off.

I turned around and found Indrea standing behind me in a fur coat. The wind blew her purple hair around her face, but her violet eyes were locked on me. Merfolk and selkies had been battling for so long that it should've felt strange to see Indrea in our side of Rathe, but instead I was relieved. She walked forward and stood over me. She was using her calming abilities on me, and I was grateful. "I'm sorry to wake you. I didn't realize you'd be asleep this early."

"Don't apologize. You did me a favor. Nightmares suck."

She wrapped her coat tightly around herself and sat down in the sand beside me. "I came for one last healing session. Just to make sure you're as strong as possible."

"I appreciate that."

She tilted her head back and admired the sky. "I had nearly forgotten how enchanting this side of our world is."

I looked up too. Blue and green lights streaked the sky. If humans saw them shooting through the dark and falling into the ocean they might think it was a meteor shower, but in Rathe it was more than that.

"She's weeping for you," Indrea said. "It must feel good to be so loved."

I was still calm, even though I should have been angry. "If Medusa loves me so much, and if she's so sad, then why would she allow this to happen?"

"Many things are beyond her control."

"If we were a mer couple, I bet she would've done something to stop it."

Indrea sighed. "We're home. There's no reason for further fighting between sea creatures. Medusa loves all of her children equally."

"I don't believe that." More calmness washed over me. "I'm okay, Indrea. Stop wasting your energy."

"Helping you is not a waste."

Once upon a time, Indrea had been like a mother to Treygan and an aunt to me. She and my mother were great friends. Ever since Treygan and I were kids, Indrea and Caspian were the Violets who had always helped us get out of trouble, or healed us when we were hurt. Me, Vienna, Treygan, Delmar, Kimber, even Pango and Koraline—no matter what happened, Indrea and Caspian were there for all of us.

"I turned my back on you," I mumbled. "Why are you helping me?"

"You did what you believed was right. You were loyal to your kind. No one can fault you for that."

"I fault myself for it. I abandoned my brother, my best friends, but worse than any of that, I abandoned Vienna. I never should've left her."

Indrea turned to look at me. She placed her hand over mine. "What happened that day? Why were you and Vienna separated?"

I tensed. Indrea's calming powers were wearing off. I stayed silent as my guilt intensified.

"Sometimes it helps to talk about it, Rownan. Bottling up your feelings never ends well."

I pulled my hand free of hers and sank my fingers into the sand. "I told her to go through the gate, to make sure her family was home safe. I went back for my mother. I promised Vienna I'd return by sunset."

Indrea nodded once. "I see."

"It's the only promise I've ever broken. To her, I mean."

"Promises are fragile things. They are easy to break, and difficult to repair once the damage is done."

"I have to fix this mess I made."

A subtle grin spread across Indrea's face; a mixture of sadness and something else I couldn't interpret. "Do you remember when you were just a pup and Treygan was going through that awkward stage of discovering his abilities, you two were underwater wrestling and he accidentally destroyed a coral reef?"

I flinched at the memory. I was digging pieces of coral out of my back and neck for days. It dawned on me that Indrea said *he* destroyed the reef, but we told her I was the one who shattered it. Treygan had been getting in a lot of trouble, and he had been warned that if he had one more slip-up he would be punished. It was so long ago, but I instinctively kept the lie going. "You mean the time a dolphin pile-drove *me* into the reef?"

Indrea laughed. "Do you think any of us believed that story? We knew what really happened."

"You knew I lied? Why didn't you say anything?"

"Because you were protecting your brother. Some acts, even lies, when done to help another soul are a noble testament to one's character."

I hung my head. "I'm not noble."

Indrea turned and raised my chin. "That was a demonstration of your true character. So was trying to save your mother's life at that gate, even though it meant putting your own life and future at risk. And, by gods, if insisting on going to Harte to find Vienna isn't a brave and selfless deed, then I don't know what is."

"It's not selfless. It's greedy." Letting Yara and Treygan come with me was even worse. Years of bottled-up grief threatened to pour out of me. I didn't know what would happen if I let it out. It would be like the levy of a damn breaking. I respected Indrea too much to make her deal with that.

She and Caspian had chosen to be trapped in Earth's realm. They weren't even there when the warning went out. They didn't race to return home like the rest of us. They *were* home, but they accepted the possibility of never seeing Rathe again, and they willingly swam through the gate, knowing they would be locked out. They did it because they cared about the sea creatures who would be trapped. They wanted to help us survive. And they did. What *they* did was brave. It was selfless. I was nothing like them. "I miss Vienna like crazy. I'm only going to Harte because I don't want to live without her. How is that brave?"

"Trust me, it's one of the bravest acts I've ever witnessed. And I've been alive a long time."

We sat silent for a few minutes, watching the waves roll onto the shore.

"The guilt is overwhelming at times," I admitted. "Because of my broken promise, she's in some damned place alone. I'll never forgive myself for that."

"Forgiveness will be one of your most important weapons on this journey. As for your broken promise," Indrea wrapped her arm around me like she used to do when I was a child, "that day when you shattered the reef, you asked me what you could do to fix it. Do you remember what I told you?"

I didn't have to think hard. Indrea's words echoed through my mind loud and clear. "You said, 'Time and the tides will fix what's been broken. Focus on making yourself whole again.'"

"Exactly. I suggest you follow that same advice for your current predicament."

"The tides can't fix this."

"You'd be surprised what forces of nature can do. You just worry about doing your part. Concentrate on making yourself whole again."

I needed Vienna to feel whole. Maybe that's what Indrea meant. I had to focus on finding her and bringing her home. Medusa's tears still streaked the sky. "Indrea, do you think Vienna is okay?"

She squeezed my injured arm, but I felt no pain. "She will be. Once she's with you again."

"So you're confident she's still alive? That her soul hasn't been consumed by evil?"

"As long as a soul remembers how to love, as long as Vienna could remember those she loved, she could fight off the evil. I don't believe Vienna could ever forget you, Rownan."

Everyone had been telling me how insane I was, and that I would never make it back from Harte, but Indrea understood. People had told her she and Caspian were crazy for voluntarily trapping themselves in Earth's realm when the gate closed, but they survived. They were proof that some risks were worth it.

"Earlier, you told me I could do this. Do you really believe that?" I faced her and saw certainty and faith in her amethyst eyes. Faith that couldn't be faked.

"I have always believed in you, Rownan. I never stopped."

I sat on the sill of the largest window of our nest, staring at the three foreboding moons in the sky. Tomorrow it would all be over.

My time with Yara was almost up. She didn't even want to spend her last night with me. Another tear streamed down my cheek. I caught it on my finger, held my hand out the window, and watched it drop, disappearing into the clouds below me.

"Why are you such a sniveling, depressed mess?" Otabia asked. "Pull yourself together!"

"Yara's with Treygan tonight," I told her. "Again. Always with Treygan."

"Can't say I blame her." Mariza flopped down in a chair. The frame of branches creaked under her weight. "I've longed to devour him for ages. I'm jealous that motley mutt can have him whenever she wants."

I used to feel the same, but ever since he went off the market I couldn't look at him that way. "He's not all that great."

"I beg to differ," Otabia said.

Mariza pouted her lips so they were even plumper than usual. "It's not fair that both of you have sampled him. Nixie drank a whole memory from him. And you," she pointed at Otabia, "you licked the entire length of his spine." Mariza sighed dreamily. "Nixie, tell me again how he tasted."

I shook my head. She was an insatiable leech. "I've already told you a dozen times."

Mariza clapped her hands. "Tell me again. Again!"

Otabia cooed. "Like the most decadent chocolate with a touch of sea salt."

If only they could see how ridiculous they were, getting all worked up over Treygan. A million other males existed in the worlds, and we could seduce almost any of them at any time, but they had to crave the ones they couldn't have.

"Let me relive it," Mariza begged, reaching for Otabia's arm.

Otabia pulled out of her grasp. "I'm tired of you sucking blood out of me. Go get your own memories."

I pulled my knees to my chest. A splatter of blood lingered on my leg. I must have missed it when I cleaned up after my feedings. I wiped it away and stared out the window again.

"We sense you're sad." Otabia sounded annoyed. "But you're also scared. We don't like being scared. It's not familiar to us."

"It makes me all itchy and twitchy." Mariza turned, draping her legs over the arm of her chair. "Knock it off."

My voice screeched louder than I intended, but I was tired of everything always being about them. "I can't help how I feel!"

Otabia paced in front of me, looking leery. "Is this where we're supposed to ask you to share your worries with us? One of those wretched moments where venting would alleviate your anger and sorrow?"

"We have to do something," Mariza said. "I can't stand all this doom and gloom putting a damper on my mood."

"It might help," I offered meekly. The last creatures in the world to be compassionate were Otabia and Mariza, but I didn't feel like flying all the way to Echo Bayou to talk to the sprites again. "Yara didn't even want to spend time with me tonight. She doesn't care that we may never see each other after tomorrow."

"Not this again," Mariza whined. "If Yara wasn't alive—"

"Don't say that!" I snapped.

"*If,* I said *if* she wasn't alive, you would be free. Cleo crossed over. You'd have no one left to answer to, no one to send you on errands or order you to do their bidding. I would kill for that."

"I'm not like the two of you. I enjoy being needed."

"Silly water sprite tendencies still lingering." Mariza tsked. "Awful idea that was, promoting such a busybody creature."

I silently agreed. I had made a mistake leaving my family and becoming a siren, but there was no undoing it, and no way out of it except death. As much as Otabia and Mariza would have liked to get rid of me, I'd never give them the satisfaction.

We were leaving in the morning.

I couldn't stop rifling through our collection of gifts. Everyone from the merfolk to the sprites had given us stuff they thought would help or protect us.

I still wasn't sure who had given us the massive black tooth shaped like an arrowhead. Rownan told me it was one of the gorgon kin, but when I asked for their name so I could thank them he said they wanted to stay anonymous. At first I was suspicious, but the gorgon kin did keep to themselves. I hadn't seen any of them since Talus rushed me away from the gate on the Triple Eighteen.

I could barely wrap my hand around the huge tooth. "Can you imagine the beast this thing belonged to? This is *one* of his teeth. How big must he have been?" Next, I held up a jar of thick, glowing goo. "The sprites said we could rub this all over ourselves if we need to find each other in the dark."

Treygan smiled deviously. "I like the sound of that."

"Get your mind out of the gutter."

"I assure you, any time I think about your body my mind is in heaven."

I threw a boot at him, but he dodged it then winked at me.

"Are we really taking these clunky things with us?" He picked the boot up by the laces and held it in front of him like it was a dead fish. "I'm not a fan of footwear."

"What if the ground is too jagged or hot or whatever to walk on?"

"Our sea creature skin is thick and resilient. More so than these unnatural things." Treygan dropped the boot and it hit the floor with a thud. "What if there is no ground? We might not even use our legs or feet."

"Seems unlikely that hell would be all water."

"Unless it's boiling water," he grumbled.

I pretended I didn't hear him and tried not to imagine us boiling to death. I sorted through more gifts: assorted knives and daggers, healing ointments and potions from the Violets, thermoses of blood from the selkies—for Rownan only, of course. "How are we supposed to take all of these things with us? It's not like we're taking luggage."

Treygan came up behind me and wrapped his arms around my waist. "They meant well. We'll take as much as we can carry."

"Carry how?"

Treygan kissed below my ear and bursts of color flashed in front of my eyes. His kisses trailed down my neck as he replied, "Holsters … packs … special gear …" I only comprehended a few words due to the tingling heat rushing through my body. He turned me around to face him. He traced my hallmarks with his fingertips, starting at my wrists then trailing up my arms and across my chest. He brushed over every swirl and symbol until he reached my hips and whispered, "It will be a shame to hide this body under a protective suit."

I rose on my tiptoes and kissed him, pressing my body tight against him. Much to my frustration, he pulled back after only a few seconds.

"I have a gift for you."

"We weren't supposed to get each other gifts." I ran my fingers through his hair and pulled him in to continue where we left off.

He kissed me swiftly then reached behind his head and took my hands in his. I groaned and stomped my foot when he pushed us apart again. "Trust me, you will like this gift, and this is the perfect time to give it to you."

My hands flopped to my sides as he left the room. Usually it was me trying to keep us focused on preparations or training. Here I was throwing myself at him, and he was more worried about distracting me with a present. I would never understand men.

Treygan returned pushing a huge box across the floor. The lid came up to my nose, and it was wrapped in blue paper with a yellow ribbon. I was sure his color selection was no accident. I batted my eyelashes at him. "Blue and yellow look very nice together."

The side of his mouth curved upward. "Almost as nice as white and indigo."

I lifted the lid, trying to peek over the rim. I couldn't see anything but silver tissue paper, so I tilted the box toward me and reached inside. I pulled out a pillow and squealed with joy. I dug through the box, pulling out a total of six pillows.

Treygan watched me, his huge grin matching mine. "I thought you might want a rematch since I won last time."

"Ha. Won by default." It was weird to see pillows in Rathe. I hadn't seen any in anyone's home, which made sense considering merfolk rested in pools but never slept, and I hadn't been to a selkie or siren's residence. "How did you even get these here without them getting soaked?"

"Same way we keep books and everything else dry. Waterproofing spells."

I hugged one to my chest. "I adore them."

"Use your selkie claws to cut them open so we can get this—what do you call it?—*smack down* started."

I smiled, lowering my chin. "I'm not in much of a fighting mood."

"Oh?" His brow rose. "What kind of mood are you in?"

I arranged all the pillows on the floor. "How about some pillow talk instead?" I sat down, retracting my wings so they wouldn't get in the way of what I hoped would be a lot of rolling around together.

Treygan silently stared at me for a few painstaking moments, but the desire in his eyes kept building.

All the tips Nixie had been teaching me about how to be seductive rattled through my mind. I reclined and raised my arms over my head. According to Nixie it was a demonstration of power and sensuality, but I felt silly and exposed. "Care to join me?"

Nixie's tip worked. Treygan licked his lips, unsuccessfully fighting back a smile. Slowly, he lowered himself on top of me. His left arm stayed braced beside my head. Hallmarks swirled over the taut muscles in his neck, chest, and arms as his right hand caressed my skin more softly than the petals of a star-flower. He stared at me in his signature way that made my skin feel like it was melting off my body. I considered morphing into human form, but human skin was more sensitive, and I could barely think or breathe already.

Treygan's gruff voice dripped with as much longing as I felt. "It's a shame we can't take these pillows on our trip."

I replied breathlessly. "Then we better get good use out of them before tomorrow."

The next morning I was wrapped up in Treygan's arms on the thatch roof of his house.

Ever since our hideout before the Triple Eighteen, roof time with Treygan had become one of my favorite activities. Medusa's sunbeams stretched long and wide through the sky.

I nuzzled my head against Treygan's chest one more time before breaking the peaceful silence. "Today is the day."

Treygan breathed deeply. "It feels surreal. And ominous."

"We can do it," I said. "We can. We're going to be fine."

He pressed his lips to the top of my head. "You sound like you're trying to convince yourself."

Maybe I was, or maybe all the warnings about how we would most likely never return were making me realize how mine and Treygan's happy ending was in grave jeopardy. Being on the roof and wondering if we would live to see another day was all too familiar, and way too soon after our last scare. "I'm having déjà vu."

"Yes, it seems unfair how often you and I have to deal with impending doom."

I curled up tighter against him. "Tell me a story."

He rolled me over onto my back and gently kissed my stomach. "Tell you a story, or write you a story?"

I smiled. Given a choice, there was only one answer.

He held his hand above my chest, wiggling his fingers temptingly as his eyes shifted upward. "Hmm, let me think of a good one." My skin ached to feel his fingers write invisible words. His beautiful blue eyes met mine. "Got it."

"About time."

He squinted, still grinning. "Patience, Yamabuki." His fingertip landed just below my neck as he started writing a story the same as always. I said the words out loud while his hand scrolled down the length of my body. "Once upon a tide ...."

He had reached my stomach. I tried to breathe steadily, but he leaned down and kissed each of my hips, then his lips slowly trailed to my thigh. My hallmarks were swirling so fast I could feel my skin rippling, but then Treygan stopped and his fingers returned to my neck.

"Let's continue our story, shall we?"

A tortured grunt was all I could manage. He smirked, then wrote down my body again. I tried focusing on the trails his finger made as he wrote letter after letter down to my toes, but it was all a blur of tingling and desire.

"You lost me," I muttered. "What did you write?"

"I'll write it again."

As if that would help. He formed each letter slower, which only made my craving for him that much stronger. His smug face proved he was enjoying teasing me way too much. I pulled his head down to me and kissed him.

"Your turn," he whispered between deep kisses. "But I want you to sing me a story."

My lips froze. "Huh?" Sing? He had never asked me to sing to him.

"You sang at Koraline's healing ceremony, and it was the most exquisite sound I've ever heard. I've wanted to hear you sing again ever since. But I knew you'd blush," he rubbed my cheek with his thumb, "like you're doing now, and clam up."

My chest was on fire. I could see shades of orange spreading down the front of me. He was right; I was blushing out of control. I stumbled on my words. "I don't think—why would—that's so … awkward."

"Why? It's just you and me."

I sat up. "That's why it's awkward. At Koraline's ceremony, everyone was singing. I can't sing solo with you watching me."

"Lloyd told me you love to sing."

"Sure, in the shower, or while I cleaned the house or gardened, when I don't think anyone is listening or judging me."

"Judging? Have you heard yourself?" He tucked my hair behind my ear. "Since your transformation to a mermaid, your voice is a step above angelic."

My chest was so orange that it reflected off Treygan's skin and made him look tan. "What am I supposed to sing?"

"Anything."

I stared at him, frozen with embarrassment.

"Please, we have to leave soon, and …" Sadness washed over his face. I would have done anything to wipe it away and bring back the smile he wore moments ago. "This might be our last time alone together."

I caressed his face, drawing an invisible line between his freckles that mirrored the Canis Major constellation. "Okay." I breathed deep and cracked my neck. "But I can't look at you. I'm going to focus on the ocean or something."

He nodded. "I'll take it."

I rubbed my dry lips together and thought of a song I made up a few years ago. I sang the first few wordless notes before easing into the first verse.

Storms surround me,
waves keep breaking,
there's no escape I can find.

I was so nervous I scrambled parts of the song, not singing the lines in order.

I'll share my soul with you, and fight what we're facing,
Is it all worth fighting for?

I held the last note, and an intense longing rose inside me. I kept singing, feeling my vocal chords vibrate as my tone went up and down, the song ebbing and flowing like waves.

I was hyper-aware of Treygan beside me. The heat from his body radiated, engulfing me. I craved him so intensely that my vision seemed screened by flames as hot as my skin. I turned to him, still singing a wordless riff, and his eyes were smoldering. I leaped forward, my wings helping me close the short distance between us in the blink of an eye. I landed on top of him, straddling him, and pushed him down as I kissed him harder than ever.

His hands tangled in my hair as he pulled me down tighter against him.

I ground my hips against him. His hips bucked in response. My lips hummed against his as I kept singing. His groaning sent me into a frenzy. I sank my teeth into his bottom lip and sucked until we both moaned with pleasure.

My own face flashed through my mind. Treygan and I were at the bottom of the ocean in the Catacombs. At the gate between Earth and Rathe. Stone was cracking away from my skin. I felt overwhelming joy and relief.

It was one of Treygan's memories.

My eyes snapped open and back to the present moment. Treygan was still tugging at my hair, kissing me, and thrusting his hips to meet mine. As difficult as it was, I forced my teeth free of his lip and stumbled backward off him, muttering "*no*" over and over.

He looked dazed and feverish. "What's wrong?"

I tried to catch my breath. I shook my head, shaking away the intense urge to climb on top of him again. "Don't you see what happened?"

He was breathing hard and his eyes seemed cloudy, but not in a good way. My wings were spread wide and I could feel my hair and eyes glowing the same way I had seen Nixie, Otabia, and Mariza's do in the past. My siren side was turned up full blast.

Treygan slowly cocked his head. "That was a siren song?"

"No, it was a song I've sung for years, but my siren instincts kicked in and I lost control."

"Fine with me." He sat up. "That was amazing."

"Treygan! I was about to steal one of your memories!"

He crawled toward me. "Take it, I have lots more. Just keep kissing me."

I backed up, and he chased after me on his hands and knees. "Stop it! Look at you! You're in some sort of lust trance."

He caught me by the leg and held me in place. I could have easily overpowered him and escaped, but he sweetly said, "I'm not in any trance. I just want you more than you can imagine."

A shaky breath escaped my lips. "I could have hurt you."

"Love hurts sometimes. I can handle it." He kissed my chin softly, then my forehead, followed by each of my cheeks.

"I almost stole your memory of me at the gate on the Triple Eighteen. I was out of control. My siren side ..." He kissed my neck and I groaned. "Please, Treygan, I'm trying to talk to you."

"No talking. And no singing." He kissed my shoulder. "If you don't sing, that part of you will stay dormant. Now, remove your talons from the roof and relax. I'm in control."

I hadn't noticed my death grip on the thatch roof, but I released it. Treygan's lips smiled against mine. He kissed me for one long, delicious moment and I wrapped my arms around him, resisting the urge to rake my nails down his back. My talons were still out, and I didn't need to injure him right before our trip.

He took my hands in his, assessing my curved, deadly nails. "Talons *and* selkie claws. Now that is impressive."

My selkie claws had shot out from my fingers on a couple of occasions, but the talon thing was new. "How is that even possible?"

Treygan shrugged. "You're multi-gifted."

"I'm a mess."

"You're amazing." He kissed each of my knuckles while keeping his eyes locked with mine. My talons transformed back into fingers. "We have to leave soon," he said. "Rownan is expecting us."

He might as well have thrown a bucket of ice water on me. "When we get back, we're going to Forbidden Apple Lagoon and we're going to spend days alone together."

"Days?" Treygan smiled mischievously. "I'm keeping you all to myself for weeks."

"Good. Let's return home as fast as possible."

Rowan

I didn't put up a fight when Yara insisted we take a boat to the Devil's Triangle. Well, as close as a vessel could get to it without getting sucked in. We needed to save as much energy as possible for whatever awaited us.

Our boat bumped along the choppy waters, creeping closer to a foggy horizon. For most of the ride, we all stayed silent. Intermittent gusts of wind howled but then stopped as if they were choked into silence. Even huge, outspoken Pango hadn't uttered a word. His wide green eyes never stopped scanning our surroundings. The whitecaps of the waves looked like huge teeth trying to chew us to pieces. No amount of planning or training could've prepared me for the sinking feeling in my stomach.

"We're getting close," Caspian shouted, slowing our speed.

Yara waved her hand above her head. "The compass is acting up."

Caspian motioned her over to him and he studied it. "The needle should start spinning soon. As soon as it does let me know, because that's as far as we can take you."

Yara nodded, gripping the compass with both hands.

Treygan started gearing up, pulling weapon holsters over his shoulders, arms, and legs, and attaching his belt and satchels around his waist. Pango handed me my jacket and belt.

I still wasn't comfortable entering Harte with our legs instead of tails, but the Violets argued that we might not be able to change forms once we arrived there, and it would be better to be stuck with legs and still have the option to swim—*if* there was water—

rather than be stuck with our tails and unable to walk on land. Still, preparing to enter the ocean and knowing I would have to keep my tail suppressed felt wrong. Our formfitting bodysuits felt even more wrong. I longed for my soft coat.

As I put on the top half of my suffocation suit, I glanced between Yara and Treygan. Would they really go through with it? I sat down and dropped my head into my hands. Freakin' martyrs. I could never be as brave or selfless as them. And for some asinine reason I was too much of a coward to tell them how much I loved them for doing this. Maybe I loved them more than I realized.

"I'm going alone." My voice was muffled by my hands. The boat engine's low hum and the wind whipping around us didn't help either.

Yara pulled her hair into a ponytail. "Did you say something?"

I dropped my hands and stood up. "I can't let you and Treygan go to Harte. It's too dangerous. I want to do this alone."

"No." Treygan didn't look up from adjusting his holsters.

"Yes," I said louder, with more conviction. "I wouldn't be able to live with myself if something happened to either one of you."

Pango slid a dagger into my jacket pocket and zipped it. "You won't be living at all if you go by your lonesome."

"I can do it."

"No, you can't," Treygan argued, pulling on his gloves. "You haven't seen Vienna in almost two decades. If and when you do find her, especially if she's sick, or hurt, or ..." He hesitated, carefully choosing his words as if others hadn't told me the same thing a dozen times already. "If she's no longer herself, you're going to lose the ability to think rationally. Your emotions will take over. We need to be there to do your rational thinking for you."

"He's right." Yara stepped closer to me. "No one—I don't care how strong they are—can find their own way out of hell. Someone needs to shine the light that guides them through the darkness." She linked her pinky with mine. "We'll be each other's light."

"Holy Poseidon," I grumbled, trying to pull my pinky away from hers with no success. "We're about to cross into the realm of the damned, and you're getting all sappy and uplifting."

Yara squeezed my finger before letting go. "There's plenty more where that came from."

I started to tell them I had a sick feeling. How I feared some or all of us would die on this trip, but Yara shouted before I could say another word.

"The compass is spinning!"

Pango pressed one hand to his forehead while fanning himself with the other. "Sufferin' suckerfish, this is really happening."

Caspian killed the motor and dropped anchor. "This is as far as we go. You three will have to swim the rest of the way."

"Oh dear, I knew this moment would arrive," Pango said. "But it's all happening too fast."

"Breathe, Pango." Treygan reached up and gripped his shoulder. "We'll be okay."

The fog grew thicker with each passing second. I could barely see the bow of the boat. Electricity seemed to buzz and crackle in the thick haze.

"This place is even creepier than I imagined," Pango said.

Yara flashed him a scathing look.

"Sorry," Pango muttered.

"Remember, we stick together." Treygan locked eyes with me over Yara's shoulder as he helped adjust her holsters. "It's the cardinal rule."

I nodded and put on my gloves, trying to ignore the knots in my stomach.

"Yara." Pango held both of her hands. "Koraline wanted me to tell you something. She told me to wait until the last second, and this seems to be it."

"What did she say?" Yara asked, sounding concerned.

"She wants you to remember Harriet Stowe's quote." Pango bent his knees so he was almost eye-level with Yara. "Never give up, for that is the place and time that the tide will turn."

"Never give up," Yara repeated. "The tide will turn. Got it."

"She said to tattoo it on your arm, but that's a bit extreme. Such a drama queen, that sister of mine."

In spite of the situation, Yara smiled at him. "I won't forget."

Treygan jumped into the water first. Yara carefully eased herself off the swimming platform like she was afraid the ocean might swallow her whole. Judging from the foreboding vibe, I wouldn't have been surprised if we all disappeared without a trace. I climbed in after Yara, not dipping below the surface because I felt safer with the boat still in sight.

Pango and Caspian leaned over the back.

"I expect a full and detailed report when you return," Caspian told us.

Pango gingerly waved. "Oh, my brave starfishies, please return soon."

We all said goodbye, then Treygan turned to me.

"You ready?" he asked.

I splashed water on my face. This was really about to happen. We were actually swimming into the mouth of the Devil's Triangle. Gods help us all. "Ready as I'll ever be."

We sank below the surface, but the soupy fog was just as thick in the water as it was above. The three of us linked hands and swam forward. I'm not ashamed to admit that Yara's fingers laced tightly with mine were comforting.

I wasn't sure if I would have been able to continue alone.

I had never flown so fast.

My heart sped up until it felt like one steady, painful beat. My lungs stung from lack of oxygen. My wings burned, but I kept pushing, trying to gain more speed. I had to see Yara again.

I had refused to say goodbye or good luck, and then, like a child, I had flown off with attitude. I had expected her to follow me and talk to me. Almost all night I stayed awake, gazing out of the nest and watching for her. I didn't remember falling asleep, but when I finally woke, Medusa's sun shined at full power. I rushed to Treygan's house, but they were gone. No note, no message left for me, nothing.

I never thought she would go to Harte—knowing she would probably never come back—without saying goodbye. How could she care so little about me?

I almost flew right over the boat. The fog was so thick I couldn't see more than a few feet in front of me or below me. I swooped down, grazing Caspian's head. Pango waved to me and pointed east. I nodded and flew off as fast as my wings would carry me.

They weren't far. Thank the gods for Rownan's and Treygan's dark hair because Yara blended into the waves and fog as if it they were already erasing her. I coasted down to them and landed on the water, skidding to a squatted position a few feet ahead of them. Just before they passed below me I reached down and yanked Yara to the surface. Treygan and Rownan popped up beside her.

"Nixie?" Yara looked surprised, but also as terrified as I felt her to be. "What are you doing here?"

"You left without saying goodbye."

"You refused to say goodbye."

"Are we still moving?" Treygan asked.

We all glanced around. We were being pulled eastward even though no one was making any effort to move. I examined the surface of the water where my boots sank into it. The water was tunneling around the heels rapidly.

I glanced over my shoulder, hoping to see where the current was carrying us, but behind me was just more blinding fog. I pointed at my boots so the others could see the rushing water. "We are definitely moving."

"The fog seems to be moving at the same speed as us," Treygan noted. "It's creating the illusion that we are staying in place."

"This is weird," Yara mumbled. She held her hands out in front of her and spread her fingers wide. The water rushed through them. "We're picking up speed."

"Everyone stay together." Treygan linked his arm tightly with Yara's. She latched on to Rownan with her other arm. Clearly, Treygan meant everyone except me. They all stared past me, their eyes widening. I was afraid to turn around and see what was causing their expressions, but I did.

The fog had thinned out. Charcoal lines curled around us like a spiraling tunnel.

"Time lines," Yara shouted. "Just like Joel said."

I snapped around to look at her. "What do you mean, time lines?"

A loud sound filled the air around us. I had never heard anything like it. Whooshing in and out like waves, but with a high-pitched, eerie echo. I stepped over Yara and sank into the water so that only my head was above the surface, just like the others. I don't know why I thought the ocean would protect me from whatever strange phenomenon was going on, but I hid behind Yara and held on to her and Treygan's linked arms.

"Time is different in Harte." Yara turned and spoke over her shoulder so I could hear her. "Joel said we'd see time lines in the fog when we reached the gateway."

Treygan glanced back at me. "We have to be out by the third sunset from today. If not, the gate doesn't open for another year and a half."

"Treygan," Yara hissed.

"She has the right to know."

My heart sank to my toes. Yara kept a lot of things from me, but this was unacceptable. They could lose track of time and never know when or how to get back. "What if you don't know when the third sunset is?"

The wind sucked us forward. I held on to Yara and Treygan so tight they grimaced.

"We'll know," Yara tried assuring me. "We have a plan."

That didn't make me feel any better. We picked up speed, moving closer and closer to the time lines spiraling through the sky. I lifted myself up out of the water just enough to confirm what I suspected. A whirlpool was forming ahead of us.

I ripped Yara and Treygan apart then turned Yara to face me. I grasped her wrist and laced each of my fingers with her gloved hand, squeezing hard. "I'm begging you, don't go. Don't do this."

She squeezed back, freed her other arm from Rownan, and pulled me so close our foreheads touched. "Believe in me, Nixie. Because I believe in you."

Her words meant the worlds to me, but they were bittersweet. "Believe in *me*? I have nothing to do with this."

"You have everything to do with this. We have a bond that I don't have with anyone else. You've been with me since childhood. You were with me when my mom died. I wouldn't be alive today if you hadn't told Treygan I was drowning. You knew my own mother better than I did. Now we're sisters, but you're also my siren."

An overwhelming need to protect her engulfed me. "Let me come with you. I can help."

She shook her head. "I need you to stay in Rathe." Sage slithered behind her neck. "I need you here, believing I will make it home. I need to know the people I love need me to return. Knowing that will give me the strength and courage to get out of Harte."

"We're getting pulled into a whirlpool," Treygan yelled, grabbing Yara with one hand and Rownan with the other.

I finally, genuinely, felt needed by her, but I still pleaded, "Don't go."

"Stay strong for me," Yara urged. "I have to come back. I can't leave you or Uncle Lloyd." She smiled, even as waves crashed against her face. "Or the sprites and all the other creatures I love so much."

The pulling sensation tugged hard at me too. I could have easily let myself be pulled in with them. I could have claimed I wasn't strong enough to fly to safety, but that would be betraying Yara. I would do what she needed me to do.

I kissed her then flew up out of the current. I was high enough to see how massive the whirlpool was. My hair whipped my face so hard I could feel it cutting my skin. I prayed into the screaming winds ripping past me. "Medusa, please help them."

I watched their three bodies circling deeper into the giant, dark tunnel. They became smaller and smaller until I could no longer see them.

Tears formed in my eyes, but they were immediately carried away by the wind. Carried away and lost in the ocean, just like Yara.

The clock had begun ticking.

Riding the spiraling whirlpool down into the belly of the ocean was the easy part.

Then stillness hit us so abruptly that I wondered if we were dead. Except I had died before, and it was nothing like what we were experiencing.

Everything went white. The lack of scenery, of sound, of … *anything* was disorienting. We were weightless. I didn't know if we were floating in air, water, or something entirely different. I flexed my biceps against Treygan's and Rownan's. Their arms were linked together too. We faced each other, forming a tight triangle. The feel of them beside me, and seeing us all still linked together, gave me hope. I tried speaking, but no words came out. Rownan and Treygan did the same thing; their mouths moved in slow motion but there was no sound.

Then the real spinning started. My head and arms were forced back, like gravity was pressing against me harder than a hurricane. My body folded so far backward I thought my spine would snap. My limbs felt like taffy being stretched until they would rip apart. Rownan slipped away from me first, followed by Treygan.

I tried yelling out for Treygan, but I couldn't open my mouth against the intense pressure. I let out a close-lipped scream that stayed buried inside me.

I fell.

And fell.

I kept falling through a soundless tunnel of white that gradually turned gray then darkened to black.

I landed facedown with a thud so hard it should have broken every bone in my body. I lifted my head and saw Rownan and Treygan sprawled on the ground just a few feet away. Then I realized the ground was only a patch of land, like a sandbar hovering in … air? Black and blue surrounded us, but it didn't look like sky or water. At least, no sky or water I had ever seen. I sat up and inhaled. My lungs strained, but at least I could breathe.

I pushed my hair out of my face and discovered some strands floating freely above my head as if we were in water. But when I gathered all of it and pulled it over my shoulder, it remained in place. The laws of gravity were nothing like in Earth or Rathe.

"Yara?" Treygan's eyes flew open, and he sprang to his feet just as fast, but then he toppled over and fell to his knees.

"I'm here. I'm okay." I crawled closer to him.

His bewildered gaze landed on me. He hugged me so tight I was certain he would crack any bones that were spared in our fall.

"Easy," I groaned. "That was a hard landing."

His grip loosened. "Sorry. I felt you slip away from me. I didn't know what to do."

"Treygan?" Rownan turned his head. "You all right, man?" He struggled to sit up, grunting while rubbing his arms and back.

I took off my gloves and assessed my own limbs. I ached all over, but amazingly all of my muscles and bones were still intact.

"What in the—?" Rownan gazed at the dark, dingy haze surrounding our floating island.

"My sentiments exactly." I motioned to the emptiness around us. No stars, mountains, water, plants, nothing. "Where are we supposed to go from here?"

Rownan walked to the edge of our plot of land. Taking off his gloves, he pointed downward. "There, I'm assuming."

Treygan helped me to my feet and we walked over to join Rownan. I looked over the edge and gasped. I couldn't tell if we were floating high above a raging fire, or if the sky/water/land below us just looked like burning embers.

"Holy Poseidon." Treygan clutched my waist, pulling me a step back from the edge.

Rownan ran his hand over his goatee. "We're going to burn to death, aren't we? Who would have thought hell would be so predictable?"

Leaning forward, Treygan squinted. "Is it just me, or are those flames getting closer?"

"Oh, gods, we're sinking." Panic rushed through me.

"Or the flames are rising up to meet us," Rownan mused.

The shifting shades of red, orange, and yellow were almost level with our island, but when they hit our sliver of land the flames—were they flames?—burst into billions of pieces.

Treygan reached forward, waving his hands through the sparks.

"No!" I tried pulling him back before he got burned, but he glanced up at me and smiled. His bare hand still glided through the fragments of fire.

"It's warm but doesn't burn. It feels like rain."

The sea of flames kept exploding into droplets as it rose around us. Rownan and I waved our hands through the glowing rain. Or embers. Or whatever.

I tried catching a few drops in my hand to examine them, but they evaporated. "Rain that starts as fire and falls up?"

Treygan shrugged. "We knew to expect the unexpected."

"What else do you suppose is down there?" Rownan stared over the edge again. "And how deep do you think it goes?"

"Or does it ever end?" I did not want to fall again. The last long trip was disorienting enough. I strained my eyes, trying to see what existed below us, but the constantly moving flames created too many optical illusions.

"For the love of Medusa," Treygan gasped.

Rownan and I snapped around at Treygan's remark. My mouth actually fell open.

A giant ship, most of it decayed or rusted, slowly floated toward us—upside-down.

"Do you think there are any people on it?" I whispered.

"I don't know," Treygan muttered. "I don't know what to think about any of this."

We all watched the ship sail closer, slightly rotating as if trying to right itself. Its iron sides groaned and creaked so loud I covered my ears. I turned away, not wanting to chance seeing someone, or something, on the ship.

I immediately regretted facing the other direction. "Guys!"

They turned, and together the three of us watched the front half of a plane flying toward us. Seaweed hung from its propeller, but it wasn't spinning.

"That looks like it's from the 1950s or '60s," Treygan said.

"Is it going to hit us?" I asked.

Rownan glanced between the ship and the plane, then down at our plot of land. "It's like everything is just orbiting around each other."

I held on to Treygan's hand. "What if we collide with one of them?"

"You'll have to fly us out of the way if they get too close."

I pinched my shoulder blades together, confirming my wings still functioned. Why hadn't I already thought of that? Sage. My hand flew to the back of my head, searching for her. She slithered over my shoulder until I could see her.

"I'm sorry," I murmured, feeling guilty for hardly acknowledging her. Sure, I was banged up and disoriented, but Sage was a part of me and I hadn't even thought to check on her. "I'm glad you're okay."

She rubbed against my cheek, but I still felt guilty.

"Where do we go from here?" Treygan asked.

The plane crept closer and tilted as if steering around us. The broken right wing passed directly over our heads.

"Maybe we're supposed to …," I didn't want to say it out loud because I couldn't imagine actually doing it, but finally I suggested, "board the ship or plane."

Treygan and Rownan looked as horrified as I felt.

"No way," Rownan said. "That would be like climbing into a used grave."

"So, this is it?" I spun in a circle. "We just stand here, watching remnants of crashed planes and lost ships float by us?"

Rownan searched the nothingness above us. "Where in the hell is Vienna?"

"Where in hell, indeed," Treygan said.

"Really?" Rownan scowled at him. "Already with the hell puns?"

Treygan shrugged. "Sorry."

Rownan closed his eyes and swayed slightly. I almost asked if he was feeling all right, but then I realized he was trying to shadow Vienna. I nodded at Treygan, encouraging him to try too. He held up a finger, telling me to wait. We both watched Rownan; his head kept moving and his eyelids flickered.

After a tense and long waiting period, Rownan opened his eyes. I already knew the outcome based on his frustrated frown. "Nothing."

"I'll give it a try," Treygan offered.

Rownan huffed. "If I can't find her, there's no way you can." He watched the ship and plane float farther away, then he turned his back to us and stared over the edge again. "She's down there somewhere. I can feel it."

"Maybe," I started, "but we don't know for—"

He dove off the ledge.

I screamed as Treygan and I both rushed to where Rownan had jumped. Rownan's figure got smaller as he fell away from us. My heart was racing. I thought about flying after him and catching him in midair, but I was so scared I couldn't make my wings open.

Treygan's eyes were wide, watching his brother fall from sight and into who-knows-what. "I knew this would happen." He stepped back and pinched the bridge of his nose. "He never listens."

"Why did he jump? I could have flown him down there!"

Treygan shook his head. "I don't know, but we have to follow him."

I grabbed Treygan's hand and rolled my shoulders, forcing my wings to loosen. Treygan always declined letting me fly him around unless it was absolutely necessary, but this felt necessary. "We are flying. Safely. Not jumping like idiots."

"No arguments here. Diving into the murky depths of a damned realm is not my preferred choice." He kissed my forehead then turned his back to me and lifted his arms at his sides.

After some more shoulder rolling, neck cracking, and a few quick breaths, my wings were functioning. I spread them wide, hooked my hands under Treygan's arms, and soared off the edge. I dove down, but caught a glimpse of something peculiar in my peripheral vision, so I flew back up.

"What's wrong?" Treygan asked.

I circled the island, blinking my eyes. "I know it sounds weird, but when we first jumped, out of the corner of my eye, I thought I saw you and Rownan, lying on the ground."

"Everything about this place is weird," Treygan said. "But I'm right here and I'm not leaving you."

Treygan was in my arms, solid and real as ever, but still, I had to make sure for my own peace of mind. Sage rubbed along my neck, urging me to find Rownan, so I flew down into the dangerous depths of Harte.

 Rowan

Somehow, instinctively, I knew jumping would be safe, which is why I took the plunge.

I had no directional control while falling, but I was able to slow down and control my landing—almost like I was manipulating gravity. I landed gently on my feet and stared up at the sky, or whatever I had just traveled through.

I jumped in place, half-hoping I could fly, but nope. Gravity was at work in this realm too. I examined the black substance oozing between my toes. It felt similar to wet sand but without the grainy texture. It wasn't hot or cold, so no need to wear the boots Yara made us pack—yet. Who knew what other kind of terrain we might encounter.

All my gear was still intact and attached to me. I tightened a couple of loose straps and rubbed my aching shoulder. Yara and Treygan would catch up, I had no doubt of that, so while I waited for them, I closed my eyes and tried shadowing Vienna again.

Shadowing was like looking through a long, dark tunnel. I had to keep crawling through it, around corners, up and down hills, searching for any trace of light. My mind crawled, dipped, clawed at the darkness, but all I found was more darkness. What if she really was dead?

No. My eyes snapped open.

Yara and Treygan stood in front of me. I didn't know how long they had been there, but Yara stepped forward and hugged me. "We're so glad you're okay." She pulled back then shoved me so hard I toppled backward and landed on my butt. "And if you act that reckless and stupid again we will leave you here to fend for yourself!"

I stood up and brushed myself off. "Sorry. I followed my instincts."

"Your instincts have always been questionable," Treygan said. "The only rule is *not* to separate, and you broke that rule minutes after we arrive. Doesn't exactly bode well."

"Seriously, I'm sorry. It won't happen again. That creepy floating island spooked me. I wanted to get away from it as fast as possible."

Yara crossed her arms over her chest. "Next time, tell us and we'll agree on a plan of action."

"I will." I raised my hand. "I swear."

"Well, it's about time." Out of an orange and silver haze that I hadn't noticed before, a woman I recognized from Lloyd's photographs and wall panels appeared. The sight of Treygan's mother, Liora, froze him in place. Beside her was Cleo, Yara's mother. I glanced around, hoping to see my mom appear too.

"Mom?" Treygan gawked.

Liora smiled as she approached Treygan. She stopped in front of him and caressed his face. "We're here to help you."

Treygan hugged her, holding her like he never wanted to let go.

Cleo strutted over to Yara and brushed her fingers against her cheek, but Yara's arms stayed stiff at her sides. After an awkward moment of silence, Yara pulled away from her and grabbed Treygan's arm, separating him and Liora.

The mothers glanced back and forth at each other and then at Yara and Treygan.

Cleo folded her hands in front of her. "We thought you could use a bit of guidance through this place."

Yara backed up a step. "You crossed over. I saw you fly into the Eternal Falls."

"Oh, darling." Cleo tilted her head and reached for Yara, but Yara leaned away as Sage rose beside her head. "I'm your mother. I will always watch over you."

Liora walked past them toward me. "Vienna is this way, Rownan."

My heart slammed into my throat. *Vienna.* They knew where she was. We'd find her and get out of here so much faster than we expected. Hope gushed through every part of me.

"Rownan, wait," Yara said. "Something is off."

Treygan hadn't said a word. He kept glancing between Yara and his mom.

"Of course something is off," I huffed. "We're in Harte. This place is awful."

Sage hissed and Yara absentmindedly touched the snake's head. "No, something about them. Our mothers are dead. They might appear to us in spirit form, but not solid like they are now. I don't understand how they could be here."

Cleo folded her hands in front of her again. "Our souls are still intact. The nature of this place allows us to exist in physical form."

All this chitchat was wasting too much precious time. I threw my hands up in the air. "Do you want to stand around having ghost discussions or do you want to help save my wife?"

"How far are you taking us?" Treygan asked his mother.

"Just around the bend," Liora told him.

"It's not far," Treygan said to Yara. "And it's not like we have an alternate route mapped out. What if they do know where she is?"

Sage lay on Yara's hunched shoulder. "Fine. But if I say we turn around, I don't want any arguments."

About time she came to her senses.

"Lead the way," I told Liora.

The three of us followed them. The scenery ahead of us shifted with each step. At first, tall mountains loomed in the distance, but then I glanced down at the black mud we were hiking through, and when I looked up again strangely-shaped trees and a stream of black water flowed past us.

"Are you two seeing what I'm seeing?" I asked Yara and Treygan.

"Yes," Treygan answered. "It's fascinating, but at the same time scary."

Yara nodded, but kept her focus locked on the backs of Liora and Cleo as they led the way.

We stopped at an opening where two massive, bare trees bowed together. Their dried and peeling branches created an archway into what looked like ancient ruins. Liora turned to me and motioned with her hand. "Go in. You'll find her waiting for you."

I stepped forward, but Yara grabbed my arm. "No. We all go in together." She flashed Liora and Cleo looks that were the opposite of grateful. "And you two are going in first."

The mothers bowed slightly then walked in ahead of us.

I smoothed down my hair and glanced at my chest and arms. Had I changed a lot since we last saw each other? Would Vienna still be attracted to me? Would she think I looked different? Would she look different? It didn't matter. I would love her no matter what she looked like. And I knew she felt the same way about me.

We approached the remains of some sort of temple compound. Liora and Cleo glided through the overgrown vegetation effortlessly, while I trampled over plants and pushed through tall weeds. We rounded a corner and there, sitting in a nest of giant twisted tree roots, perfectly framed between two crumbling pillars, was Vienna.

I couldn't move. I couldn't speak. She lifted her head, and we just stared at each other. Eighteen years had passed since we had seen each other. I had imagined our reunion a million times over the years. I had rehearsed all the things I would say. How I wouldn't wait one second to kiss her again. But here we were, just staring at each other, unmoving and silent, with an audience watching us.

I slowly stepped forward, unblinking, afraid to break eye contact with her in case she disappeared. I stopped at the pile of tree roots. "Hi."

"Hi." Her smile wasn't a fraction of how bright it used to be, but it was her. My Vienna.

Her black fur coat concealed her body, except for her hands and dirty feet propped up on a root. Her flawless face looked the same—almost. She was thinner, and she didn't have her usual glow, but sixteen years in a hellhole would make anyone lose their glow.

Did she know who I was? Did she know who *she* was? What had this place done to her mind and soul?

"V, I missed you so much." I choked on the words. Our reunion wasn't going anything like I had planned.

She stood. Her long black hair fell to her feet. "I missed you too."

"You know who I am?"

"Of course."

I stepped closer, lifting my foot over a thick section of root. "I was terrified this place would have destroyed you or that you'd be …."

"Dead?" she asked. Her smile stretched across her pale face. Pale was normal for her, but her eyes weren't the right shade of brown. They were darker. Her inner light was gone.

I swallowed hard. "I couldn't even think it. I knew I'd find you. My heart knew you were still alive."

"I knew you were alive too." She maneuvered over a few coils of root, using her hands to crawl over the largest section. She stopped in front of me. I held my breath as she reached up and touched my cheek. I flinched.

"Your hand is warm." A selkie's skin was supposed to be cold. Her touch had always been so invigorating.

"It's this place. All the fire makes me too warm." She ran her fingers over my lips. "Kiss me."

I had been waiting for the chance to kiss her again for almost two decades. I leaned down, but like an intrusive dickhead, Treygan coughed and interrupted the moment.

"Rownan, we need to get out of here."

Vienna hadn't budged. She was still looking up at me, lips pouting, waiting for me to kiss her.

"Let's find some place private," I whispered.

She flashed me another hollow smile. "Yes, some place private. Come with me."

"No," Yara practically shouted. "We need to stay together. You swore, Rownan. Now that we've found Vienna, we need to go home—fast."

"Just a few minutes," I argued. "I haven't seen her in eighteen years!"

"Yara's right," Treygan said. "The longer we're here, the harder it will be to find our way out. You two can make up for lost time once we get back to Rathe."

"Let the poor dears spend a few minutes alone," Liora said. "It's only fair considering what they've been through."

Cleo sat on a stone wall. "I agree. A few minutes won't kill anyone."

Yara and Treygan exchanged glances, but then Yara nodded at me. "Five minutes at the most. I'm serious, Rownan. Every minute spent here is too long."

Blood rushed through every part of me. I ached to share myself with Vienna again. Even one drink would satisfy me until we got home. We hadn't shared our souls with each other in so long. "Thanks. We'll be back soon."

"Five minutes!" Treygan repeated. "Not a minute longer."

I grabbed Vienna's hand and headed for a nearby archway framed by more tree roots.

"Not that way." Vienna tugged me and pointed to a temple farther away. "That one."

“We don’t have much time.”

“Trust me.” She ran her long fingernails across the top of her breasts. “The ambiance is better in there.”

My entire body ached with longing. Five minutes wouldn’t allow me to do a fraction of the things I wanted to do to her, but at least it would give us time for a quick reunion. A tiny release to last us until we returned home. Then, time would stop altogether. I planned to ravish every part of her.

I shouted over my shoulder to Yara and Treygan. “Five minutes doesn’t start until we’re inside.”

It was too easy.

Even without Sage whispering warnings to me, I would have been suspicious of how perfectly this had played out. I turned my cheek, hoping our "mothers" were far enough away not to overhear me whisper to Treygan.

"This went a little too perfectly, don't you think?"

He glanced at me and pursed his lips. "Maybe Medusa is helping us."

My eyes flickered to the inky, starless, moonless sky. "Highly unlikely."

Treygan may have wanted to believe Medusa was helping us, and that our spirit guides were the real deal, but I knew better. First off, Medusa didn't reign over this world. Second, if Treygan truly believed that Liora—dressed in a spotless white gown, in hell—was his mother, he would be gushing over her, asking a million questions, and offering her unnecessary apologies for killing her during his birth.

Instead, we stood divided, two and two, mothers apart from their children, waiting for Rownan and Vienna to do gods-knew-what in a decaying temple while Treygan and I twiddled our thumbs and tried to keep our souls intact.

I leaned against the rock wall and studied my supposed mom.

"How are you, darling?" she asked.

"Why do you keep calling me darling? You never called me that when you were alive." She didn't reply. Just shrugged and smiled, but her smile sent a chill up my spine. "You seem different than the last time I saw you."

Her cold eyes darted up then back down to her feet. "You were a child back then, of course you remember me differently."

My back went rigid. I had seen her only a week ago in the Inbetween. Sage curled around the back of my neck, hissing softly. Treygan shifted closer to me. Liora kept her penetrating stare locked on me.

I had talked with Liora's spirit right before the Triple Eighteen. I offered another test to confirm what I had suspected all along. "You too, Liora. It's been a long time."

Treygan watched them with as much venom as I felt. I didn't need to tell him. He had figured it out too.

"Yara, don't be silly," Liora said, proving she wasn't who or what she claimed. "We've never met."

Treygan and I reached for our weapons, but the mom lookalikes were faster than us. They both leaped through the air, knocking us flat on our backs.

My mother's imposter screamed like some kind of rabid animal. Her mouth stretched wide, revealing a toothless black hole. She leaned close to my face like she wanted to swallow me. I kicked and fought to push her away, but she had my arms pinned at my sides.

Sage shot forward and bit her cheek, sending my fake mom leaping backward. I scrambled toward Treygan. Evil Liora held him down while screaming the same way Cleo had. Sage extended longer than I had ever seen her stretch and sank her fangs into Liora's neck. Liora shrieked and rolled to her side.

Treygan jumped to his feet, whipping out a dagger. I reached for my thigh holster, but my hands shook so badly that I fumbled my dagger and it fell to the ground.

Both mothers flew at me again. My claws instinctively shout out. I caught Evil Cleo by the throat, but Liora sailed over my head.

Treygan shouted my name as fire ripped across my back. I fell to my knees. The pain was overwhelming. Sage bobbed behind me, tugging at my scalp, but commanding me to stay down. The searing pain in my back kept me anchored in place.

My fingers, still lodged in Evil Cleo's neck, changed from selkie claws to siren talons then back again. A wheezing sound gushed out of the puncture wounds, along with black smoke. Beneath my hand, Cleo's body dissolved into a pile of black sand.

Sage no longer whipped through my hair. I was dizzy. I couldn't feel my legs. I toppled forward, face-planting into Evil Cleo's remains.

"Yara?" Treygan's voice was delicate and cautious. He kneeled beside me, pulling me into his arms. He gently brushed the sand off my face. His eyes were wider than I had ever seen.

"What happened?" I managed. The fire in my back was fading, but an intense aching took its place. Sage purred against my cheek. I could sense her sadness.

"I'm so sorry. I should've been faster." Treygan nostril's flared and his eyes were glassy. "How bad does it hurt?"

I had only seen his face etched with such concern and sadness one other time, on the Triple Eighteen when I was turning to stone and he couldn't do anything to stop it. Something was very wrong with me. I managed to turn my head enough to see the statue of Liora. Treygan had turned her to stone. She was frozen in motion.

Held high on either side of her were my wings.

"Noooooooo!" I groaned, trying to roll out of Treygan's arms so I could get to them. *My wings.* She had ripped off my wings. I would never fly again. Treygan held on to me. I didn't have much energy to fight. Tears pooled in my eyes as Sage slithered up and down my arm.

The Liora statue disintegrated into another pile of black sand. My beautiful pearl wings landed on top of it. A strong wind blew, and the sand formed a small tornado that carried my wings into the air. Evil laughter echoed above us as they swirled out of sight.

I buried my face against Treygan's chest, fighting the urge to break down and sob. He kissed the top of my head and squeezed me tight. "I know it hurts. I want nothing more than to sit here and hold you, but we have to find Rownan."

We knew this place would be awful. I expected to fight. I expected to get hurt. But my wings—the part of me I inherited from my mother—were gone.

"Yara, can you walk?" Treygan probed.

Sage nudged me. I rolled onto my knees, but I was so lightheaded. My limbs felt like they weren't attached to me. "Go. Help Rownan."

"I can't leave you."

I willed blood to travel to my limbs, demanding my legs become useful. Sage pressed her head against the back of my skull, trying to help me up. I tried so hard to stand, but I collapsed again.

Treygan's arms were under me in an instant, carrying me. Every jostle hurt as he ran toward the temple with me in his arms.

"Three entrances," Treygan said. "Which one do I choose?"

"I don't know."

"The middle." Treygan rushed toward it. "Agreed?"

I nodded my heavy head.

Left. Sage whispered to me.

"Left!" I groaned. "The left one."

He didn't question me—just changed course, and into the muggy, dark ruins we went.

She always loved it slow. The slower the better.

I slid Vienna's coat off her shoulders and let it fall to her feet. I brushed my fingers up her arms. She watched them as if I was touching her for the first time.

"Do you need a drink?" I asked her. "You look weak."

"A drink?"

"Of my blood."

"No, I need you." She grabbed me with such intensity that I was knocked off balance. She tried to kiss me, but I slipped. She missed my lips and ended up almost biting my chin.

"I know it's been a long time, but don't be so rough."

Her eyes were so different. Beautiful ice crystals used to form when she stared at me with love or lust, but now they were dark and empty.

She rushed at me again. Something inside me screamed that this situation was very off. I dodged her next kiss and held her at arm's length.

"V, why do you love me?" She first asked me that question when I proposed. We had asked each other the same question more times than I could remember. Our answer was always the same.

"Because." She leaned forward, pouting, but my locked arms kept her from reaching me.

"Because why?" I wanted her to say the right words. I wanted it to be her more than anything.

"Many reasons," she whispered.

I clenched my teeth, realizing this person, this *thing*, was not my Vienna. "Wrong answer."

Her eyes hollowed and I shoved her backward. "What are you? Where is my wife?"

Her tongue rolled out of her mouth like a long carpet, changing from pink to black as it hit the ground and slithered toward my feet. I stomped on it and she screamed like a teapot boiling.

I reached for my knife, but she catapulted through the air and knocked me down. We wrestled as she morphed into a creature with speckled skin and black holes for eyes, but then she became Vienna's lookalike again.

"You're not her," I grunted. "Where is she?"

"Fool," it hissed, elbowing me in my jaw. "Give me your soul."

Her mouth opened as wide as my entire head. I grappled for a tight hold on her neck, pushing her off me with all the strength I had. Whatever this creature was, it was strong and not giving up.

Vienna's features solidified. For a moment her eyes almost looked real. Her voice softened, sounding exactly like Vienna's. "Please, Rownan. Don't do this. I love you."

Part of me wanted to believe it could be her, possessed by some demon that I could exorcise from her. It caused me to hesitate, and the creature used the opportunity to bite my forearm. I cried out, but tightened my grip on its neck. This thing was not Vienna. It couldn't contain the soul I loved so dearly.

I dug my heels into the ground and took a quick breath for strength. My claws shout out of my fingers and into the demon's neck. She hissed, and the holes smoked, but it hardly fazed her. She kept thrusting her face at me. Her disgusting tongue flopped side-to-side, smacking against my neck and shoulders as I thrashed out of its path. My arms shook from exertion.

She pinned my forearms over my head. Her bony hands seared my skin. I cried out in agony. Her mouth opened wide, a swirling black vacuum, and she rushed at my face for what I suspected would be the final time.

But then her mouth turned to stone. The rest of her hardened into rock in seconds. She hovered less than an inch from my mouth.

"Move!" Treygan yelled.

I wiggled my right arm furiously, breaking her stone fingers and freeing myself from her grip. I dug at the dirt to free my other arm and then rolled out from under her, shoving the statue so it wouldn't fall on top of me. I scurried to my feet, wobbling and almost falling back down. Treygan rushed over to me, carrying Yara in his arms.

"What the hell was that thing?" I gasped, trying to catch my breath.

"We don't know. But our mothers were the same thing."

I leaned against a wall, raising my head to look at my brother. "Thank you. If you hadn't shown up, I would've been a goner."

The statue began cracking. Even though I knew it wasn't Vienna, it was hard to watch her crumble and melt into a black pool that looked like tar. The liquid slid up into the air like a floating blob then turned to smoke and swirled around me. A bodiless whisper said, "Her soul is ours. You're too late."

Distant laughter echoed through the ruins as the black smoke rose through an opening in the ceiling.

"We have to get out of here," Yara said shakily, looking more scared and weak than I would have ever thought possible.

"What happened to—?" Then it registered. "Holy hell. You're wings are gone."

Yara dropped her head to Treygan's chest. "Please, let's go home."

Treygan hugged her tighter to him. "I hate to say this, but we have barely survived an hour in this place and there are three of us. Vienna couldn't have survived this long by herself."

Anyone else would be easily convinced this place would have killed or consumed Vienna minutes after her solo arrival, but no one knew her like I did. I knew she was still alive.

"No," I argued. "She's here and I'm going to find her, but I can't do it without you guys."

"Try shadowing her again," Treygan said. "Do you get any sense that she could still possibly be here?"

"I feel it. I know she is."

"Just try," Treygan demanded.

I closed my eyes and searched for her. Nothing.

My eyes fluttered open to find Treygan watching me with a crinkled brow.

"She's not dead," I told him. "I would know if she was." My heart was hopeful, even in this wasteland of despair. I would find her. She was here somewhere, and I would search every crevice, shadow, and demon until I found her.

I cried out so long and hard that the leaves around us curled in on themselves. I was curled up as well, in too much pain to move. "They hurt so much."

Keeley flew around me, examining me with tears in her eyes. "They're fine. I swear, nothing is wrong with your wings."

"There must be," I groaned.

Jenna continued to pet my cheek. "The boys went to get help. Hang in there. I promise you're going to be okay."

"I hate seeing her like this," Keeley whispered.

The pain wasn't subsiding, but time allowed me to think about why my wings were hurting so badly. "Oh, gods."

I lifted my head and Jenna and Keeley both froze, watching me intently.

"What? What is it?" Keeley asked me.

"It's Yara."

"What?" Keeley looked confused.

"Ohhhhhh." Jenna drifted backward and sat on a daisy. "What do you think happened?"

"I don't understand!" Keeley glanced between Jenna and me.

"Sirens feel other sirens' pain," I explained to Keeley. "If there's nothing actually wrong with my wings, it could mean something happened to Yara."

"Maybe it's Mariza or Otabia," Jenna offered.

I shook my head, clenching my teeth at the furious stinging in my back.

As if on cue, Otabia's caw pierced through the bayou. Mariza's shrill squawking echoed Otabia's. I answered them, my loud call sending Jenna and Keeley backing away from me. They looked up at the sky where Otabia and Mariza's black and brown forms swept over the tops of the Weeping Willows.

"They scare me," Keeley whispered.

"Should we leave?" Jenna asked.

"No," I told them. "They aren't as scary as they seem. Don't worry."

Otabia and Mariza's wings blew leaves all around us. They landed gracefully on the riverbank.

"What in the hell was that?" Otabia asked me. "Did you hurt yourself?"

Mariza made a disgusted face as she pulled the heel of her boot out of the mud. "I loathe this place."

"It wasn't me," I said, sitting up. "I think it's Yara."

Otabia walked closer, staring at me. Her pupils enlarged, the way they always did when she thought hard. "Do you know how badly she must have been hurt for all three of us to feel her pain?"

"While she's in Harte," Mariza added, flying up to a tree branch. She sat on it and used leaves to wipe the mud from her boots.

"My back is still burning," I said. "What if she's dying?"

Otabia waved her talons dismissively. "She's not dying. We'd feel that too."

I hoped she was right. "Something horrible must have happened."

"Maybe she lost her wings," Mariza said. "Easy come, easy go."

"Shut up, Mariza!" I snapped. "How can you be so heartless?"

Mariza laughed. "When have I ever pretended to have a heart?"

I snarled at her and she snarled back.

"Stop it, you two," Otabia ordered. "We didn't come here to discuss Yara or give the false impression that we care about her. We wanted to make sure you were all right."

"I'm not all right. If Yara is in pain then so am I. What if she dies in there? What will happen to me?"

"You will live," Otabia assured me.

Mariza flicked a leaf off her hand. "And we'll throw a party and get on with our lives."

I snapped my teeth at her. I wanted to rip every hair out of her head, but she wasn't worth my energy.

"I would be devastated," I admitted. Yes, I was assigned to be Yara's siren as part of the gorgon sister trinity, but my feelings ran deeper than that. I genuinely cared about Yara. Cleo had me protect her for years. I had watched Yara grow up and go through so much in her short life. She and Treygan had just started their life together. She deserved a long, happy existence. "We have to get them out of there before it's too late."

"We?" Otabia grimaced.

"You have lost your batty little mind," Mariza said.

Jenna and Keeley were hiding behind plants. I could never ask them to come with me. I'd have to go alone. "I'm going," I said. "I should have gone with them and I didn't, but I'm going back to the Triangle and I'm going to find them."

Mariza flew down from her branch, landing directly in front of me. "No, you're not."

Otabia advanced on me too. "Our connection to you is infinitely stronger than your connection to Yara. If you suffer in there, so will we."

"Exactly," I argued. "The same way I'm suffering from Yara's pain."

"Your connection to her can't be that strong yet," Otabia snapped.

"I assure you, it is."

Mariza crossed her arms over her chest. "I refuse to endure more pain and emotional torment because of that half-breed sea monster. Give her the damn mirror."

Otabia's eyes flared with fire and she swiped her talons at Mariza's mouth. "Silence!"

"Mirror?" I questioned. "The all-seeing mirror?"

Mariza nodded, darting away from Otabia. "It still exists. Stheno and Euryale have it hidden in the grotto."

Otabia slowly and deliberately stepped toward Mariza. "Shut." Another step. "Your." Another step. "Mouth."

Mariza fluttered backward, putting a safe distance between them.

"That mirror was destroyed," I said. "Stheno and Euryale told us it was destroyed ages ago."

Mariza's lip curled. "They lied."

"Last warning," Otabia snarled. "Shut your trap."

Mariza curled her fingers into fists. "We tell her, or she enters Harte and we suffer."

"Tell me what?" I probed.

Otabia shook her head. Her black bangs swept across her forehead.

Mariza crouched the way she always did before an attack. "It doesn't just view Rathe, it views all of Poseidon's worlds."

Otabia pounced, but Mariza did too. They collided in mid-air, grabbing each other's hair, yanking so hard it looked like their flailing heads might snap off. Their wings flapped and rustled as dark feathers drifted to the ground. Jenna and Keeley trembled so hard the plant they hid behind shook.

"Enough!" I flew at my pain-in-the-ass sisters, breaking up their fight, and keeping myself positioned between them. They continued swiping and spitting at each other. "Stop it! Tell me the truth!"

Otabia snapped her teeth and kicked at Mariza a few more times while Mariza stuck out her brown tongue like a spiteful child.

"Mariza," I glared at her. "Start talking."

"They will punish us severely for this," Otabia hissed. "Stheno and Euryale will have our heads."

"So, they become angry for a few days." Mariza shoved my hand off her chest. "They still need us if they want to have any kind of pleasure or excitement in their dismal existence. Besides, Nixie can tell them she discovered it all by herself. No need to rat us out."

"I won't rat anyone out," I promised them. "You're saying the mirror still exists and I could see Yara in Harte?"

"It does," Mariza said. "And you could."

Otabia turned her back to us.

"How come I didn't know about this?"

"It's one of their many secrets." Mariza shrugged. "Stheno and Euryale are greedy. They don't even let us use it."

"Where is it hidden?" The grotto had many dens and corridors, but Stheno and Euryale mainly stayed in the front few caverns. The mirror could be hidden anywhere, and if it was buried or hidden in a tide pool then it could take me weeks to find it.

"They will never allow you to use it," Otabia said. "If they find out we told you it still exists, they will make our lives hell."

"But why can you know about it and I can't?"

Otabia's pupils contracted then expanded, over and over. As they always did when she was biting her tongue.

"Because you aren't a *real* siren," Mariza said with too much satisfaction. Otabia looked away.

My wings drooped. I lowered to the ground. I felt as if I'd been shot. "What is that supposed to mean? I'm as much a siren as either of you."

"No," Mariza said. "You weren't born a siren. You were— what did they call it?—promoted." She snickered. "You are much softer than us. You don't even have a pure gorgon to bond with."

"I have Yara!" I argued. "Stheno and Euryale should want her to be kept safe. She's the third of their trilogy."

Mariza laughed. "Yara is the most motley mess of a sea creature in history. Do you really think Stheno and Euryale take her seriously? No one knows what she is. Not even Yara."

"She is more powerful than any of us!"

"No, she's inexperienced. And her human genes make her vulnerable and weak. Stheno and Euryale are insulted that Medusa sent her to them in her condition."

I tore my eyes away from Mariza and looked at Otabia, hoping she would tell me Mariza was lying. But Otabia wouldn't look at me, which meant Mariza was telling the truth. They considered Yara a joke. They considered *me* a joke.

"And to think," I said, "all this time I considered you my sisters."

"We are sisters." Otabia sounded exasperated.

"Sort of," Mariza jabbed. "We've always known you had a stronger connection with the sprites. You behave so much differently than Cleo. She hardly ever separated from us."

"Until she fell in love with Vyron," Otabia grumbled.

"Seductive selkies," Mariza snarled. "That's how these huge messes begin, when creatures start mingling outside their own breed. It's not natural."

They could have continued the conversation without me for all I cared. I had never felt so disconnected from them. I backed up to the plant where Jenna and Keeley were hiding and put my hands behind my back, waving them to come to me. Both of them nestled into my wings. I flew away, leaving Mariza and Otabia to finish their bickering by themselves.

Never again would I forget who my true family was.

Treygan's hands trailed gently over my back, examining the wounds where my wings had been ripped off. He applied a healing salve the Violets had given us.

"That's enough." I pulled on my suit jacket, woefully aware of the slits in the back that were no longer needed. "We need to conserve the salve."

The Violets had given us a whole jar of the stuff, but I only brought a tiny portion in a small tube because it was easier to carry. As the ointment soothed the burning, I wished I had packed more.

"Are you still in pain?" Treygan asked.

"A little, but mostly just lightheaded."

"There's no blood coming out, but you must have lost a lot." He handed me a bottle of water. "Drink this."

I took the bottle from him but dropped it when I saw what was inside. "I take it you didn't put the bugs in there?"

"What?" Treygan leaned down and picked up the bottle. Centipedes swam inside, their hundreds of legs stirring up tiny bubbles.

"How is that even possible?" He pulled out his remaining bottle and then dug through my pack to check mine. All of them were contaminated. "These bottles were sealed."

"How is any of this possible?" I kicked a bottle near my feet and it rolled away. "I don't need water. I'll be okay."

"Our time window just got shorter," Rownan said. "With no water, we'll dehydrate. And I doubt any water sources in this world are safe to drink from."

"He's right. Do you think you can walk?" Treygan asked me.

"We'll take turns carrying her," Rownan said. I glared at him and he put his hands up. "Just until you're feeling better."

"I'm fine," I grumbled, attempting to stand. My limbs felt like cotton and the ground swayed. Sage curled around my neck, trying to steady me.

Treygan lifted me into his arms. "Forget your pride. For now, I'm carrying you."

I nodded, resting my head on his shoulder.

"Logically," Rownan said, "if those demon bitches led us here then we're probably as far away from Vienna as possible. Let's head back the way we came."

Treygan followed Rownan out of the temple. The warmth of his body kept me from shivering at the memory of the attack as we passed by the area where we had fought the imposters. We exited through the same arched trees we had entered through.

"I'll follow you," Treygan told Rownan.

Rownan glanced left and right then marched straight ahead. I wrapped my arms more securely around Treygan's neck as he followed him.

After only a minute of walking, Rownan stopped. "Are we trapped here?" He spun on his heel to face me and Treygan again. He spoke faster than normal. "We dove off that floating island and down here into the trenches. How will we get back up to the gate we came through if you can't fly?"

I glanced at Treygan, hoping he had a reassuring answer, but worry lines pinched the corners of his mouth. The consequences of losing my wings hadn't occurred to me yet, but now that Rownan pointed it out, panic catapulted through me.

"There has to be another way to the gate." Treygan tried sounding calm. "We'll worry about that after we find Vienna."

I nodded, not wanting to dwell on how much more impossible this mission had just become with the loss of my wings. Rownan wiped his hand over his face then continued forward.

Eventually, the solid ground transitioned into sand. A wide strip of maroon powder lay rolled out in front of us like a blood-red carpet. We had reached what resembled a beach except there was no water. One side dropped off into a deep canyon of what looked like cracked concrete, like maybe an ocean had existed at some point but it had dried up. On the other side was a gray mist so thick we couldn't see past it. I almost suggested we enter the mist, but Sage encouraged me to stay quiet and let Rownan lead.

"I'm feeling better," I told Treygan. "I think I can walk."

"You sure? I'm not tired. I'm fine carrying you."

Noble as always. "Really, I'm good."

He set me down and held my hand. I still felt somewhat unbalanced, but I managed. Rownan was already marching ahead onto the beach, so Treygan and I followed.

We had almost closed the distance to Rownan when I stopped short and cocked my head. "Do you hear that?"

"Hear what?" Treygan asked.

"It sounds like rain."

Rownan paused, pointing out over the barren canyon. "Looks like rain too. Sort of."

We all watched a pink, glistening curtain creep across the spanning horizon of concrete.

"It's heading this way," Treygan said.

Sage nudged my chin. "Maybe we should find somewhere to take cover."

"Good idea."

We turned to enter the gray mist behind us, except it had cleared and the landscape was covered with black plants and trees.

"I'm not going in there," Rownan said. "I'm not scared of a little bad weather."

As if insulted by his words, the rain reached the beach. The first drop hit my hand and I yelped and stumbled into Treygan. "It burned me!"

Treygan and Rownan were hit with drops on their faces almost simultaneously. Both of them winced.

The skin on my hand was bubbling. "Find shelter!"

We took off running for the trees. A few more drops hit us as we ran. We were all shrieking or gasping from the burns.

"There! A cave!" Rownan shouted.

Again, too easy, but at that point it was either let the rain melt our skin or run into a cave and deal with whatever awaited us inside. The rain pounded louder behind us. I wanted to fly so badly. I could have gotten us inside so much quicker.

A few more drops pelted us before we made it to safety. Treygan and I dashed into the cave first. Rownan ran in seconds behind us. We were all gasping and groaning from the pain. I made the mistake of wiping my face and ended up burning my fingertips. I cursed under my breath and fell against the cave wall.

Treygan shook the burning raindrops from his hands. "Everyone okay?"

"Rain that makes our skin boil—literally." Rownan bent over, bracing his hands on his knees. "What next?"

"Don't ask," I moaned, digging out the tube of healing salve from my pack. "I'd rather not find out." I tossed the tube to Rownan. "That should help." His face was already blistering worse than mine or Treygan's. He nodded gratefully.

I eyed the cave. The back wall was only a few yards away. Thankfully, from what I could tell, no soul-sucking creatures inhabited the space. Outside, the rain poured down. The weight of what had almost happened to us hung heavy in the air.

Treygan stood near the opening, watching the deadly storm. He glanced down at his jacket, which looked the same as mine and Rownan's; tiny circles of singed fiber had formed everywhere raindrops landed, but at least they hadn't burned through.

"Our faces would have melted off," Rownan grunted.

I swallowed hard, staring at the inflamed boils on my hands.

Treygan's frown was contagious. "We should rest."

"I can't rest in this place." Rownan handed the salve to Treygan. "We have to find Vienna."

"We can't go anywhere until the rain stops." Treygan gave me the tube without taking any for himself. "Now might be our only chance to let our bodies recharge. I have a feeling we're going to need all the strength we can muster once we get out of this cave."

Treygan was right. And I was so tired. My eyelids were heavy. I dabbed the absolute least amount of ointment needed on my burns then did the same to Treygan's. We might need the medicine for worse injuries later. I didn't want to think about anything worse, but I was sure it was possible.

I reached for Treygan. "I'll rest if you rest with me."

Rownan removed his gear and stood at the cave's opening. "I'm not tired. You two rest and I'll keep watch."

"We're right here if you need us," Treygan told him.

"I know. Merfolk don't sleep." Rownan looked me up and down. "Do you still sleep? I mean, you're not pure mer."

"No," I admitted. "Not since I was transformed into a mermaid."

He nodded. "Get some rest."

Treygan and I nestled into a dark, dry spot in the back of the cave. He curled up behind me, offering me his arm as a pillow. My body went limp, but my mind wouldn't relax. I watched Rownan pace back and forth at the cave entrance.

Treygan's breath made my ear tingle. "Hypothetical situation. We find out Vienna is gone, and for some reason I don't make it back, but you and Rownan do." He hesitated. "Rownan would take care of you. I hope you know that."

I rolled over to gawk at him. "Are you trying to tell me, in some sick way, that if you and Vienna end up dead, you'd want me and Rownan to be together?"

"It's not ideal, and I'd humbly request you have a relationship with absolutely no kissing, or touching, or any kind of physical intimacy, but yes, he'd take good care of you."

"You've lost your mind."

"Have I? He's loyal and brave. He loves deeply."

"He loves Vienna. And I love you. And we're all going back to Rathe. We're going to live happily ever after, and I'm going to try really hard to forget that you ever tried to convince me to be with your brother."

Treygan kissed my shoulder. "I like hearing you so confident."

Truth be told, I wasn't confident at all. We had burns on our skin, we were trapped in a cave for who knows how long, and demonic creatures had attacked us and ripped my wings off. Our odds of surviving this trip weren't looking good.

"I'm very confident," I lied, relieved that I had the ability, because my words—untrue as they were—seemed to put Treygan at ease.

"We survived the Triple Eighteen. We can survive this, right?"

If only we could go back in time to the Triple Eighteen. That drama seemed like child's play compared to our current situation.

"Rest," Treygan whispered. "You're safe in my arms."

And because Treygan couldn't lie, I took comfort in his words, and slid away into a cloud of happy memories—far away from Harte.

We weren't sleeping, but my body and mind had settled into rest mode.

A wind blew hard, gusting through the cave entrance and stirring me awake. My hair flew around my head. "What was that?"

"Storm gust," Treygan murmured.

A voice called my name in the distance. It was barely audible through the wind and rain, but I jumped to my feet.

"Uncle Lloyd!" I shouted, running to the cave opening.

Rownan reached out and stopped me.

"Yara!" Uncle Lloyd faintly called again.

"Oh, my gods!" I shrieked. "Your father is out there!" His skin would be melted off judging from how hard the rain was coming down. "Uncle Lloyd! We're here! Follow my voice!"

Rownan's hand coiled tighter around my wrist. "It's another imposter."

He appeared out of the pink mist, covered head to toe in a slicker suit and fisherman boots. I waved my arms frantically over my head. "Over here!"

He staggered toward us. Not thinking, I stepped out of the cave to help him, but the burning rain sent me darting back, hissing in pain. Uncle Lloyd kept trudging forward until he stumbled his way inside.

I reached for him.

"Wait!" he gasped. "Don't touch me. All this rain will burn you." He attempted to undo his jacket, but stopped when his fingers sizzled. The slicker was covered in burn marks and reeked of burnt plastic.

"Why are you here?" I studied his face, looking for signs that he was an evil demon, but it was really him. Sage was calm and so was my intuition.

"I had to come." He still gasped and wheezed. I glanced around as if I'd magically find a towel or drink to offer him, but of course there was nothing except a shocked Rownan and Treygan in the empty cave with us. "I have information."

Looking apprehensive, Treygan knelt beside him. "What kind of information?"

Uncle Lloyd's cloudy eyes blindly searched the rest of the cave. His failing vision was another sign that he was the real deal. "Rownan, I'm so sorry."

Rownan flinched. "Sorry for what?"

Uncle Lloyd's hands shook the way they always did when he was upset. "Vienna. She … there's no point in searching for her."

Rownan's jaw tightened. "Why?"

Uncle Lloyd bowed his head. "Many years ago, she tried exiting Harte through the same gate you entered, but it killed her."

My breath caught in my throat. My heart felt heavier than stone, and my grief sent it crumbling into a billion broken pieces. "Rownan, I'm so sorry."

Treygan stood and placed a hand on Rownan's shoulder.

Rownan was frozen in place, his eyes wide. "That's a lie."

Uncle Lloyd sighed. "It pains me to have to tell you, more than you can imagine, but it's the truth."

Rownan lurched forward. "Who told you that?"

"Stheno and Euryale told the sirens. Nixie told me."

"Why wouldn't she have told us this before we came here?"

Uncle Lloyd flashed a sad grimace in my direction. "Apparently, the gorgon sisters were happy to be rid of Yara."

I knew it. Stheno and Euryale did hate me. They wanted me to go to Harte so I wouldn't come back. I hung my head. Treygan and Rownan were in this evil realm because of me.

"We have to go home," Treygan said. "The minute the rain stops, we're out of here."

"I still don't believe it," Rownan growled.

"Rownan," Treygan gripped his arm. "Stheno and Euryale have no reason to lie."

"How would they know what happened to Vienna?"

"They know everything," Treygan said.

Rownan's jaw clenched so tight it looked like it might break. I had to get everyone out of here. If anything happened to any of them, Uncle Lloyd, Treygan, or Rownan, I would never be able to live with myself. "How do we get home?"

"We go back to the gate," Uncle Lloyd said. "Yara will have to fly us out one at a time."

I froze. I could feel Treygan's and Rownan's eyes on me.

After a few silent moments, Treygan asked, "What's the alternative plan? Yara no longer has her wings."

"What?" Uncle Lloyd squinted.

With a tremor in my voice, I explained, "Evil creatures ripped them off as soon as we arrived."

"Dear gods." Uncle Lloyd rubbed the back of his neck. "I know of no other way."

Treygan and I exchanged defeated frowns. The inevitable truth escaped my lips in a whisper. "We're never going home."

"Don't say that," Treygan said. "There has to be another way."

"Not for us." Uncle Lloyd sighed. "We all have human blood in our veins. That was the only gateway we could cross through. And it's hidden high in the sky."

"This is all my fault." Rownan leaned against the cave, his head in his hands. His shoulders bounced like he was silently crying.

"Actually," Uncle Lloyd mumbled, "it's mine. It all started with me. I never should've fallen in love with Liora. Never wed outside of my species. And I most certainly never should've made a deal to be turned human. My greed led us to this. I'll never forgive myself for how badly my sons have suffered because of my choices. And Yara too. I'm a monster in the truest sense of the word."

"No." I rubbed his hand. "You've always tried to do what's best for everyone. This isn't your fault. And it isn't Rownan's, either."

"He's right," Rownan snarled. "All this trouble started with him." He turned and pointed at me. "Then *your* parents broke the rules and fell in love because they saw him and Liora together and thought they could get away with it too. The curse was a chain of events that started with him."

I stood, balling my fists at my sides. "How can you say such a thing? He's your father!"

Rownan raised his chin, his eyes smoldered with rage. "It's the truth."

I glanced at Treygan, expecting him to stick up for Lloyd, but Treygan said nothing. Worse, he nodded as if he agreed with Rownan.

Uncle Lloyd clutched his chest, groaning loud and long.

"What's wrong?" I hurried to his side again. "What's happening? What hurts?"

He clawed at his chest and shoulder. His eyes were bulging and drool dripped from his mouth. I turned to Treygan. "Do something!" He just stood there, watching but not moving.

Uncle Lloyd squeezed my hand so hard I whimpered. "I'm here," I told him. "I'm right here. It's going to be okay."

He shook violently then went rigid. His eyes were wide open, unblinking.

"Uncle Lloyd?" I squeezed his hand, but he didn't squeeze back. "Please, say something."

A rock formed in my throat. He wasn't breathing. He wasn't moving. "No," I pleaded. "No, no, no."

I began doing CPR. He had taught it to me years ago. I tilted his neck, breathed into his mouth, pumped hard on his chest, and then repeated the process. Nothing happened.

I went through the steps again, desperately blowing as much air into his mouth as I could, pressing down on his chest with all my might. Tears streamed from my cheeks, splashing onto his unblinking eyes.

Treygan's hands rested on my shoulders. "You have to let him go, Yara. He's gone."

"No!" I choked.

He grabbed my hands. "We knew it was coming. At least he didn't die alone."

There was a cold resolve in Treygan's voice. How could he not be upset?

"No!" I pulled my hands free of his and leaned forward, laying my head against Uncle Lloyd's chest. "Please don't leave me. I need you. You can't die!"

There was no heartbeat. No breath. I was helpless to save the man who had always taken care of me. My sunshine was fading from my life.

I cried out. "This can't be happening!"

Treygan pulled me into his arms. "He's gone." I struggled to pull out of his grip and hug my uncle again, but Treygan held me too tight. "He meddled for the last time. They killed him."

"They can't." My words were strangled by my sobs. "It's not fair."

"It's the way our world works. He did this to himself."

Crying harder, I beat my fist against Treygan's chest. "How can you say that? How can you be so cold? He's your father!"

"Yara!" Treygan yelled my name, but his lips didn't move. The way I heard him was different from when we talked through our minds underwater. I kept pounding his chest, trying to push him away from me. He shouted my name again, but the voice wasn't the vapid, cold-hearted Treygan in front of me.

"Yara!" Treygan repeated. "Snap out of it!"

I looked down at Uncle Lloyd, feeling emotionally destroyed and mentally disoriented. Sea scorpions crawled out of every hole in the burned slicker. I jumped back, horrified.

Treygan shook me hard. "What's wrong? Yara?" His eyes were wide with panic and worry. "You spaced out for a few seconds and started pounding on my chest."

Rownan stood beside him, skeptically watching me.

I turned around to reach for Uncle Lloyd, but he was gone. The cave floor where he and the scorpions had just been was empty. "Where'd your father go?"

"What?" Treygan turned my chin so our eyes met again. "Yara, look at me. What just happened?"

I tried fighting back my flood of sadness. I wiped at my tears, but my eyes and cheeks were completely dry. "Your dad was here. He had a heart attack. He died."

Treygan's eyes narrowed and he glanced sideways at Rownan.

"What the hell is going on?" Rownan murmured.

Treygan studied me like I was an injured animal who shouldn't be spooked. "You saw something that wasn't real."

"No," I said. "It was real." My lip quivered. "He came here to help us, and it killed him."

Treygan slowly shook his head. "No one has come into this cave except the three of us."

Something about the cave was off. The lighting was different. The temperature wasn't right. I focused on Treygan. His eyes were almost black. My Treygan's eyes were blue.

"*This* isn't real."

Treygan's grip on my arms loosened. "What isn't real?"

"This conversation with you."

His brows lifted. "No, Yara. This is real." He held my face in his hands. "I am real right now. My father is not here. He is home in Eden's Hammock. He's not dead."

Rownan stepped closer, looking at me the same way Treygan had earlier, apprehensive but concerned—which wasn't normal for Rownan.

"Vienna is dead," I said. "She died trying to get out of this place. Stheno and Euryale confirmed it."

Rownan and Treygan frowned at each other, but Treygan kept my face in his hands.

"That's what they want you to believe," Treygan said. "It's not reality. Don't fall for their tricks."

"Vienna is alive," Rownan retorted.

I shook my head. "You two aren't the real Treygan and Rownan."

Imposter Treygan rested his forehead against mine. "You're stronger than this. I am real. You have to believe me. *This* is real." He leaned in to kiss me. Just like the other evil creatures, he wanted to suck my soul out of me. I shoved him hard.

Treygan stumbled backward. "Yara, please, don't do this."

"Stay away from me." I reached into my arm holster for my dagger. A line of black dust swept across my vision, but when I tried focusing on it, it moved again.

Rownan stepped back. "She's losing her mind. She's pulling out weapons on us!"

I held my dagger in front of me. I knew what was real and what wasn't. The pain of Uncle Lloyd's death hurt too much. I knew his touch. His words. He didn't look or sound like an evil imposter, but these versions of Treygan and Rownan—with their black eyes and evil dust swirling around us—were definitely demons.

Treygan held out his hands in front of him. "I won't move or touch you again until you say it's okay."

"This is crazy." Rownan backed farther away. "She has lost it."

"Think about it," Evil Treygan said to me. "If we are imposters, why haven't we attacked you yet? It would be two against one. We would easily win. And if we aren't real, then where are the real Treygan and Rownan?" He pointed to the entrance of the cave. "Scorching rain is still falling. It's not like we could have left."

I glanced back and forth at the two of them, processing what Treygan had said. The black smoke still weaved in front of me. "It's an illusion. You make me see what you want me to see."

"No," Rownan argued. "Obviously you experienced an illusion of our father dying, but right now, *this* is reality."

I gripped my dagger tighter. They were messing with my mind. The other attack wasn't successful, so they were trying a different tactic.

"Listen to Sage," Treygan said. "She's dancing around your head like crazy. She must be trying to tell you something."

Sage. I hadn't seen or heard Sage since I woke up from resting. I felt for her, but she was missing. No tugging at my scalp, no hissing, nothing. "She's not here. More proof that this is all a mirage."

A sharp pain seared the flesh on my hand. Sage appeared in front of me, her tongue darting out at me. "Sage?"

I'm here. She mentally whispered.

I stared at the two marks from her fangs. She hadn't bitten me hard enough to draw blood. When I looked up again, the lighting in the cave had returned to normal. The temperature seemed right again. The line of black dust dancing across my vision had stopped. Could that have been Sage trying to communicate with me?

"This is real?" I wasn't sure if I intended to say it as a question or statement.

"I swear," Treygan said. "This is real."

I slowly stepped closer to him. His dark blue eyes watched me intently. I tested him. "Tell me a story."

Relief washed over his face. He extended his hand. "My fingers can't reach your skin when you're so far away, and I promised not to touch you until you say it's okay."

I dropped the dagger and rushed into his open arms. He hugged me tighter than ever. His comforting scent of honey and clean ocean air wafted over me.

"Damn, that was intense." Rownan slumped against the wall. "I thought we lost you, Yara."

"I didn't." Treygan's chest rose and fell against mine as he kissed me. "I knew you were stronger than that."

A seed of hope blossomed inside me. "Lloyd isn't dead?"

Treygan smiled. "He's probably home asleep in bed at this very moment."

That was good enough for me. We had no idea what was happening in Earth's realm, but as long as Uncle Lloyd hadn't really come to Harte and died, I had an extremely precious reason to find a way home.

"We need to get out of this cave," Treygan said. "It's making us stir crazy."

I didn't think our hallucinations had anything to do with the cave. Harte knew how to hit where it hurt. But had some unseen force corralled us into this small space for a reason? We were trapped like animals. "What if the rain never stops?"

Treygan walked to the cave's opening and crossed his arms over his chest. "Eventually, every storm runs out of steam."

I snickered. "This one literally steams."

Rownan's head fell back against the wall. "Can we please go one day without some play on words about hell or burning or anything about this messed up world?"

"You're a bit cranky," I said.

"You think? We're trapped in a cave by skin-sizzling rain while Vienna is out there, maybe burning to death, or being tortured by who knows what, and all I can do is sit here doing nothing."

"I'm sorry," I offered. "I know this is a million times harder for you than it is for me or Treygan."

"A million doesn't come close."

"Noted." I didn't want to argue about who loved who more. Love was love; it couldn't be measured or weighed to see who had less or more of it. "Again, I'm sorry."

Treygan stood beside Rownan. "It's your turn to rest. Get some sleep. It's not like we can do anything until this rain stops."

Rownan rubbed his bloodshot eyes. "I could use some sleep. You'll wake me up the second it stops raining?"

"Of course," Treygan told him. "We want to get out of here too."

Rownan stripped off his jacket and lay down in the back of the cave, using his jacket as a pillow. It seemed like only a few minutes had passed before Rownan's breathing deepened and he snored softly.

I glanced at the watch Delmar had given me. He thought it might work in Harte, but sadly, he was wrong. The hands hadn't budged since we had sailed into the Triangle. Tracking time was impossible in Harte. I took off the watch and tossed it on the ground. One less thing to weigh me down.

"Otabia and Mariza won't help me," I told the sprites.

Every last one of them had gathered around the bayou. It was past their bedtime, but they all made an exception and attended the emergency meeting. Their loyalty was touching, but they had no idea what I was about to ask. I wouldn't be surprised if all of them said no. I couldn't blame them. I would have said no too.

"We'll help you!" Jenna shouted.

Many yesses and cheers erupted around me.

Tucker was the voice of reason. He was the least shy of all the guys. Not that any of them were as outgoing as the girls, but Tucker took the lead while a group of boys hovered behind him. "First, we should probably know what you need help with."

"Well," I began, fiddling with my hands, "You've all heard the legend of the gorgon sisters' all-seeing mirror." Nods and acknowledgments buzzed all around me. "I found out it still exists."

The sprites oohed and ahhed. I glanced at Jenna and Keeley, who watched me with innocent, unknowing smiles.

"And … well …" I stood and took a deep breath. "I'm stealing it from the grotto."

Silence. The only sounds were random single music notes coming from the lightsing bugs each time they lit up. But even their lights were dim, and their low tones sounded ominous.

Keeley's teensy hands covered her mouth.

Jenna leaned forward. "Did you say *steal* it from the grotto?"

I nodded. Tucker flew backward and huddled with a group of sprites who looked as shocked as him.

"I know it's dangerous," I added. "I realize none of you have ever been in the grotto, and it frightens you—"

"Venus Flytraps frighten us," Tucker said. "Stheno and Euryale terrify us!"

I hung my head. "It was an absurd idea. I shouldn't have asked."

"You still haven't actually asked us to do anything," Keeley pointed out. "What would you want us to help with?"

"You're small enough that you could fly through the tunnel into the grotto with me. I'll distract Stheno and Euryale while some of you fly in and search all the caverns for the mirror."

Their twinkling eyes were wide with fear.

Tucker spoke in a hushed voice. "Surely, they'd burn off our wings or worse if they found out we had violated their sacred and forbidden home."

Many sprites wrapped their wings around themselves protectively. Tucker was right.

"I'm sorry I asked." My shoulders slumped. I knew I would never find the mirror by myself.

"We'll do it." Jenna and Keeley stood holding hands. "We'll help you."

"Jenna, no!" Tucker argued, flying to their side. "Keeley, it's too dangerous."

Keeley grinned. "But think of the adventure! Imagine the feeling of helping save someone so important."

"It's the chance of a lifetime," Jenna cooed.

Tucker's eyes lit up as if he was star struck. He muttered something I couldn't hear.

"What?" I asked him.

Tucker turned to face me. "The adventure of a lifetime." He threw his hands above his head like a true champion. "I'm in!"

They were the only three sprites who volunteered to help me, but three were enough.

I was upset with myself for putting my three favorite family members in danger, but I couldn't do this on my own, and I had to get the mirror so I could check on Yara.

Otabia and Mariza stooped atop one of the cliffs of the grotto. Otabia shook her head, giving me a final warning not to proceed. Mariza stared down at us with her eyes gleaming. She would love to see us get caught and be subjected to the wrath of Stheno and Euryale. That was probably her intention in telling me about the mirror in the first place.

It didn't matter. They couldn't stop me. If my plan worked the way it was supposed to, then we would be in and out of the grotto before Stheno and Euryale woke up. I would have the mirror, and I would never set foot in there again. It wasn't like Yara would ever be trapped inside the way they were. The grotto could implode—with Stheno and Euryale in it—for all I cared.

The sprites and I landed on a boulder outside the entrance. "Remember, only follow me halfway through the tunnel," I warned. "Wait until you hear my siren song, then you can come in."

"What if your trick doesn't work?" Keeley asked.

"It will work," I told her. "Stheno and Euryale salivate for any memories, but they'll be excited by a change of source. I'm sure they've grown bored of Mariza and Otabia after all this time."

Jenna nervously stroked one of the leaves on her head. "And you're sure the poison will work on them?"

"It's not poison," I corrected. "It's serum to put them to sleep for a little while."

"Liquid lullaby," Tucker said, trying to make all of us feel better about the crime we were about to commit. "Everyone enjoys a nice nap."

They were worried and scared—it showed all over their faces. I was too, but I had to be the confident one in this mission. I would never let anything happen to them. That I was sure of.

I crouched, preparing to morph into bird form. "Ready?"

All three of them nodded.

I threw back the vial of Liquid Lullaby—as Tucker innocently called it—almost choking on its sickly sweet taste. I only had a few minutes to regurgitate the concoction before it put me into a deep sleep.

My bones cracked and my skin tightened, bristling with a full coat of downy feathers as I shrank into my heron form. I sailed off the cliff with Tucker, Jenna, and Keeley flying after me. We dove into the water and I led them to the secret tunnel of the grotto's entrance. Like true, brave soldiers they didn't hesitate and followed close behind me. I slowed halfway through and craned my long neck—our signal for them to hold until my next command.

Then I continued forward.

I burst through the tidal pool, instantly changing back into siren form. The main cavern was empty and the torches on the walls burned dimly. I pulled my hair back, leaned forward, and vomited the awful memory I had recently consumed, along with the Liquid Lullaby.

I hadn't even finished wiping the blood and saliva from my mouth before Stheno and Euryale's rattling tails echoed through the grotto. They slithered my way so fast it could only mean one thing: they were already frenzied. I knew I could count on Stheno and Euryale's hunger and greed winning over rational thought about why, for the first time ever, I had regurgitate memories for them.

They rounded the corner pushing and shoving each other in a battle to get to the puddle at my feet. Their pinwheel eyes were spinning furiously. They groaned with thirst as saliva dripped from their fangs.

Their serpentine torsos stretched long as their black tongues dove into the puddle simultaneously. I stepped back, half-worried they might accidentally eat my feet in their ravenous consumption.

Somewhat disgusted, I watched them lap from the puddle and throw back their heads, swallowing as much as they could as fast as they could. They had never been so out of control when feeding from Mariza or Otabia. This meal bordered on barbaric.

I had expected some questions, at least a trace of skepticism or questioning of my motives, but me regurgitating for them was like throwing a freshly decapitated body to a pair of starved sharks.

True, the memories I stole were more pungent than usual, but it was by no means our best catch ever. I had been there for the pinnacles of Otabia and Mariza's careers. Euryale and Stheno had fed on much darker and richer meals than this one. But you would never know it by the way they slurped and gulped down my recent catch.

My prey was a recently released convict who had fled to the Bahamas. He had committed such heinous crimes, and planned to do many more. I found him strutting out of a hotel with two teenage girls slurring and stumbling at his side. He had baited them on the internet with false promises of lucrative modeling careers. Upon meeting them in person, he weakened their defenses with liquor and drugs. My sisters and I trailed them to an abandoned warehouse that served as his makeshift home and a factory of horrors.

Seven girls were shackled and gagged inside, bleeding and broken like traumatized animals. The newest two would have made nine victims total. If only they knew how close they had come to suffering a nightmare worse than anything they could have imagined.

I relished strutting into that dark and dingy warehouse. Not because of the bruised, naked, whimpering girls watching me and trembling with fear that I might be another torturer. What I relished was the sick hunger in the despicable man's eyes. There I was, a fiery redhead in high-heeled boots and a form-fitting bodice, radiating such a powerful aura of seduction that he was paralyzed with lust. My sultry sisters, being centuries more experienced, oozed sexual prowess without even trying. Little did he know that as horrid as his crimes were, they were child's play compared to what we were about to do to him.

Otabia and Mariza flanked me on either side, purring with anticipation.

The tent forming in his shorts made me laugh out loud. Usually, I let Mariza and Otabia battle over ripping off the pathetic proof of supposed manhood, but I needed to make sure this experience was as tantalizing as possible for Stheno and Euryale. This time I would do the honor.

I stepped closer, licking my lips and pressing my chest against his as I grabbed hold of the tacky fake gold chain around his neck. I hummed a few notes, barely a taste of my intoxicating siren song.

His breath was as putrid as his soul. "I've been dreaming about girls like you."

I smiled and pressed my nails into his hairy chest. "The hunter becomes the hunted."

His eyes widened with alarm, but then I sang. Otabia and Mariza joined in behind me. All the female victims around us calmed and quieted. Men can't resist a siren's song, but women are soothed by its power. Those poor girls were long overdue for soothing.

I released my wings and spread them high, contemplating the most torturous way to suck the degenerate dry, then closed my mouth over his. When Otabia and Mariza's talons tore into him he tried to scream, but I breathed it back into him, not allowing him his much needed release and forcing him to choke and writhe. It went on like that, gradually intensifying his agony for hours.

Even regurgitated, his terrified screams, sobbing, and pleas for mercy, lived on through the blood dripping down Stheno and Euryale's faces.

They were enjoying the memory of his punishment almost as much as I enjoyed administering it. But they were already swaying. The sleeping potion was taking effect. Soon, the beautiful faces of the nine avenged girls would lure Stheno and Euryale into a satisfying and peaceful sleep. Because after all was said and done, the most rewarding part of our outing was tenderly removing all the horrifying memories from the innocent girls. Their bodies would forever be scarred, and they wouldn't remember why, but their minds and souls were cleansed.

That's the burden and the beauty of being a siren. Some consider what we do sinister, but we know part of our work is saintly.

Stheno and Euryale passed out in what was left of the blood. I sang my cue for Jenna, Keeley, and Tucker to come in. They flew through the pool, shaking the water from their tiny wings.

"It worked?" Keeley whispered.

I gloated. "Of course it worked. Let's get moving. Jenna, you're with me. We'll check every room and tunnel on the right side. Keeley and Tucker you do the same on the left."

"What about the middle?" Keeley asked.

"That was Medusa's wing. They haven't entered her space since she died. Even Yara isn't allowed to go in there."

Keeley nodded as she and Tucker flew off and we started our search mission.

I was prepared to search for hours, but after searching only three caverns, Jenna squealed with excitement. "Look! Look, Nixie! Is this it?"

I ran over to her. She fluttered by the corner of an elegant gold mirror. My heart sank to the heels of my boots. "Yes, I'm sure that's it."

"Why do you look so sad?"

"I always envisioned it as a hand mirror." I ran my nails along the exquisitely etched frame. Wider than me with the top coming up to my chest, it leaned against a wall. "Don't you see? It will never fit through the tunnel."

Jenna flew from side to side, assessing it. "Oh dear. You're right. It's much too big."

"How did they originally get it in here?"

Jenna shrugged. "Magic?"

"Sadly, I don't know any magic to get it out."

"What should we do?"

I had no clue if it would work, but my intuition took over. "Get back."

"Why?"

"Just do it, Jenna."

She flew backward until she reached the other side of the room.

I took a deep breath, swallowed hard, and prayed to Medusa that this would work for Yara's sake. I held my hands over my face for protection, then kicked the mirror—shattering it into pieces.

"Nixie!" Jenna yelled. "What have you done?"

"Seven years bad luck is worth it if this works."

I carefully picked up a shard of the mirror the size of my hand. "This will easily fit through the tunnel."

"But it's broken. Will it still work?"

"Let's get Keeley and Tucker and get out of here so we can find out."

I woke up expecting to relieve Yara and Treygan of their lookout duties, but both of them were passed out. "Some guards you turned out to be."

The rain had stopped. How long had we been out of it?

"Hey, rest time is over!" I stood and walked over to them. I nudged Treygan's shoulder with my foot. "The rain stopped. Let's go." He didn't move a muscle. "Yara?"

Snapping them out of rest mode should have been easy. One half of their mind stayed conscious while the other rested. Treygan said he was always vaguely aware of what went on around him.

That's when I noticed how pale they were.

No way. It had to be another illusion or trick of some kind. They couldn't be dead. Crouching down beside them, I placed my ear against Treygan's chest. No heartbeat. No breath. I pulled back and stared at him. "Wake up, man!"

I shook him hard, but he was cold and stiff. I placed a hand on Yara's arm. She felt the same. "No," I said out loud. Then louder, "No!"

I ran the scenario through my mind. We were alone in the cave. No other imposters or creatures pretending to be someone else. No black smoke like Yara had seen. The lighting in the cave was different, but it had stopped raining outside, so that made sense.

I had watched Yara bang on Treygan's chest during her hallucination. No matter what she saw, she was still in her body. Even if I was imagining this, they should've been able to hear me.

"Wake me up!" I screamed. I yanked Treygan so he was sitting up. "If you're not dead, snap me out of this nightmare!" His head fell back, totally limp. I hugged him to my chest. "Treygan?"

How could they be dead? I would have woken up if someone had entered the cave. And why would they be killed but not me?

Yara lay still on the ground beside us. Treygan was lifeless in my arms. I gently lowered Treygan's body and crawled over him, shaking Yara. "Yara, wake up."

Her head rolled to the side and I scrambled backward. A creature that looked like a viperfish with legs gnawed on what was left of Sage's body. I tried shooing it away, but it snapped its sharp teeth at me. Foam dripped from its lips in bright green and yellow bubbles. It turned its attention back to Sage's corpse and continued eating.

I pulled my dagger from my hip and stabbed the vermin without hesitating. It squealed and hissed as black goo oozed out of its skin. Gagging at the rank stench, I stabbed it again and again. When it no longer moved or made any sound, I flung it against the back wall.

The skin on Yara's neck was peeling away and covered in foaming teeth marks. "Oh, gods, no." My voice echoed through the cave. This couldn't be happening. "Yara?" I shook her again, but she was limp. "Treygan?" I searched his body and found the same foaming wounds on his leg. "No!"

I ran for our packs, frantically searching for the salve. Fumbling to remove the lid, I hurried back to them and rubbed the ointment on their wounds. "Please work. Please don't let me be too late."

I stared, waiting. Begging and praying for them to breathe and open their eyes. When I realized it wasn't going to happen, I choked back a sob and punched the cave wall, shouting at the top of my lungs. "What have I done?"

I fell against the wall, continuing to punch it until my self-hatred and heartache manifested into tears. I waited five ragged breaths before turning around. I begged for it to be an illusion. I would have traded my own soul to turn around and see them alive. Through my blurry eyes, I stared at Yara's and Treygan's lifeless bodies—even Sage was an innocent victim. All of them gone. Because of me.

I shouldn't have let them come. Treygan and Yara were supposed to have more time together. So much more time. I pulled at my hair, fighting back rage. "I'm so sorry. You have no idea how sorry I am."

I slumped down beside them and placed Treygan's hand over Yara's. "I pray you're together in a place even more beautiful than Rathe. Please believe me, I never meant for this to happen."

I kissed my fingers then touched them to Yara's cheek. I wiped away the tear rolling down my face and stood, listening to the eerie silence. Pieces of my broken heart scraped at my insides. I was alone. I was brotherless. I was a murderer.

I couldn't leave them. I promised Yara and Treygan we would stick together. I needed to keep that promise. Their bodies needed to be brought home, their souls honored with heartfelt ceremonies by their loved ones. I pulled Treygan back up to a sitting position. I hoisted him over my left shoulder then reached for Yara. I dragged her to me and lifted her into my arms like a baby. Rising but stumbling sideways, I tried to keep Treygan balanced over one side of my body. They were heavier than they looked.

I carried them out of the cave, but I had only made it a few steps when a spasm locked up my back. Grunting, I dropped to my knees and set Yara down. I heaved Treygan off my shoulder, flinching at the tremors of pain shooting down my spine and leg.

How could I keep carrying both of them? Especially through a damned realm where I had no idea what awaited me, or where I was going, or how I would ever get out. My body was already failing me. Failing had become the theme of my life.

"Tell me what to do," I said to Treygan. "You always knew the right thing to do."

I stretched out on my back beside my brother, the top of our heads touching, like we used to do when we were kids. We would lie on the rocks at the gorgon grotto—the melding point of the dark and light sides of Rathe. We would stare up at the sky and talk about all the places in Earth we were going to visit, and all the human adventures we wanted to experience.

We went through with so many of them. Vienna came along on more trips than I could count. Treygan never minded. He always welcomed her. Never once did I feel even a hint of jealousy or resentment that I could love, kiss, and be physically intimate with another soul without turning them to stone. Never once did he complain that he would never be able to have what I had.

He loved unconditionally and selflessly. And I took all I could because he was my brother and my best friend, and being around him made me happy. We led an amazing and exciting life together.

Until the gate closed and our differences made us enemies. For me, survival trumped brotherhood. Even though it shouldn't have. Treygan knew that. He fought tooth and nail for the first couple of years to keep our bond unbreakable. But I turned my back on him. I was a selfish, bitter coward. Partly because it became crystal clear who was the better between the two of us, and it wasn't me.

What Treygan didn't know, what I never told anyone, was that every night I prayed for him. Every single night for years I had fallen asleep begging Poseidon and Medusa to gift him with happiness.

They gave him Yara.

Not because of me or my prayers, but because he deserved her. Because he deserved happiness. And like a selfish, stupid coward, I ruined one of the most rare and magical loves any of the worlds had ever seen by allowing them to be killed by some sneaky venomous creature.

A special place existed for souls like me—it was called Harte.

Medusa's pearl shined brightly, radiating beams of color in all directions. All around her head the petals of her flowery vines bloomed. Her star-filled eyes shined as bright as her crescent moon smile as she recited Koraline's favorite line from the famous gorgon poem. "Beauty is sometimes hidden under a veil of tragedy."

The agape pearl in the hollow of Medusa's throat began spinning.

Poseidon appeared. His eyes raged fiercely with white-capped waves. He towered above me with his ethereal trident raised at his side. His voice boomed like thunder. "You must choose."

When I had visited the Inbetween, I had no clue what the foreboding dark sea represented. It was so ominous compared to the beautiful towering waterfall. But now I had figured it out.

The ominous sea was Harte. It was Medusa's biggest and ugliest mistake—one that couldn't be erased. Sealed off, apologized for, contained, but not erased. When souls died, they had to make a choice. Had anyone ever willingly chosen to dive into the horrifying sea instead of the Eternal Falls? They would be out of their minds to do so.

Just as we were out of our minds for willingly entering Harte.

But that made me wonder. We were *visiting* Harte. Did that mean the living could visit the Eternal Falls too? Or, a much more tragic thought, did Rownan, Treygan, and I voluntarily give up our lives when we crossed into Harte?

I raised my head to meet Medusa's gaze. "Are we already dead?"

She reached forward, her fingers flowing like gentle waves toward my face, but just before I felt their caress, Koraline's voice shouted from behind me. "Never give up! The tide will turn."

My eyes snapped open and I sat up.

We couldn't be dead. I was no genius, but I would know if we were dead. I intimately knew what death felt like, and this wasn't it.

Treygan stirred beside me. What did he think about while he rested?

Sage slept peacefully on my shoulder. I glanced at the cave's opening, expecting to see Rownan, but he was gone.

"Treygan!"

He shot upright. "What? What's wrong?"

I scrambled to my feet. "Rownan's gone!"

Treygan scanned the empty cave, as if it were so big that I might have overlooked Rownan. "But it's still raining. He wouldn't have gone out there. He knows we have to stick together."

"Then where is he?"

Treygan walked to the entrance and cupped his hands over his mouth, shouting, "Rownan!"

No one answered.

Sage swayed beside me as I stood behind Treygan. "What does this mean?"

Treygan reached back and pulled me closer to him. "I don't know."

"I'm scared."

"Me too."

"Wait." Treygan let go of me. "I can shadow him." Thank gods one of us had the ability to think rationally. "Give me a minute." Treygan rolled his shoulders and closed his eyes. I held my breath, waiting what felt like centuries for Treygan to tell me he could see Rownan and that he was okay.

I waited.

And waited.

I didn't want to interrupt him, but my anxiety kept building. Outside, the rain pounded harder, or maybe it just seemed to get louder because of Treygan's deafening silence. He had said a minute or two. At least five minutes had passed. I paced, tapping my knuckles together and chewing my lip. How far could Rownan have gone?

My chest tightened. The long wait with no word from Treygan could only mean one thing. I couldn't wait anymore. "You can't find him, can you?" Treygan didn't respond. Not even an eyelid flicker. "Please, say something. Do you see any trace of him?"

No reply.

I had seen Treygan shadow Rownan before. This time seemed different. Something felt wrong. I touched Treygan's arm. "Treygan?" He still didn't react. Even with him standing mere inches from me, I felt alone. "Please take a break. I need you here. I'm worried about you."

Still nothing.

"Treygan!" I snapped my fingers in front of his face then clapped my hands. This wasn't normal. He would never ignore me. Especially knowing I was already scared. I shook him, but he stiffened. Every muscle in his body locked up. "What's wrong with you? Treygan!"

I peeled open his eyelids. His pupils were so huge and silver they almost eclipsed the whites of his eyes. "Oh, gods," I muttered. He was reliving a memory. I had seen the same thing when he shared memories with Caspian and Indrea. "Where are you? Treygan come back!"

I wished with all my being to see clouds pass over his beautiful eyes and take me into his soul so I could see what he was seeing, but I couldn't get through to him. He was already too deep in the memory.

Sage hissed in my ear, startling me. I was part siren. I could create storms. Maybe I could create clouds in Treygan's eyes and force my way in.

"It's worth a shot," I told Sage. She settled on my shoulder in agreement.

I stood tall and bowed my head, focusing on pushing my energy down my arms and through my fingertips. Out of habit, my shoulder blades spread, allowing the ghost of my wings to release. I imagined storm clouds forming around us, then I drew my hands inward, pressing on Treygan's temples.

My fingers tingled as silver clouds glided over his pupils. I plunged into them and felt the familiar tug at my chest. In the blink of my own eyes, I was Treygan.

And I was screaming in agony.

I watched helplessly through Treygan's eyes as he turned me to stone with a kiss.

I fought—hard—to remember the moment wasn't actually happening. Treygan's despair, his heart break, his anger and guilt, were *not* my own. It was in the past, and his feelings were not mine. But then it worsened.

Treygan wasn't just reliving the Triple Eighteen; he was experiencing a twisted version of it. In Treygan's nightmare, I remained stone. The gate didn't open. Talus the gorgon flamed through the water and ripped Treygan away from my stony form. Talus carried him, kicking and screaming, past all the merfolk and selkies who had been trapped in Earth's realm. They had all turned to stone too. Treygan was so horrified, so consumed by guilt and heartbreak that he begged Talus to kill him.

Talus kept rushing him away, dragging him through a dark gateway, into Rathe. But he whisked him through it so fast that Treygan didn't even have time to realize he was back in his own realm. Talus dropped him outside of the grotto like a bag of trash. Stheno and Euryale rose out of the water, their eyes flaming, black seaweed hanging from all the snakes hissing around their heads.

They each grabbed one of Treygan's arms and pulled him under into murky darkness.

Somehow, through all of that, Treygan kept calling out, whispering or crying my name.

The real me couldn't tell him anything. I could barely cling to the truth that I wasn't him and the nightmare wasn't real. But I kept clutching at reality, holding tight for both of our sakes.

The scene we were experiencing must have been what Treygan feared might have happened. It was draining his soul and weakening him so fast I wasn't sure I could stop it.

I fought to take control of his limbs. It was like trying to catch a fish in water. Every time I grabbed on to him, he would slip away again. He clung to the image of my stone form, letting it destroy him from the inside out. He pictured his mother turning to stone seconds after giving birth to him. The memories were debilitating him. But I was stronger.

I focused on the feel of his muscles, imagining I could manipulate and control them like strings on a puppet. I forced his hand to touch the wet mud of the grotto. Then, using his index finger, I slowly made him write *not real*.

He read the words. They registered. But he struggled to believe them. I was getting the hang of controlling his hand like it was my own, so I kept writing. *Not stone. In Harte. Come back.*

The hope hit him light a lightning bolt. His head snapped up.

I was shoved in the chest, back into the present, and Treygan's cobalt eyes focused on me.

"There you are," I said, sighing with relief. "Welcome back."

He hugged me, rocking me. "Thank you." He pulled back, holding my face in his hands and staring into my eyes.

We didn't need to say anything. He knew I had experienced what he had. He knew I felt what he felt and how awful it had been. If I hadn't known how much he loved me before, I certainly knew it now. One of his deepest fears was losing me.

"I'm right here," I assured him.

He pressed his forehead to mine. "We stay together. Always."

"Always," I promised. "But what about Rownan?"

He blinked and turned to look at the rain outside. "I never got that far. Whatever happened to me happened instantly."

"This is bad," I said. "They're using our fears against us. Mine was Uncle Lloyd dying."

"Mine was turning you to stone. Losing you forever."

"They make it seem so real. It feels so real while it's happening."

"The question is who are *they*? And how do we stop them?"

"I wish I knew."

Treygan leaned against a wall as I made slow laps around the cave. Where could Rownan have gone? Did someone or something take him? If so, how did we not hear it?

I tripped over something on the ground and it skidded into the shadows. I crouched down, reaching into the dark, narrow cubby at the back of the cave. My fingers closed around something solid. A handle. I pulled out a dagger. Hanging from the tip of the blade was the watch I took off earlier.

Treygan closed in behind me. "What did you find?"

"My watch. Stabbed."

"I assume you didn't stab it."

I shook my head. "This is Rownan's dagger."

"Why would he stab your watch? And please tell me you weren't wearing it at the time."

"I took it off earlier."

"This gets weirder and weirder."

A scary thought hit me. "What other weapons did Rownan bring?"

Treygan's jaw shifted. "I'm not sure."

We were both worried, hoping Rownan hadn't ventured out into Harte unarmed.

"We have to find him," I said.

Treygan nodded and glanced at the rain. "But how? This place seems to outsmart us at every turn."

I hated that he was right. Soul-sucking demons, nightmarish illusions, murderous weather, and now Harte had managed to separate Rownan from us.

"I have a feeling we haven't seen the worst of this place yet," Treygan said.

I chewed on my lip, trying not to imagine what could be worse than what we had already encountered. "They'll probably keep trying to separate us."

"I won't let that happen."

He said it out loud, which meant he wholeheartedly believed it, but I wasn't so sure. Harte kept hitting where it hurt the most. Treygan feared losing me, and I feared losing him. Harte would probably feed on that. What if we were both lured into hallucinations and neither one of us could snap the other back into reality?

I had an idea.

"I need to do something." I grabbed one of the big scallop shells I had seen half-buried in the back of the cave. I set it upside-down on the ground at the entrance. I pried a thick vine from the cave wall and used my dagger to cut off a long portion. It was flexible, but still stiff enough to serve my purpose. Using the long piece of vine, I pushed the shell out into the rain, careful not to let any drops hit my hand.

Treygan eyed me skeptically.

The shell filled up with rain. I hooked its rim with the curved end of the vine and slid it back inside. Some liquid splashed out, but I had enough to do the job. I wriggled out of my jacket then knelt on the ground and dipped the tip of the dagger into the steaming shell. Then I drew an N on my forearm, but my sizzling skin made me gasp.

"Yara, stop!" Treygan rushed over to me, but I was already burning the second letter into my arm.

"We're getting mentally weak," I explained. "Koraline wanted me to tattoo this on myself so I wouldn't forget."

I dipped the dagger into the scalding rain and kept writing.

"Tattoo? I doubt she meant literally." He grabbed my hand, but I pulled away from him, still burning Koraline's words into my arm so I wouldn't forget. "Never give up."

I held up my arm so Treygan could read the pink letters rising on my burned skin. "This isn't going away. If at any time you question whether I'm real, make sure this is on my arm. If it's not, then it's not the real me."

His eyebrows twitched and he blew out a breath. He delicately held my arm in his hands, examining my new brand.

"Never give up. The tide will turn," I told him. "We're going to get out of here."

He stripped off his jacket, took the dagger from me, and turned away. He squatted by the shell while I stared at his back muscles, flinching and rippling. He never made a sound, even though I smelled his skin burning. Treygan rose and walked around me. He positioned himself behind me, wrapped his arms around my torso, and pulled my back tight against his chest. Taking my left hand with his right, he lifted our forearms, his beneath mine, and there were Koraline's words burned into our skin.

Never give up.

The tide will turn.

His brand had more letters than mine. It must have hurt like hell.

"Together," Treygan said, "we can survive anything."

I turned around and kissed him.

Rowan

With every step I took, I mourned them.

The terrain was covered with tall, thick plants. Bugs and scorpions crawled across my boots while snakes hissed and snapped at me. I used my claws to slice my way through the infested jungle.

A few times I wanted to quit. Sit on the ground, let some evil thing come for me and kill me or eternally trap me in the wretched wasteland. I deserved whatever punishment Harte wanted to dish out.

But I kept moving. Too scared to be still and sit alone with my guilty thoughts.

Step after lonely step, I waited for something to pounce on me. Nothing ever did—which intensified my fear even more. When something or someone finally did find me, what kind of suffering would I have to endure?

My body was numb with grief. My heart kept breaking into pieces over and over. Every time I thought of Vienna or Treygan or Yara, another part of me died.

I rested against a huge tree with no leaves. At first, I thought the bark had streaks of red running through it, but when I touched one of the veins blood coated my fingers. My mouth watered. I was beyond thirsty, but I wasn't about to drink from anything or anyone in Harte. The thought alone made me shiver.

I closed my eyes, not wanting to see the ugliness around me anymore. Without even trying, I began shadowing. Mainly, it was my way of hiding in the dark tunnel of my own mind, a temporary escape from Harte, but then a dim light appeared.

Huddled on the ground, in the middle of a pool of amber light, was Vienna.

She had her back to me, her face hidden from my sight, but her shoulders rose and fell with each breath she took. She breathed deep and slow, and her left foot occasionally twitched the way it always did when she slept. I knew without a doubt she was no hallucination or evil imposter.

I opened my eyes and ran as fast as my legs would carry me.

The stench of rotted corpses made me dry heave.

How could Vienna sleep in such a disgusting and dreadful place? Decaying sea creatures were scattered all over the tiny beach. Based on the skeletal remains, I guessed the carcasses were some breed of seal. Dead fish washed in and out with each weak wave that lapped the tiny beach.

How could water find its way up this high? My fingertips were sliced and raw from climbing the steep cliffs to reach the isolated beach where I now stood—with Vienna at my feet.

At first, I didn't want to wake her. She looked so peaceful, lying there asleep, still so beautiful even after so many years in this godforsaken place—even as she lay curled up with a slimy, mold-covered piece of driftwood. Her hair had grown so long. Wet strands clung to her skin, ending in a tangled pile around her feet.

Every part of me screamed this was the real her, but I still silently prayed she wasn't some sort of mirage.

I leaned closer. No visible injuries. She was much thinner, especially in the face, but not a scratch on her. It was almost too good to be true. She had always been too good to be true. Why should this moment be any different?

We didn't have much time. I didn't even know how long I had been in Harte, but my internal clock assured me we were within the three-day window to get back through the gate. I had to wake her and get us home.

I kneeled beside her.

"Vienna." I laid my fingers on her bare shoulder. Touching her. For years I agonized about whether I would ever feel her soft skin again. I fought back the overwhelming urge to cry tears of joy and sadness all mixed together. But a crying mess was not how I wanted Vienna to see me for the first time in so long. "V, I'm here."

She stirred with a sweet sigh and rolled over. Her eyes half opened and her smile grew bigger.

My heart exploded with joy. "You have no idea how much I've missed that smile."

She reached forward and touched my chin. "You almost look real."

I placed my hand over hers, still fighting back tears. "I am real."

She tilted her head and her arms went limp. "That's what they all say."

I leaned closer, clutching her hand against my chest. "Vienna, it's me. I'm here to take you home."

"Of course you are." Her expression remained dreamy and unchanging. "Let me sleep. My dreams let me exist with the real Rownan in a much happier place."

I grabbed her shoulders and yanked her up. "Vienna, it's me. This is no hallucination or evil creature pretending to be me. I'm really here. And we don't have much time left. We have to get out of here and get back to Rathe. Your family misses you. I've missed you more than you could possibly imagine."

Her eyes narrowed. "You hellions. Why do you keep trying? It's never going to work."

Of course she doubted me. I had seen what this place did to Yara. "I can only imagine what horrible tricks they've pulled on you since you've been here, but I swear to you. I swear on your brother, Dresden, your mother, and my own life, I am your Rownan. Through and through, I am one hundred percent real."

She shook her head then draped herself over the long piece of wood beside her. "This was Rownan. *He* was real. We spent two long, happy years together here. But your dark, twisted world killed him."

For two years she'd believed some evil creation was me? I couldn't think about what that meant. What might have happened between her and some … hellion? "That's driftwood. Not me."

"He's still here with me. His body may be dead, but his soul is still with me. I feel it."

Her delusions ran deep. She loved a piece of wood covered in black and green mold. She believed it was my body and that I was dead. How could I overcome that? "Look around this place and tell me what you see."

"I know what you're thinking," she said. "But I'm not delusional. I'm surrounded by dead selkies that wear the faces of my family and friends. You send them so I'll think I have no reason to live." She smiled, a little too psychotically for comfort. "But the joke is on you. I'm numb to your corpses. My family and friends are healthy and happy, safe at home. Your tricks will never make me believe otherwise."

"Good. Because that's the truth. But that," I pointed to the wood she was curled up beside. "You believe that is my— Rownan's—body? Is it decayed too?"

"Of course not," she sneered, gathering a pile of her long hair in her hands and clutching it to her chest. "Our love keeps him from decaying. As I said, his soul is still with me."

My mind raced to come up with things I could do or say to make her see the truth. I held out my arm. "Drink some of my blood. Feel my love for you. You'll know I'm real. That connection can't be faked."

She backed away. "I'm not stupid. You won't bleed because you're not real. You have no soul."

"What if I do bleed? Then will you believe me?"

"That's impossible."

I slashed my forearm open with my claws, and held it out to her. "See?"

She glanced at it then shook her head. "You're all the same."

I looked at my arm and I was stunned. Not one drop of blood. My skin appeared to be torn open, but nothing leaked out of it. "What's wrong with me?"

"You're an evil phony. But you're acting has improved."

Desperate, I grabbed her, hoping to kiss her and make her feel it was the real me. She slashed open my cheek with her claws then squirmed out of my grasp. I touched my face. It hurt, but again, no blood.

She stood with her feet planted wide apart in the sand, her arms held at her sides like she was ready to fight.

"No need to be defensive," I said. "I would never hurt you."

"None of you can hurt me. When will you stop trying?"

"I will figure this out," I assured her. "Somehow, I'll prove to you that I'm real and I'll get us out of here."

She spit in my face. "Over my dead body."

The rain finally stopped. Treygan and I walked out of the cave, and I gasped at how drastically the scene outside had changed. The sky was pitch black and resembled a massive brain with long, tubular strands curled and wound around each other. The pattern stretched from horizon to horizon, and at times looked like it was moving. A few feet of burnt-orange sand led to an ocean of murky moss-green water.

"Are we going to swim in that?" I asked.

"Seems we don't have a choice." There was no other land to walk on. The dark water surrounded our cave. A quick glance around the rock wall confirmed more water behind us. Our cave had somehow become an island.

I stepped to the edge of the water. "Why do I get the feeling there's something lurking in there that will eat us?"

"I'll check it out first and make sure it's safe."

He only took one step before I grabbed his arm. "Oh, great idea. You'll get eaten and I'll be left here festering with guilt and despair because I let you go in alone."

"Then we'll go together." He unlaced his boots.

I grunted in agreement as I squatted down and took off my boots too.

"I miss being in the water," Treygan said. "This is a welcome change from that cave."

"I miss the water too. I'm just not sure I want to be in *that* water." I motioned to the dreary abyss around us. "How did this happen? How does an ocean suddenly form out of nowhere?"

"I can think of much worse things to encounter." His head snapped up. "Wait. Maybe that's it!"

"What's it?"

"I missed the water. Lying there in the cave, I was wishing we were swimming in the ocean again. I craved the ocean, and here it is."

"That's the big magic secret," I said sarcastically. "In hell, anything you wish for will appear." I threw my head back and shouted at the sky, "I wish for my wings back. I wish Rownan was here. I wish we'd find Vienna alive and well so all of us can go home. I wish for Uncle Lloyd to be in perfect health." I rolled my eyes at Treygan. "Oh, and I wish for an endless amount of more wishes when we get back to Rathe."

"Let's test my theory. Don't be afraid. Don't imagine anything in the water that could hurt us."

"Easier said than done."

"Visualize this ocean being as safe as ours in Rathe."

I eyed him skeptically. "You think whatever we're afraid of is going to materialize too?"

"That's what happened with your hallucination of Lloyd dying. And me turning you to stone. Maybe that's the trick to this place. Our negative thoughts and fears try to consume us. Think positive. Believe that nothing can hurt us, and hopefully nothing will."

I considered his logic. Although it seemed inevitable that this place would hurt us in every way possible, I was willing to try anything. I closed my eyes and pictured a healthy Rownan swimming up to meet us. I opened them, and Treygan was watching me.

"Nope," I said. "No Rownan."

"I doubt it's instant. Focus on him being safe and believing we'll find him. I'm going to try shadowing him."

"Are you sure you should try shadowing him again? Look what happened last time."

Treygan winked. "Now I *believe* it's going to work. Mind over matter."

I still wasn't sure about Treygan's theory, but I created a happy scene in my mind: Rownan and Vienna together again, smiling and holding hands. They were together in Rathe, celebrating holidays with their families and coming to visit me and Treygan.

Treygan's voice grounded me back in Harte. "I found him. He's with Vienna."

A jolt of hope shot through me. "The real Vienna?"

"We can only hope so."

Up until that moment, I wasn't sure if I truly believed Vienna could still be alive. I must have believed it somewhat because I agreed to come to Harte to help find her. But now that we were here and I had experienced firsthand how dangerous and hurtful Harte was, I wasn't sure if anyone could endure it, much less survive it for sixteen years. "Treygan, do you really believe Vienna could have lasted so long?"

"I'm forcing myself to have faith for Rownan's sake." He unbuttoned his pants. "Let's dive into this friendly and peaceful water and swim to the happy couple."

"Why are you taking off your suit?"

Looking down, he paused. "I assumed we'd use our tails to swim."

"And what happens if the water turns boiling hot or freezing cold?"

"You aren't supposed to think negatively."

Was he kidding me with this crap? Did he want us to leave our gear and weapons behind too? Were we continuing our mission armed with nothing but positive thoughts?

I kicked sand at him. "I'm being realistic! Yes, it would be wonderful if I mentally manifested a herd of winged rainbow unicorns rising out of the sea so we could all ride off into the sunset while holding hands and singing merry songs, but until that happens we need to be prepared for fire-breathing unicorns who can melt our skin and stab us to death with their poison-filled devil horns."

Treygan stared at me, his lips parted. Then he burst out laughing.

At first I was upset, but then my hissy fit replayed through my head and I laughed too.

Treygan pulled himself together. "Yara, we have to make it back to Rathe, because it will be tragic if I never get to tell anyone about your unicorn rant."

I chuckled one last time then pulled myself together too. "I'm glad I amuse you."

"You do." He wrapped his arm around my neck and pulled me close to him, kissing the top of my head. "And I'm grateful for it because things were way too tense."

I nodded. "But we're keeping the suits on, right? Because if a demonic unicorn does stab me to death, I'd like my tombstone to read, 'Here lies Yara Jones. She was stupid enough to go to Harte and get killed, but at least she kept on her temperature-controlled, super durable, fire- and ice-repellent suit."

"We'll wear the suits." He grinned down at me. "How could I ever dismiss such a *solid* argument?"

I pointed at our boots sitting in the sand. "But we can't swim with those on."

"I agree. We'll have to take our chances and hope the unicorns don't have a foot fetish."

And so we waded in. As much as I wanted the ocean to be safe, I still kept an eye out for fire-breathing unicorns.

Treygan might have been on to something with his positive thinking theory because we swam for a long time without incident. Eventually, I grew tired and surfaced. So did Treygan.

"Why am I so exhausted?" I asked him, rolling onto my back to float for a few minutes and regain some energy.

"We can't be sure how long we've been here. We haven't had food or water since before we arrived. Exhaustion is to be expected."

"Do you think we've been here longer than one day?"

"I honestly don't know."

"Definitely not three, though, right? No way could we have been here for three days already."

"No, I figure we have at least another day to get out of here."

That helped me relax. Not much, but a little. My focus drifted to the dark sky above us and I went completely still. My heart pounded so hard the water was vibrating.

Treygan noticed. "What's wrong?"

I didn't want to speak. I worried I would draw attention to us. I very slowly pointed up. Treygan looked at the sky, and then he went rigid too.

High above us, but not high enough, was a terrifying new addition to Harte. Enormous eel-like creatures lined the sky, forming what looked like slithering bars of a cage. The creatures were scarier than anything I had ever seen.

Slowly, Treygan took hold of me and pulled both of us beneath the water. It was dark, but I could still see Treygan's eyes.

What are those things? I asked.

Soul suckers. Lloyd warned me and Rownan about them. He said they looked like giant lamprey.

Why didn't anyone tell me about them?

We didn't want to scare you.

As if I wasn't scared of Harte for countless other reasons. You should have told me!

This isn't the time to argue, Yara. Let's keep swimming so we can get away from them.

What if they see us? What if they swoop down and snatch us out of the water? I was panicking. Not good. Not good at all.

Don't think like that.

We kept glancing upward as we swam. I shivered thinking about what might happen if the creatures saw us, or sensed us swimming below them. Maybe they already knew and were just waiting for the right time to devour us.

How much longer until we reach Rownan? I asked.

I'm not sure. I don't know this world. I can see him, and I'm following his trail, but I have no idea how far away he is.

I averted my eyes so Treygan wouldn't hear my thoughts. This mission was taking too long. We were separated from Rownan and running out of time. *We're never getting out of here*, I thought to myself.

Sage brushed across my chin. *You will,* she assured me.

For the first time since she had become part of me, I didn't believe her.

I kept my distance. Vienna and I exchanged silent glances and occasionally she told me to go away, but I just sat there, trying to figure out what to do.

Eventually, she drifted back to sleep, so I quietly crawled closer. If I could move the driftwood away from her and get rid of it, then I could take its place. Maybe she would believe I had come back to life. As slowly as possible, I attempted to roll her off of the log, but she woke up swinging her fists.

"Don't touch us!"

"Okay, okay." I backed up with my hands in front of me, showing I had no intentions of hurting her. "I won't touch you."

The fire in her eyes calmed and she hugged the driftwood tighter. What did she see when she looked at that moldy log? Did she really see *me*? Did a hunk of old wood really feel like me?

I settled into the sand a few feet away from her. "Your mother and brother miss you."

"Don't speak of them," she snapped.

"How about us? Can I tell you stories about us?"

"There is no us. You're not my Rownan."

"Okay then, how about your childhood?"

She looked at me skeptically. If I could prove I knew everything about her, then maybe she'd believe I was truly me. She didn't say no, so I proceeded.

"When we were seven years old, your mother was really into gardening. She had these beautiful frost-rose bushes that she cherished. She warned us never to play near them." I smiled at the memory of Vienna so young. "You weren't good at following directions, though. We were building a fort and you climbed one of the trellises and slipped on the ice. You ended up falling into a rose bush."

Vienna's eyes were locked on me. Her expression was impossible to read, so I continued. "You cried like someone had cut off your limbs. I helped pull you out, but you were covered in thorns. I wanted to take you to Indrea and Caspian so they could heal you, but you wouldn't let me. You thought you'd get in trouble, so we ran from the house and hid in Seal Cove while I carefully pulled every thorn from your skin."

She blinked then looked away.

"Do you remember that, V?"

"I remember," she said quietly.

"How would I know that if I wasn't really me?"

She picked up a clump of muddy sand and rubbed it around in her hand, staring at it oozing between her fingers. "I don't want any of this to be real. I want to go home. I just want to go home."

"I can take you there." I leaned forward, hesitant to move any closer because I didn't want to spook her. "Please, Vienna. Come home with me."

She threw her head back and rubbed her lips together. After a few moments of staring at the sky, she asked, "Why do you love me?"

My heart fluttered with a surge of hope. Why hadn't I thought to ask her that? No, it wouldn't have worked. She had to ask me first so I could give the right answer. The only answer I had ever given her. I crawled up on my knees, reaching out to touch her, but she cowered back so I dropped my hand. "Because you are my everything."

Her head snapped to attention. Her eyes were wide.

"It's me, Vienna. I swear it's me. Please believe me."

"I want to. I want to so badly, but—" she twisted a strand of black hair around her pale finger while staring at the log beside her. "If you're Rownan, then who did I spend two years with? Who is he?"

"I don't know who that was, but it doesn't matter. It's the past. I am me." I placed my hands on my chest. "Me. Right here. With you. Right now. Ask me anything, V. I'll do whatever it takes to prove I'm not an imposter or a wicked trick of your mind."

Her eyes lit up. "I almost forgot." She reached into her coat and pulled out half of a broken shell and held it in front of her so I could see it. "What is this?"

"A shell."

Her hand lowered. The light in her eyes dimmed. "Just a shell?"

I was confused. Obviously, I was supposed to know something more about the shell. My gut told me it was important, that it had deep meaning, but I searched my memory and found nothing. "It's a very pretty shell."

She snatched it back and stuck it in her coat pocket. "You're not him! If you were him, you would've known."

"Known what? I am him! I mean, I'm *me*! I can't remember everything. Tell me a little about it and maybe it will tug a memory loose."

"Tell you a little about it? You're a phony! You're the best imitation yet, but I can't be fooled. Go torment someone else!" She turned her back to me. "You will not get my soul. You'll never make me believe you're Rownan."

I hung my head. I had failed her. I had failed us both. Again.

I couldn't keep track of time, but what felt like hours passed with us sitting several feet apart in silence. I sat with my back resting against a rock. My head hung heavy in my hands.

Vienna stood. I lifted my head and watched her gather all her hair, twisting it into a heap on top of her head. She used bones from a carcass to pin it in place. She walked closer to the water, picked up a dead fish, then hurled it as far out to sea as she could throw. She picked up another and did the same thing, grumbling, "Filthy, stinking place."

I stood and walked to the water, but stayed a safe distance from her. I picked up a dead fish and threw it hard, taking out as much of my frustration as possible. It felt good, so I threw another one, and another.

"What are you doing?" Vienna asked.

"Helping you, I guess, I don't know."

She squinted then turned away from me, ridding the beach of more dead fish, one at a time. I kept helping.

After hurling dozens more fish into the ocean, I took a break, resting my hands on my knees and catching my breath. Why was I so exhausted? "Reminds me of that time we swam up to Maine and found those seal poachers partying on the beach." A bittersweet grin tugged at my lips. "You and Dina talked the guys into taking off all their clothes, and then you threw everything into the ocean, including their boots. You told them to walk home naked."

Vienna smiled hesitantly. "They were so mad they chased us into the water."

"Which is exactly what you planned." I chuckled. "Not only did they have no clothes, they were soaking wet, and it was freezing."

"They deserved it."

"They deserved a lot worse."

Her smile turned to a confused frown. "Dina wanted to drown them, but you said we couldn't kill them or we'd be just as awful as they were."

I nodded.

Vienna wrapped her arms around herself. "I know you're not him. You can't be, or you'd have known that shell as well as your own coat. But whoever you are, thank you for making me smile. For helping me remember why I love him so much."

I swallowed down the lump in my throat. "I'm sorry I don't remember the shell. But I'm glad I could make you smile again. Knowing you aren't here alone is enough for me."

A long comfortable moment of silence passed. I took a chance and held out my hand to her. "Will you dance with me?"

She wrapped her arms around herself. "I don't dance."

"Yes, you do. You love to dance. We won countless contests together."

She bounced on the balls of her feet, biting her nails. "You should go."

"You just thanked me for making you smile."

"That was wrong of me. Please go away."

"I left you once. I won't leave you again. I can't."

She dropped her hands at her side. "Don't you get it? I don't want you here. I don't want to look at you, or talk to you, or anything. You're not my Rownan. You're an infectious disease that makes me weak."

I inhaled sharply. "Wow, harsh words, Vienna. I'd accuse you of ripping out my heart, but I already gave it to you, willingly and completely, a long time ago. Now you're just clawing at the empty hole inside me."

"Leave me alone!"

I stepped forward and looked her straight in the eyes, mocking her earlier words. "Over my dead body."

I see Rownan and Vienna, Treygan said. *They're standing on a beach, talking.*

Do you really think it's them?

I'm sure of it.

We reached a forest of seaweed and both of us slowed to a stop. I eyed the eerie scene ahead. *I don't think we should swim through there.*

A loud screech pierced the sky. A shadow from one of the creatures passed over us, briefly darkening Treygan's face. *We're out in the open. At least in there we'd be harder to spot from above. Plus, Rownan is this way. I sense him.*

Swaying black seaweed stretched wider and deeper than I could see. Who knew where the dark underwater jungle ended? But Treygan was right—we would have to swim through it. Turning back wouldn't get us closer to Rownan and Vienna.

Treygan reached out to me and I took his hand. We swam forward and I cringed as slimy seaweed brushed against me. We swam slower as the seaweed grew thicker.

My foot caught on something and I jerked to a halt.

Treygan floated forward until our linked hands pulled him to a stop too. *What's wrong?*

I'm stuck on something.

I'll take a look. He dipped toward my feet and a rope of seaweed followed him. At first I thought it was just caught in the drag of the water, but then it curled around his leg and yanked him away from me.

"Treygan!" I shouted, swallowing a mouthful of water.

More vines wrapped around my arms. I punched and fought against them, but they wound tighter. Treygan was pulled farther away from me, flailing and thrashing against his own ropes. He was shouting my name and I yelled for him again, but seaweed tightened around my neck, choking me into silence.

Oh, gods, this is it. This is how we die. Strangulation by seaweed.

But no, that would have been too easy. The seaweed didn't keep choking me like I expected. It launched me upward, lifting me above the surface of the water. My arms were bound at my sides. I couldn't move my head or legs. I lay there, helplessly staring up at the screeching black creatures in the sky.

One of their long bodies split into three sections, a head forming on each segment. Three pairs of glowing eyes raced toward me, slithering like snakes.

Sage! Sage, help me, I mentally begged her. She stretched forward, hissing and snapping her fangs. Then I regretted ever asking her to help.

The three creatures opened their massive mouths, and they had something much worse than fangs. Their round mouths were filled with circular rows of razor-sharp teeth. Treygan was right. They were mutant, larger-than-life lamprey.

I couldn't turn my head, but from the corner of my eye I saw another creature split into three and dive toward the water. They were heading for Treygan. My chest ached and my body was convulsing with fear. We would be eaten alive.

One beast stopped inches from my face. A huge, pointy tongue darted out of the center of its circle of teeth. The stench of death made me gag, but because I couldn't swallow it burned my throat.

I closed my eyes, too terrified to watch the hundreds of teeth tear through me.

Sage swayed and snapped. She tugged at my head as her body lashed out over and over.

Stop, Sage. Don't make it worse.

The beast's hot breath blew so hard against my face that my skin rippled and tightened. I waited, dreading the moment its teeth would clench down on me, but it didn't happen. I felt one hard yank at my scalp before a deeper pain took over. That instant, I knew the beast had Sage.

Emptiness spread throughout my entire being, something not physical. I had never felt anything like it. Through my tears, I watched the beast pull back, moving up and away from me. Impaled by the beast's teeth hung a severed Sage.

I tried to scream, to break free and reach for her, but I couldn't move. Tears dripped down the side of my face and behind my ears. I closed my eyes again, knowing I couldn't handle seeing Treygan snared in the beast's teeth too.

My left hand snapped free and dropped behind me. I opened my eyes and saw the other trio of beastly heads pulling back, but two of the three were dripping a black substance and the other was making a god-awful screaming sound.

My neck was suddenly freed too. I turned and saw Treygan below me, slicing the seaweed with a dagger. I breathed a sigh, a mixture of relief and despair.

The seaweed holding me up collapsed, and I splashed into the water. Treygan clutched me to him. I pawed at my head, desperately pleading for it to be an illusion, wanting so badly to feel Sage's scaly skin. But she was gone.

The thought of her lifeless body in their huge teeth sent more tears spilling down my cheeks. How could I have been so careless? Why didn't I protect her?

Treygan pulled me under and held my face in his hands. *I'm so sorry about Sage, but we have to get out of here. Those things might descend again.*

I nodded, unable to form a coherent sentence.

With one arm, Treygan held me tight at his side as we swam. With his other hand he sliced through seaweed with impressive speed.

We reached a cave and swam into it, surfacing and taking a moment to rest. The rock ceiling hid us from the beasts' view.

"Sage," was all I could mutter to Treygan.

He held my head against his chest. "I know. I'm so sorry."

"She was part of me."

"I know," he whispered. He pulled back, lifting my hair and examining my scalp where she and I used to be connected. He leaned closer and pressed his fingers against my scalp. It stung, but it was nothing compared to the pain in my heart.

"Strange," Treygan murmured.

I whimpered. "What's strange?"

"There's a slit, but it's not bleeding, or even inflamed." We exchanged worried glances. "Everything is wrong and unpredictable here."

"I hate it." I felt like I might puke. "Why did we come? We were idiots to think we'd survive this place."

Treygan lowered his eyes. "I tried turning those creatures to stone. I tried turning the seaweed to stone. I couldn't. Not even a crackle."

My nausea got worse. "How can that be?"

"I don't know."

I pressed my hand to my mouth. "I feel sick."

"Sick to your stomach?"

"Sick everywhere. That helpless and exhausting sick when you know how wrong and hopeless everything is."

A loud roar sounded outside the cave. I turned slowly, afraid to see what was making the noise. My eyes widened.

A wave formed, flowing downward *out of the sky*. The water around us rushed out of the cave, pulling us with it, and rose up to meld with the huge wave forming above us. Treygan kept a tight hold of me, but I barely had any strength left to fight.

The beasts appeared in the rush of water, writhing as their teeth spun open and closed over and over.

My eyes met Treygan's. *I will always love you.*

Never give up, he mentally shouted. *We'll get through this!*

The wave ripped us forward and I was launched through the sky—flying without wings. I crashed, hard, onto jagged ocean rocks. I was sure every bone in my body was broken, along with my will to live.

We had been flying toward the mer side of Rathe. That was the last place anyone would look for me. It would give me and the sprites time to make the mirror work. But as we flew, a pain ripped through my head, making me buckle in the air.

I fell into the water, a tangled mess of pain and heartache. Jenna and Keeley pulled me back to the surface.

"Nixie, what's wrong?" Keeley asked.

I was crying, clutching the back of my head, overwhelmed by grief. "It hurts."

"Your head?" Jenna asked. "Like a headache?"

"No," I groaned.

They each positioned themselves under one of my arms and flew me to land. When we arrived at the beach outside of Caspian and Indrea's home, I couldn't move. I just laid there in the sand, curled up in a ball and groaning in agony.

Jenna petted my hair as Keeley flew off to fetch Caspian and Indrea.

"Do you think it's Yara again?" Jenna asked.

My mind wouldn't allow me to accept that the pain couldn't be mine. It hurt too badly. Maybe Stheno and Euryale woke up, discovered the broken mirror, and were punishing me with some kind of crippling pain only they could conjure.

Indrea's feet thudded through the sand as she ran to me. Each of her steps caused my brain to rattle. She dropped to her knees beside me, rubbing my arms. "I'm here, Nixie. Try to take deep breaths."

I felt calmer, but the pain wasn't lessening.

"Can you tell me where it hurts?" Indrea asked.

I placed one palm against the back of my head, and the other over my heart.

"Your head and chest?" Indrea's purple eyes looked so concerned. How could she care so much about me? I wasn't even mer.

"Maybe it's the silvery snake," Jenna said. "Maybe Yara's snake is sick."

Keeley flitted side to side. "Maybe Stheno and Euryale are stealing her soul like we stole their mirror."

Tragically, that was the more likely scenario given how much pain rippled through me.

"What?" Indrea asked, looking confused.

Keeley explained. "We did a bad thing. We broke the gorgon's magic mirror."

"And then we stole a piece," Jenna said meekly.

"They did nothing." I couldn't hold my eyes open anymore. "I broke it. I stole it."

Indrea took my wrist in her hands. "Her pulse is weak. Help me get her inside."

Caspian dabbed my head with a wet rag while Indrea held her hands over my body, murmuring one healing spell after another. My wings were smashed between me and the table I was sprawled out on, but I didn't care. The minor discomfort was nothing in comparison.

"They're coming," I murmured. I sensed them getting closer, moving faster than usual. "They're furious."

"Who?" Caspian asked.

I didn't have enough energy to answer. They would be here soon enough, so why waste my breath?

"Keeley, Jenna," I mumbled. "Hide."

The roar of siren wings shook the table beneath me as my sisters landed on the stoop and kicked the door open.

"What the hell have you done?" Otabia snarled.

Caspian sprang to his feet and stood between us. "Keep your distance. Nixie is hurt and weak."

"You're damn right she's weak." Mariza leaped over him, landing on the other side of me. "And she's an idiot!"

"You broke the mirror!" Otabia screeched. "How could you be such an imbecile? Stheno and Euryale will torture you until there's nothing left!"

"Everyone, calm down," Indrea ordered. "Nixie is no condition to be screamed at. She's very sick."

Otabia and Mariza's wings kept rustling and fire raged in their eyes.

"She's not sick." Otabia pushed past Caspian as if he was light as a cloud. "It's Yara again. You're letting her pain and miseries affect you as if they're actually happening to you." She leaned close to my face, snarling at me. "Have we taught you nothing?"

Jenna's voice shook as she tried defending me from her hiding place under the table. "But they're connected. If Yara is hurt or sick, so is Nixie."

Otabia squatted down, glaring at her. "Don't explain the siren connection to me, you little cretin. I know how it works."

"Don't call her a cretin," I managed to grumble.

"Oh, now you can speak," Mariza snapped at me. "How convenient."

"Get up!" Otabia commanded.

"She can't," Indrea argued.

Otabia rolled her eyes and grasped my wrists so hard I flinched. "Yes, you can feel Yara's pain. So can we—somewhat—but that doesn't mean you are sick and weak. Do we look any sicker or weaker to you? Get up!"

She yanked me to a sitting position. Mariza shoved me in the back so hard I slid and stumbled off the table. Indrea and Caspian caught me, and I managed to stay sitting up.

"This is not the correct way to go about this," Indrea said sternly.

Otabia stepped forward, her black wings spread high behind her, rippling like a dire wave. She lowered her face so that she was almost nose to nose with Indrea. "Don't tell me how to deal with my own sister."

Indrea raised her chin. "Don't disrespect me in my own home."

Otabia growled at her then turned to me. "You are a disgrace to our kind. Stheno and Euryale will be enraged when they see what you've done." Otabia's talons curled under my chin as she lifted my face to look at her. "Now you'll never see your precious Yara again."

"I kept a piece of it," I said.

"A piece? What good will a piece do? You destroyed it!"

"It might still work." It sounded crazy even as I said the words, but deep down I believed it.

Mariza laughed menacingly. "Such a fool you are."

"What if she's right?" Indrea said. "It doesn't hurt to try."

"We can't try, you idiots!" Otabia swept one wing across her chest. Black feathers rained around us. "Only a gorgon can see into the mirror. And none of them would ever help us, knowing the consequences and the wrath they'd face from Stheno and Euryale."

A smug smile spread across my lips. "You're wrong. I know one gorgon who would do anything to help Yara."

My eyes met Indrea's. "We have to visit Lloyd."

I crawled down the jagged rocks, back into the water. Everything was dark, except the glowing green crests of the waves. The ocean looked sickly and contaminated. Every bone in my body felt splintered. Electrical spasms shot through my muscles, causing me to twitch and whimper in pain. Through it all the stinging spray of water crashed against me.

I remembered the soul suckers, Sage, and being catapulted against the rocks.

Where was Treygan? I fought against the roaring current. I couldn't allow myself to be carried too far or I would never find him.

I plunged below the surface, searching for him, but underwater I couldn't see anything. I tried activating my underwater vision, but it didn't work. A new wave of fear rushed through me.

What if Treygan was dead? I sobbed, accidentally ingesting water. It tasted so horrible I threw it right back up again.

Everything hurt. Physically, emotionally, mentally, it hurt to exist. Why couldn't this place just kill me and get it over with?

Calm down, I told myself. *You have to calm down*. I thought of Indrea, sending her calming waves. I would have given anything to be back in Rathe or Earth with the merfolk again, and to have Treygan by my side.

A speck of blue and silver flashed in the distance. I shook my head and wiped the water from my eyes. I squinted, focusing so hard my head ached. I found it again, far away and being carried away too fast, but that shade of silver was Treygan's skin and the dark blue was his hair.

"Treygan!" I screamed for him and my mouth filled with water. I spit it out then dove beneath the waves, swimming as fast as I could, but my suit and gear were hindering me. I stripped off my jacket, along with the packs and holsters attached to it. I struggled through immense pain as I wiggled out of my pants, freeing my legs from their bindings.

For half an instant I worried my tail wouldn't form, but it did. Pumping my tail and body with all the desperate energy I had left, I swam as fast as I could to Treygan. I got close enough to see his limp arms whipping around him with every motion of the waves. He was floating, but the raging ocean was carrying him away so fast.

Please don't let him be dead. Please, please, please.

My body screamed in agony with every move I made. I dug deep, through the burning and stabbing pain, and gained speed. Harte would not win. I refused to let it separate us.

Treygan was a little more than an arm's length away. I stretched for him, calling out his name, but I couldn't reach him. I pumped my tail harder, using my arms to propel me forward. I reached for him again, willing my fingers to stretch longer. They momentarily grazed his hair, but I couldn't get a grip on him.

Then his body buckled in half and something yanked him underwater.

I didn't shout, or even think, I dove down, desperately trying to grab him.

Underwater, the only reason I could still see him was because of the huge, glowing, enchanting eyes of a kraken.

Never would I have thought a kraken—the giant squid-like monster I had read about and seen in movies—could have *enchanting* eyes, but that was just the tip of the iceberg. He was breathtaking.

The ocean calmed as if the kraken kept the water and everything around him tranquil. Treygan looked like a toy doll, wrapped in one of the kraken's massive tentacles. As horrifying as it should have been to see Treygan unconscious and caught by a monster of Harte, I was rendered motionless with envy. I wanted to be held by the kraken too.

He did not have the head of an octopus. He didn't have deadly jaws of razor-sharp teeth. He was the most exotically gorgeous creature I had ever seen. Dozens of tentacles of all lengths and thicknesses gracefully danced around him in translucent shades of black, blue, and silver, stemming from his sculpted torso which was the size of a mountain. And what a majestic mountain it was. Covered with etchings similar to my own hallmarks, his steel-gray pecs and abs were chiseled so perfectly they could have only been sculpted by the gods. Or maybe he *was* a god.

Atop his head were long, antler-like branches of black and blue coral. I longed to swim into them, to feel them against my skin, but I kept still, held in a trance by the kraken's glowing eyes. He blinked, and the bright blue light dimmed enough so his black pupils could be seen. His alluring eyes left me breathless.

His black lips parted and I drifted closer, pulled toward him by his tantalizing gaze. My eyes struggled to close as millions of bubbles kissed my skin, but I fought to keep watching him. Every tilt of his chin or bat of his seaweed eyelashes made my heart leap. The tip of one of his tentacles grazed the back of my tail, gently inching its way up, wrapping itself around my hips as another tentacle traced along my spine. A third tentacle brushed my cheek and caressed my neck. I arched my body, my chest aching to be touched by him too.

His mouth opened wide, taller than a cave entrance. It was filled with white light. I coasted in, finally closing my eyes and letting his warmth and beauty spread over me.

I woke up face-down, groaning with bliss. I assumed I was lying on a bed of silk, but when my eyes fluttered open I found myself on a beach. The sand felt like rose petals, and it smelled like them too. Waves of ecstasy flowed throughout my entire body as someone behind me ran their lips and tongue up my back and breathed softly against the nape of my neck.

"More," I murmured.

He flipped me over in one swift movement. I gasped as I came face to face with the kraken. We weren't underwater anymore. He wasn't a massive, towering, creature of the sea. He was human, not much bigger or taller than me, but his eyes were still enchanting, and my gods, he was still breathtaking.

He hovered over me. One of his muscular arms was braced in the sand while the other was wrapped around my waist, his strong fingers kneading my hip. I ran my hands through his long dreadlocks, pulling him closer to me.

"Enjoy this," he whispered. "I will do things to you no mortal ever could."

I nodded and his warm lips closed over mine. His physical form might have been proportionate to mine, but his power was larger than life. His tongue circled mine so masterfully that I didn't have to make any effort. He was in full control of our kiss. He teased my lips with the tip of his tongue then traveled down to my neck.

I sighed, closing my eyes. I don't know how, but gradually he kissed me in multiple places at the same time. His hands were everywhere: my lips, face, neck, shoulders, wrists, fingers, chest, stomach, hips, and thighs. It was as if he had invisible extensions of himself that could pleasure my entire body simultaneously. I needed him closer to me. I needed so much more of him. I raked my fingers down his back and he bit my shoulder. We clawed, kissed, and rolled around together.

"More," I begged again.

He pulled my hair, yanking my head back. He sucked on my neck until I felt like we were floating.

I whispered the only thought in my hazy mind. "I'm in heaven."

My eyes snapped open. *No. I'm in Harte.*

My fingers were tangled in his dreadlocks. I pulled them free and stared at my hands as the kraken continued kissing me. What was I doing? I loved Treygan.

"Please stop," I gasped, but I didn't sound convincing.

The kraken grinned at me as his hand crept between my thighs, making me moan and thrust my hips again.

Just a few more minutes, I thought. It felt too good to stop. It wouldn't be fair to me or him. We wanted each other so badly. We were already so worked up. We had to finish what we started.

His deep voice dripped with passion. "I can give you everything you desire."

I purred in response.

"Yes," he whispered, snaking his sinewy body against mine. "Give yourself to me, angel mermaid."

Mermaid. I was so much more than a mermaid. And I had a name. A name he didn't even know. Why was I letting a stranger do these things to me? I had never been so out of control with lust. I had to pull myself together.

I tried pushing him off me, but his dozens of invisible tongues and fingers whirled into action more intensely. My head spun. My toes curled. My loins ached, screaming for more of him. I wanted it. I wanted him. It was time to take what I wanted.

I sang. My siren song spilled out of me like a damn breaking.

He pulled back and gaped at me. A momentary wince of confusion swept across his face, but then his eyes glassed over and I saw my own reflection in them. My hair rose like flames around my head and my eyes glowed white. A ring of fire circled us, formed by my own burning desire.

I wrapped my legs tightly around him, yanking him hard against me as I lifted us into the air. In an isolated, quiet place in my mind, logic reminded me I had no wings, but my siren power pushed the limitation away. I didn't need wings to fly. We were fueled by rapture.

I had a kraken locked between my thighs. And I was going to feed on his soul.

I sang another seductive riff and lifted his chin. He was so dark, so delectable. The taste of him still lingered on my lips, reminding me how satisfying his soul would taste.

"What are you?" He dipped his head forward, trying to kiss me again.

I smiled seductively. "I'm a sea monster who is about to devour you."

"Devour me," he whispered.

I bit into his bottom lip, kissing him so hard we swirled through the air. He groaned so loud it shook the sky around us. I swallowed the first sip of his blood and moaned at the flurry of memories. Together, we spiraled into a dark world of beautiful delirium.

He had seduced hoards of women. He had been the source of endless ecstasy. Not one female ever struggled or denied him. They craved him, and blissfully thanked him afterward, begging for a next time. Countless women devoted themselves to him, physically fighting each other for his attention and affection. And here I was, removing so many memories of them from his mind. It didn't matter. They were his playthings. And being played with by him was more than enough for them.

My feeding was cut short as my head and arms, were ripped backward.

We were back in the ocean. My legs were still wrapped around his torso, but his human limbs had turned into tentacles. His dreadlocks were replaced by coral again. He was much taller than me, but nowhere near as big as the mountain-sized creature I first encountered.

You're a siren, he mentally communicated. *And a mermaid?*

My selkie claws shot through my fingers. I leaned forward until our faces were inches apart. For the first time ever, a coat of soft white fur formed on my chest and shoulders. I rubbed against him, purring in his ear. *And a selkie.*

He lowered his head, rubbing his lips against my silky coat.

I pulled his face away, needing to see the look in his eyes when I showed him my last surprise. *And last but not least, I'm human.*

I morphed into human form. Warmth spread through me as one of his tentacles wrapped tightly around my waist. Two other tentacles caressed me, tracing every inch of the curves and contours of my naked human body.

He's not worthy of you, my exquisite kraken said.

Who isn't?

One of the kraken's tentacles rose, holding a limp, unconscious body. I tried to recall his name. *Treygan?*

The kraken lowered Treygan to his side. *Stay with me. You and I could be the most powerful couple in all the worlds.*

I can't. My gaze drifted to Treygan, trying to remember something important. *I love him.*

Love is an illusion that never lasts. What we have is primal.

His offer shouldn't have been so tempting, but it was. Why?

I morphed back into sea monster form, trying to focus my bleary thoughts. *No, this is only lust.*

His smoldering eyes caused my body to erupt with more tingling. *Lust is more powerful than love.*

It took me a minute to force my next sensible thought. *I don't believe that.*

He grinned. *Give it time. You will come back to me.*

The kraken might have been sexy as hell—literally—but he was an idiot if he thought I would return to Harte. *Not a chance.*

His grip around my waist tightened and we rose to the surface. A small raft that looked like it had been made from pieces of ship wreckage floated inches from us. He released me and nodded at it. "Use the raft to safely find your way. When you're ready, it will carry you back to me."

"You're letting me go?"

"You'll return."

I had expected a fight. I had no idea how I would fight a kraken, but I never expected him to just let me go so easily. "I don't want to lie to you. I won't come back."

"We've shared ourselves with each other. We're part of each other now. You won't be able to resist the memory of me. Someday, you will surrender to your desire and return to me for eternity."

My hallmarks swirled through my skin. I missed the kraken already and I hadn't left him yet. Would I think about him once I was gone from here? No. I loved Treygan.

Good gods, how could I tell Treygan the truth about what happened? Would he ever forgive me? Would I run back to the kraken if Treygan no longer wanted me?

I couldn't think that way. Treygan and I could survive anything. I did not love this dark, intoxicating creature.

"Will you give him to me?" I asked hesitantly.

The kraken lifted Treygan to the surface then pushed him into my open arms. "He will never be worthy of you."

The kraken leaned across Treygan's limp body and kissed me so deeply my head spun. I had to get away from him. I had to stop letting him kiss me and touch me. What was wrong with me? Kissing someone else with Treygan passed out in my arms. I was despicable.

"When you're ready," the kraken said, pulling the raft closer, "you know how to find me."

I lifted Treygan onto the raft and pumped my tail, swimming us away from the kraken as fast as I could.

He whispered, "See you soon," but I heard his words as if he had breathed them into my ear.

I silently prayed he wasn't right.

Darkness fell over us like a heavy cloak dropped out of the sky. The waves stopped breaking on the shore. My claws sprang free, ready for anything. I held my hand up in front of my face. Not even a shimmer from my claws—just pure pitch black.

"Vienna?"

She breathed steadily a few feet away. "What?"

"Why is it so dark?"

"It happens frequently. Right before they throw a new scenario at me."

My hearing had gone into hyper alert mode. I kept turning my head, trying to pick up on any and all sounds. "Scenario?"

"Mm," she mumbled in acknowledgment.

I stood. "We should stay together. Would it be okay if I came closer to you?"

"Are you scared?"

"Honestly, a little, yes."

Vienna huffed. "No selkie would be afraid of the dark."

"In Rathe, that would be true. There, the dark is comforting, calming, and there's always magic in the air. But this place would scare anyone. The dark makes it worse."

I sensed her stand up. Her footsteps in the sand grew louder until I felt grains shift beneath my feet.

"Boo." She was so close to me her breath blew in my face. It didn't even smell bad. How was that possible?

I didn't move away. I ached to lean in and kiss her, but I would probably end up getting clawed to shreds if I tried.

She pressed one finger into my chest. "Sometimes it's better that you can't see the ghosts and monsters lurking in the dark."

My heart sped up. I didn't know if it was from fear of what might happen around us or excitement because of our close proximity to each other. "I always prefer to see what I'm dealing with."

She laughed quietly, almost menacingly. "You have no idea the horrible things I've seen here. The nightmares I've had to live through." She paused. "Actually, you probably do know. You helped create them."

"I would never." I reached for her, but then stopped. She still thought I was a demon or imposter. Energy radiated between our hands. I didn't need to see. I could feel how close I was to touching her.

The ground started vibrating. Vienna pulled back. "And another round begins."

"Another round of what?"

"You know what."

The sand turned solid. "I don't, Vienna. Tell me what's happening."

"You should be scared of the light. You want to know what's happening? I'll show you, *Rownan*." I had never heard her speak my name with such venom. A dim light formed in front of her. As it got brighter I realized she was holding a jellyfish the size of my head.

"Where did you—?" I didn't finish my question. I was silenced by fright.

Black moths swarmed around us so thick they looked like a moving wall. The beach we had been standing on had turned to ice. Huge bugs and snakes slithered beneath the surface, pooling into writhing shadows under our feet.

A much bigger shadow caught my attention a few steps away. I recognized the shape of a selkie tail and ran toward it. I couldn't make out a face, but it was a male selkie trapped under the ice. I dropped to my knees, placing my hands flat above him. He flipped over and pressed his face to the ice. His eyes were wide and terrified. He was *me*.

He tried to scream, but water rushed into his mouth. I jerked backward, trembling. "That's not me."

Another body floated under my feet. Her long, black hair pressed against the ice first. I shook my head before she flipped over. *She's not Vienna*, I told myself. She rolled over, clawing at the ice as her pale face smashed against it. Her eyes were bleeding blue blood. I cringed and looked away, focusing on the real Vienna.

She just stood there, holding the glowing jellyfish, watching me with an aloof expression on her face.

"This isn't real," I said.

"The fear is real," she whispered.

I moved toward her. A hole in the ice opened and dozens of snakes and insects skittered onto the ice, forcing me back again. "You don't seem scared."

She grinned, but it was a tired, couldn't-be-bothered grin. "Because nothing changes. I always end up back on the beach of bones. Alone and physically unharmed. Death would be better than this. But death never comes."

Black snow fell between us. Or so I thought. Until I looked closer and saw it was millions of black moths pelting the ice. The ground below us started cracking.

I shielded my face with my arm as I pushed through the waterfall of moths. They stung my skin like each one was a razorblade. A crack in the ice splintered and spread apart, forming a gap between us. I leaped over the steaming opening and landed near Vienna, but she jumped to the other side.

The two masses of ice drifted farther apart. I jumped again, but barely made it across the gap. My upper body hit the ice ledge, knocking the wind out of me. My lower body hung over the bottomless pit below. My legs felt like they were on fire even though there were no flames. I clawed at the ice, trying to pull myself back onto land.

"V, help me."

She flinched, but then her face hardened. She backed away and threw the jellyfish into the black abyss below me. I watched it fall, its glowing light fading as it fell farther and farther. Then I lost my grip and slipped, tumbling through the pitch black fire that I was certain would consume my body and soul.

I felt the sand against the side of my face before I opened my eyes.

Vienna sat across from me, her arms wrapped around her legs, and her lips pursed and twisted to one side. "It's almost believable."

I blinked and carefully brushed grains of sand out of my eyelashes before sitting up. We were back on the beach of bones. It was light out. No ice. No bugs or moths. Had I dreamed that entire nightmare? "What's almost believable?"

"You." She rested her chin on top of her knees. "That you could really be Rownan."

Assuring her I was truly me hadn't worked so far. If I let her talk out her thoughts, maybe she would convince herself. "Why is that?"

"Every other time, after every other scenario, I've ended up back here alone. That's how it started. After the very first Rownan. After I deliberately crashed our boat into that mountain and he was swallowed by those creatures, and I woke up here."

"Why'd you crash the boat?"

"He said it was the gateway home, but it wasn't. I knew it was some sort of portal to an even worse part of this place."

"How'd you know?"

"Instinct."

I nodded. "You've always had sharp instincts."

"You all try to take me deeper into this hell hole, but I won't fall for it. I know what the real gate looks like." She rubbed her shell between her fingers, hugged her knees to her chest, and closed her eyes. "And now I have no reason to leave this beach. Ever."

"Tell me about the Rownan you were with for two years." I glanced at the piece of driftwood a few yards away. At least she had been leaving it for longer periods of time.

"No bad things happened when he was around. That's how I knew he was real."

"That didn't seem strange to you?"

"Did what seem strange?"

I rubbed my hand over my goatee. "That nothing bad ever happened. In hell."

"That's how it always was with Rownan. He didn't let bad things happen to me." She stared off at the ocean. "To us."

Guilt knotted my stomach and heart together into one tangled mess of sadness. "Except for the day Rathe's gate closed."

She flashed me a smoldering glare. "You don't know the whole story."

That was the worst part of it. I did know the whole story. And I hated that Rownan—that part of me—for hurting her, for leaving her alone. I let a horrible thing happen to her. To us.

We sat silent, watching each other. That was enough for me. Just being near her again was more than I expected when I first heard she had gone to Harte.

This place was evil, but the scenario we had just suffered through didn't harm us. We were back where we started, physically fine. I could endure any nightmare if I knew I would always end up back at Vienna's side. I had no grand plan to get us home to Rathe. No way to convince her I wasn't a fraud. So I just sat there, enjoying her presence.

But after a long time of listening to nothing but waves, I missed her voice. "Tell me more about the time you and the first Rownan crashed the boat."

I held out the shard of mirror. "This is a piece of—"

"The all-seeing mirror," Lloyd finished.

"How did you know?"

He pointed up at one of his wall panels. "I have some all-knowing devices of my own."

I eyed the carvings, not understanding what he was talking about. Maybe his poor health had made him senile. I tried handing him the mirror again. "You were a gorgon. Can you see anything when you look into it?"

"Maybe I could, if the powers that be hadn't taken my sight from me."

"What?" His eyes were gray and cloudy. How had I missed that? "Lloyd, I'm sorry."

"Meh." He waved it off like being able to see wasn't important. "Probably best I can't see what it might show. If I saw Yara or either of my sons suffering, I'd probably rush into that world like the glutton for punishment that I am."

I doubted Lloyd could even get out of bed. He wasn't rushing anywhere, no matter how badly he wanted to. I tossed the mirror onto the blanket near his feet. "I broke the mirror and angered Stheno and Euryale for nothing. Splendid."

Lloyd took a breath to speak, but ended up coughing and wheezing. Indrea placed her hands on his chest and his coughing calmed, but not much. Caspian placed his hands on top of Indrea's, and Lloyd breathed normally again.

"Thanks," Lloyd said to them. "But don't waste your energy on me."

"We can at least help calm it," Caspian told him.

Lloyd nodded. "As I was saying, a gorgon must activate the mirror, but I've heard any sea creature can use it to view our worlds."

My head snapped up. "You mean you could make it work and I could see Yara in Harte?" Indrea and Caspian looked hopeful too.

"I can give it a shot," Lloyd said. "But it being broken might put a kink in things."

"It's just as good as having the whole mirror," I assured him.

"Why would you think that?"

"I don't know why. I just do." Somehow, something—maybe a sixth sense—told me the mirror would help me figure out how to help Yara. I believed that with every part of me.

Lloyd held out his hands, motioning for me to give him the mirror. I gently laid it in his hand. "Careful. It's sharp."

He closed his weary eyes and chanted a bunch of gibberish I didn't understand. The mirror, which had been showing a reflection of the ceiling fan above Lloyd's bed, fogged over as he breathed on it. Its surface rippled up like miniature waves which spread like a parting sea. A still lake formed in the middle of the waves, changing from silver to black. What started as two faint clouds slowly solidified into Yara and Treygan.

"Are they dead?" I whispered, a lump forming in my throat.

"What do you see?" Lloyd asked.

"Yara and Treygan are sprawled out on the ground with their eyes closed." Indrea leaned closer, squinting. "They don't look injured, or even sick. Just … motionless."

Yara's wings were flaccid behind her. "Her wings look fine. So, what was the searing pain in my back about?"

Caspian shook his head. "I don't understand any of this."

"Show us Rownan," I told Lloyd.

He chanted the same incantation again. Treygan and Yara's image faded and Rownan came into view. "He looks the same as Yara and Treygan," I reported to Lloyd. "Passed out on a beach of some sort, but no sign of injuries."

"I'd like to summon a view of Vienna," Lloyd said. "Will you tell me what you see?"

My heart felt heavy as a stone. I nodded, but realized Lloyd couldn't see me. "Yes, of course."

Lloyd chanted, but just as he said Vienna's name Otabia burst into the room.

"Fools!" she squawked. "You're wasting your time." I didn't peel my eyes away from the mirror until Otabia said, "Nothing is as it seems in Harte."

"What does that mean?" I asked her. "And how would you know?"

Mariza danced seductively around a stiff Otabia. "Otabia knows all about the only soul to survive Harte." She ran her talon-like nails down her sister's arm. "Secrets, secrets. My, how they fester."

Otabia turned and snapped her teeth at Mariza. "You annoying harpy. Shut your beak before I break it."

I stepped away from the mirror. "Otabia, what do you know about the merman who escaped from Harte?"

"I know he's none of your business."

I stomped over to her. "Tell me what you know or I'll claw it out of you."

Otabia cawed with anger. Mariza smiled and shrieked, excited by the argument.

My wings spread wide and I let out a screech that muffled their annoying racket. "Both of you shut up!"

I grabbed Otabia by her neck, lifting her off her feet. Her black boots kicked the air as she tried breaking free of my grip. My wings rippled behind me and the candle on Lloyd's nightstand roared to life. "You tell me now, or so help me gods, I will poison you when you least expect it and let you die a long, slow, and miserable death.”

Mariza laughed and clapped her hands.

“You’ll be next,” I told Mariza. She stiffened and shut up.

Lloyd called out from his bed. “Nothing is as it seems. He told me that too. He said Harte preyed on his fears, played tricks with his mind and soul until he didn’t know reality anymore, or if he was even still himself. He worried he had left his true self in Harte.”

“What?” I loosened my grip on Otabia’s throat, but when she tried to slip free again, I tightened it and pinned her against the wall. Her black lips parted, trying to speak. Her eyes bulged so wide they looked like they might pop out and fly across the room. I let her go and she fell into a heap on the ground, rubbing her neck and taking deep breaths.

“You’ll pay for that,” she uttered.

“You’ll pay a lot more than me if you don’t start telling me what you know. How dare you keep such a crucial secret from me! I’m your sister!”

“I kept it a secret for your safety. You aren’t strong enough to go into Harte!”

“I’m not going there! But you could have told Yara what you knew. She would have had a much better chance of coming back alive.”

“No,” Otabia hissed. “That’s just it. No one who goes in can get out on their own.”

“Liar! The merman did. He lived and came back to tell about it.”

Otabia’s nostrils flared as she straightened. “Because *I* made the mistake of going there and bringing him back.”

I stopped breathing. Caspian and Indrea gasped.

Lloyd’s head fell back against his headboard. “Ah. Of course.”

Mariza’s eyes were wide, and when they met mine, her focus darted to her feet.

“*You* have been to Harte?” I asked Otabia.

She rolled her shoulders. "You want to know the truth, here it is. I loved him."

"*You* loved a *merman*?" My mind was blown. Otabia didn't love anyone but herself.

"I knew we couldn't be together," she began. "We were different species. It was forbidden. I broke his heart, even though I loved him. I denied his affections to protect him. I broke him so badly that he threw himself into Harte. I had to get him out of there. Or so I thought. What I didn't know, what I couldn't have known, was how awful that place truly is. That no soul will ever be right again after they have been inside." She stared at the floor. "Including me."

I felt her heartache, but I needed to focus on Yara. "How did you get him out?"

"I flew him out. It's the only way. The only two gateways are in the sky. Well, the sky is more like a waterless ocean above the ground. As I said, nothing is as it seems. Once a creature enters, unless they can fly, they can never exit."

I stated the obvious. "Like Yara."

Otabia shook her head. "She'd never be able to fly."

"I just saw her. Her wings are fine."

"That place has broken her spirit by now. She will believe she is doomed, therefore she will be. Her body—"

"No," I said through clenched teeth. "Yara is stronger than that."

"No soul stands a chance in Harte. I was almost consumed, and I wasn't there nearly as long as they have been. I still have nightmares. I'm still lured back in my dreams. I still question reality at times."

"How long were you there?" Indrea asked.

"Minutes," Otabia replied. "The longest, most agonizing, most dangerous few minutes of my life."

"She's been damaged goods ever since," Mariza added. My attention snapped to her. She knew too? Of course she knew. She and Otabia had been together since their creation. Mariza strutted closer to me. "Why do you think we crave such dark and lustful experiences? Haven't you ever questioned our greedy appetites? Wondered why we subject so many men to our wrath, or why we steal entire souls instead of just consuming a memory or two?"

I glanced between Otabia and Mariza. "We're sirens. It's our nature."

Otabia smirked. "It's lustful greed. I unleashed an appetite that will never be satisfied. All because I went to Harte."

"You're not strong enough to enter Harte," Mariza told me. "Even if you were, so much light still exists in you. That place would fill you with darkness, just like it did to Otabia. As much as we fight with you, you are our sister, and we don't want to lose you."

"Even if you did survive," Otabia added. "We don't want you to be as dark and ravenous as us."

It would have been touching if my mind wasn't racing a million knots a minute.

"You didn't know when you went to Harte, right?" I asked Otabia. "You didn't know the dark would become part of you?"

"No. I thought it was something outside of myself. I didn't realize it was a part of me waiting to be awakened."

"But I do know. I won't let it awaken that side of me. I'll fight it."

"There is no fighting it." Otabia sighed. "It's more powerful than you can imagine."

I stared into Otabia's big black eyes for what felt like eternity. The room was so quiet you could hear a feather drop. "I'm going in to get them."

"Them?" Otabia's eyes widened.

"Yara, Treygan, Rownan, and Vienna."

"No you are not," Mariza said through clenched teeth

Otabia's black wings rose high and wrapped around me. "You're mad. Saving Yara alone would take so much time the dark would consume you. It would be impossible to save all of them. Impossible."

"Maybe impossible for you, but I can do it."

Mariza screeched with rage outside the wall of Otabia's wings. "We'll be hurt by this too! We'll feel whatever you feel. You're risking us all turning even darker."

I pushed Otabia away from me, prying my way out of her wings. "I'd say I'm sorry, but I'm not. I won't leave Yara in Harte." I walked over to the bed and held Lloyd's hand. "I won't leave any of them there."

Lloyd squeezed my hand and lowered his head.

"We will tie you down!" Mariza cawed. "Cage you if needed. We won't allow this to happen."

"We can't stop her. No one could have stopped me." Otabia lifted her black eyes, and for the first time in a long time, she looked at me with worry and maybe—impossible as it seemed—love. Her shoulders slumped. "You probably won't make it out, but in case you do, I'll tell you where I went wrong so you don't make the same mistake."

Treygan's eyes fluttered open.

"Oh, thank gods." I hugged him so tight his ribs smashed against mine.

He glanced around at the water surrounding us, then at our raft. "Where are we? What happened?"

Treygan had been passed out for a while. While sitting beside him and praying he would wake up, I had stewed with guilt and self-loathing for what I had done with the kraken. I wanted to believe I had been tricked, caught up in some powerful trance where I had no control over what I did, but that seemed like a cop-out. I should have said no. I should have fought the kraken, not indulged in a steamy make-out session with him.

"Where's your suit and gear?" Treygan smoothed down my hair, cradling my face in his hand and checking me for injuries. My hallmarks were a mix of blue, gray, and green—sadness, anger, and shame. "Are you okay?"

"Okay is a very subjective term in this place."

He cracked a smile, but worry tugged it down into a frown again. "How long was I out?"

I shrugged. "I've lost track of time."

His brow lifted and he scanned the river we were floating down. The land was covered in flames. We had no choice but to stay in the river, out of the burning inferno on either side of us.

"Let me try shadowing Rownan," Treygan said. "If he has stayed awake, he'll be a better judge of how long we've been here."

Treygan slipped away into shadow mode. I fidgeted with my hands, cursing them for touching the kraken so intimately. I cringed at the memory of my nails raking down his back. How could I ever tell Treygan what I had done? He'd never forgive me.

"Strange." Treygan's voice startled me. "I saw him and Vienna, but it was like looking at them through a sheet of ice."

"Nothing here surprises me anymore," I murmured.

He lifted my chin. "Hey, talk to me. Something has you upset. What happened while I was unconscious?"

"We're in hell. And it's beating us every step of the way. You don't want to know what happened while you were out because it's so heinous that you'll never look at me the same."

"Yara, I expected heinous. Actually, I expected a lot worse than what we've endured so far. You can tell me anything, and I will still look at you the same. If anything, I'll be proud of you for surviving whatever you had to face."

"Proud of me?" I laughed like a crazy person. I sounded maniacal, even to myself. For the first time since he woke, I really looked at him. He said we could survive anything, so we would see if he really meant it. "You were pulled underwater by a—" I paused, flinching at the change in his eyes.

"By a what?" he asked.

I couldn't think about anything except how different he looked. "Your eyes are darker. They aren't as blue as they used to be."

"I was promoted to Indigo. Of course my eyes would darken."

"Oh."

He pulled back. "It's amazing how one word can be filled with so much disappointment. My tail and hair darkened. You had to have known my eyes would turn indigo too."

I eyed him skeptically. What if he wasn't the real Treygan? The kraken could have swapped him for an imposter. What if he was the kraken in the form of Treygan?

As if reading my mind, he opened his jacket and pulled his arm out, showing me the branded words. "It's me, Yara. Only my eyes have changed." I glanced away, but he held my hand, pulling my attention back to him. "I'm still me."

"It's just … they were such a pretty blue."

He let go of my hand. "You don't like my eyes now that they're a different color? That seems a bit shallow."

"You're misunderstanding. It's not that I don't like them. But my first time sharing your soul was such a life-changing experience for me. The strongest part of my memory of that event was your intense blue eyes. It makes me sad to think I'll never look into your eyes and see them that same way again."

"I'm sorry, but it's not like I can change them back." His voice grew louder and irritated. "I loved your gold tail. Most of my memories of us together are when your tail was gold and your hair was yellow, but I don't throw that in your face."

A dull pain ached in my chest. "You liked me better as a Yellow?"

"I didn't say that." His nostrils flared. "I wouldn't have even brought it up if you hadn't mentioned that you don't like my eyes."

"I didn't say I don't like them."

"You're implying it."

"I don't imply things. I say exactly how I feel. You of all people should know that."

He turned away from me and stared at the river for a painful few seconds of silence. "Can we please stop arguing? Neither one of us can change how we look."

"So, you *did* like me better as a Yellow?"

Treygan let out a frustrated sigh and raked his fingers through his hair. "That's not what I said." He turned around and leaned close to me. "You are beautiful. Yellow, white, or polka-dotted, you are and always will be beautiful in my eyes—no matter what color they turn."

I sat there, staring at him. Gorgeous as he was, it occurred to me that one day, eventually, he would become a Violet. His eyes would turn purple. What if they were light purple like Indrea's? He would look totally different. I felt horrible for even thinking I might not be as attracted to him if he was a Violet, but the thought kept tugging at me. I wanted him to stay the same Blue I fell in love with. I didn't want to think about how Treygan might change again. None of it mattered anyway. We'd never leave Harte.

"What now?" he asked. "Your forehead is wrinkled which means you're thinking intensely about something you don't want to think about."

How could he know me so well? I didn't want to talk about it anymore. "I'm fine."

"And there's another one."

"Another what?"

"Another lie."

I stiffened.

"Did you think I'd never figure it out?" he snapped. "You've lied at least three times since your transformation. How long were you going to hide *that* ability from me?"

I fumbled for an explanation. "I didn't … I thought maybe …."

"You negotiated for it, didn't you? When you met Medusa. You actually requested the ability to lie again."

I lowered my guilty eyes.

"Most sea creatures don't live a shallow existence," Treygan said, "but apparently our new leader insisted upon it."

"I requested that ability to protect you!"

"Protect me? From the truth? I don't ever want to be protected from the truth!"

"You don't know that." The kraken's kisses flashed through my mind again.

Treygan turned his back to me. "Pride, wrath, greed, we're being sucked in by every type of sin."

Don't forget lust. I hated Harte. I hated what it was doing to us.

We drifted for what must have been miles past fire, ice, and crumbling mountains, but we never saw another living soul. I was so exhausted I collapsed, lying flat on my back.

Treygan turned around. His voice was still cold. "Are you okay?"

"Weak and lightheaded. And I'm so hot." I reached into the water, splashing my arms and face. "Even the water is too warm."

He leaned closer and wiped sweat from my brow. "It is sweltering." He stripped off his jacket the rest of the way and draped it around my shoulders. "Put that on. It will help cool you down."

I gratefully accepted and slid it on. The rubbery material cooled my arms and torso, but sweat still seeped out of the rest of my skin. "Are we floating in the right direction? Toward Rownan?"

"I'm not sure. My senses are off and I'm disoriented." Treygan scanned the raft and river. "Maybe we should swim. It would be faster."

"No," I practically shouted, picturing the kraken lurking below us. "Let's stay out of the water." I could tell Treygan wanted to ask me why, but he didn't. He knew I was keeping secrets from him. "I'm sorry for lying. I'd never lie unless it was to keep you from being hurt."

His eyes met mine, softening more the longer he stared at me. He wrapped his arms around me and kissed my head. I thought about how his embrace dulled in comparison to the kraken's. And I hated myself for it.

I drifted in and out of a hazy cloud of worry, guilt, anger, and a dozen other negative emotions. Occasionally, I would think of Rownan and Vienna and remember our mission, but mostly I just wanted to slither off the raft and drown myself for being such a weak and awful person.

My pinky was hooked around Treygan's. That's as much skin to skin contact as we could handle because we were so miserably hot. I was lying in a pool of my own sweat, but I didn't have enough energy to move to a drier spot on the raft.

Treygan let go of me and rolled over, splashing into the water. My fingers reached for him, but that was all I could muster. I didn't even have the strength to sit up.

He surfaced and draped his arms over the edge of the raft, dropping his head onto his forearm. "I needed water."

I managed to nod.

"You should get in too. It helps. Not much, but some."

"No," I mumbled. I didn't want to ever dip foot or fin in the kraken's ocean again.

"This river seems never-ending. I don't know where it's taking us. We need a plan. Maybe swim somewhere."

"Just leave me."

Treygan stretched forward, relinking his wet pinky with mine. "Not a chance."

"What if we surrender to it?"

"Surrender to what?"

I struggled to take a big breath, knowing it would take so much energy to say everything I was thinking. "The darkness. People who are insane don't know they're insane. They live in their own reality. We could exist the same way." My lips felt heavy. My words slurred. "If we don't remember a different world, if we don't remember light and love exist somewhere else, we'd be content."

"You're talking nonsense because you're dehydrated," Treygan said. "We're going to get out of here."

"I don't want to fight anymore."

"You're exhausted. I am too, but we have to keep going until we find a way out."

"No one has ever found their way out." I closed my eyes, lured into the enticing darkness. "And stayed sane."

"No one has ever died, negotiated a deal with Medusa and Poseidon, and been given a second chance at life either, but you pulled that off. Finding a way out of here should be simple compared to that."

"My wings are gone. Even if we find the gate …" I was too tired to finish.

"We'll find another way."

"And if there is no other way?"

He ran his fingers through my hair. "Then we hang in there until someone comes for us."

"No one would come *with* us. No one will come for us either."

"They'll come for you," Treygan said. "You're too important."

"I'm no one. I'm a fluke."

He pulled himself onto the raft and laid so close to me our noses almost touched. "You're everything. You're my happily ever after, and our story is not going to end here. I won't let it."

I didn't have enough energy to argue anymore.

His thumb caressed my cheek. "You and I are going to put all the storybooks to shame." Treygan shook me until my eyes opened. I didn't even realize they had closed. "Let's play the game where I write a message on your body and you tell me what it says."

I mustered a nod.

His finger glided down my leg as he wrote *never give up*.

I dreamed a dozen dreams, but they weren't mine.

I was Treygan as a child, playing games with other children, climbing a glacier with a teenage version of Rownan, sharing a sundae with him and Vienna, extreme jet-skiing with Delmar, even watching myself as a child build sandcastles on the beach at

Uncle Lloyd's house. I was full of happiness and hope. I hardly had a care in the world.

A wave of water crashed over me. Or I was sinking. I opened my eyes and discovered both of my assumptions were wrong. Treygan had shoved me under a waterfall.

"Snap out of it," he shouted, pulling me out of the downpour. "We're here."

I shook my head, trying to reorient myself. "Were you sharing your memories with me?"

"You were in a very dark place. Your soul needed some positive emotions poured into it."

I did feel better. Not completely like myself, and I was still dismally aware that we were in Harte and would probably never get out, but I wasn't feeling suicidal like when we were on the raft.

"This is it." Treygan pointed at a towering rock cliff.

"Rownan is up there?"

"And Vienna."

"You're sure?"

"Positive."

I wanted to contribute something to this rescue. Since my wings had been ripped off and Sage was killed, I felt useless. The least I could do was control water and lift us up the cliff.

"I've got this one," I told Treygan.

I held my hands to my sides, wiggling my fingers and trying to summon the power to make the waterfall reverse its flow upward, but nothing happened.

Treygan watched me for a minute then tried helping me. Neither of us caused even a tug in the waterfall.

I slapped the falls in frustration. "Our powers aren't working in this hellhole!"

"We'll climb it," Treygan said.

"Climb it? How?"

"Use your selkie claws. They're as strong as picks."

I tried unsheathing my claws, but nothing happened. "My claws aren't working either."

He faced the steep rocks and started climbing. "Then we use pure strength and determination."

Great. Two things I had hardly any of. I planted one foot on a rock and heaved myself up. Each advance upward made my muscles burn. By the time we had reached the halfway point, the skin on my hands felt like it had been ripped off. If only we still had our gloves.

After a while I made the mistake of looking down. We were up so high the ground beneath us swayed. I stared at the rocks in front of my face, trying to push away the dizziness rushing through me.

"We're almost there," Treygan assured me. He was beside me, looking much more comfortable and confident than I felt.

I nodded and watched him climb higher. His muscles visibly trembled from overexertion. Worried, I called out to him. "Be careful!"

His foot slipped. Pieces of rock crumbled around my head, and in what felt like slow motion, Treygan's body fell past me.

I reached out just in time, catching his forearm and squeezing for dear life. My hand slipped down his wet skin until our hands connected. With my other hand, I clung to a rock ledge so hard my fingers felt like they were breaking.

"Don't let go!" I grunted, trying to swing him closer to the wall.

A familiar screeching from the sky sent shivers down my spine. *Please no, not now,* I mentally begged, clamping my eyes shut tight. I knew it was a soul sucker. I couldn't look at it or fear would make me weaker.

"Swing me one more time," Treygan yelled. "Just a little closer and I can grab the wall."

Sweat poured down my face and back. My hand felt more slippery the longer I held on to him. My muscles burned ferociously, but I dug deep, summoning the last bit of strength I didn't have. I swung him one more time.

I screamed bloody murder when he slipped out of my grasp.

Yara waded out of the water and onto the beach, gasping for breath. "Thank goodness, I found you." She desperately hugged me then tried to kiss me, but I turned my face and her lips caught my chin. "Treygan is dead."

I held her at arm's length, still in shock from the sight of her. "I thought both of you were dead."

"No, but Treygan's gone and we need to get out of here."

Treygan really was gone. I felt the pain of losing him all over again. Yara's focus was locked on me. After all we had risked coming to Harte to find Vienna, Yara didn't even glance in her direction. "Yara, this is Vienna."

Vienna wrapped her arms around herself, watching us.

Yara still didn't acknowledge her. "Did you tell her about us?"

"What?"

"Did you tell Vienna it's over between the two of you and that you love me?"

I stepped away from her. "What the hell are you talking about?" I turned to Vienna, but she was already walking away. "Vienna, she's lying." I gaped at Yara. "Why would you say something like that?"

Yara grabbed my hand. "You know how much I love you. You said you wanted to be with me."

"You're crazy!" I yanked free from her grip. "V, she's lying. She loves Treygan. They were a couple."

"What?" Yara gasped, acting appalled. "I would never be with a merman. I'm a selkie."

Vienna sat beside her driftwood, petting it as she watched us.

"You're mer *and* selkie," I reminded Yara. "And siren, and gorgon, and human."

"Both of you get off my beach!" Vienna shouted.

"I'm not going anywhere," I said. "Yara, get the hell away from us. This place has made you crazy. My brother hasn't even been dead for a day and you're claiming you never loved him?"

"We're running out of time." Yara gripped my hand so tight I flinched. "The third sunset is happening in a couple of hours. We'll be trapped here if we don't leave right now."

Could that be true? Had three days passed already? Or was this another trick?

Trick. My chin jutted forward, realizing what I was dealing with. "You aren't Yara. There's no way Yara would ever act this way or say that about Treygan."

Yara's imposter sprang forward, but I was ready. In one swift move I pierced her through the heart with the claws of my free hand. She laughed, hanging from my hand, kicking like a crazed doll. She spit black dust into my face. The sand below her dangling feet parted and sucked her away.

I stepped back, watching the sand shift and seal the opening. "I knew that wasn't her," I told Vienna. "The real Yara and Treygan died."

"The *real* Yara and Treygan," Vienna snickered.

A blood-curdling scream rang through the air. I ran to the other side of the beach where it dropped off into a deep canyon.

For a moment I could only make out a head of white hair, but then a dark blue speck came into view. Imposters of Treygan and Yara were climbing the steep rock wall below us.

"Not again," I muttered.

"Who is it this time?" Vienna asked.

"More demons."

They struggled with every move as they climbed up the cliff. I stood back a safe distance as they pulled themselves over the edge and onto our flat beach.

"Really?" Treygan gasped, sprawling onto his back. "Couldn't lend us a hand?"

Yara was on her hands and knees, looking up at us. "Vienna," she said through her pained breaths. She swayed and stammered as she struggled to stand. "Nice to finally meet you."

"Don't be fooled," I warned Vienna. "Keep your distance."

Yara cocked her head. "What?"

The fake Treygan managed to stand up. "Fooled? By us?"

"I know what you are," I snarled at them. "My brother and Yara are dead."

"Oh no." Treygan's head dropped back, lifting to the sky. "Son of a—"

"I hate this place!" Yara punched the air. "Hate it, hate it, hate it!" She looked like a child throwing a tantrum. "Who knows how much time we have left before we're stuck here for eternity with sand-breathing demons, rain that melts our skin off, and sex-crazed krakens, and now *he*," Yara pointed at me, "thinks we're dead."

"Calm down," Treygan told Yara.

"Calm down?" She laughed like a deranged bird. "Why? Rownan is probably going to kill us because he thinks we're evil phonies, and clearly this mission to rejoin the happy couple wasn't successful, because look at them." She swiped her hand at me and Vienna. "They won't go within five feet of each other, and Vienna looks at all of us," she glared pointedly at me, "and I do mean *all* of us, like we're going to burn her at the stake. This story has no sunshine ending. This is it, boys. Welcome to hell. You know what the song says. You can never check out or leave."

Treygan shook his head. "That's not what the song says."

"What?" Yara snapped. "The gorgon merman is correcting the human about human song lyrics?"

"You're only one-fifth human now," Treygan reminded her. "And are you certain all those band members are human?"

Yara gaped at him silently.

In spite of the insane scene taking place, I chuckled. Vienna shot me a scathing look, but I shrugged. "Don't you see? It's really them. No demons would be this unhinged."

I walked over to Treygan and squeezed his shoulders. "I saw you. Both of you were dead in the cave."

"Illusions," Treygan said. "But we did lose Sage to the soul suckers in the sky."

I glanced up. The sky was black but clear. "Those toothy beasts Lloyd warned us about?"

"You didn't see them?"

"No."

"We have to get out of here," Yara insisted. "Now."

"How?" I asked her. "You can't fly."

"We'll retrace our steps and go back the way we came. We'll figure out how to pass through the gate when we get there."

"Past the soul suckers? And, I do believe you mentioned something about a kraken? Doesn't sound like the best plan."

"So, we're just going to camp out here on this carcass-infested beach? Lovely."

Treygan stepped toward Vienna, but she backed away. "Vienna," he said gently. "Come home with us. You don't belong here."

Vienna stared at him coldly without uttering a word.

Treygan looked at me questioningly. I lowered my eyes, unsure of what else to do or say.

He gripped my arm. "Rownan, it's now or never. We have to leave immediately or we'll be trapped here. Forever."

I felt as if I had lost my heart in the years of living without Vienna. Now, after only a short time in Harte, I worried I had lost my mind too. I had to make a decision.

I crouched in front of Vienna. "Please, V, I'm begging you. Come home with me." She shook her head, digging her feet deeper in the sand. "Nothing I can do or say will make you change your mind?"

She whispered two simple but impossible words. "The shell."

I sighed. She thought a piece of driftwood was "the real Rownan." Who knows what the shell could be. I would never remember something she had created in her own Harte-infested mind. "Okay, then. I have to accept that I can't make you leave this place."

A tear streamed down her cheek. I slowly reached up and wiped it away. She'd never let me kiss her, so I kissed my finger that had just touched her cheek, and turned away from her.

Defeated, I walked over to Treygan and Yara. "Harte has warped her mind. She'll never believe I'm really me. She doesn't believe it's possible that I'm still alive. This is her fate. To stay here."

"I'm so sorry, Rownan," Yara whispered.

I nodded, gritting my teeth and flaring my nostrils to try to breathe normally. How had we come so far and failed? I clenched my fists, wanting to punch something, but it wouldn't change anything. This was how it had to end. We were out of time.

"Time to go," I said.

Treygan stared at Vienna over my shoulder. "Vienna, please?"

I glanced back at her as she put her hands over her ears and hummed loudly so she couldn't hear him. "Like I said, it's hopeless."

"You did all you could," Treygan told me. "And then some."

"I know."

Yara reached for my hand and I took it, walking between her and Treygan to the edge of the cliff. We all stared down the steep drop-off.

"How long will it take to climb down?" I asked.

"We can jump," Yara said. "Aim for this side and we'll land in the water."

I nodded, cracking my knuckles. Still denying I was actually making this decision. Hating myself for failing. For dragging so many people I loved into such an awful place.

"Thank you," I told Yara and Treygan. "For coming here and trying. For continuing to search for me after I left you. I'm sorry you had to suffer. I love both of you and I always will."

I shoved Yara off first.

Her arms windmilled, trying to grab on to me as she disappeared over the edge. Treygan's head whipped back and forth between me and Yara as she plummeted, screaming the whole way until she splashed into the water below.

"Why did you do that?" Treygan shouted.

"Go," I told him.

He cocked his chin. His eyes were wide. "You're staying?"

"I have to."

"No, you don't. She's not herself anymore. I can tell just by looking at her. She lost her sanity. It doesn't mean you have to."

"Without her, I lose everything."

"You'd rather stay here in hell for eternity?"

"It will be an eternity with her, so yes."

"Rownan, no. You can't do this."

I tried shoving him off the cliff, but he moved too quickly. We wrestled, grunting and swiping at each other, but a broken heart will overpower a solid one every time. Broken-hearted souls are desperate and reckless because they have nothing to lose.

I muscled Treygan to the ledge. His feet moved in place as pieces of rock broke away beneath him. "I'm not letting go, Rownan."

"I'll never forgive you if you don't."

"I'm willing to take that chance."

"I'm not. Love you, bro." I extended my claws deep into his arms. His one second of shock was all I needed. I pushed him hard to make sure he would clear the cliff during his fall. I watched—more pieces of my heart crumbling into oblivion—as he fell, flailing, then splashed into the water far below me.

When I turned around, Vienna's eyes were wide. "You said that was really them."

"It was."

"Why didn't you go with them?"

"I'm not leaving you. You want to stay here and be insane, then I'll stay and be insane with you." I flopped onto the sand beside her, resolved to stay. The smelly, wretched beach was where we would spend the rest of eternity. Together. Being together was the only thing that mattered to me. "You never really lost me, you know. In my heart, we were never apart. I promised you I'd always find you. And I did. You're stuck with me."

"What did you say?"

"I said you're stuck with me."

Her bottom lip quivered. "Before that. About your promise."

"You were always afraid of losing me. Ever since Gran warned you about our love being so powerful that it would be tested by awful fate. Well, I promised you we would always be together. I made that promise when we were teenagers, and I meant it."

Slowly, she crawled closer to me. She lifted my face with her hands and stared into my eyes. "If it's really you, why can't you tell me what the shell means?"

It hit me like a ton of sand. Vienna crawling toward me like that, and holding my face in her hands, it was the same thing Nixie had done the night I was wasted out of my mind.

"Nixie," I whispered. Vienna flinched, but I held her hands tighter against my face. "I asked Nixie to drain my memories of you."

"What?" Vienna gasped.

"When I thought I couldn't enter Harte, when I thought I'd lost you forever, I drowned myself with liquor then begged Nixie to steal all my memories of you so I wouldn't have to miss you anymore. That must be it! She must have taken my memories of the shell."

"But you remember other things."

"Yes." I nodded fiercely. "She stopped when she felt how much I loved you. She said I had to find you. She refused to devour all trace of a love as rare as ours."

"No siren would be that sentimental."

"Nixie would." I scrambled to my knees. "V, you have to believe me. Nixie took those memories. That's the only reason I don't remember the shell."

She looked skeptical, but then, "Say it. Say your promise the way you always said it."

Something had changed in her. Would my promise be what she needed to hear to make her believe I wasn't an imposter?

I inhaled shakily and stared deep into her eyes, so deep that only she and I existed. Harte and all its ugliness disappeared. "You won't lose me. Even if you do, I'll always find you again."

She pressed her hands to my face as if she was seeing me for the first time. She pawed at me gently, but with so much passion. Every time any part of her hand touched my lips, I kissed it.

"It's you." She smiled as a tear ran down her cheek. "It's really you."

Cradling her head in my hand, I moved her backward until I was lying on top of her. She gazed up at me with so much love I could have died right there and been eternally happy. Her light had returned. I knew without a doubt she was truly seeing *me*. "For the love of gods, I've been waiting for this for nearly two decades. May I *please* kiss you now?"

She nodded enthusiastically. My lips closed over hers.

It didn't matter that we were in Harte. I was home.

I didn't cry when I told the sprites I was going to Harte.

Even when all of them broke down sobbing and begged me not to go, I kept a straight face. Jenna and Keeley had followed me to the outskirts of Echo Bayou, still pleading with me. I told them I would be a disgrace to myself and every sea creature in Rathe if I didn't try to save Yara. I kissed both of them goodbye and never looked back.

Yara stood no chance of leaving Harte without being flown out. None of them did. I had to do the right thing.

Later, I sat in the back of the boat, watching Caspian, Delmar, Pango, and Merrick navigate us to the Triangle. Kimber sat beside me, silent as always. I looked at her and she turned to face me. Her warm, sky blue eyes were such a drastic contrast to her mouth of stone.

"Can I tell you a secret?" I asked her.

She nodded.

"I'm scared."

She placed her hand over mine. Even though she couldn't speak, I felt as if she was telling me it would be okay. Or maybe that was just what I wanted to hear. No one, especially on a boat full of merfolk who were unable to lie, could make me that false promise. But the fact that Caspian, Indrea, Delmar, Kimber, Pango, and Merrick were escorting me to the Triangle did bring me some small sense of comfort.

None of them were going in with me. They couldn't fly, so they would be useless in the rescue mission. Mariza and Otabia refused to help. I would be on my own in Harte.

Indrea was sitting across from us, watching the horizon. The clouds were thickening and turning gray. My throat was dry. I couldn't sit still.

"Indrea." My knees bounced nonstop. "Could you help me calm down?"

She smiled sweetly. "With pleasure."

She bent over me and smoothed down my hair. She didn't need to touch me to calm me. We both knew that, but her nurturing touch helped immensely.

My legs stilled and my heart wasn't racing as fast as it had been. "Thank you."

She sat beside me and held my free hand while Kimber still held the other.

"Words can't express how much I admire your bravery," Indrea said.

"Thanks, but keep the calming juju coming, please."

Indrea nodded, and we sat in silence as we traveled closer to hell.

My last visit to the Triangle just days earlier was very different. Back then, all of nature had been violent and angry. Today the ocean was calm. The fog was still thick and dark, but there was no wind, and no powerful current pulling us in.

"Are you sure this is the right place?" I asked.

Delmar held out a compass so I could see the needle spinning in circles. "This is it. According to our calculations, if you fly east less than one nautical mile you should see it."

I stood with shaky knees. Even Indrea's powers couldn't tame the sick feeling in my stomach.

"Remember," Pango said, "you don't have much time. The sun will set just over an hour from now. Get in and get out. If you can't find them right away, you have to accept that there's nothing more you can do."

Merrick slightly bowed his head as our eyes met. "Don't risk your own soul, Nixie. That's the last thing Yara and Treygan would want."

Delmar gripped my shoulders. "I'm sorry you have to go alone, but we are with you in spirit. We'll be right here waiting for you to return."

Alone. That was the scariest part about this. Yara, Treygan, and Rownan had gone as a team. I had no one.

My throat still felt like sandpaper. My back twitched and my wings itched.

"She won't be alone," a shaky voice said behind me.

Delmar dropped his hands. Keeley and Jenna landed on each of my shoulders.

"What are you two doing here?" I asked, shocked and worried about their safety. "How did you get here?"

"We hid in your wings," Jenna admitted.

Keeley flew up and touched my cheek. "We couldn't let you go by yourself."

"You two aren't going," I said firmly. "It's too dangerous."

"But you're going. Why is it okay for you to go and not us?"

"I'm much bigger," I argued.

Jenna looked crushed. "You've always said our size doesn't matter. That we could do anything big creatures can do."

"It doesn't matter. And you can do anything. Just not this."

"You don't believe in us." Keeley pressed her hands over her heart as if I had shot her with my words.

"Of course I do. I just don't want the two of you risking your souls in Harte. I don't want you to get hurt."

"We'll forever be filled with guilt if we don't go," Keeley said.

"And we'll feel like cowards," Jenna added. "Do you want us to live the rest of our lives feeling useless?"

Being useless was the worst thing in the world to a sprite. And to a siren. It's why I was offered the promotion to siren. Our beliefs and work ethics were so similar.

"You're our family," Jenna said. "Family sticks together."

"They even go through hell together," Keeley added.

Until that moment I had been worried I would have to leave Treygan, Rownan, or Vienna behind. Maybe even all three, depending on how long it took me to save Yara. I had no miracle plan for how to rescue all of them in such a short time, especially without sacrificing my own soul like Otabia had warned me about. One or more of them would hate me for leaving someone behind. As much as it worried me to put Jenna and Keeley in such danger, it could be the answer to saving more than just Yara.

"Fine," I said reluctantly. "Because you're family. And because I know you're brave and strong enough to survive this."

Both of their eyes widened with a mixture of pride, satisfaction, and fear.

"But you listen to everything I tell you," I insisted. "I know more about this place than you, so do not separate from me, and swear to obey everything I say no matter what."

"We swear," they both vowed.

I suddenly felt much more confident about this mission now that I had help from two of the bravest souls I knew.

Pango leaned in close to my ear, trying to speak softly enough that the sprites couldn't hear him. "Maybe they shouldn't go with you. They're so tiny."

I shoved him away, looking up and down his 6'5" frame. "Body size is no indication of courage or spirit. Those two tiny sprites can do anything they set their minds to."

I had never seen Delmar look so concerned. "What if you lose them?"

I raised my wings high behind me. "I don't lose." I rose up in the air with Keeley and Jenna on either side of me. "We'll see you soon. And we'll have all the love birds with us."

As we flew toward the Devil's Triangle, Keeley held her fists out in front of her. "I'm ready."

Jenna flew back and forth, nervously chanting, "I am strong. I am a sprite. I can do anything."

I saw the gate. The huge hole in the ocean was churning in on itself, creating a massive whirlpool. I gathered Jenna and Keeley closer to me with my wings. "Hang on tight, girls."

I heard Nixie calling my name. I covered my ears with my hands. "I hate this place. No words can adequately express how much I hate it."

Treygan pulled my hands down. "What do you hear?"

"Nixie calling my name over and over."

His eyes widened. "I heard her call my name too."

"Are we both having the same hallucination?"

Treygan looked up at the sky. "Maybe it's real. She's crazy enough to come here."

"Dear gods, I hope not." My head snapped up as Nixie's voice shouted my name again but louder and with more force. "She's getting louder."

"I don't see any sign of her."

I listened as Nixie screamed at me to wake up. To get back in my body. "Get back in my body?"

Treygan's lip twitched. "What?"

"She just said 'get back in your body.'" I looked down at my arms and hands. "You don't think …" Hope flooded through me from my toes to my fingertips. "Maybe this is all a bad dream. Maybe Vienna never went to Harte and we never left Rathe. Maybe Harte doesn't even exist, and this is just a nightmare I'm trying to wake up from. Maybe Nixie is trying to wake me."

"I wish that was the case, but no. This is real. Harte has always been a scary reality."

"Of course you'd say that if I'm dreaming."

"You can't dream because you don't sleep."

"But I'm still part human. Maybe I can still dream." My heart ached. "Oh no. What if you're a dream too? What if being turned into a mermaid was a dream and *you* don't really exist?"

"Please don't make me snap you of out of another hysterical downward spiral. I'm real. You're awake. And Harte, unfortunately, is real." He pinched the bridge of his nose. "So is Nixie's voice. Now she's screaming at me again."

I pulled his hand away, getting ready to continue my argument about dreaming, but then I noticed something about his face. "Your constellation is gone."

"Beg your pardon?"

"Your freckles along the side of your face that match the Canis Major constellation, they aren't there."

He touched his cheek and gave me a strange look. I glanced at the brand on his arm then down at myself. "Am I exactly the same as you remember me?"

"Of course not. You've lost your wings, and …" He hesitated, then sadly said, "Sage."

I read the burnt words on my arm, still there, looking as inflamed as ever. "Yes, but besides that, is there any minor detail on me that's missing?"

He stepped forward and lifted my arm, bending it to examine my elbow. He squinted. "Your scar is gone."

I twisted my arm to look at the faded scar from when I had received stitches. "It *is* gone."

"What does that mean?"

"Nixie is telling us to get in our bodies because we aren't in our bodies!"

"How is that possible?"

"How is anything possible in this place? Harte is all about consuming our souls, right? Maybe our—" I gasped mid-thought, remembering when I dove off the floating island when we first arrived. Even though Rownan jumped before us, I could have sworn I saw his body lying on the ground. "We left our bodies! Our souls separated from our bodies right after we arrived. Our souls jumped from that island, but our bodies didn't."

"Then what do you call this?" He motioned to his torso.

"An illusion. Just like everything else here."

"If so, how do we get back into our bodies?"

Nixie was still screaming at me. "We wake up."

"How do you propose we do that?"

I listened to Nixie while assessing the dark world around us. "Just like when we soul share. Focus on something real in great detail. I'll focus on your freckles. You focus on my scar."

Treygan apprehensively nodded then closed his eyes.

"See you soon," I whispered.

My eyes fluttered open.

Treygan lay beside me on his back. The freckles on his pale cheek came into focus.

"Yara!" Nixie yanked me up and hugged me tight. "Thank gods."

I rested my chin on her shoulder as I groggily watched an old ship and plane float through the air behind her. I managed a couple of raspy words. "You came."

Sage slithered against my cheek. She was alive. I wriggled my wings, feeling them attached and unharmed. I wanted to sing with joy, but Treygan's body was still motionless beside us. I let go of Nixie and leaned over him, crawling onto my knees. I smacked him lightly on the cheeks. "Wake up, Treygan!"

"I already tried that on both of you," Nixie said. "It doesn't work."

"What were you doing just before I woke up?"

Nixie blushed. I had never seen Nixie blush. "I kissed you. Deep. And, well …."

"What? Now isn't the time for you to start being shy."

"I imagined sucking your soul back into your body."

I turned and kissed Treygan, putting as much passion as I could into it. I pictured every time he had smiled or laughed, the look on his face when he saw me outside of the gorgon's grotto for the first time, our first kiss. I let so many intense and happy memories charge the energy between us. I imagined breathing his soul into his body. *Come back to me.*

His chest heaved, so I pulled away. His eyes flew open.

He didn't even speak, just yanked me back down to him and kissed me hard. When he finally let go of me, he whispered, "You're brilliant."

"You two stay here," Nixie ordered. "I have to find Rownan and Vienna."

"They're on a small beach at the top of a cliff," I told her, but Treygan stopped me.

"Are they? Or is that just where their souls are?"

I glanced around. "But this is where we landed. Rownan should be here."

"He's down there!" Nixie shouted, standing at a crumbling edge of our floating island and pointing. "I'll be right back."

She dove off and I faced Treygan. "But where is Vienna's body?"

Treygan rubbed the back of his neck. "I have no idea, but look." He nodded at something behind me.

I turned to see Jenna and Keeley holding hands and watching us. "What are you two doing here?"

"We came to help," Jenna squeaked.

I rushed over to them. "You shouldn't have come to this place."

"We're going to help carry everyone out," Jenna said.

"Nixie couldn't save all of you on her own," Keeley added.

Nixie landed beside us with Rownan unconscious in her arms. She laid him on the ground and yelled all the same stuff she had yelled to me and Treygan.

"You have to kiss him," I reminded her.

An all-too-familiar screeching started.

I ran to the ledge. The soul suckers were slithering far below us, rising fast. "They're coming!"

"Get his soul back inside his body right now!" Treygan shouted at Nixie.

She leaned over and kissed him, her wings quivering behind her.

The soul suckers' multiple heads formed. At least four different trios of heads were coming our way. That made twelve massive mouths of sharp teeth. We were grossly outnumbered.

I whipped around at the sound of Rownan's voice. "Vienna? What happened?"

"No time to explain," Treygan said. "We need to leave right now."

Rownan sat up, looking disoriented. "Where are we? Where's Vienna?"

"Probably long gone," Treygan said. "Nixie, Yara, fly us out of here."

"No!" Rownan scrambled to his feet, backing away from us. "I'm not leaving without Vienna."

Treygan tried explaining as fast as he could. "We separated from our bodies. Only our souls dove off this island and into hell. We're back in our bodies and we're out of time. Those creatures are coming to eat us alive."

Rownan's eyes were wide like he was trying to process everything, but he shook his head. "We have to find Vienna's body."

"Rownan." I stood in front of him. "Feel how weak you are. It's because our bodies have been lying here with no food, water, or movement for nearly three days. Vienna would have been here for *sixteen years*. I'm sorry, but her body would never survive that long." I took his hand. "We have to go. Now."

I flew upward, holding on to Rownan. I lifted him off the ground a few inches, but he kicked and squirmed his way free of my grip, landing hard.

"Let me make this clear," he growled. "I'm not leaving here without Vienna."

The three-headed soul suckers rising around us silenced everyone. They shrieked long and loud, and the stench of death nearly knocked me over. The sprites were visibly trembling and the color had drained from them.

I swooped down and tackled Rownan, binding his arms at his side in a tight bear hug. "Nixie, get Treygan!"

In an instant, she and Treygan were beside us. "Jenna, Keeley, in my wings, *now*!"

We flew high into the air, darting between the heads of the beasts. Rownan thrashed in my arms screaming to let him go and demanding we find Vienna.

"Where's the gate?" I shouted to Nixie.

"I think this way, but I'm not sure. The trip here was disorienting."

I knew what she meant. I had no idea how or why we had landed where we did when we passed through the gateway. "Look for an opening in the sky, a tunnel or hole."

"No," Nixie explained. "It looks like a black crescent moon. A nail puncture in a cloudless sky. It will seem like we'll never reach it, but keep flying toward it and eventually we'll cross through. Then hold on to him tight, because it's a hellish ride."

How did Nixie know any of this? There was no time for questions. We kept flying as Rownan continued yelling at me and thrashing. I was so weak and tired. Struggling to keep hold of him was not helping the situation. "Hold still!" I yelled. "We're not leaving you here!"

"Don't do this!" Rownan begged. "Don't take me away from her again."

The desperation and despair in his voice slowed my flight. Nixie pulled ahead of us.

"Yara," Rownan pleaded, "I don't know what's going on, but if I need to bring back Vienna's body then help me find it."

"You're not understanding."

"No, *you* aren't understanding. I know where her body might be."

I closed my eyes, trying to shake the mental image of Vienna's rotten corpse. No way could her body have survived sixteen years of this place without her soul in it.

Rownan was desperate. "She's on a boat. I know it. Please, take me to it and let me end her nightmare!"

Nixie and Treygan had doubled back and hovered in front of me.

"Come on!" Treygan demanded.

"We're running out of time," Nixie warned. Jenna and Keeley peeked out from her wings.

"How long have you been here?" I asked Nixie.

"Too long. Let's go!"

"How much time until the sun sets?"

"Maybe thirty minutes!"

My eyes locked with Treygan's. "Go," I told him. "We'll only be a few minutes behind you."

Rownan's muscles softened in my grip. I heard him murmur words of gratitude.

"Absolutely not!" Treygan said. "We stay together!"

"We're going to do a quick search."

"Of what?" Nixie said.

"Rownan thinks Vienna's body is on a boat."

Nixie rolled her eyes. "For gods' sakes, Rownan, haven't you already put everyone in enough danger? Vienna's body is a deteriorated mess by now!"

Rownan went rigid. "I'll only believe that when I see it. I need to be sure before I leave here. If not, I will kill myself the moment we get back, I swear."

Treygan closed his eyes, his mouth curving into the heaviest frown I had ever seen.

"Five minutes," he said.

Nixie groaned.

"Then we are out of here with or without Vienna. Agreed?" I squeezed Rownan in frustration.

"Agreed," Rownan said.

"I saw a couple of floating vessels on my way in." Nixie swung her head to the side and flew off. "This way."

I followed, glancing down at the soul suckers still writhing and screeching below us. They weren't chasing us. I couldn't help but wonder why.

We approached a huge Navy warship. It groaned and creaked as it sailed through the dark sky.

"It would take us an hour to search that thing!" I said.

Rownan shook his head. "That's not it. She's on a sailboat called *Home Sweet Home*."

"A sailboat?" Nixie shouted. "There are no sailboats here."

Sage rose high above my head, pulling me upward. *This way.*

"Follow us!" I shouted. "Sage is leading me."

We soared past a graveyard of ships and planes of every shape, size, and age.

On one boat, a human man stood at the wheel, his long hair blown by an invisible wind as if he was jetting through the open water. He was smiling and seemed happy as could be. He saluted us as we flew by him. I would never understand this place.

I tried recalling my conversation with Vienna about the first Rownan imposter. She said they had sailed on a boat called *Home Sweet Home*, and that she had purposefully crashed the boat into a mountain to avoid a black tunnel.

But all the boats we saw were in the sky. Could there be a mountain in the sky? I hadn't seen any, but this morbid place seemed infinite. How would we ever find one small sailboat in my allotted five minutes? I would have to convince Yara to keep searching until we found Vienna. I tried asking Yara how Sage could possibly know where we were going, but we were flying so fast the wind muffled my voice.

I closed my eyes, shadowing Vienna, but I kept seeing her on the beach. She was sitting in the sand, hugging the piece of driftwood and crying. I wanted to be with her, even if it was only my soul. I kept willing my soul to join hers again, but nothing happened.

Yara's hands gripped tighter around me as we flew.

So many things sort of made sense now: why we didn't bleed, why I couldn't find a pulse when I checked Yara and Treygan in the cave, how I fell into a pit and woke up without a scratch on me. But all the experiences, the hallucinations, the pain that felt so real, even Vienna's breath in my face. How did any of those things happen?

"There!" Yara's voice snapped me back to the present.

Ahead of us, impossible as it seemed, was a mountain in the sky. Massive tree roots sprouted from the bottom of it, twisting and wrapping up the mountainside. Ensnared by the roots and secured to the mountain were several vessels, but only one sailboat.

From far away the sailboat looked so small and beat up—and empty. As we flew closer it got bigger, and so did the possibility that Vienna might be aboard. On the back of the boat were cracked, faded letters: *me   we   Home*

"That's it!" I yelled.

The tattered mainsail still flapped in the wind. The other sails were filthy heaps of material on the deck. We landed on the rotting planks. My feet carried me forward even before Yara let go of me.

Like a magnet, I was drawn mid-ship where one pile of sail appeared to have long, black threads tangled through its folds. But I knew that shade of black, and I knew they weren't threads at all. They were Vienna's hair.

I reached forward, but Treygan grabbed my arms and held me in place. "Rownan, you need to prepare yourself for what you're about to see."

"She's fine."

His brow wrinkled. "Her body hasn't had a soul inside it for a long time."

"Time doesn't work the same here. That human history buff told Yara that." I pulled out of his grasp. "Help me move this sail."

I leaned down, gathering the fabric and pulling it back. Treygan and Yara grabbed the other end. The material seemed endless. We kept pulling more and more out of the way until I flung the end of it aside and dropped to my knees.

I heard Yara gasp. Maybe everyone gasped. I was too focused on Vienna to care about anyone's reaction. We had found her.

She was so skinny. So pale. Her hair was at least five times longer than the Vienna on the beach. Every bone in her body protruded beneath her taut skin. Her veins were visible and a scary shade of blue. She was in selkie form. Her tail was bald in spots, and her entire coat was dull. I leaned down and rested my ear against her chest.

Nothing. Nothing. Nothing.

Then, one weak beat.

"She's alive!"

"Rownan," Yara began.

"I'm not hallucinating. She's alive." I looked at Nixie. "What do I do to get her soul back in her body?"

Nixie's wide eyes blinked fast. "I don't think you—"

"I know how bad she looks!" I said. "But I swear on every soul in Rathe, she has a heartbeat. Help me get her soul back inside her body so we can go home!"

Jenna flew off Nixie's shoulder and nudged Treygan's back. "You listen," she told him.

Treygan kneeled on the other side of Vienna and pressed his ear to her chest. His eyes stayed on me for a few seconds. Then his forehead flinched and he shot up. "He's right. She has a heartbeat!"

Nixie spewed out orders. "Tell her to get back in her body. Tell her the place she's in isn't real."

I recited everything Nixie said before she even finished. I pressed my lips to Vienna's ear repeating all of it over and over, getting louder and more demanding each time.

"Kiss her," Nixie ordered. "Imagine pulling her soul back here with your breath."

I kissed Vienna's dry lips, and flashes of us laughing, kissing, and talking raced through my mind. I opened my eyes and stared at her motionless face. "Now what?"

"I don't know," Nixie said. "It worked every other time."

"Kiss her again!" Keeley yelled.

I kissed her multiple times, begging her to get back in her body, but she wasn't stirring or responding at all.

Yara spoke quietly, probably intending for me not to hear, but it was the same question I had been wondering. "What would happen if we took her body back before her soul returned to it?"

I paused to hear Nixie's reply. "Worse than a horror movie."

I continued pleading with Vienna's unconscious body. "Please, this is it, V. This is where you have to trust in me and let me take you home. You know it was me on the beach. It was me who just kissed you. Please, for us, for your family, for all your friends back in Rathe who have been waiting sixteen years to see you again, for you and our future, get back in your body."

I kissed her again. Nothing.

I looked up at Yara. She had tears in her eyes. Treygan and Nixie wore pained expressions. Keeley shook her head.

"Now what?" Jenna whispered to Nixie.

"I don't know," Nixie answered somberly.

I stared down at Vienna again, smoothing stray wisps of hair away from her face. "I won't leave you, V. I can't."

Nixie squatted down and touched my arm. "We're almost out of time."

"Go," I told them, pulling Vienna against my chest. "You did all you could and I'm grateful, but you have to go. I'm staying."

"Don't do this," Treygan begged me.

"You won't talk me out of it. Stop wasting precious time and go. Live your lives, be happy, love each other. Go!"

Nixie stepped onto the edge of the boat. "We did all we could."

"It would be cruel to force him to leave her," Jenna offered meekly.

"No!" Treygan grabbed my hand, but I squirmed out of his grip. "I will carry you out of here kicking and screaming if I have to."

Yara leaped forward as if she had been shot. "Blood!" She dropped to her knees on the other side of Vienna. Sage swayed between us. "Selkies share themselves through blood. It's your life force."

"She can't drink from me," I said. "She's unconscious."

"You have to try," Yara urged.

Hope ricocheted through my chest. As I laid Vienna back down, Yara's claws shot out and pierced my inner arm. Blood surfaced, and Yara wiped it on Vienna's lips. I squeezed more blood out and parted Vienna's mouth to rub some on her stiff tongue.

Still nothing.

I lay down beside Vienna and pulled her body against me. "You stay, I stay. I promised you forever, and I meant it." I kissed her head then whispered in her ear, "You are my everything. Even if you lose me, I will always find you again."

"She swallowed!" Yara shrieked.

I bolted up. Keeley and Jenna flitted above us.

"She's right!" Keeley clapped her hands so fast they blurred. "I saw her throat bob up and down!"

"Vienna?" I caressed her face. "Can you hear me?" Her dark eyelashes twitched. "Thank you, thank you, thank you." I kissed her lips. "Come on, Vienna, come back to me. I'm right here."

Her lips parted and she murmured, "Row."

"Yes. Dear gods, yes, I'm right here, V."

Yara was using her claws to cut Vienna's long, tangled hair free.

Treygan bent over us. "Vienna, hang in there. We're taking you back to Rathe. You're going to be all right."

I sobbed. It was uncontrollable. Because her eyes opened.

"It's you," she whispered.

"It's me." I couldn't stop touching her face and kissing her.

"Home?" she croaked.

"Yes, home. We're going home."

"I'll take her," Yara said. "We have to get out of here before the gate closes."

As much as I didn't want to let go of Vienna, I knew someone had to fly her out of here, and I trusted Yara to be gentle with her. "She's fragile."

"I know." Yara carefully gathered Vienna in her arms. "I'll take good care of her."

"Rownan, who do you want to carry you?" Nixie asked. "Me or the sprites?"

Keeley and Jenna were hovering side by side, holding hands. Judging from their misty eyes, they had been crying too.

"It doesn't matter," I said. "Just keep me close to Vienna."

Nixie nodded and scooped me up. Then she turned to Treygan. "Jenna and Keeley are stronger than they look."

Treygan lifted his arms. "I have total faith in them."

I had no idea what happened with Treygan and the sprites after that. My full attention was locked on Vienna. She had closed her eyes again but still wore a peaceful smile across her bloodstained lips.

Yara was being extremely careful with Vienna. She had her eyes glued to her, watching over her like a protector. Which is exactly why Yara never saw the boom of the sailboat swinging behind her.

I called out to warn her, but it happened too fast. Sage launched upward, trying to stop it, but the beam struck both of them and Yara was knocked out. She crash-landed on the deck with Vienna under her, and the rotted floor collapsed under them.

Treygan ran to her side and pulled her out of the hole, "Yara?"

Nixie let go of me, and I was beside them in an instant, knee-deep in broken floorboards as I lifted Vienna into my arms. She groaned, and I breathed a sigh of relief. I looked up at Yara and Treygan. Treygan wasn't having the same luck. Yara and Sage were out cold.

"What do we do?" he asked me.

Jenna had her hands over her mouth. Keeley watched through her fingers spread over her eyes.

"Well isn't this just perfect?" Nixie threw her hands in the air. "What else can possibly go wrong?"

"Her soul isn't stuck anywhere," Treygan said. "She's just unconscious. We can still take her home, right?"

"I hope so," Nixie replied. "I don't understand all the rules to this place!"

Treygan looked at Keeley and Jenna. "Can you each carry one of us?"

The sprites glanced at each other with bulging eyes. Jenna was the first to speak.

"Yes." But it sounded more like a question. "Yes," she said again with more conviction. "We are strong. We can do anything."

"Jenna," Nixie said. "Take Vienna."

"What?" I gasped. "She's the smallest! Why can't you take Vienna?"

"Vienna is the lightest body," Nixie explained impatiently. "She and Vienna are a good match. I'm going to have to carry Treygan and Yara."

She was right. We only had three winged creatures to carry out four people who couldn't fly. I eyed Keeley. She looked more nervous than anyone.

"I'm counting on you, little one," I told her.

She took a deep breath and stretched her arms. "I'm ready."

Treygan cradled Yara against him. "I'll carry Yara," he told Nixie. "You carry me."

"Your muscles are too fatigued." Nixie gripped his bicep. "They're already shaking."

Treygan didn't look happy about it, but he handed Yara's body over to Nixie. She wrapped one arm around Yara's waist and hoisted her upper body over her left shoulder. She pulled Treygan against her with her right arm. "Ready."

With all bodies—and souls—accounted for, our trio of winged angels carried us off the boat and into the dark sky of Harte.

I had done what Otabia told me—I kept counting.

Through every conversation, every step, every struggle, I counted. Even if I was talking or doing something, a part of my mind counted. Maybe I had missed a few seconds here and there, but we had approximately thirteen minutes until the gate closed.

My brave sprites flew ahead of us. I couldn't see them, and Vienna and Rownan looked as if they were soaring through the air on their own. I pictured Keeley and Jenna underneath them, struggling to carry all that weight above their heads. The soul suckers Lloyd and Otabia warned me about screeched below us.

"Faster!" I yelled.

Jenna shot forward. Keeley wasn't far behind her.

Yara and Treygan's weight was no problem for me, but they felt so different. Treygan was tense and constantly moving. Every time he turned his head or leaned to look below or behind us, my muscles had to work harder to keep a grip on him.

"Stop fidgeting," I told him.

Yara was limp and draped over my shoulder. Her hair tickled my back and her hip bones ground into my collar bone. But at least she kept still.

Finally, the black crescent moon came into view. "There it is! Go, girls! Fly directly into the moon!"

The heat of the soul sucker's breath hit me like fire swallowing my legs. Glancing down, I saw the beast's open mouth full of teeth. I darted out of its path.

Treygan let go of me and reached for something in his jacket. "Stop fidgeting!" I yelled again.

The soul sucker followed us, one of its heads extending rapidly in our direction. I climbed as fast as I could, trying to spot Keeley and Jenna again. I found nothing but black sky.

Cold shot through my chest. Where were they?

They couldn't have been eaten. They were ahead of us. Maybe they had made it through the gate. *They're fine.* I had to tell myself that or my despair would make me lose focus.

I kept darting side to side, flying high then dipping low, trying to confuse the soul suckers, but each time one or more of their heads trailed us.

One of them bumped my feet, jostling all of us. Yara slid off my shoulder, but I caught her under the arm and kept her clutched at my side. The jolt sent Treygan sliding out of my grip. Our hands connected before he fell away.

I screeched, panicked, and adjusted to keep hold of both of them.

Treygan swung his free arm up and held on to my wrist. He dangled below me like bait on a hook. Bait that probably had the soul suckers foaming at the mouth.

"Hold on," I shouted to him, lifting him close to me again. I flew back toward the area where I thought I had seen the moon.

At least a dozen soul suckers followed.

I had no idea how such tiny creatures could be so strong, but Keeley's hands pressed into my ribs, lifting us into the fog of the moon.

Vienna was close enough for me to reach. I grabbed her hand and she squeezed as tight as she could manage. She was weak, but at least she wasn't the rotted corpse everyone had tried convincing me she would be.

"It'll get rough," I warned her. "Don't let go."

She nodded, her lids drooping heavily over the dark circles under her eyes. She was far from healthy, but she was alive. She was alive, and we were on our way home.

Gale force winds blew against us. We bobbed up and down as the sprites fought to keep flying forward. I felt so helpless. If I had wings I would have bulldozed us a way out of here.

"You can do it!" I yelled, hoping Keeley could hear me. "I believe in you!"

We surged forward so hard that I pulled Vienna along behind us. My body ached to kick and help propel us forward. If only my tail could help us swim through the sky. All I could do was have faith that Keeley and Jenna, small but so courageous, would have the strength to get us out.

Keeley never said a word. She just groaned and yelled as if she was pushing through the worst pain she had ever felt. "You're doing it, Keeley! Keep going! I can see the opening!"

The wind whipped so hard I thought Vienna and I would be ripped apart. I held her hand so tight I couldn't tell the difference between her fingers and mine.

Vienna tried pulling her hand free. "That's not the gateway. Let go of me!"

"It is the gate." My pulse throbbed between our palms as I fought to keep our hands linked. "Stop struggling!"

She kicked and thrashed, trying to break free as she screamed and cursed me. We bobbed and flailed through the air. Keeley struggled beneath me, her small hands kneading my chest, trying to rebalance my weight above her.

"Liar!" Vienna yelled. "I won't be tricked!"

The realization hit me harder than the wind. Vienna had entered Harte through Rathe's gateway. We used the Devil's Triangle. Of course they didn't look the same. Harte's demons had been trying to lure her into a deeper level of hell for years. She thought this was another trick. "V, it's not what you think!"

She was fighting so hard to free herself from Jenna. She would fall into a sea of soul suckers. I hadn't come this far only to lose her again. "Keeley, get me closer to her!"

We collided, and I threw my arms around Vienna, pinning her against me and clinging to her so tightly that the devil himself wouldn't be able to take her from me.

We shot out of the turbulence and into a tunnel of swirling water. The spray felt like bullets hitting me. I tried looking at Vienna, but I couldn't turn my head or open my eyes. The pull from the spinning was too strong.

Then the pelting spray stopped. We sailed upward through an orange and pink sky. My head drooped from exhaustion. Below us was the ocean. Earth's ocean.

The sprites had saved us.

"Keeley!" I shouted weakly. "You did it!"

A boat filled with familiar faces staring up at us came into view. Tears of joy streamed down my cheeks. I had never been so happy to see Delmar, Kimber, Pango, and the rest of the crew. We didn't so much land as crash onto the deck of the boat. I rolled to my side, knowing Keeley was crushed beneath me. Vienna crashed just as hard beside me. I immediately pulled her off Jenna.

Both tiny, angelic sprites lay face down on the deck boards. Their backs rose and fell rapidly. Their wings were motionless.

I gently rolled both of them over.

Keeley's eyes opened. "Are we dead?"

I smiled. All the merfolk had gathered around us. Kimber was cradling Vienna in her arms. I lowered my face so Keeley and I were almost nose to nose. "No, you're alive. And so are we, thanks to you. You and Jenna are heroes."

"Heroes," Jenna sighed, eyes still closed, wearing an exhausted grin. "I always wanted to be a hero."

Indrea kneeled besides us, snapping into action. "Who is hurt the worst?"

"Vienna," I said.

Delmar was holding Vienna's wrist. "Her pulse is almost non-existent."

Indrea rushed over to Vienna and I grabbed Indrea's arm. I took a breath, my lungs aching at the gravity of my words. "Her soul was out of her body the whole time. Until a few minutes ago."

"Holy Hades," Pango gasped. "It's a miracle she's still alive."

Indrea patted my hand. "Love kept her alive."

I closed my eyes. The adrenaline, the realization that we were out of Harte, and having Vienna by my side again was overloading my system.

Indrea's voice was calming as always. "Just lay beside her while I work on her. Being with you is the best medicine for her right now."

Kimber delicately handed Vienna to me. I placed one hand behind Vienna's head, letting my arm be her pillow. I lay on my side, my other arm wrapped tight around her. "I'm here," I whispered into her ear. "Soon we'll be home."

She let her head fall against my neck while Indrea worked on her.

"Where are the others?" Caspian asked.

"They were right behind us," I said. "Nixie was carrying Yara and Treygan."

"Why Yara?" Delmar asked. "She can fly."

"She got knocked out. Nixie had to carry both of them."

"Good grief," Pango sighed. "Could the odds be any worse?"

Keeping Vienna's head tucked under my chin, I watched glimpses of color from the setting sun peek through the fog. I silently prayed to Medusa and Poseidon, begging to see Nixie's red wings above us with Yara and Treygan in her arms.

But minutes passed with no sign of them.

Jenna sat up. "I'm going back in!"

Keeley sat up beside her. "Me too."

"No," Delmar said. "You can't. There's not enough time."

"We can't leave them in there," Keeley argued.

"They'll make it out," I offered. "I know they will." But even as I said it, my doubt grew stronger.

"And what if they don't?" Jenna asked.

"You're exhausted," Indrea reasoned calmly with her. "No good could come from you going back in. What if the gate closed before you came out again?" Jenna crossed her arms over her chest. "I'm sorry, girls," Indrea told them. "We can't allow you to go back in at this point. It's too dangerous."

The boat kept rocking. Vienna cooed softly, asleep in my arms. Delmar offered hope that they would make it out. Pango kneeled at the bow of the boat, his chin resting on his praying hands. I almost didn't hear Jenna's quiet voice behind me.

"They will make it out. I'll make sure of it." Jenna flew from the boat.

Caspian caught Keeley by the wings. "Oh, no you don't."

"She can't go alone!" Keeley yelled, kicking the air furiously.

Jenna's shimmering yellow wings left a trail of light through the fog. I hoped beyond hope it wouldn't be the last time we saw her.

I flew against the wind as fast as I could. Six minutes left—or was it four? I lost count. I had no idea where the gate was.

I was a siren who could control fire, but I had never known true heat until I was caught in the vacuum breath of a soul sucker. We were pulled backward toward its inferno of a mouth. I kicked and flapped my wings harder than ever, but we were sucked in.

With my elbows, I blocked the beast's jaw from closing all the way. I screamed when teeth tore through my flesh. Yara was still draped over my shoulder, only an inch above the teeth, but Treygan was below me, deeper in the huge, tubular mouth of the soul sucker.

My skin burned so intensely from the heat that I assumed my flesh was melting. Treygan swung and struggled below me, but I kept my grip on his hand. I didn't know what he was trying to do, but then he roared and the beast screeched so loudly my ears rang. Black smoke rushed up around me and the circular mouth of teeth opened and fell away, allowing me to soar up into the dark sky again.

I glanced down and saw Treygan hanging like a charred rope from my singed, black arm. A dagger glistened in his hand. I couldn't see the full extent of damage the beast had done to my arms, but I could feel it. Yara still lay unconscious over my other shoulder. I kept flying higher, desperately searching for the gateway again, but I found nothing except empty sky and my own despair.

Treygan was becoming unbearably heavy. My arm was numb in the places that didn't pulse with crippling pain. As much as I didn't want to accept it, I had to let go of him if I had any hope of saving Yara. But actually doing it—letting go of Treygan's hand, knowing what that meant—seemed impossible.

I gazed down at where our hands joined. I wanted to say goodbye. I needed to apologize for being so weak. All I could see was his hair and a hint of his forehead and nose. It was better that way. If I had seen his face, his selfless and caring eyes, they would have haunted me eternally.

I closed my eyes, fighting back tears. "Please forgive me, Yara." I whispered into the wind, "I'm so sorry, Treygan."

The heavy weight of him fell away.

My injured arm no longer felt like it would rip into pieces from the strain.

But I hadn't let go of his hand yet.

"Got him!" Jenna yelled. She lifted him over her head, smiling at me as she rose to my eye level. "I'm here! I've got him!"

"Jenna!" I squealed, releasing my death-grip on Treygan's fingers and using both hands to secure Yara in my arms.

"Jenna's got you," I told Treygan. I said it again, assuring myself because it almost seemed too good to be true. My eyes were teary, a mixture of shame, joy, and intense physical pain. "She's got you."

My arm wouldn't have lasted another second if she hadn't come along. Jenna had saved me from having to release Treygan to certain death in a sea of soul suckers.

Treygan noticed my shredded arms. "Nixie, you're injured."

"I'll be fine." A second wave of adrenaline and hope rushed through me. I dipped my head to check on Jenna. "You sure you can handle it?"

Her arms were locked above her head, Treygan draped over her like a living cape. "I can handle it."

I cradled Yara against my torso and yelled. "Let's go home!"

Jenna enthusiastically nodded.

Jenna led the way, directly to the gate. I stayed behind her in case she needed help. The moon was so close I felt like I could reach out and touch it, but the hot breath of a soul sucker engulfed my legs again. The soul sucker's body broke off into three heads.

"Get to the gate!" I shouted. "We can outrun them!"

Jenna peeked back at me, and her eyes flew wide open at the sight of the beast. Her wings flapped harder as she and Treygan surged upward. Treygan still had the dagger clutched in his hand.

"Faster, Jenna!"

Treygan was looking back, shouting something I couldn't hear. The heat and the pull of one beast sucking us in intensified.

"Left!" I yelled, swerving out of the path of the beast. By the time I realized Jenna hadn't heard me, it was too late.

She and Treygan were sucked past me. I reached out, trying to grab Treygan's hand, but he rushed by me too fast.

I doubled back, chasing after them. Jenna hung on to Treygan's hair, her body stretched out behind her as they were sucked closer to the beast's mouth. I managed to grab Treygan's foot. I squeezed hard, struggling to keep hold of Yara while trying to pull Treygan and Jenna out of the powerful vacuum.

I was no match for it. I was going to lose everyone, including myself. We had come so far, but this was the point of no return. The soul suckers and Harte had won.

Treygan shouted, "Save Yara! Let go, Nixie!"

Jenna was terrified, crying, screaming, still clutching Treygan's hair.

"I can't," I grunted, fighting against the pull, but my arms felt so weak and useless. I hugged Yara tighter to my body with one hand while squeezing Treygan's foot with the other. If I let go, I wouldn't be able to live with the guilt. I would have to live mourning Jenna and Treygan forever, knowing it was me who killed them. I would have to tell Yara that I failed her and let Treygan be eaten alive by a soul sucker.

No. We were a sinking ship, but we would go down together.

The heat scorched my hands and face. The beast's teeth looked close enough to snap shut around Jenna.

Treygan's eyes met mine. I couldn't hear him over the roaring breath of the beast, but I could read his lips. "Let go!"

I shook my head as he tried kicking free. Sweat dripped from every pore on my body. His foot was slippery, but I held on. Treygan's head fell back in the same hopeless defeat I felt.

"We die together," I said, even though no one could hear me.

Sage whipped forward, snapping into consciousness. She bit Yara's cheek and Yara jolted awake. Yara flew out of my arms so fast I barely had time to blink. She looked around frantically then flipped over, grabbing Treygan's other foot. Her wings flapped furiously. "Nixie, get Jenna!"

I sprang into action, swooping past Treygan. Jenna was flapping her wings so hard they were a blur of yellow. I snatched her up in my hands and surged backward, but I wasn't powerful enough to pull us out of the beast's vacuum. Treygan's arms were free, so he hooked his hands inside my elbows, fighting to keep me away from the beast's teeth. I lifted my legs toward my chest as one tooth grazed the heels of my boots.

I don't know how Yara did it, but she spun us like a chain. I was whipped upward, away from the beast's deadly teeth. Now Yara was closest to the beast's head.

She kept one hand locked on Treygan's ankle as she pulled a giant tooth from a holster on her thigh. Just before they were sucked into the beast's mouth, Yara drew her arm back. Using the giant tooth like a knife, she stabbed the top of the beast's head.

The soul sucker let out an ear-piercing screech followed by a gasping noise. The pull of the vacuum decreased significantly. I flew higher out of its path. Yara kicked the tooth in deeper, clogging what I realized was a singular nostril on the soul sucker's head. The vacuum suction stopped entirely as the beast shook from side to side trying to dislodge the obstruction.

Jenna flew from my hands and stood on my shoulder, grabbing hold of my hair. "Nixie, your arms. You're badly wounded."

She was right. My muscles and tendons felt like they had been shredded. I cradled my bloody arms against my chest. "I'll be fine."

Yara turned to face us and yelled, "Go!"

She didn't need to tell me twice. We flew side by side, racing toward the moon. She had Treygan, I had Jenna. We could do it. We were going to make it. We were free and clear. The soul suckers were far below us.

Until two more splintered out of the moon.

"Where the hell did they come from?" Yara shouted.

I slowed, not knowing what to do. Jenna grabbed my hair tighter.

Treygan called my name. He fumbled with a pack on his side. "Here!" He tossed me another tooth. I tried to catch it, but my hand was numb. The tooth grazed my useless fingers and fell away.

Treygan waved his dagger as Yara banked left. One soul sucker followed them. The other was coming directly at us, so I darted to the right. We passed under it, inches from its slimy chin.

We entered the gray fog. A violent wind pushed against us.

"Hang on tight!" I screamed to Jenna.

"I am!"

I wanted to cry when the heat hit my legs and scorched my wings. The soul sucker was too close. My hair felt like it might rip from my head as Jenna hung on for dear life. The vacuum was even more powerful than before. Then the tugging at my scalp stopped.

I quit breathing.

Jenna had let go. She tumbled through the sky, straight into the beast's mouth as if caught in a tractor beam.

"Nooooooo!" I screamed.

Jenna never looked back. Even the beast's tongue was covered with teeth. Like a tiny leaf being sucked into a whirlwind, Jenna was swallowed by the soul sucker.

I doubled back. Shaking. Still not breathing. I didn't know what to do. I was in denial. I couldn't accept what I had just seen. She couldn't be gone.

"Jenna!" I shouted as loud and long as I could.

More soul suckers slithered to life below. Glowing eyes opened on their eel-like heads. I saw no sign of Yara and Treygan. Maybe they had escaped. I hoped it more than anything.

I waited for the soul sucker that had swallowed Jenna to open its giant mouth again, which only took a few seconds. I flew in, zipping down his dark gullet before his teeth snapped shut.

The smell alone should have killed me.

Getting in was easy compared to getting out.

The wind and water mercilessly whipped against us. I felt like I was frozen in a block of ice, and no matter how hard I tried, I couldn't budge. But through it all, I made sure of one thing: I did not lose Treygan. Like a limb that I refused to part with, I kept Treygan attached to my side.

I vaguely recalled breaking through the surface. I was so woozy I might as well have been sleepwalking. My mer senses led us to the boat. I crashed into it, eyes closed, past the point of exhaustion. I wanted to gasp for deep breaths, but I didn't have enough energy.

Rownan's voice was a relief. "You made it. I knew you would."

Treygan peeled himself out of my grip. He caressed my cheek with his quivering hand. "You did it."

"We did it," I murmured.

He collapsed, his head on my chest. I silently thanked all the gods and goddesses everywhere a million times over.

"Praise Poseidon, it's a miracle," Pango said. "With only seconds left."

Seconds left. My eyes snapped open. The winds were calm. The sky and ocean weren't angry, and it was getting dark. The sun had set. "Where's Nixie?"

Delmar knelt beside me, holding my hand. "She didn't make it out."

"No!" I tried to sit up. Treygan lifted his weight off me.

Delmar put a hand under my shoulder to support me. "There's nothing you can do. Time is up."

"No!" I tried scrambling to my feet and getting my wings to flap, but my body failed me.

Treygan clutched my hand. "I'm sorry, Yamabuki. I'm so sorry."

"Not Nixie." A choked yelp stuck in my throat. My eyes filled with tears. "And Jenna. They were right beside us. They can't be …" Treygan held me as I cried for my siren, my sister, my savior, my friend. And the tiny angel who had saved our lives.

Indrea knelt beside me and placed her hands over my chest. Caspian pressed his hand to my forehead. They worked as a team, giving me all the calming and healing power they could. But no matter how powerful they were, there was no way they could fix my imploding heart.

Some of my strength returned after only a minute or so. I stood up. "I'm going back in."

Treygan grabbed my hand. "You can't."

"Let go of me! I'm not leaving them in there." I broke free from his grip. "They saved us. We can't just leave them!" My wings spread wide. "I'll be back—with both of them."

They all stared at me like I had lost my mind. I flew out of the boat, zipping through the sky. There was no fog. No wind. No funnel churning in the ocean. I hovered above the spot where I was sure the gateway had been. A glint of electric blue caught my attention.

"Keeley," I whispered, flying over to her.

"Where are they?" she asked me, not taking her frantic eyes off the water.

"We'll find them." I dove in, swimming down until I hit the dark, sandy bottom. The gate had to be somewhere. I would rip it open with my bare hands if I had to. I dug so fast my fingertips burned. I unsheathed my selkie claws and kept plowing.

Treygan appeared at my side. He tried stopping me from digging, so I swatted him away and threw a few frustrated punches at him. He caught one of my hands in his, wincing at my claws cutting his flesh, but he held tight. *The sun set*, he said. *The gate is closed. It won't open for another eighteen months*.

Tears poured out of me, disappearing into the godforsaken ocean, just like Nixie and Jenna. I hated Harte. I hated the Devil's Triangle. *I failed them.*

Treygan held me and let me sob as we slowly floated upward.

The boat's engine vibrated the water around us. Its humming grew closer until it purred directly above us. Together, we surfaced.

"Where are they?" Keeley flitted back and forth so fast the water rippled under her toes.

My voice cracked with defeat. "I'm so sorry, Keeley."

"No!" She flew at my face, shaking her finger. "You get them out of there! My sisters will not be eternally trapped in hell."

"Keeley," I uttered. "I can't—"

"Don't tell me you can't! You find a way, Miss Almighty Powerful Sea Monster. You find a way. Right now!" For such a small thing, she was intimidating. "What do you feel? You *feel* that she's still alive, don't you? She felt everything you felt while you were in there. She was so sick and in so much pain. I know you can feel her too. How can you just leave her in Harte if she's still alive?" She balled her fists at her sides and screamed at me so loud my hair blew backward. "Don't you give up on them!"

She was right. I could still feel my connection with Nixie. She was in a lot of pain, but she wasn't dead. Sage coiled on my shoulder as I turned to stare at the area where the opening had been. Eerily calm waves had replaced the giant whirlpool that had churned and sucked us into the dangerous depths of Harte. I had seen the ocean floor and dug through the sand with my own hands. The gate had closed without a trace.

Keeley practically stood on my nose. "Don't give up on them! They didn't give up on you."

I lifted my arm out of the water, but the words I had burned into my skin were gone. I looked at Treygan and mumbled, more to myself than to him, "Never give up."

"What?" Treygan asked, drifting closer to me.

"The tide will turn," I whispered.

Keeley threw her arms above her head as she stomped the air. "Don't just float there. Do something!"

A scene played out in my mind like pictures in a book. "The tide will turn." I smacked the water with my hands, excited by my epiphany. Koraline's quote might have given me the answer to saving them. "The tide will turn!"

Everyone on the boat exchanged confused glances. Treygan stared at me with questioning eyes.

"Delmar, Kimber, Merrick, Pango." I pointed where the gate had been. "Part the water."

Pango and Merrick just stared at me. Delmar glanced at Kimber. "What?"

"At my welcoming ceremony, I watched all of you lift a castle out of the water. You parted the water. Do that again."

Pango leaned on the railing of the boat. "Yara, it took teams of merfolk to lift that castle. Lifting from above and below."

"I'm not asking you to lift anything. Just make a damn opening in the ocean!"

"Wait," Treygan touched my arm. "If you're about to do what I think, you aren't considering a major problem with your plan."

Treygan had a knack for reading my mind, and thank goodness for that, because I was too frantic. If he hadn't stopped me when he did, I probably would have lost everyone.

We worked out a plan within minutes, but with every second that passed it felt like Nixie and Jenna were slipping further away.

Treygan tugged on the anchor chain. "Pango, what's our anchor situation?"

"Three total. The main, backup, and dredge. Strongest ever made."

"You'll have to serve as a fourth," Treygan said. "With your strength, it should be enough to hold."

Pango nodded. "Got it."

"Rownan and Vienna are secured down below?" Treygan asked Indrea.

"Yes. Tethered with safety lines, just in case."

I didn't know how safe Rownan and Vienna would be in the sleeping quarters of the boat, but it was all we could do. Selkies couldn't offer the kind of help we required, and Vienna wasn't strong enough to do anything but recover.

"Everyone, in the water," Treygan ordered.

All of our trusting merfolk family dove or jumped into the water around us. Treygan, Pango, and I reached the ocean floor. Pango's tail morphed into legs and he planted his feet in the sand. Treygan went to work. Shaky breaths rattled through me as I watched Treygan put his insane plan into action. He formed thick stone around each anchor for extra security. Then he swam back to me and Pango.

He created a slab of rock on the ocean floor. He slowed down, but not much, as he encased Pango's legs and torso in stone.

You're our anchor, Treygan said.

Pango grinned. *Haven't I always been?*

Treygan squeezed Pango's shoulder then faced me. *You'll have to help me if we're going to do this quickly.*

He had much more faith in my stone-making skills than I did.

What if I crush them? What if I can't control it like you can?

You won't crush anyone, Treygan assured me, forming a huge slab of bedrock below us. *You'll do great. Use that as your base and build upward until you can connect someone. Start with Delmar.*

I did what Treygan taught me in our days of training, imagining stone forming like a giant puzzle building upon itself. When I reached Delmar's fins, I froze. What if I hurt him? Worse, what if I killed him?

I glanced up, looking for Treygan to help me do it correctly, but he was an indigo blur in the water, erecting pillars of stone.

Slowly, I formed a foot or so of stone around Delmar's fins and tail. I couldn't do it as fast as Treygan. I was too worried about crushing Delmar. Treygan was beside me in an instant and Delmar was encased up to his waist before I could thank Treygan for helping me.

I swam to the surface, needing to make sure everyone was okay.

"Holy Poseidon." Delmar tucked his long hair behind his ears. "I can't move my lower body—at all."

"I think it just might work," Caspian said.

"Is anyone hurt?" I asked.

No one was. Not one complaint of pain or discomfort.

Treygan surfaced beside me. "Okay, Yara. Your turn. Anchor me."

"I can't."

"I can't encase myself, so you have to or I'll be swept away."

"Maybe this wasn't the best idea."

"Do it," Treygan said. "Now. For Nixie and Jenna."

That was the only reminder I needed. I dove down, concentrating on my gorgon ability and feeling its power simmering inside me. I started at the bedrock base and kept expanding the stone. I built upward until I reached Treygan's tail, sculpting all around him, up to his abs, but it didn't seem safe enough. I added more, encasing him up to his chest, and then I surfaced.

He smirked. "Went a bit overboard, didn't you?"

"Better safe than sorry."

"You did an amazing job. Now, go. Nixie and Jenna need you."

Keeley hovered above our heads with one of my packs. "I found the one you wanted."

"Good. You stay with me." I flew into the sunless sky, gazing down at Treygan, Caspian, Indrea, Delmar, Kimber, and Merrick, and deeper to where Pango anchored the boat that Rownan and Vienna were stowed away in. I was putting all of them at risk. I grumbled to myself, "What am I doing?"

"You're saving my sisters," Keeley reminded me.

I took the empty bag from her and punctured a few air holes in the leather with my talons. "Get in and do not come out no matter what."

"Yes, ma'am." She flew inside, but darted back out and kissed me on the chin. "You can do it. I believe in you."

That makes one of us.

She flew into the pouch and I tightened the strings then double-knotted them. I strapped on the pack and took a deep breath. I stared at the pale moon now visible in the darkening sky. *Please help me pull this off, Medusa.*

We had already taken too much time. I had to work fast. I scanned the horizon and connected with the wind. My instinct was to create a hurricane, but I pushed away the desire and focused on my purpose.

"Open it!" I yelled to the merfolk below me.

They all sang together and lifted their arms. The water slowly spread apart.

I said another prayer and closed my eyes, visualizing the funnel, making the air gather and swirl in a powerful whirlwind. My tornado began brewing.

"You're doing it, Yara!" Treygan shouted.

I flew higher, stretching the waterspout taller. Digging deep, I summoned every bit of my siren strength. I raised my hands, struggling against its increasing power. My muscles trembled. Keeley's pack slapped my chest over and over. My hair whipped against my face and eyes, almost blinding me. I couldn't hear or see everyone below me. I felt alone, but I knew I wasn't.

I conjured power from every species that existed in me: siren, mer, selkie, and gorgon. The tornado whistled and screamed so loud my ears rang. My bones threatened to snap like twigs and my muscles fought to keep from being ripped to shreds. I resisted the suction that tried to pull me into the tornado. *I'm stronger than you*, I silently told it. *I control you.*

I pictured Nixie's fiery but fiercely loyal eyes, and Jenna's big, contagious grin.

Uncle Lloyd's voice echoed in my memory. "Love is when you care about someone so much you would risk everything to keep them safe."

My skin tingled with love for them. I didn't care if the tornado broke me into pieces. I would give my life if I had to. Anything to get Nixie and Jenna out of Harte.

I chanted Koraline's words in my head. *Never give up. The tide will turn.*

I groaned and thrashed as surges of strength rippled through me. Sage stretched tall and proud, somehow remaining upright against the wind. *The tide will turn.*

With one final yank, I flipped the tornado upside down. The force of it threw me backward. My wings snapped back on themselves. I momentarily toppled through the air and was almost sucked into the funnel. But I fought back and pried my wings open, kicking, flapping, and pumping my way out of the pull toward the ocean.

I steadied myself and hovered there, in awe of the monstrous churning force of nature in front of me. Then I raised my arms and threw them back down with all my might, driving the upside-down funnel deep into the hole the merfolk held open.

It worked. The brunt of the tornado's power was in the water, but I wasn't sure how long I could hold it. The force of the tornado was even stronger than I anticipated. It was a living, breathing thing that existed because of me. It was *part* of me.

I felt when it stopped at the ocean floor, spinning the sand, weakening when it had nowhere else to go. My muscles were rigid, but I dug deeper, searching for more strength. *I am a sea monster. The ocean will not beat me.*

I clenched my fists and dug my heels into the ocean foam bubbling around me. My teeth rattled from the tremors. I roared uncontrollably.

Then, finally, I broke through. Plumes of smoke shot through the middle of the funnel like a geyser. The gate was open.

Nixie! I mentally shouted. *We're still here. We didn't leave you. Get out of there!*

I should have been exhausted, but adrenaline made me stronger. I could see everyone below me. I drifted down closer to them.

"I don't know how much longer we can hold it!" Delmar yelled.

"I can feel her!" I told them. "She's panicking and weak, but she's fighting. Keep it open!"

Come on, Nixie, I urged. *Come, on!*

It felt like eternity stretched out in front of me. My merfolk grunted and groaned below. Their muscles strained and rippled as they struggled to hold the ocean open against the raging storm. Their hallmarks swirled through their skin and changed colors like a fireworks display in the water.

Indrea let out one last painful shout and collapsed face-first into the ocean, but the stone around her body kept her in place. Caspian reached for her, but he couldn't move anything but his upper torso. The hole in the ocean closed significantly without their help.

Nixie! I mentally shouted. *Hurry! It's closing!*

I felt her hope disappear. It was replaced by worry and dread.

No! You fight, Nixie. You get back here! I tried emanating my own determination so she would feel it. *I need you,* I mentally whispered. *I won't be me anymore without you.*

The hole closed even more.

I hovered above Treygan and harnessed my ability to control water. I pulled with everything I had, grunting and straining with the rest of my mer family while still keeping the tornado spinning.

A huge wave of water rushed toward me. I bowed my head as it crashed against me, but I kept fighting. The hole widened.

I could feel Nixie's pain intensifying. Her hope was almost non-existent.

Now, Nixie! I screamed at her. *As your assigned gorgon, I command you to push through your pain and fly through the gate right now!*

I took two more shaky breaths. Praying between each one. The wind howled. Water churned so fast I couldn't tell where the ocean ended and the sky began. Something black shot up in front of me. Hints of red shimmered high above the tornado. *Nixie.*

She was the most beautiful sight I've ever seen. She was covered in black slime, but traces of her bright red hair and wings shined through. She hung in place momentarily, like a black and red feather lifted by an updraft. I let the funnel of water collapse, and then gravity yanked her down.

I rushed forward, catching her in mid-air. She smelled as bad as the breath of a soul sucker, but happy tears spilled from my eyes. She made it. She was out of Harte.

The others had let the hole snap shut beneath us. Treygan busted free of his stone encasing and started freeing the others.

I carried Nixie's body to the boat and gently set her down. Keeley kicked and punched against my chest from inside her pouch. I sliced open the string with a flick of one talon and she flitted out, landing on Nixie's shoulder.

"Nixie," Keeley whispered, pushing and pulling her long, wet hair from her face. "Nixie, please wake up."

Nixie didn't budge.

"She's not dead," I said. "I feel it. She's alive."

"Where is Jenna?" Keeley asked me.

"She …" I searched the sky and glanced out over the ocean. "I don't know."

Keeley's eyes welled with tears. "She had to make it out. She's so tough. She probably flew out and you didn't see her. I'll find her." Keeley flew off, searching for a tiny yellow body I was sure I hadn't seen.

The others climbed aboard one after the other. Delmar rushed below to check on Rownan and Vienna. I sighed with relief when Pango's huge body rocked the boat as he climbed inside. Everyone was accounted for—except for sweet, brave Jenna.

"Is she all right?" Treygan asked, kneeling beside us. Nixie's crimson eyelashes fluttered as she groaned.

"Nixie, you made it. We're all here." I patted her cheek until her eyes opened.

"My wings," she whispered.

"Your wings are intact," I assured her. Her arms looked like shredded meat. "The Violets will heal your injuries."

Keeley landed on my shoulder. She was sniffling and wiping her eyes. "Jenna went back in to help you, Nixie. Did you see her?"

"My wings," Nixie murmured again.

Keeley's head snapped up. "Her wings!"

She dashed behind Nixie and pushed her onto her side. Treygan helped, holding an exhausted Nixie against him. Nixie's wings were tattered, closed tight against her back and covered in black slime like the rest of her. Keeley pulled at one, but it was rigid.

"Keeley, stop," I said. "You might hurt her."

Keeley scowled at me. "You don't understand!"

She tugged harder, freeing Nixie's right wing and fanning it open as far as she could. Treygan glanced at me apprehensively, and I shrugged. Maybe it was some water sprite way of healing that we didn't understand.

Keeley grunted, tugging on Nixie's left wing. "Relax your grip, Nixie! I can't open it."

Nixie grumbled something I couldn't understand. Then her wing loosened and Keeley fanned it open. I gasped.

There, whimpering and nestled tightly in Nixie's down feathers, was an unconscious and slime-covered Jenna.

Keeley squealed and flew forward. "Oh, Jenna!"

She covered her sister's face with kisses, not minding the putrid-smelling slime at all.

"You did it, Nix." I said into her ear. "You saved all of us. Even Jenna."

Nixie could barely hold up her head. I felt the stinging of her wounded arms and the burning of her legs as if they were my own. Her red eyes darted aimlessly, confirming the dizzy sensation I'd been feeling was hers. "Jenna's okay?"

"She's going to be fine," I told her. "You're a hero."

Jenna stirred awake. She wiped the tar-like slime from her buttercup face and let out the biggest yawn I had ever seen. "Can we go home? I'd very much like to take a long nap."

Treygan and I smiled at each other. Caspian and Indrea kneeled beside Nixie and went to work. Merrick steered the boat as we bounced across the ocean, all souls accounted for, and headed back to the gateway to Rathe.

I went below to check on Rownan and Vienna. Meeting Vienna for the first time in Harte hadn't felt real. It was like we met in a nightmare and now I needed to see her in the waking world to make sure she was real.

After only a few minutes of sitting with her and Rownan, the pain and lightheadedness I'd been feeling from Nixie dissolved. I was relieved that her pain had subsided, until a familiar ethereal feeling washed over me. I'd only ever felt that otherworldly sensation one other time—in the Inbetween.

I bolted up the small ladder to go above deck. Everyone was circled around Nixie. "Nixie!" I rushed forward, kneeling at her side. "What's wrong?"

"She has lost too much blood," Indrea said gently.

"No." I clutched Nixie's thigh. Her eyes were closed and she was so cold. Siren skin was supposed to be hot. "Give her my blood."

"We don't have the supplies to do a transfusion here," Caspian explained.

"I can fly ahead. I'm fast. Tell me what supplies we need."

"Yara," Indrea placed her hand on mine. "She's fading too quickly. There isn't time."

"Nixie, don't do it. Don't cross over." I gripped her hand. I refused to believe it. We had made it out of Harte. Nixie couldn't die after all we had been through. After everything she did to save us. "We have to do something."

Indrea's eyes were glassy. "All you can do is say goodbye before it's too late."

Because of our connection, I could feel the life draining out of Nixie. She wasn't in pain anymore, and I had experienced firsthand what that meant on the Triple Eighteen. A boulder formed in my throat as I gazed down at my siren. Her eyelids opened just enough for me to see her passionate ruby eyes were dimming. I leaned forward, desperately wiping slime from her as if that would save her. "Hang in there, Nixie. You can't die on me. I need you."

"Yara," she uttered weakly.

"I'm here. I'm not leaving you. You hang in there." My voice croaked. "I demand that you survive this."

Sage slithered down one of my arms. The sprites landed on my shoulder, sniffling and crying just below my ear.

"Thank you," Nixie whispered.

I leaned closer, fighting back tears as I wiped slime and blood from Nixie's cheek. She was so cold. "Shh, just rest. You'll be fine."

She lifted her trembling arm and pressed her hand over mine. "You saved me."

I choked back a sob. "I only saved you if you live."

She shook her head slightly. "You didn't give up on me." She coughed, and blood came up.

"Nixie," I whimpered, wiping the blood from her mouth. "Please don't leave me."

She had a faraway look, like she was staring at something far above me. "The waterfall. It's so beautiful."

"No! Don't cross into Eternal Falls." I gripped her tighter. I knew what she was seeing. I knew how tempting the Inbetween was. "Tell Medusa I won't allow it. She can't take you."

"I'll always be with you." Her eyes drifted closed.

The sprites flew forward, crying, whimpering "I love you" and hugging her neck.

"Nixie!" I shook her, but she had gone completely limp. The damn of tears I had been holding back broke free. I collapsed on top of her. Treygan tried to comfort me. Caspian and Indrea tried to calm me. None of it worked.

Nixie was gone.

My world was whole again.

Vienna grew stronger each day. The more time she spent with her family and friends, the brighter her eyes and smile became. My awful memories of Harte were already starting to fade. For Vienna, it would take much longer to forget. Some nights she still woke up from nightmares, clutching me and making sure I was real. She had lived in Harte for longer than any soul should have. Only someone as loving and extraordinary as Vienna could have survived a place filled with so much ugliness.

The season changed into Stheno's icy reign. Vienna and I sat on our front porch together watching the snow fall.

"Sometimes I see movement out of the corner of my eye, or a simple shadow, and panic hits me," Vienna said. "For a brief moment, I think I'm still in Harte."

"I'm sorry for that, but you're home. I won't let anything hurt you ever again."

Vienna reached forward, trying to catch one of the colored snowflakes. "Why do you think she's crying?"

"Medusa is very emotional, but I think they're tears of joy."

"I hope so." She wrapped her coat tighter around herself. "I wish Yara could ask her."

"I'm sure Yara wishes that too."

Medusa's tears had been falling from the sky off and on since we returned, but her moon seemed to glow brighter while Stheno and Euryale's moons grew dimmer. I had asked Indrea about it, and her best guess was it only seemed that way because Medusa's moon and sun shined so bright in comparison.

"Indrea says it's because Medusa is proud." I wrapped my arm around Vienna, running my fingers through her chin-length hair. "After so many years of tragedy and sadness, we finally have peace and joy again. It's what Medusa always wanted."

"I'm not sure it's what Stheno and Euryale want."

"They've always been the dark energy of the sisters, but Medusa fills our world with enough light to counter their darkness."

"Quite the balancing act," Vienna said.

"Life always is."

Vienna held up her empty mug. "I'm out of frozen java."

"I'll get you some more." I took her mug and kissed the top of her head. "Wait here. I'll be right back."

I stood up and turned to go inside, but stopped. My own words brought a bittersweet smile to my lips. I returned to Vienna and gathered her in my arms, carrying her into our house.

She giggled. "What are you doing?"

"I can't chance being separated from you again. Not even for a minute."

She kissed me. I didn't pull away until we were in the kitchen. I set her on the counter and whipped up a new drink for her.

"Besides you and my family," Vienna said, "I think I missed frozen javas the most."

"A world without caffeine is indeed hell." We smiled at each other, but sadness tugged at her lips. "What's wrong?"

She shuddered. "I can't completely shake the feel of that place. All the evil, the wrath, the hatred, even the putrid smell."

"Give it time." I stood between her legs, lifting her chin to look at me. "We'll replace all the negative memories with positive ones."

She stared at me with her beautiful dark eyes. Wrapping her legs around my waist, she pulled me closer. "There is one sin I don't mind giving in to."

I licked my lips, already knowing her answer. "Which one?"

"Lust," she whispered against my neck.

For the dozenth time, Vienna and I generated enough heat in our kitchen to melt the selkie side of Rathe.

I hid behind an apple blossom tree, holding my breath and pressing myself against the trunk. I imagined a protective bubble around me, blocking Treygan's mer senses from detecting me.

I heard his footsteps getting closer and held back a nervous giggle. I closed my eyes and imagined myself blending with the tree, hoping he wouldn't see me. If I could stay hidden for two more minutes, I would win the bet.

He walked closer. I barely opened my eyes, watching him through my eyelashes. He wasn't looking in my direction, but his head was cocked. He looked alert, like he suspected I was nearby. He took a few more steps and sniffed the air.

Then he turned and headed in my direction. He was so close I could have reached out and touched him. I was sure he had spotted me since he was looking right at me.

"So close," I said. "I only had one more minute to go."

His eyes widened, and grew wider as he scanned me up and down. "How are you doing that?"

"What?" I glanced down and gasped. My toes and feet were grass. My legs looked like the bark of the tree I was leaning against. I held out my arms, and at first they looked like bark too, but as I moved them they morphed to look like star-flowers. "Oh, my gods! What happened to me?"

"You don't know how you're doing that?" Treygan touched my stomach. "It's an illusion. Your skin still feels the same."

I touched my stomach, amazed it didn't feel dry and rough like tree bark because it looked so real. "What in the worlds?"

He took my hand and pulled me away from the tree. My skin faded back to normal, hallmarks and all. His smile was blinding. "Now *that* I have never seen before. Yamabuki, I think you've just discovered yet another amazing ability you inherited."

"To look like a tree? I'm not sure I want that ability."

"I bet you can blend to look like anything in nature. That could come in handy in certain situations."

"Like when?"

His eyes shifted, trying to come up with a good answer. "Spying?"

"I have a mirror for that."

"Then I don't know. But it's unique, and I'm envious."

I laughed and leaned against the tree again. I glanced down. "It's not working anymore."

"You must have done something to trigger it. We'll have to explore this newfound ability later. Right now we need to head back."

We waded into the lagoon. A surge of relief warmed my body as my legs morphed into my tail. "How did you find me?"

"Your apple blossom scent."

"But this whole place smells like apple blossoms."

"You have an exceptionally delicious scent that no tree, not even one filled with star-flowers, could ever live up to."

"And now I can look like an apple tree too."

"As pretty as Medusa's trees are," he traced my hallmarks with his fingertips, "I prefer you to look just like this."

"Like a mermaid?"

He grinned. "It's still my favorite sea creature."

We held hands as we swam away from Forbidden Apple Lagoon. I was already itching to return.

I spent most of my days making rounds to see all the sea creatures, but each evening we would go to Uncle Lloyd's to watch the sunset. I would sit at his side as he slept through the night, and when the sun rose—and I was sure he would live to see another day—I made him breakfast and wheeled him out to the garden for fresh air and sunshine.

I sliced up a monstera fruit and set it between us on the table. "You're looking good today."

"I feel pretty good." Uncle Lloyd stretched his arms above his head. "It's great to have all of you here. Does wonders for my soul."

Treygan pulled out a chair and sat beside us, lining up Uncle Lloyd's medications. Vienna and Rownan were laughing and cutting flowers on the other side of garden.

"Do you have enough strength for a celebration?" I asked. "Maybe even a ceremony?"

Uncle Lloyd's eyes lit up. He turned to Treygan. "So, you did ask her? I take it she said yes?"

"I didn't ask her anything yet." Treygan smirked. "I didn't want Yara telling our children that their father asked her to marry him while we were in hell. Yara deserves a proper proposal, and I need time to figure out how and when to do it."

Treygan was planning to ask me to marry him? My heart leaped at the thought, but for all good reasons.

"I'm confused," Uncle Lloyd said. "Then who …?"

"Rownan and Vienna want to renew their vows. They want to do it here. With you."

Rownan walked up behind his father and squeezed his shoulders. "You couldn't make it to our original wedding. I'd like you to be present for our renewal of vows."

Uncle Lloyd's lips tightened the way they always did when he was emotionally touched. "I'd like that very much."

Vienna and I smiled at each other. Her beauty still left me staring at her in awe at times. She lit up every time Rownan looked at her.

"You and Treygan will be next," Vienna said to me.

"When the time is right." I squeezed Treygan's thigh. "We're in no rush."

Uncle Lloyd chuckled. "I hope I live long enough to attend that one."

"You will." Treygan winked at me. "I promise, you will."

Rownan squinted at us, sensing our secret, but I changed the subject. "Jenna and Keeley will be here soon."

Uncle Lloyd grinned. He adored Jenna and Keeley. They had been helping him with his latest wood carving while I returned to Rathe during the day. When Uncle Lloyd had finished his last piece of monstera fruit, he released the locks on his wheelchair and rolled himself into the house while we all gathered the dishes.

Rownan touched my elbow. "What was that about?"

"What?" I asked innocently.

"That secret wink Treygan gave you. Is there something you're not telling us?"

I glanced between him, Vienna, and Treygan, and grinned. "Let's just say I did some bartering with Stheno and Euryale."

Vienna's eyebrow rose. "Is the curse on Lloyd lifted?"

From inside, Lloyd called for Rownan. I nodded toward the house. "Someone needs you."

"We *will* discuss this later." Rownan took my dishes from me then he and Vienna went into the house together.

Treygan wrapped his arm around me. "I still don't understand what could have been juicy enough to strike a deal like that with Stheno and Euryale. What memories did you give them?"

A vague, faceless image of someone with a head of coral, or maybe it was dreadlocks, flickered in my mind, disappearing as soon as I tried to focus on it. "I don't remember. Isn't that the whole point of letting them take a memory from me?"

"Good point." Treygan kissed my shoulder. "Whatever it was, it must have been powerful."

"It was an experience from Harte. I would happily give them all of those memories."

"Keep some," Treygan said. "You never know when you might need to negotiate with them again."

"Very true." I raised my face to enjoy the warmth of the sunshine and bask in how much my entire family of sea creatures had achieved in the last several weeks. Something tickled my cheek and I opened my eyes to see Jenna and Keeley flitting in front of me.

Jenna kissed Sage's nose. "Hello, stinky breath."

Sage rubbed against her affectionately.

"Come on," Jenna said, ushering me up by my pinky while Keeley did the same to Treygan. "It's time for the big reveal."

Treygan and I grinned at each other and followed them into the house. Rownan, Vienna, and Lloyd stood beside Lloyd's newest carving, which was covered with a sheet. Candles had been lit, and sunlight poured into the room through the large bay window.

Lloyd tugged the sheet away, letting it slide off the gleaming wood and onto the floor. I sucked in a breath because it was more beautiful than I imagined. Nixie's portrait was breathtaking.

Lloyd said a few sentimental words. Rownan did too, and he and Vienna thanked her for saving their lives. The sprites petted Nixie's carved wings while they told her how much they missed her and loved her. Jenna choked up when she thanked her for saving her from the soul suckers. Treygan was just finishing his heartfelt speech when I felt a twinge of sadness that wasn't my own. Shadows stretched across the room as Otabia and Mariza joined us.

"You're late," I said.

"Better late than never." Otabia held my hand while Mariza strutted to the portrait and laid a bouquet of red Calliandra flowers at Nixie's feet.

Uncle Lloyd turned to me. "Yara, would you like to say a few words?"

I could have said wonderful things about Nixie for days. My heart overflowed with love and gratitude for her, but Nixie had asked me to keep it simple, so I said what mattered most. "She will always be with us."

Everyone nodded or bowed their head then the room slowly cleared out except for me, Uncle Lloyd, and Nixie's life-sized portrait.

"It's ready." Uncle Lloyd winked at me. "Liora said it should work."

I stepped forward, eye to eye with my beautiful, devoted siren. As Lloyd recited a familiar incantation in the gorgon language, Sage rose then bowed with respect. I stared at the smooth, rounded mahogany that created Nixie's lifelike pupils.

I hadn't saved Nixie's life. And I had to live with that guilt each and every day. But at least her soul was saved. It wasn't the ending I had imagined, and it certainly wasn't ideal, but at least no one was still trapped in Harte, suffering alone in hell. Vienna had endured enough of that for all of us.

When the wooden eyes in front of me glowed ruby red, I smiled. "Let the renegotiating begin."

THE END

Acknowledgments

I'm a small fish in a big ocean of amazing people. Seriously, I have the best job in the world, but what makes it even better is the people who support and help me along the way. A heartfelt thanks to all the usual suspects:

Mom, my #1 fan, you're there for every step of every book. None of my stories would be a reality if it weren't for your belief in me and your encouragement.

Dad, my personal Imagineer, thanks for all the advice and ideas, including the "giant lamprey" now known as soul suckers. This book's dedication said it all.

John, my Peter Pan, for putting up with me, my musings, and my time-consuming dream on a daily basis. I love you more.

My beloved M-N-Ms: Megan, Natalie, and Marie...

Megan McBride, leave it to you to tell me to kill my darlings. And of course, I obeyed. I promise, someday I will write you a romantic kraken story.

Natalie Bahm, we should meet for butterbeer more often. Play dates with you and your kids keep my imagination going full speed.

Marie Devers Jaskulka, two bits of your sage wisdom that always stay with me: 1.) Don't be a serial series starter. 2.) Shut the F up and write. I'll continue to do both.

M-N-M, you three have been there since the very beginning. I said it before and I'll say it again, I would be lost without you.

Steve Graham, you deserve an award for your art skills, and for putting up with my endless requests. Thank you for making my books beautifully badass.

Melissa, Michelle, Diane, Becca, I can't keep you gals straight anymore, but thanks for everything. Kidding. Sort of. But seriously...

Melissa Williams, you did it again. The cover is enchanting.

Michelle Davidson Argyle, thanks for holding my hand at the start of my publishing journey, and continuing to walk the path with me as a dear friend.

Diane Dalton, your editing skills continue to amaze me. This book is so much better because of you.

Becca Brown, for enthusiastically supporting my Hans Solo in carbonate decision, and telling me when enough was enough with the unicorn jokes.

Magan Vernon, your text messages keep me going every day. Keep calm and love our book boyfriends.

Becca Zeno, for cheering me on and inspiring me with your spirit and determination. I can't wait to see your books published soon.

Sarah Kennedy, for the hauntingly beautiful song you wrote, sang, and recorded for this series. You are a shining, cherished star.

Krista, April, and Andrea, just because I love you and I know you'll read this. Thanks for being such supportive friends since way back when.

Emmaline, Rhett, and everyone at Rhemalda Publishing, thank you for giving me my start as an author. You'll always hold a special place in my heart.

The Indelibles, you're all rock stars and I treasure each of you.

And always, to my readers, I'd thank each of you individually if I could. I'm still reaching through these pages and hugging you. My gratitude still is, and will always be, deeper than the oceans.

Karen Amanda Hooper

Born and bred in Baltimore, Karen has been making up stories for as long as she can remember. In high school she discovered her passion for putting her thoughts onto paper, but it wasn't until her late twenties that she wrote her first novel.

Due to her strong Disney upbringing, she still believes in fairy tales and will forever sprinkle magic throughout all of her novels. Karen is currently sunning and splashing around Florida with her two spoiled rescue dogs.

To learn more about Karen, visit her at
www.KarenAmandaHooper.com